PILLARS OF CLOUD

CONNOR IRVING

THE SALT OF ANGELS BOOK 1

Tea With Coffee
—Media—

CONNOR IRVING
FANTASY AUTHOR

Acknowledgments

I started writing 'Pillars of Cloud' back in 2016 when I was 13. Throughout those 6 years, the plot, themes and characters changed numerous times and it wouldn't have been possible without the help and support from a great number of people.

I firstly want to thank my family, my mum, Carol, and my dad, Pete, for listening to me talking about my writing and surrounding Mythologies for countless hours; and for assisting me in naming several characters. And a special thank you to my sister, Keira, for reading snippets of early drafts and for the suggestion of the word silhouette.

Of course, I want to say a huge thank you to the team at Tea With Coffee Media for working on Pillars of Cloud and turning this dream into a reality. Special thanks to Lynn for taking the time to edit the book and to Victoria for creating an amazing cover.

And I would like to say a final thank you to a couple of my friends and former teachers. Firstly to Faye, Emily and my partner Finn for reading chapters and snippets and for giving me praise and constructive criticisms which helped make Pillars of Cloud what it is today. To Mrs Clayton for encouraging my interest in writing and stories when I was only 10 years old. And to Mrs Perry who was the first to read and review my very first draft and showed nothing but support.

Contents

Chapter 1

*Octo urbibus caelitibus invitis et potestatibus
Pandaemonii, evoco ex infernis igneis Lilitu, virginem
umbrarum, matrem daemonum, magnam diabolam, ut
regnum caeleste et omnes obvios deleat. Haec est voluntas mea,
sic sit.*

The man chanted, his voice echoing with the
crackling of flames. He stood, in a suit of all black, before
a pentagram carved into the floor. Most of his face was
hidden by the waves of his greasy hair, but certain parts

of his skin could be seen. It was so pale and so thin that it seemed to have a sheen in the light shining through the roof of the neglected ruins that had once been the home of an ancient king. As he chanted, he moved his hands in circular motions with his palms facing forward and with each rotation magical crimson energy shot from his hands and began dancing between his fingers and running up his arms and around his body. His breathing grew heavier and his voice louder as he neared the end of his chant and when he completed it, the magical energies shot violently from his body and surged down onto the pentagram before him. It hit with such force that the ground shook aggressively.

He watched with great interest as the crimson energies were drawn beneath the surface of the grey stone floor and then released again as a dark red mist. He had seen the effects of magic before, but he had never used it. It had been something he had feared since he was a child, but that was a long time ago. The mist spread across the entire pentagram before beginning to twist upward in a spiralling crimson pillar. Through the gaps in the spinning smoke he watched as something began to take shape in the eye of the storm. His view of the event was hindered as the pillar began to implode. For a moment, the man worried that he had not done the spell correctly, that he had set up the pentagram wrong, but his worries subsided when the smoke once again spun around violently, shooting outward and spreading across the room before dissipating into nothing.

Where the smoke had been, there was now a woman. She was tall, her bronze skin dark against the shining white of her dress which made her long hair look like spilled ink. She took in a deep breath and the lingering red smoke shot from the back of the room and slithered into her nostrils like twin snakes. As she exhaled, her full red lips opened, flashing her shining white fangs momentarily until she opened eyes that were endless black voids with no whites, similar to the eyes of a shark.

"My Lady," the greasy-haired man dropped to one knee in a bow, his voice shaking a little. Before him was Lilith, the Queen of Hell. She had been the First Woman until she refused to be submissive to Adam and was cast out of Eden. Lilith became the mother of Demons and sovereign of the seven planes of Hell. She was also the reason he had killed his own brother and she still had some influence over him so he couldn't hate her.

"Get off the floor, Cain." Lilith said, he instantly got up. When he was a baby, Lilith had used her blood to make him unable to deny her desires and she had used him to exact revenge on Adam and Eve by having him kill his brother, Abel. He had been cursed with immortality for that and Lilith had been the one person to stick by him, however, she only turned up when she needed him to do something.

"It is about time you summoned me; I was beginning to think you had forgotten me."

"I could never forget you, my Lady,"

Lilith's mouth twisted into a thin smile as she chuckled slightly and looked around, recognizing the ruins of the castle. It had been the home of King Bladud until he had offended her. She had destroyed him and his kingdom. It was right in the centre of ley lines, areas where magical energy was most powerful and so was perfect for summoning beings from Hell.

"So, you have procured what I wanted?" her voice was smooth and harsh, like an icy spring.

"Indeed I have, much to the dismay of Sammael," Cain said. Sammael was a Lord of Hell and consort to Lilith.

"Then take me to them," the Demon commanded.

Cain, unable to deny her, nodded as his eyes flashed red. A pillar of the same red smoke spiralled around both Cain and Lilith as it whisked them away from the ruins of Bladud's castle. When the pillar of cloud dissipated, they were in an empty field surrounded by tall bright trees and an array of beautiful flowers, the sun was shining gloriously and there was not a cloud in the sky.

Lilith smiled as she felt the heat of the heavenly body on her face. It always amused her that the Alium, a community of mortals, maintained the illusion that they were safe in daylight, in order to stay alive. The mortals were more commonly known as Stagnants, a pejorative used by the supernatural community. Most demons were safe anyway and the Greater Demons only cared about stagnants that could see through the veil. The veil was a magical curtain hiding the Alium from the stagnants. It was the Faeries and Vampires that they really had to worry about.

Lilith grimaced as her dark eyes scanned the field.

"There's nothing here, Cain." Her tone was dangerous, the Queen of Hell hated being taken advantage of or tricked.

"Not to the naked eye, my Lady," Cain said as he continued to look forward, willing anything to be revealed. Lilith was impatient and he had seen her angry before. It was not something he wished to see again.

Nothing was said between them for a few moments, which felt like a millennium to Cain. Lilith took a deep breath, readying herself to speak, when the air before them rippled and began peeling away. The scene changed entirely and the empty field was replaced by a large building of dark grey cobblestone, the door was a dark brown with no handle and above it was a large window. Most of the window glass was normal, but some of the panes were an intense black, in the shape of a cross adorned with a crescent moon. It was the symbol of Lilith. Even from a quick glance at the exterior, it was clear that this was a temple to the Demon Queen. As she made her way forward, the door swung open to allow entry. They stepped inside and it became even more apparent that this was a church to Lilith, the air was warm with the heat trapped by the stone walls. Tapestries hanging from the walls depicted the life of Lilith - her creation, her fall, her coronation. There were black pews running down either side of the room creating a long aisle down the middle covered in a crimson carpet, Lilith's ceremonial colour. The aisle led to a large stone altar at the other side of the room. On the surface of the altar was a red cloth, a golden chalice and a shining silver athame with an ornate black handle. On the front of the altar was a phrase in the most ancient of languages, Tamil. "நான் தலை வணங்கமாட்டேன்".

Cain glanced at the altar, mentally translating the phrase to "I will not bow" and thinking privately that the quotation was very appropriate for Lilith's temple.

There was an air of illness within the church and an off-putting smell of brimstone. It was obviously a place of darkness. The roof was high and only the tapping of Lilith's white heeled shoes broke the silence. The sound echoed upwards.

"Magnificent," she whispered, mostly to herself though she knew others could hear her. She had not created this place and she knew it was not the work of a Stagnant cult, the magic hiding it was too strong. It could only be a Demon, a Prince or Lord of Hell.

"Why, thank you," said another behind Lilith and Cain, the voice cutting through the eerie silence. Both turned to see a man before them, his skin the same bronze as Lilith's, his hair the exact same shade of the darkest black but his eyes were not like Lilith's, they were like emeralds shining in a cavern.

"Sammael," Lilith strutted over to her husband and threw her arms around his neck, he coiled his around her back before they unwound themselves.

"I did not expect you to help."

"Cain was very persistent, he refused to leave my palace in Pandemonium unless I helped him." There was a clear annoyance in Sammael's voice.

Pandemonium was a plain in Hell belonging to Lilith, Sammael, as her consort, had his own palace there.

"Then show them to me," Lilith said excitedly.

Sammael nodded, he walked past Lilith and Cain to lead them toward the altar, his face stony. He had never wanted to reveal this secret to Lilith. He had hoped to conceal the knowledge of this event, one that he would have been able to forget after seventy or eighty years - no time at all in the life of an immortal. He had been mortified when Lilith had discovered the secret. He thought she would be angry about it but was shocked when he discovered how pleased she was, a plan instantly forming in her mind. She was crazy, but she was brilliant. At the altar he adjusted the collar of his silver suit and played nervously with one of his lapels before waving a hand above the red cloth. As the shining silver rings on his fingers moved above the red cloth, the air shimmered and stripped away the illusion covering it. Four baskets were revealed, four wooden Moses baskets each holding a small infant. Two of the children were swaddled in pink blankets, the others wrapped in blue. Two boys and two girls. Sammael's cheeks flushed with colour as they were revealed. Two of the children, the first boy and girl were the product of his infidelity with a beautiful woman from Egypt. The the other two had been conceived by Sammael and another gorgeous woman from Greece.

"Perfect," Lilith gasped as she bent down to get a closer look at the sleeping children. "Absolutely perfect." She had not been around a baby in a long time, but she knew she had to remain quiet or they would wake and start crying; she despised the sound of babies crying.

"My Lady," Cain began speaking at normal volume but dropped to a whisper as soon as Lilith shot him a dark look.

"What are they perfect for?"

"Yes, Lilith, you have explained part of your plan, but not all of it. What do you require my children for?" Sammael whispered, his green eyes illuminated with intrigue.

"They're our children now, Sammael, or at least they will be when I feed them my blood as I did with Cain. As you know, we have been subject to the rules of Angels and the Seraphic Laws for thousands of years. They have restricted the rights of all of the Alium, but it has been bearable."

Lilith spoke of the laws that had been set by the Seraphic Council, the governing body of the Alium made up of the leaders of each Pantheon of gods - powerful Angels confused as gods by Stagnants over many years. There were laws that restricted the movements of Demons, controlled Vampire feeding, banned necromancy and gave Faeries guidance in how to deal with humans. The laws were supposed to protect Stagnants, but most of the Alium believed them to merely be a way for the Angels to control the gods and had fought against the laws being passed originally. The punishment for breaking these laws was a trial before the Council and a sentence to be passed.

"Well, there have been rumours within the Alium that the Seraphic Council wants to pass a new set of rules called the Arcadian Laws; these are more restrictive, and many are cruel. The punishment for even bending these Laws will be instant death, or for those who cannot die, an eternity trapped in purgatory. These Laws cannot be passed for another few years as is stated in the Seraphic Laws and these children are half Stagnant, half Alium, a brand-new race. This will delay the Arcadian Laws being passed even further as they will be unsure whether these children come under their laws or mortal laws and will want to wait to see if they can add more to the Arcadian Laws to restrict these beings as well. I want these children to be raised in captivity by Angels. whilethe Angels are not with them, you Sammael, their father, will train them in the arts of Demonic magic. When they are old enough, we will free them and they will lead an army of the Alium in a war against the Angels. We will take control of all realms and put an end to the Arcadian Laws before they begin."

Lilith spoke with conviction, there was a rage behind her words. She had been punished throughout her entire life for not conforming to the rules and she was not willing to let the Angels diminish her power and her rights any further.

"How many years are left of the Seraphic Laws?" Cain asked.

He recalled them being passed, it was early in the fifteenth century when he was moving through France, he hadn't been able to stay there though, he never got to stay anywhere. That was his curse for killing his brother, he would be forever walking across the earth, alone.

"There are ten more years until any new laws can be passed, and they will have to wait a further eight years until these children are of age before they pass the Arcadian Laws in order to account for all species of the Alium."

Lilith made her way around the altar to stand behind it. She picked up the athame that lay between two of the Moses baskets and traced the edge of the blade down her palm, normal flesh would have sliced open and bled, but not Lilith's, her skin was tough as iron.

"Do they have names, Sammael? You are their father; it makes sense you would name them."

Sammael felt very uneasy listening to Lilith, there was no disdain in her voice, no disgusted undertone when discussing the children brought forth by his infidelity, yet he couldn't shake the feeling that Lilith was furious with him. Then again, he had given her the tools for her plan, maybe she was as pleased as she claimed.

"They do have names," Sammael said. He chose his words very carefully, Lilith would know and be angry if he were lying, but she would be incandescent with rage if she knew that the baby's mortal mothers had named them before their deaths.

"The first boy and girl are the children of an Armenian noble, he is called Loukas, and she is Estrie. The other two are the children of an Egyptian descended from the Ptolemaic dynasty, the girl's name is Mania and the boy is Astaroth."

"Beautiful names," Lilith said. She was hovering a hand above each child for a moment, the air between her palm and the babies shaking and shimmering slightly.

"They all have such raw magical potential, especially this one," her hand hovered above the child Sammael had named Estrie.

"I sense a dangerous amount of power in this one. Keep an eye on her, Sammael."

"I am sure that you will also be watching her closely." Sammael said.

"Not for the first eighteen years." The corners of Lilith's mouth turned up as she saw a look of confusion and a little bit of fear run into Sammael's eyes; he hadn't been a very hands-on parent with their Demons, caring for children did not come as naturally to him as it did to Lilith. Perhaps that was because he had never been human.

"If the Angels think I am caring for and training the children, they will kill them before they reach eighteen and will foil my plan. We will allow the Angels to think they are the only people raising the children in captivity and they will keep them on Earth as they will not want the *polluted* in Heaven. In secret, Sammael, you will train and teach them the history of the Alium, the cruelty of the Angels and how to control their powers. After eighteen years, just before the new laws are to be passed, you will free them, summon me and then we will gather our army hidden in Hell where the Angels cannot venture."

The Demon Queen had been thinking this through. It was not a spur of the moment idea; she had carefully planned each point since finding out Sammael had had various children with a number of women three months previously.

"That is an intricate plan for the future, my lady. What now?" Cain asked.

"Now, Cain, you are about to witness what I did to you as a baby to make you so obedient."

There was a gleeful tone to her harsh voice as she spoke of the past. Cain had been her secret weapon against Adam and Eve, the tool she had used to bring their perfect house crumbling down; even thinking of the pain she caused the two of them made her ecstatic.

With all eyes on her, Lilith raised the shining silver and black athame once again, she muttered something in an ancient language under her breath and the blade began glowing with a faint red light. She repeated the action of drawing the metal against her tough skin, only this time it did open, and a black-silver liquid poured out across her palm. It was her blood, her demonic ichor. She placed the athame back onto the crimson cloth, a drop of ichor fell from the blade onto the fabric, it hissed and burned through it immediately, creating a small hole. The Demon then picked up the golden chalice which stood between the other two Moses baskets. She placed her bleeding hand above the chalice, tilted her palm and squeezed. Ichor dripped into the golden cup, filling it quickly. When Lilith decided it was full enough, she withdrew her hand and uttered a new incantation in the ancient language. The cut sealed instantly and the ichor on her palm was wiped clean. She picked up the full chalice and walked back around the altar to face the sleeping babies.

With her back to Sammael and Cain, Lilith waved her free hand and the air around the babies shimmered as their mouths opened. Lilith pressed the chalice against each of the baby's mouths and poured a small amount of her ichor into each of them; none woke or moved as it entered their systems. Lilith's dark eyes widened, as did her smile. She replaced the chalice and turned back to face Cain and Sammael. The ichor insured that the four children would be obedient to her forever. They were her children now. She had always wanted a partly-human child; she had the chance once, but it was torn from her by God.

"Lower your spells, Sammael, it's time." Lilith said.

Sammael knew exactly what she meant, he was being told to lower the spells hiding the church from the sight of anyone, the spells that had prevented Lilith from seeing it before Sammael had wanted her to find it. If he did that, the Angels would immediately be alerted to the presence of the dark magic she had performed, magic that broke at least three of the Seraphic Laws, they would swoop down from the Heavens and send her back to Pandemonium. This was the best they could do with Lilith, she was impossible to kill and far too powerful for mere Angels to place her in purgatory.

"Are you sure, Lilith?"

"Completely. Lower your spells and then get out, the Angels cannot know you are here, or they will send you to Hell with me."

The Angels feared her more than Sammael, she was always calm and collected, a dangerous state for a Demon of any rank.

Sammael nodded as Cain started.

"What about me? Am I to leave?"

"Yes, Cain, you are to leave. It is unlikely that you will ever see me again now that I have four of you, now that I have a family." Lilith saw the hurt flash across his face. He had done everything she ever asked, he had always been more her son than Eve's, but not by choice. Cain had considered himself a part of Lilith's family, or at least one of her closest friends. She had never seen him as anything more than a pawn for her revenge, he was a constant reminder of Adam and Eve. She needed him, but she hated him. He took a deep breath as he readied himself to speak again.

"Go." Lilith commanded. Cain had no choice but to conform, he closed his mouth and lowered his head, his greasy hair fell into his face once again as he made his way out the door to continue his eternity-long venture.

The moment Cain was out of the door, Sammael raised his arms and flexed his fingers.

"Tutela carmina, nos non abscondam."

Streaks of magical energy the precise colour of Sammael's green eyes began pouring off of the walls and flying straight into Sammael's body. As the magic was stripped from the dark grey walls, they grew darker, the building shook aggressively, and the tapestries went up in dark green flames, dropping the white ash onto the ground and filling the room with a thin layer of black smoke. The babies coughed in their sleep and Sammael repeated his enchantment. The church shook again, the black wooden pews snapped and toppled over as some of the walls cracked with a loud crunch, there was a loud smashing noise as the stained glass window shattered inwardly, splattering broken shards of glass along the floor at Sammael's feet. The shattered window allowed the smoke to be cleared from the room. The Lord of Hell repeated his chant for a third and final time, more green energy rolled off of everything in the church and straight into him. The door shook violently with a loud explosion that sent small splinters of wood flying through the air in all directions. Quickly, Sammael raised his hand to create a small invisible force that bounced the shards of spiked wood away from the sleeping children. Once done, he lowered his arms and turned to Lilith to smile before being covered by a spiralling pillar of green cloud. When it cleared, Sammael was gone.

Lilith only had a moment alone as the last of the green smoke dissipated. Immediately, two twinning pillars of white cloud spiralled before her. They spun quickly, creating winds which blew Lilith's hair and cleared the floor of broken glass and wood. When the shards had been pushed into the corners of the room, the pillars began slowing until they disappeared, revealing two beings who had not been standing there before. Both were slightly taller than Lilith, their skin was a darker brown than Lilith's and their hair was light brown. Both had shimmering golden eyes and giant grey wings extending from their backs. They were Angels, dressed in the silver armour of the Seraphic army. Simultaneously their wings flexed before folding themselves tight against the backs of the Angels as they drew swords from the air.

"Nakir, Adriel; how delectable to see you both again."

Lilith had met many Angels in the past, though it had been hundreds of thousands of years since she had last seen these two. On the day that she became a Demon, she was transported to Heaven and tried before a court of Angels who wanted to *fix* her. She had declined their offer and destroyed areas of Heaven during her escape. She had killed many Angels and injured many more, Nakir and Adriel among them.

"Lilith, you have broken the Seraphic Laws by creating monstrosities once again… " Adriel began, his voice was loud and echoed around the room.

"Monstrosities?" Lilith demanded loudly but calmly. "They are my children."

"And children of yours are Demons - monsters." Nakir said.

Lilith smiled; the two Angels recoiled at the sight of her fangs.

"You are half right, Nakir, these children are half Demon, but they are also half human; your Seraphic Laws do not apply to them nor will any new Laws you… "

Lilith cut herself off. No one was meant to know about the design of the Arcadian Laws. She would never divulge her informant's name.

The Angels knew Lilith was correct about the Seraphic Laws, they included nothing about being half Alium and half Stagnant, nor did their plans for the

Arcadian Laws. Alium members below the age of eighteen could not be punished under any law unless they committed one of the cardinal sins.

Nakir gritted his shining white teeth and glared at Lilith who was watching them with one hand on her hip and a smug look on her face.

"Be that as it may, you are a Demon and you have broken the laws, it is time for you to go back to Hell."

Both he and Adriel raised their blades, aiming for an attack from Lilith.

"Very well," Lilith said. Both Angels looked bewildered as they wondered why she was giving up so easily. Lilith had never given in before.

"But before I go, I want your word that no harm will come to my children."

Adriel sighed heavily and lowered his blade. An Angel's word was his bond, literally, Angels could not lie. If they made this promise to Lilith, they would be bound to it for eternity and the very fabric of the Universe would prevent them from harming the creatures.

"Very well. In the name of all Angels, no harm will come to these children," Adriel said and watched as Lilith's shoulders dropped slightly as she relaxed.

"Unless they attempt to harm any member of Heaven or Earth." Adriel expected this to rile Lilith but it did not.

Lilith flicked her hair off of her shoulder so that it cascaded down her back and then spread her arms out in a T-shape with her head thrown back.

"Okay, I'm ready. Send me back to Hell."

Despite acting rather blasé about being sent to Hell, Lilith was dreading it. The ritual for sending her back was a painful one filled with intense Angelic magic that not only hurt but made her feel physically ill.

The two Angels dropped their swords and before the swords hit the ground they disappeared into thin air. Nakir and Adriel each drew another blade, seemingly from nowhere. These blades were daggers of pure gold, much smaller than the previous swords, and they seemed to radiate Angelic energies. Nakir and Adriel both walked in different directions around Lilith and plunged one blade at equidistant points a little before her. Each created another blade for themselves and walked around her a little bit more. Standing in the T-pose bored Lilith and she was now waiting impatiently, twirling a lock of her long black hair between her thin fingers. The Angels stabbed the knives into the ground again. Nakir then created one final blade and went behind Lilith as Adriel walked past the other Angel and back around to stand before Lilith.

"Ignes." Both Angels said as Nakir drove the final blade into the ground. The final blade sparked and set off a trail of fire running from knife-to-knife trapping

Lilith in the pentagon shape in the centre of a star, the flames continued to run until they formed a circle around the star making a pentagram out of flames of white, heavenly fire.

"*Olim iterum revertar.*" Lilith snarled angrily. "One day I'll be back."

"*Non diu.*" Adriel responded- Not for a long time. It was a horrendous experience for a Demon to be dispatched back to Hell; the more powerful they were the more energy was used and the more painful it was going back. Lilith, being the most powerful of Demons, was in for a world of pain; one that would take years of recovery in Hell before she could return to earth.With the flaming pentagram ready, Nakir returned to the side of Adriel.

"*Dios, Satani probat!*" they said together and slowly the flames began to get hotter and brighter. They said it again and the fire rose, higher and higher. There was little sound coming from Lilith apart from her deep breathing. The Seraphic energy was already affecting her.

"*Dios, Satani probat!*" The Angels chanted again.

The flames grew to a bright, even white and for a moment they stopped dancing before beginning to spin rapidly; they spun so fast that there were no individual flames, only a tornado of white light, a pure heavenly fire. The screams of Lilith began with howls of torture as her skin was caught by the leaping flames within. The pillar of fire became thinner and thinner, and the shrieks of Lilith grew louder. There were no gaps to see what was happening to the Demon, but from her harrowing cries, the Angels could only assume that it was a pain like no other. Then the screaming stopped and instantly the fires died, revealing a scorched pentagram on the ground and nothing more. The swords had been melted by the heat of flames and Lilith was back in Hell.

The Angels nodded to one another, a job well done, before they made their way to the altar to look at the four half-breed children, the four Cambions - half Alium, half Stagnant beings: the first of their kind. The Angels knew exactly what they needed to do but they were prevented from doing that until they attempted to harm someone from Heaven or earth; until then they would have to raise the Cambions and keep them away from society.

Chapter 2

Nakir and Adriel did not want the four Cambions in or close to Heaven since having anything slightly demonic on the Celestial plain was always a bad idea. Instead, they decided to keep the children on earth where they could visit and keep an eye on them. They renovated the Church of Lilith into a prison; it was large and comfortable with various rooms which they could venture into and out of at will. The walls were lined with enchanted Damascus Steel, the most heavenly of metals. The door was coated in the blood of Angels to prevent them from leaving. For the first few years of their lives, Nakir and Adriel remained in the church with them. The

Angels taught the Cambions self-control when they began to display signs of magic and attempted to teach them about the glory of God and his Angels. This usually ended with the children screaming all the way through the Angel's prayers. Despite the best efforts of the Angels, it was clear that these small half-breeds were not good. There was something evil rooted deep within them, something caused by Lilith's blood and Sammael's lineage. Despite being inherently bad, they did not attack the Angels at any point. It was as if they knew about the deal Nakir and Adriel had made with Lilith before her departure.

The Angels remained in the prison and Sammael had no opportunity to teach the Cambions for the first eight years. During that time, he contacted them via hypnomancy. He invaded their dreams and told them that he was their father and that he would one day free them from their prison and take them to save their mother, meaning Lilith.

After eight years, the Angels decided that the half Alium, half Stagnant children were old enough to care for themselves most of the time and returned to Heaven. Each day they visited the children two or three times to give them food and make sure they were alive. When the Angels were away. Sammael was free to enter the prison to train them. The first time he visited he was treated like a celebrity, they were all excited to meet him for the first time. Luckily, Damascus steel had no effect on him so he was not trapped and could escape before the Angels returned. His magic also passed under the radar as the Angels assumed the children were practicing.

Over their time together, Sammael noticed things about his children, he saw that Astaroth and Loukas were good friends, but Mania and Estrie rarely spoke to one another, even when confined together. Mania was more of a solitary being, even she and her full blood brother, Astaroth, did not speak much; she spent a lot of time on her own and her personality changed often, sometimes she wanted to be left alone while the others practised their fire manipulation, sometimes she wanted to burn the church down. She was interesting to observe.

Estrie, on the other hand. loved attention in any form, she was always talking to someone and was usually too loud, as Lilith had picked up when first seeing her. Estrie had a raw ability when it came to magic, but she had very little self-control and her magic would often explode when she got upset or annoyed. The relationship between Estrie and Loukas was interesting; Estrie was protective of him but from what Sammael could see there was nothing he needed to be protected from. Loukas was not shy, but did seem to be secretive. He was popular with the other three, even with Mania and he wasn't as loud as his sister but could hold his own within the group. He was often a mediator whenever an argument broke out and he was the only one who was able to calm Estrie. Despite Estrie having extreme natural powers, her magic was not as strong as Mania's blood brother, Astaroth. Sammael kept an eye on Astaroth most of all. He was always calm, and the others listened to him instinctively. He was a natural leader with great power and built-in self-control, Sammael knew Lilith would be impressed with this one.

The Lord of Hell spent ten years training the Cambions in the art of demonic magic. He taught them how to control their powers and how to draw strength and power from the plains of Hell in order to manipulate the elements and bend the forces of nature to their wills. He taught them the history of the Alium, how they had been separate for years until the Angels wanted to band all supernatural entities together in a group and make them subjects of the Seraphic Laws. The Cambions learned the story of Lilith, her fall from mortal grace and rise to immortal power. They were aware that their biological mothers were mortals, but to the children, Lilith was their mother. Sammael explained Lilith's cause and the oppression that the Arcadian Laws would bring, he told them of their roles and how they were the only beings who could put a stop to the new laws since they were not classed as Alium or Stagnant and so were not to be included in Seraphic and Arcadian Laws.

After eighteen years of being trapped, ten of which they were tutored by Sammael, it was time... it was time that they be released. They were powerful enough, they hated Angels and they were old enough to be tried before the Seraphic Council. The Council would determine if they were more Alium or Stagnant and if they needed to add new Arcadian Laws that encompassed them into the Alium before passing the laws in a few months time. One night after a planning session with Sammael, the Cambions decided that it was time to put their escape plot into action.

It was rare that Adriel went anywhere without Nakir, they had fought side by side ever since Lilith's attack on Heaven in the early days of human creation. They had become two of the closest warriors of the Seraphic Army; perhaps even closer than Lucifer and Sammael *had* been before their fall.

That morning, however, Nakir had been called to check out a Demonic disturbance somewhere else, meaning that Adriel had the assignment of collecting the Cambions from their prison and bringing them before the Seraphic Council alone.

Easy, he thought. He was an Angel, a soldier of Heaven, they were four glorified Stagnants; or at least they were in his view. He hoped the Council would see it his way and they would be finished with the Cambions for good and could finally pass the new Laws that would monitor the behaviours of Alium scum.

Adriel emerged before the door of the Church prison in a swirling cloud of bright white smoke. The air around him was crisp, it was very early in the morning and the sun was just starting to rise, casting a faint orange glow across the dark grey stones and casting reflections in the Damascus steel. Adriel could feel the celestial energy pouring from the enchanted metal. It relaxed him as it would any Angel; but it had quite the opposite effects on lesser Demons. It was similar to the effect that iron had on Faeries. His plan was to enter the Church while the four were still asleep and use his magic to keep them that way as he transported them to the Seraphic Council chambers in Olympus, to the home of the Olympian Angels and the head of the Council.

When Adriel placed his hand on the door, it flashed white for a second before swinging open. Only a hand with Angel Ichor could open the door to the prison. He kept his blade sheathed by his side as he entered and was surprised to see that they had all returned to the room where he had banished Lilith eighteen years before. Usually, when he entered the church, he had to go through various rooms in order to find them all. It unsettled Adriel that they were all seated on adjacent sofas, in complete silence. At the sound of Adriel's approach, the four of them turned to look at him. His wings twitched nervously.

"Adriel." Astaroth greeted him, as was to be expected. It was always surprising for Adriel when he heard Astaroth speak, his voice was deep and quiet with an unplaceable British accent. Astaroth looked at him with his slick red-raven hair and his bright cyan eyes.

"How can we help you?" Estrie spoke from the opposite sofa. She was strikingly similar to Lilith, her hair a waterfall of black, her skin beautifully tanned; even her eyes were such a dark brown they could have been confused as black. As usual she was dressed glamorously, a mix of silver and white. If it were not for the smirk on her dark lips, she would have looked angelic.

"Don't you usually visit us later than this?" Loukas said, turning his head slightly to the side. Adriel could believe Loukas was half Demon, he was almost identical to Sammael, tall and tanned with emerald eyes and a tousle of black curls on the top of his head. His voice was similar to Sammael's as well, rough but quiet.

Adriel began to speak, but was cut off.

"What was the plan? Were you going to keep us asleep using magic and take us to be tried without telling us?"

Adriel had no words for Mania. Out of all four Cambions, Mania was the one who scared him, her eyes were brown, but no matter how the light caught them, they looked a dark red. Unlike Astaroth, who had taken after Sammael, Mania resembled their mother and her hair was naturally cherry red, as were her lips.

They all stood and faced Adriel with menacing looks in their eyes and on each face. The Angel, feeling threatened, drew his sword from his side, like the metal in the walls, his blade was Damascus steel. He pointed the blade toward the Cambions and spread his wings out fully behind him into arches of white light.

"Go on, attack me," he baited them. He believed them unaware of his promise to Lilith. If they attacked him, he could kill them, but he could do nothing until they made the first move.

"No." Loukas said. "If we don't harm you, you cannot harm us." He didn't want to fight; he didn't want to kill. He knew he was different from the others in that sense, but he had no interest in spilling blood.

"Why don't you just let us out of here?" It was worth a try.

Adriel chuckled. "You want me to let you go? Why, so you can go and find Lilith? So you can play happy families? She has a plan for you, I don't know what it is, but she'll have one, that is the only reason you are alive. Once you have served your purpose, you will be cast aside like the last one."

Loukas clenched his fists by his side, the one thing he had been sure of was the love of Lilith, the love of his mother. Despite never having met her, deep down he craved her love, her protection like he yearned for love from Estrie, and Mania and Astaroth and from Sammael.

"You're lying. She would never do that. She loves us." He said through gritted teeth as he felt Estrie place a hand on his shoulder, but this time it didn't calm him. He was a Cambion, a Demon... if Lilith, Mother of Demons, did not love him, who would?

"You mean like she loved Cain, the first version of you?" Adriel said.

He could sense the anger rising from all of them, slowly bubbling, ready to overflow and become an attack. The Angel watched as looks of confusion ran over their faces. They knew nothing of Cain.

"Do you not know about Cain? Lilith fed him her blood as a baby to make him obedient, she used him to destroy Adam and Eve and then she threw him away. That is your fate."

"Liar!" yelled Loukas as he shook his shoulder to remove his sister's hand. Loukas' magic was ruled by his emotions, and Adriel had triggered his strongest one - fear.

His voice created a powerful gust of wind which shot forward. As it approached, the wind picked up a tiny shard of broken glass, a remnant from eighteen years before. It flew toward the Angel and hit, sending the small piece of glass deep into Adriel's cheek just below his golden eye.

"That," Adriel said as he drew the small shard of glass from his skin, it was no longer clear, but coated in shimmering golden ichor, "was an attack."

In one swift movement, Adriel swung his sword and flew at Loukas.

Estrie watched as the Angel soared through the air toward her brother. She knew Loukas would defend himself, but he wouldn't go for the kill, not like the others would. She loved her brother, but she wished he would just let his demon side in as she had. Adriel got closer and Estrie pushed Loukas to the side and created a fireball in her palm which she launched toward the Angel. It struck one of his wings making him drop to the floor, landing on his feet.

Estrie flicked her long black hair over her shoulder and began strutting toward Adriel, her glistening silver heels tapping loudly on the stone floor. She created a long blade of dark metal. She held it in her hand and brandished it angrily before him. The Angel made the first move, swinging his blade, Estrie jumped back and felt the breeze caused by the blade close to her chest. She retaliated with an equally quick and powerful strike which was parried by the Angel. With each swing their blades clashed loudly. With her free hand, Estrie created a small bolt of lightning, it shot from her fingers and struck Adriel in the face, he cried out in pain and dropped his sword. Without taking a moment to think, Estrie lunged with her blade and drove her blade straight through the Angel's silver armour and into his stomach. Adriel yelled loudly as the metal cut through his bronze skin and brought a hand away from his eye, which was leaking ichor thanks to the bolt of lightning. She drove the blade up and he grunted and coughed up ichor before dropping to his knees, clutching his wounds.

Estrie ripped the blade from the Angel and watched as he fell forward, his armour clattering loudly. She turned back to her friends, her expression stony and unreadable. She had accepted her demonic side, but that didn't mean she liked it. It was a part of her..She was young, and she knew she was pretty; she had no desire to kill anything, only to protect herself and her friends. Estrie really wanted to go out into the mortal world and have fun. She knew of Stagnants that did that, some of them even got paid for doing it; she had been keeping up to date with them for years with a secret phone that

Sammael knew nothing about. She knew he would be unhappy that she used mortal technology, but it was fun.

She was just nearing the other Cambions when Astaroth spoke.

"Estrie, behind you," she turned and saw the Angel hurtling through the air toward her, blade back in his hand. She barely had time to drop to the floor and roll out of the way, sending her ichor-covered blade sliding toward Astaroth who grabbed it.

"Why isn't he dead?" Estrie shouted as she got back to her feet. She uttered a low growl when she saw that her white blazer was stained with Adriel's ichor; she loved that outfit and Sammael had said that ichor was almost impossible to get off of skin and fabric.

"For a mortal to kill an Angel, one must pierce its heart. Only an immortal can destroy an Angel by other means." Mania said.

Despite being half Alium, the four Cambions were not immortal in any sense, they were difficult to kill but it was possible; given time they would also die of natural old age, something that would not happen to other immortals who could be killed, such as Angels and Faeries.

"Sammael has taught us this, don't you listen?"

Mania seemed distant; her crazed, brown-red eyes were fixated on Astaroth as he battled with Adriel, narrowly avoiding the Angel's strikes.

"Do I seem the type to pay attention in school?" Estrie said.

"Will you be quiet!" hissed Loukas as he fired a ball of dark green energy soaring toward Adriel, who was close to impaling Astaroth with his sword. Astaroth was his closest friend, not that he'd ever been given the chance to make any others, but still, he valued Astaroth greatly and despite his feelings about his Demonic side, he would never abandon his friend or let harm come to him. The energy ball shot through the air and struck Adriel in the shoulder. The Angel cried out and dropped his blade; in the split second between silence and the metal of the sword slamming onto the floor, Astaroth wrapped his hand around Adriel's throat and held him up before throwing him onto his back violently. Roaring loudly, Astaroth raised his sword and drove it down forcefully, there was a loud crack as the blade snapped open the Angel's silver breastplate followed by the squishing sound of piercing flesh. Adriel screamed as his ichor sprayed out of him and ran down the silver of his armour; his screams ceased when Astaroth drove the blade up in a swift movement and pierced the golden heart of Adriel.

Astaroth removed the blade with an aggressive tug and grunt, then threw it to the ground into a puddle of ichor pooling around the deceased Angel. He brushed a black hair out of his face and turned to face the other Cambions. They all looked impressed, but concerned since none of them had killed before. They had never witnessed a murder; especially not something so Heavenly, it was impressive that Astaroth had done this. It was an experience none of them would forget, no matter how hard they tried.

The silence was broken by a whooshing noise created by a swirling pillar of green cloud followed by clapping as it died down and revealed Sammael.

"Well done, that was very impressive." The Lord of Hell said as he stopped clapping. His green eyes and black hair stood out against the bright white of his suit. He began to make his way toward the door.

"This way, we cannot create a portal to Hell in here, it will alert the Angels."

"We cannot leave, the door is spelled so only the hand of one with Angel ichor may open the door." Loukas said confidently. He liked to show his intelligence or power when in the presence of his father, he knew Astaroth was his favourite, but he wanted to be as close as he could.

"How did you – ?" the green eyed Cambion asked as Sammael opened the door to the church.

"I am a Fallen *Angel*, my ichor still has remnants of Seraphic Ichor, your blood however, is Demonic and Stagnant. You have no Angelic ichor. I suggest you find a way out or I'll have to go to Hell without you and the Angels can have you."

Sammael disappeared out of the door.

"Okay, let's think, how do we escape?" Estrie said. She put a finger to the side of her mouth and pouted her thinking face. After barely three seconds she dropped her arms and sighed.

"Ugh, it's too hard, we best give up." She sat back on the couch.

Mania glared at Estrie, she didn't like the girl and had done her best to avoid any and all contact with her over the last eighteen years. Some days she wanted to slap her, other times she wanted to gut her.

"It's simple," she walked toward the body of the Angel, hissing as she drew the blade from the ichor, the golden liquid stinging her hand. She swung the sword down twice and sliced off both of the Angels hands, a maniacal look in her eyes and a smirk fighting to emerge.

"Take a hand, use it to pass through the door then throw them back in for the last two."

She dropped down and grabbed one of the severed hands with ease, gore didn't scare Mania, she found it fascinating. In fact, one of the rare occasions she had spent any time with Estrie was when she had used her magic to retrieve something called a television and they had watched a horror movie together. Of course, Estrie had screamed the entire time, but Mania had found it quite enjoyable.

With the Angel's hand in hers, Mania walked toward the door, her cherry hair swaying at her waist, she placed the severed palm on the door and it swung open, allowing her to pass. Once outside, she threw the hand back into the room. Astaroth grabbed the other hand lying in the ichor and copied his sister's action, with Estrie and Loukas following suit.

Sammael was waiting for them outside, his arms folded, his bronze skin shining in the light of the rising sun. He smiled, flashing his perfect teeth as he saw them; in this light it was easy to see how he had once been an Angel.

"I thought it would take you longer than that."

There was an undertone of pride in his words, they were his children, and he was pleased to see they were intelligent and powerful. The Lord of Hell clicked his fingers and a swirling cloud of green with a strong pull began spinning before them all.

"This is a portal to Hell; it is time to meet your mother." Sammael said before stepping into the pillar of cloud and disappearing from sight.

Astaroth, Mania, Loukas and Estrie looked at each other. They had been waiting for this moment their entire lives, everything they had been taught had been leading to their first meeting with Lilith and helping her stop the Angels. Taking a deep, collective breath, the four Cambions entered the portal and began their quick, loud descent into Hell.

Nakir was concerned when he returned to Heaven after dealing with a Demon to find that Adriel had not returned with the Cambions. Adriel was one of the best soldiers in the Seraphic army, but Nakir knew that the Cambions were very strong and powerful. If they chose to fight against Adriel there was a very slim chance he would actually win. Fearing the worst, Nakir flew to Gabriel's Peak, the highest point of Heaven, to ask the Archangel Gabriel, the leader of the Seraphic Army, if he could go to Earth and check on his brother. He was granted permission but was instructed to take another Angel, Barachiel, just in case.

Nakir and Barachiel travelled to Earth and landed just outside of the Church. The door was open, which was the first worrying sign and there was a strong smell of brimstone; a clear indication of Demonic activity. Nakir stationed Barachiel outside and made his way into the building. He was horrified when he saw the two severed hands leaking golden ichor and losing their colour. Nakir told himself that they might not be Adriel's hands. This thought was proven to be false when Nakir turned to see the body on the floor surrounded by a pool of drying gold ichor. He ran over and dropped to his knees beside the motionless body of Adriel.

"Barachiel!" Nakir yelled. He did not cry. Angels were warriors and emotions, as well as tears, were foreign to them.

Barachiel entered the Church, his glowing eyes following the same path to Nakir., to the hands and then the body. He ran to the other side of Adriel and knelt, asking "The Cambions did this?"

"They are not Cambions, there is nothing Stagnant about them. They are Demons." Nakir said through gritted teeth as he got to his feet.

"We must gather the Seraphic Council, these creatures are eighteen and they have slaughtered an Angel. They can be held accountable to any laws we now pass; it is time we use the Musas." With that, Nakir snatched up Adriel's blade from the ground and marched out of the church.

Chapter 3

"What do you mean we cannot hunt them down?" Nakir demanded. He slammed his hands down on the white table before him angrily and stood up. "They killed Adriel!"

Nakir was in a room of pure white with the walls, doors, floor, ceiling and even the furniture all made of blindingly white Seraphic stone. He was speaking before the Seraphic Council, a group made up of a representative from each of the main four Pantheons: Greek, Norse, Egyptian and Celtic. There were also representatives from each sector of Angels: Cherubim,

Angel, Archangel and Seraphim. He had explained what he had seen in the Church prison and had proposed that they send a party after the Cambions. The idea that had been rejected by the Council.

"You have no proof that they were the ones who murdered your brother," said a woman. Her hair eyes were golden and her brown hair was tied neatly on the top of her head. She wore the silver breastplate worn by all Angels and her thin, crystal-like wings could hardly be seen. Her wings and the long spear by her side made it clear that she was an Olympian Angel of the Greek Pantheon, once mistakenly considered a god. She was Athena, Angel of Wisdom and Battle Strategy.

"For all we know, a greater Demon killed Adriel and took the Cambions to Hell for Lilith." She spoke with reason and her tone was calm and compelling.

"That does sound like a more logical explanation, why would the Cambions attack Adriel now after never showing hostility toward Angels before?" chirped a small golden eyed, red haired Angel with a thick Irish accent. He was Ecne, a member of the Tuatha De Danann, the Celtic Pantheon of Gods.

"I think it would make more sense if we disregard the Cambions now, and focus on the Arcadian Laws. They are due to be passed in two months and we still have to finalise them."

It was of no surprise to Nakir that Tyr would be the one to say this. He was the Norse Angel of War and Laws and he thought of nothing else.

The Council began discussing the Laws, which of the old ones they desired to keep the same, which they thought needed updating or removing. It was an endless cycle of noise entering Nakir's head and irritating him. He remained silent for a few moments, allowing the voices to wash over him as he took deep breaths.

"Enough!" he shouted, slamming his hands on the table again, creating a loud bang. "Adriel has been killed, and I *know* that those four *Demons* are responsible for it! They are dangerous to Alium and Stagnant alike and it is your duty to protect them, so do it!" his voice shook but his words were clear. His friend had been murdered and deserved to be avenged.

The Seraphic Council looked at Nakir, their golden eyes filled with bewilderment. Emotions were foreign to them, especially among immortals.

"What would you have us do, Nakir?" a man with a thick Egyptian accent questioned. He was wearing a robe of gold and a headdress which hooked down like a beak; he was Thoth, Angel of Wisdom in the Egyptian Pantheon.

"Use the Musas," Nakir said calmly. They were finally listening. "Should a large meeting of any Alium be announced, send in the Musas, have them check it out and if it is Lilith or the Cambions, have them infiltrate their group. Use them to gain inside intelligence." He had thought this plan through and believed it would work.

"Please."

"All those in favour of Nakir's plan, say aye," Athena said.

Whether it was because of Nakir's desperation or because they believed in his plan, or just to shut him up; a chorus of ayes ran around the table ending with Athena. Nakir thanked them all and left the council room so they could continue their planning of the Arcadian Laws. He smiled, knowing that Adriel's death was not going to be in vain, his death would have purpose and would contribute to bringing down the Alium evil. With that proud thought, Nakir launched himself from Heaven to go back, once again, to Earth. He must search long and hard for his secret weapon, the Musas.

"Pandemonium, the capital of Hell, the first of all Demon realms. A place of death, destruction and torment, home to Lilith; mother of all Demons and

Queen of Hell." Sammael said, swinging his arm out to present the vista before the group once they had emerged from the portal.

"You should put that in the brochure," Estrie said as she looked in the direction her father had indicated.

Pandemonium was the capital of Hell, one of the eight realms of the Alium world. Like each of the other realms, there were eight cities within the realm large enough to be compared to the continents of the Stagnant world. The names of the cities were Pandemonium, Fasts, Irae, Desidia, Avaritia, Gula, Libidine and Livor. The capital was a vast wasteland; the air was veiled in a thin layer of mist the same shade of red as the sky above her head and the sand beneath her feet; it gave everything an odd crimson tinge. There were small white temple-like buildings with domed roofs scattered across the land. The sky was filled with large, winged demons screeching as they flew through the air.

Scattered around were tall broken buildings of dull crystal, smashed glass and dirty white stone. They had once been great buildings and palaces in Heaven until the fall. Estrie wasn't sure if it were her imagination, but she thought she could hear screaming, not the screaming of Demons, but of people. She zoned out of that when her eyes adjusted to the mists of Hell and she saw the fortress of bright white stone shining in the distance.

The air before the group seemed to shake for a moment as the red sands were lifted from the ground. They realised that the air was not shaking but someone was moving so quickly that each individual movement was a blur. When the person arrived, the air stopped moving and the sand fell back to the ground and they saw a woman. Her skin was pale, and her brown eyes were wide and adorned with long black eyelashes. She had voluminous brown hair that made her face seem very thin and her cheekbones very sharp. She smiled, parting her full red lips to reveal two long fangs.

"Everyone, this is Amber Alarie, the world's oldest Vampire." Sammael introduced her.

"So, these are the Cambions," Amber said. There was something about her voice, a mix of different dialects with French at the forefront; she had been alive for thousands of years, it was understandable she might pick up a few accents over time.

"The world's oldest vampire?" Astaroth echoed. "I thought the Elders were the oldest?"

He spoke of Tremeur, Maslin, Chapin and Bellamy Chevalier; the four Vampires that made up the Rättslig, the Vampire Council who tried and punished Vampires who broke the law.

Amber chuckled. "They are the oldest recorded Vampires, that is correct. I was the first Vampire ever to be created, I turned many Vampires, but as the population grew and the Aurum and Argentum were created I went into hiding and haven't surfaced since."

Amber referenced the two most powerful Vampire clans.

"After that I was forgotten about; many wrote me off as dead, some even labelled me a myth and so I have remained in Hell ever since."

"Amber, take them to the fortress," Sammael said in a bored voice, he had heard this story too many times before. "Don't feed on them and don't let the Hellhounds near them. I will return soon." Amber bowed a head to Sammael before he disappeared in a spiral of green smoke.

"Suis-moi," Amber said, the French in her accent shining through.

"Sammael taught us Tamil," Estrie sighed heavily. "Not Spanish, we don't know what you're saying."

Amber turned and looked at Estrie with great confusion; she wasn't sure whether or not the girl was joking. When Estrie shook her head and widened her eyes, Amber realised she was not joking. "That... that was French. I said "Follow me." Amber shook her head and continued walking.

The group entered the nearest of the white stone temples, the inside of each was white and small, there was a hole in the floor of the temple that led underground. They followed Amber down the stairs into a tunnel lit by torches of bright red flames on walls of red, gritty stone; a compact form of the sand above them. As they walked, Mania, who seemed obsessed with the Vampire, was spouting questions nonstop, which Amber seemed to enjoy. Talking about herself was one of Amber's favourite pastimes.

Astaroth remained by his sisters' side but did not say anything. He was busy thinking about meeting Lilith for the first time; it was exciting but nerve-wracking at the same time. Estrie had no interest in listening to the Vampire and held back slightly. Loukas did the same, his sister had a way of isolating herself and not realising until it was too late, he didn't want her to be alone.

"So," Estrie said. "Isn't Hell lovely? I'm sure you and the other Demons will get on nicely."

"Es, please don't" Loukas hadn't spoken to anyone but his sister about his dislike of his Demon side, she felt a similar dislike, but not to the same extent. Being in Hell was highlighting his fears to him, he was a damned monster surrounded by damned monsters. In the event of his death, this is where he was going to end up.

"Why not?" she chuckled. "We might be able to find a nice Demon boy for you to fall in love with," She couldn't help herself.

"Estrie, stop it! Stop mocking me!" Loukas hissed.

His sister was forever reminding him of his fears and his flaws. He was fine with being gay, happy even, but could anyone, male or female ever truly love a Demon? Loukas didn't think so and Estrie knew it, he didn't understand why she enjoyed tormenting him. He didn't mock her for her obsession with Stagnants and their technology. Why would you intentionally upset someone you were supposed to care for?

"Fine, sorry," Estrie knew she had crossed the line when he referred to her by her full name instead of her nickname. She grunted angrily. In her mind it was only a bit of fun.

"I guess we should listen to the boring Vampire woman."

Together they moved forward to join the rest of the group, just as Amber began her life story.

"I was twenty when it happened. Something, I don't know what, attacked me and suddenly I couldn't go out during the day without my skin sizzling, I couldn't step foot in a church, and I had an aching hunger. I tried to eat but it always came back up. I didn't know what was wrong with me and I couldn't explain it to anyone or I would have been labelled a Witch and killed. Instead, I pretended I was ill and remained in my home all the time during the days. At night I ventured into the woods and I realised I could do other things. I could see in the dark, I could run faster than any normal human and I was stronger than the strongest of men. Then it happened, a small animal ran past me and I caught its scent. I hunted and killed that rabbit, I drained it of all its blood, and I immediately felt stronger and more powerful. I knew that if I wanted more strength, I would have to feast on a human, but I didn't want to hurt anyone.

I locked myself away for a decade. I refused to see visitors. I only went outside at night to feed on animals, but my hunger grew greater and greater. One night, as I was hunting a deer in the woods, I came across a boy, only eighteen but I couldn't control myself and I fed on him. Trying to escape me, he bit my hand and accidentally swallowed some of my blood and when I drank from him, I drained him until he died. With my blood in his system, he came back to life as a vampire; that was how I learned of my final power, the power to make more of my kind. I hated myself for it, I thought I was a monster, but I did it again and again and again. I couldn't stop myself; the blood was too good, and I knew they would come back anyway as long as they had my blood in them.

I had to kill the boy, the one I had first transformed. He turned his sister and then killed dozens of men without shifting them into vampires. He was making our existence too obvious. After that I lost control again and I returned to my hometown and turned my five best friends into Vampires. I couldn't forgive myself for what I had done to them and so I burned down my house and threw in the body of a woman that I had killed and when my friends rose from the dead, they believed I had burned to death and so they believed themselves to be the first Vampires and after many years they titled themselves the Elders. I believed that I would age as a normal human and that I would eventually die, but that never happened so I hid for years, watching as the Vampire population grew, how they created talismans that allowed them to walk in the sun and I never revealed myself to the world again.

Now I am ready to reveal myself once more, if I help to put a stop to these Arcadian Laws, I will be able to return to Vampire society, hailed as a legend and a hero and I will take my place among the Elders as Vampire royalty."

Mania, Loukas and Astaroth listened intently as they walked, their eyes filled with interest and intrigue. Estrie, on the other hand, found the tale rather boring and tedious, probably because it wasn't about her. She pushed her way to the front of the group just as Amber finished.

"Are you done yet?" she questioned, only to receive a dirty look from the Vampire in response. "Oh good, we're here,"

Estrie led them up the steps of a small temple and to the foot of a white marble palace. The palace seemed to shine as it would have in Heaven, the front wall was smooth and decorated with a large black cross crowned by a crescent moon, the symbol of Lilith.

"I hate to tell you guys this, but there is no door."

"Oh, shut up, Estrie!" Mania snapped. All she had heard during Amber's tale was the same huffing and sighing Estrie had been making her entire life, it was clear she liked to be the centre of attention, but there was no need to be rude.

"Ooh, I've never seen you show so much emotion," Estrie said smugly. "Lone wolf's got fangs!"

"I may usually look calm, but in my head, I kill you at least seven times a day." Mania snarled.

"As much as I would love to see a cat fight, we have a schedule to keep," Amber said as she bit her palm and rubbed a couple of drops of her blood onto the wall before her. A small arch appeared in the wall, it pushed backwards and then separated in the middle to create an entrance. Amber led them into a parlour that was created with bright white stone and appeared to be empty.

Two sets of red carpeted stairs on either side rose to the balcony and to doors leading to different parts of the fortress. In the centre of the room, exuding the most light, was a statue of Lilith, naked with a large snake wrapped around her shoulders covering different areas of her body. It was a monument depicting her placement of the snake in the garden and her time spent in Eden.

"I wish I was that body confident," Estrie said. She and the others knew it was a joke. Estrie had no confidence issues at all.

"Go and pick rooms for yourselves, they're all the same, and then wait for Lilith in the assembly room, she will be here presently." Amber said as she walked off into the palace, leaving the Cambions to find their own way around.

It had been five years since the deaths of Chidiebube and Ginika Musa. They had just moved from Lagos, Nigeria, to a small country house in the south of England and they had been walking to a shop in their local village. No one was quite sure what happened next. Some claimed there had been a wild animal, others claimed it had been a man with a knife, all that was completely clear was that the throats of Chidiebube and Ginika had been slashed and that they had bled out on the side of the road as people panicked and tried to call for an ambulance; but it was too late. Every year, on the anniversary of their death, their children, Mahina, Mariah and Moroccan Musa visited the scene of the attack to grieve. This year was no different.

It was mid-August; the air was thick, and the sun was beating brightly on the ground - not typical weather for England. The Moroccan son hated that the world seemed so happy, every year the weather was exactly the same on this day, as if whatever force was in charge of the universe was celebrating the deaths of his parents. That wasn't the only reason he also disliked it being bright, whenever the sun was shining, it highlighted what made him different to those around him. His hair; like his sisters, was a shimmering silver that seemed to glow with the rays of light. Most people assumed they all dyed their hair, but it was their natural color. When they had moved from Nigeria, he was thirteen years old, Mariah was fourteen and Mahina was eighteen. Their hair had slowly lost its darkness and been replaced by the metallic colour and the same had happened to their eyes. No one had been able to explain it, not Chidiebube and Ginika, not even doctors. When he had been in school, Moroccan had been mocked for his hair, mocked by the other boys for dying it. His sisters hadn't been harassed about their hair. They were told they looked pretty, and people told them how incredible it made them look, especially Mariah. She had always been the good-looking one of the family.

The three of them never spoke much when visiting the site of their parent's death, they never had anything to say. Instead, they remained silent, wrapped up in their own thoughts and memories of being rushed out of school and to the hospital where their parents were already dead. Mariah had cried for hours whereas Moroccan refused to believe it. That same day, they had been placed into the care of their eldest sister. They had inherited their parent's house and a large sum of money to help them pay for things until she began working and earning enough to sustain herself and her siblings.

Mariah wiped a tear from her cheek and turned to face her siblings. Mahina's face was mostly covered by an array of glistening curls, she had a hand on Morrocan's shoulder whose face was hard and unmoving. Mariah didn't understand why he never showed emotions, never released his feelings in any visible way. She assumed that this was the way of men; she had often heard it said, but she rarely saw it in practice. Their father had been an emotional man, but he was always positive, forever smiling. It seemed that neither she or Moroccan had inherited that part of him, neither of them smiled much but at least she tried. Mahina had always tried her best to be positive for her siblings and none of them, even Mahina herself, could tell whether her happiness was genuine or an act for the benefit of others.

"Five years," Mahina said awkwardly. It was uncomfortably tense between them. As siblings they loved each other, but they were very different.

"And we still don't know what happened," Moroccan responded. He had carried a bitterness inside him for five years over the fact that no one cared enough to find out what truly happened to his parents. It was labelled a death under mysterious circumstances and no eyewitnesses could agree on what had happened and there was no evidence to provide any leads. They had just moved to the area and they didn't know anyone, which gave no one a motive.

Mariah nodded in agreement, her silver bob bouncing on her shoulders. She too was upset that they didn't know who killed their parents, how it had happened or why. She looked up to the sky, allowing the sun to brush across her face, the rays seemed to reveal bright silver flecks on her dark skin. It pleased her that the sun was out today of all days, it lifted her mood a little. Sometimes she liked to think it was her parents telling her they were okay now. She squinted slightly as the light stung her chrome-coloured eyes, she thought she saw a bird flying in the sky, no, not a bird, it was too big to be a bird. What was it? As it got closer, the shape blocked the sun and became a shadow, the silhouette of a man - perhaps it was a paraglider.

"What in hell is that?" Moroccan said, looking in the same direction as his sisters. Mahina moved to stand before the two of them as it approached ever closer.

"I can assure you; I am nothing from Hell," the creature said as it landed, the sun bouncing off of its armour and the unusually large white wings. His skin was as bronze as his hair and his eyes were the gold of all angels.

"I am Nakir, warrior of Paradise."

"An Angel," Moroccan laughed. He had been raised to believe in God and Angels, but his faith was not that strong. He could not understand why any greater power would allow his parent's deaths. Despite Mahina's best efforts, he had turned his back on religion the day their parents died.

"Yes, an Angel," Nakir echoed.

Mariah dropped into an awkward curtsy. Unlike her brother she had a deep religious faith. She was pulled upright by Mahina.

Moroccan rolled his eyes. "Why would an Angel visit us?"

"Heaven needs your help, in fact, every realm needs your help." Nakir said in all seriousness.

Moroccan couldn't hold back his laughter this time, until he was silenced by one dangerous look from Nakir.

"You do not believe; I can prove it to you."

"Go ahead," Moroccan crossed his arms as Mariah gave him an angry look.

"It will require yourself," Nakir pointed to Moroccan. "Hold out your arm and say *'Meridiem'*."

Moroccan sighed and pulled up the sleeve of his hoodie and stretched out his arm. "*Meridiem*," he said, his voice dripping in boredom.

For a moment, nothing happened, and he gave an ironic smile. His smile faltered as the tips of his fingers and the centre of his palm began glowing with a bright white light. The glow intensified for a few moments before dying down and disappearing from Moroccan's hand.He stared at it for a moment with fear in his eyes, but he did not say a word.

"Now that I have your attention, let me explain," Nakir grinned. "The three of you are part-Angel, you are the children of Ginika Musa and throughout your mother's family line back to the beginning, you have Angelic blood. This comes from your very first ancestor, Mukuachukwu, a strong woman who caught the eye of the leader of the Seraphim Angels, Seraphiel. For this to happen is virtually unknown and giving birth to mixed angel and mortal children is now illegal. Seraphiel and Mukuachukwu conceived a child, a child that was half-Angel and half-human. From that time, there has always been Angel blood in your family and although it is now diluted, it is still very powerful.

We have decided to reveal this to you now because we need your help. There is an immense Demonic threat surfacing even as we speak, and when the time comes, we are going to need you to infiltrate them. They are unaware of your existence, however they knew of your mother's birth. They sent a Demon to kill her, and your father was an added casualty. If you join us, you will not only help the world, but you will be avenging your parents' deaths."

Nakir looked between Mariah and Moroccan hopefully, he hadn't lied to them, Angels could not lie, but he had left out how dangerous this mission was going to be.

Mahina, Moroccan and Mariah exchanged glances and Moroccan nodded at his sisters.

"Tell us everything," Mahina said.

"Do you have somewhere we can go, there is going to be a lot of information?" Nakir asked.

"This way," Mariah said and the three Musa siblings began to lead the Angel toward their home.

Chapter 4

Astaroth, Estrie, Loukas and Mania all found rooms along the same corridor of the fortress. Each of the rooms had the identical layout, a large arched door that led into a sitting room of glowing white stone. It was neatly furnished with two soft black sofas facing one another with a black-legged, glass coffee table between them. In each corner of the room were more square tables with glass tops and on each one was a tall lamp with a black shade, lit by a magical flame that would remain lit to the exact preference of the guest staying in the room. There was another archway on the other side of the room that was covered by a thin black curtain.

This opening led to the bedchamber. This chamber was also made of the same white stone and had the same glass tables and magical lamps in each corner. Located against one wall was a large four poster bed hidden behind dark curtains hanging on black poles. Across from the bed was a dark vanity table and a mirror and next to the table was a large wardrobe fully stocked with clothes selected by Lilith. There were only three walls in the bed chamber, the furthest wall had been replaced by pillars that one could slip between onto a personal balcony looking out at the blood red vista of Pandemonium. Everything in the rooms and, in fact, all of Hell stood out against the bright white of the fortress.

It was clear that the fortress had once been a monument of Heaven - no Demon could make something so beautiful.

Estrie threw open the double doors of the wardrobe to see what style Lilith preferred. She was horrified to see dozens of dresses that would cover her neck and arms and would touch the floor when worn. And even worse, the majority of them were brown. She grabbed one of the thick, brown dresses and flicked her wrist, instantly the white and silver suit she had been wearing was replaced by the hideous gown. She shook her head and tapped the dress. Immediately the top of the dress separated from the skirt to reveal the majority of her stomach and hips. The colour changed, and the collar disappeared to be replaced by a plunging neckline. The skirt also changed to black and ripped down the middle before wrapping their now separate parts around her legs to create tight, black skinny jeans.

Estrie smiled as she tapped her neck and a chain of silver slithered around and slipped down to grace the revealing border of the neckline. She tapped her fingers lightly and numerous shimmering rings appeared. With one more flick of her wrist, a pair of black heeled shoes appeared on her feet and her outfit was complete.

"What the hell are you wearing?" Astaroth had entered her room silently through the thin black curtain. His cold blue eyes looked her up and down.

"I could ask you the same question," Estrie retorted. Astaroth was dressed like Sammael usually was, in a suit, only this one was made of a shining black satin. As she said this, Astaroth looked himself up and down before shaking his head and looking back to Estrie.

"Our mother chose this for me," Astaroth said. Estrie hated it when any of them referred to Lilith as their mother. She was not their mother and they didn't even know her.

"I doubt she'd let you walk around like that."

"You're right," Estrie said. She giggled when a look of confusion ran across Astaroth's face, never before had she admitted someone else was right; especially not in front of them.

"I should fix my hair," she finished. Estrie ruffled her dark hair a little and pushed it down the front of one shoulder.

"Estrie," Astaroth warned.

"It's too late to change now," Estrie responded lightly as she strutted past Astaroth as though she was on a catwalk. He had no time to respond as she strode past the dark curtain and began making her way through the fortress. Astaroth walked quickly after her, hoping to prevent her from causing any trouble this early in their arrival.

It took the two of them a while to find the Assembly hall as Amber had not given any directions and there did not seem to be anyone else about the fortress. In each corridor there was something new that Estrie saw and wanted to play with: an ancient sword, a powerful grimoire, a bust of Sammael.

Astaroth found it was like leading a child around. They ended up bumping into Loukas and Mania who seemed equally lost and were equally as disparaging of Estrie's choice of clothing. After wandering aimlessly for a while, the group found what seemed to be the only door they hadn't yet tried, located close to the library filled with books on Demonic history and infernal magic. It was a double door, like all the others, with an arched shape and was pure black with silver embellishments. Astaroth knocked on the door and then pushed them both open. When the doors swung open, the four Cambions entered.

The Assembly hall was a large room lit by candles hanging from a metal chandelier and, like the lights in the other chambers, this light was controlled by the will of the person in the room. Now they were bright and illuminated everything. Other than the chandelier and the large, circular table of black wood, the room was quite dull; probably so anyone in there would pay attention to the actual meeting that was taking place.

There were two people already seated in one of the fourteen black chairs. Amber sat with her legs kicked over the edge and Lilith sat with perfect posture, resting her arms on the armrests of the chair. As the group entered the room, the Demon Queen's eyes shot to them immediately with a gaze like a dark void. She rose and began walking toward them. She was in a long-sleeved black jumpsuit and a pair of heeled boots which made her seem even taller. She crouched slightly to hug Astaroth but said nothing. Astaroth felt her jump as she hugged him and slowly drew back, a look of concern seemed to wash over her face for an instant. She then moved to Mania who accepted the hug awkwardly, followed by Loukas who embraced the woman he called 'mother' as fiercely as she hugged him. As Lilith drew away from Loukas, her eyes fell to his sister and remained on her for a moment before her face changed into a grimace.

"That is not a dress from your wardrobe," Lilith said to Estrie.

"Actually," Estrie began as she looked down at her clothes. "It is, I just tweaked it."

"Sit down!" Lilith snapped. Quickly the four Cambions moved to take their seats, Estrie sat next to Amber while Loukas, who looked almost identical to Sammael in his silver suit, took the chair next to his sister. Astaroth seated himself next to Mania, leaving the chair opposite Lilith empty for his father.

There was complete silence until a swirl of green magic appeared just in front of the door. It spun quickly for a moment and then dissipated to reveal Sammael in the same white suit as earlier.

"Oh good, Sammael the Whore has arrived; now we can begin." Lilith said. Her tone was light, but the look in her eyes made it clear that she was not entirely kidding. Sammael had cheated on her, granted it had worked to her advantage, but his infidelity still infuriated her; she was the *first* woman, *all* other women were just variations of Lilith.

"Very droll, Lilith." Sammael grinned wickedly as he took his seat, he knew Lilith was still angry, but it was best not to react or make any catty comments back. He had learned that the hard way.

"So, Sammy-boy, where've you been?" Estrie said as she casually kicked her legs up onto the table, receiving a growl from Lilith as she saw Estrie's shoes.

"All in good time," Sammael responded. His green eyes fell onto Estrie's shoes, his eyebrows lifted as he shook his head, moving his eyes to Estrie who promptly took her feet from the table.

"I am sure Lilith is about to explain."

As if on cue, Lilith rose from her seat. ready to do exactly as Sammael said. She coughed gently to grab everyone's attention before she began.

"Welcome to Hell. I am sure you know who I am, but I am a lady and I believe in proper introductions; I am Lilith, the Queen of Hell, but you can call me Mother. My ichor runs through your veins, it was I who requested that Sammael raise you and teach you the ways of our world. I have heard great things and can see that you are all going to be valuablet assets to our cause."

"If you are wondering what our cause is - which I am sure you are not as you have been raised to fight for it - it is this. For thousands of years, members of the Alium have been oppressed by the laws of Angels known as Seraphic Laws. A plot was discovered years ago in which the Angels planned to bring out new laws as soon as they could, the Arcadian Laws. These rules and regulations oppress our people even more. They are controlling, restrictive and some of them are cruel to the point of barbaric. Thankfully the four of you were born, delaying the Arcadian Laws from being passed so that the Angels could write more that would incorporate you when you became eighteen and they could set the Laws in motion. Now we are but a few weeks away from the Angels announcing them in full and putting them into place."

"We, Sammael and I, have decided that now is the time we start to build our army, an army that the four of you will lead as we march on Heaven. Of course, to build an army, we will need allies and for that, the Alium need to be aware of our cause. Sammael visited different sectors of the world today, speaking with the Witches, Warlocks, Sirens, etc. and has managed to get many of them on our side. He also alerted leaders of some Alium species to expect an embassy tomorrow. You will be those ambassadors: Astaroth, you will visit the Wraiths and the Ghosts: Mania, you will call on the Werewolves; Loukas, I would like you and Amber to meet with the leaders of the Argentum and Aurum Vampire clans. At these meetings, you will tell them a little of our cause and invite them to a gathering and a ball. I will inform you more on that tomorrow. If we can get them on our side, added to my Demons, we will have a chance at defeating the Angels."

Estrie sat up quickly, her eyes wide with fury at being left out. "Ahem!" she fake coughed loudly. "What am I to do?"

Lilith's head turned in Estrie's direction slowly, her face blank of any emotions. "I am hoping you will accompany me to Faerie tomorrow, but first we need to get the Queen to agree to a meeting."

"How do we do that?" Estrie was curious, she had never met a Faerie before; it would be an interesting experience to visit their homeland; not as interesting as visiting the Stagnant world though, not that Lilith or Sammael would ever allow that.

"We are awaiting an ambassador of Faerie," Sammael said.

"And here he is," a new voice said as the doors to the Assembly hall flew open and a man walked in. He was beautiful, anyone would have thought so, he was tall and tan, the muscles of his arms evident in the black sleeves of his tight shirt which was completely open at the front showing off his cobblestone-like abs. Glimpses of his legs could be seen through the rips in his tight black jeans and his face was perfectly symmetrical and angled, his eyes were a deep blue and his hair the same colour as bone. As he strutted in, his Cuban heels tapped loudly on the floor and all eyes were on him.

"Mordred," Lilith got up and walked toward him. She had known Mordred for years; he was the son of a powerful Faerie and the nephew of one even greater. He had been a key element in the fall of Camelot and was a great ally to have. She placed her hands on his arms, squeezing tightly as she kissed both of his cheeks.

"Lilith, wonderful to see you again," Mordred's voice was smooth, almost enchanting; if he was not a Faerie, he could have been a formidable Siren.

"Indeed, please, take a seat. We have plenty to discuss." Lilith gestured to the chairs with a welcoming arm.

Mordred's lapis eyes scanned the room resting on each person for no more than a second, the corner of his mouth lifted slightly after looking at Estrie and Loukas but dropped again when watching Astaroth and Mania.

"I would, Lilith, but I was under the impression that this meeting would just be me and one other person; not a group."

Lilith's face twitched slightly; she was not used to people making demands. Normally she would have killed him for such self-importance, but she needed the Faeries on her side. Their Queen was a bitch anyway, she didn't need the entire realm disliking her as well.

"My apologies," she turned back to the group. "If you would please leave us."

"No, please stay," Mordred said before anyone could move. "I no longer wish to speak with you, Lilith, but I will speak to him," he pointed a long finger toward

Loukas who looked up in bewilderment. "Come, take me to the sitting room of your chamber; we can have a drink and discuss business,"

"Um, okay," Loukas stood up, giving everyone in the room a confused look before leaving the room silently as he led Mordred to his chamber. The large doors slammed behind them loudly.

Lilith moved back to her seat as she pursed her lips and made a face. "He's never not wanted to talk to me."

"Don't pout," Estrie said. "It's unattractive for a woman your age."

Loukas and Mordred sat on the two facing sofas in the sitting room only a few feet from Loukas' bed chamber. They were totally silent for a short moment as Mordred looked directly at Loukas, but the Cambion was avoiding his eyes and looking at anything else he possibly could.

"Well," Mordred said, breaking the silence and drawing Loukas' green eyes to him. "Aren't you going to offer me a drink?"

"I don't have anything to drink,"

"Well then, it is a good thing that my magic works here." Mordred snapped his fingers and two large cocktail glasses full of a bright purple liquid appeared on the coffee table between them,. He pushed one toward Loukas and picked up his own, taking a sip.

"How did you … I thought Faeries required an incantation?"

When Sammael had raised them, he had taught them that Faeries worshipped a Pantheon known as the Tuatha De Danann and that, in order to use magic, they had to pray every time and use an incantation; if they did not, they would be denied.

"I use the magic of the Fommorians, not of the Tuatha. It was originally the magic of Unseelie, but when the Queen took over both Seelie and Unseelie, she allowed us to use it,"

Mordred spoke of the two Courts within Faerie, Seelie was known to be the kinder, gentler Faeries group, whereas members of Unseelie were more cunning and often cruel.

"That means I only need to ever do one prayer and I have access to magic for life. Try your drink."

Loukas was nervous, he had never been in the presence of a Faerie, let alone a member of the Unseelie court. He picked up his glass and tipped the liquid into his mouth, somehow it was both sweet and sour, hot and cold. He assumed it was a Faerie drink, it was nice.

"If I'm honest, I don't really know what I'm meant to be organising here," Loukas chuckled a little and hiccupped, he was feeling a little lightheaded even after just a sip of the Faerie drink; he didn't know if Faerie wine was more intoxicating or if it was just because he hadn't had much alcohol in his lifetime. Even Sammael, a Demon, had been strict on alcohol consumption.

"Lilith wants a meeting with the Queen of the Faeries, so she can have one." Mordred explained as he drank a little more from his glass, smiling over the rim.

"That was easy," Loukas responded and stood up to escort Mordred to the door. "Thank you."

"Oh, we're not done yet," Mordred said. Loukas sat back down.

"No, you see, Faeries give nothing for free. My price: I want to take you out tonight."

Loukas coughed into his drink and placed it back down onto the coffee table with a clink.

"Me?"

"Well, you and your sister; but mainly you." Mordred winked.

"Why?"

"I am a very gifted telepath; I can break into the minds of anyone. Even those like you who attempt to block telepaths. I heard what you thought when you first saw me," Mordred smiled again, his teeth a perfect white row.

"Oh," Loukas blushed. He knew exactly what he had thought upon seeing Mordred, probably the same thing most people would think.

Mordred chuckled. "Don't sound so concerned, I was very flattered. The real reason I want to take you and your sister out is because of what I heard when I dug a little deeper. Both you and your sister have the same desire, the desire to see and even live in the Stagnant world." Mordred said. "I want to take you to a mortal club, let you both live out your fantasies for one night."

The idea excited Loukas, but he knew it would excite Estrie even more. His sister was obsessed with Stagnants and their lives; especially ones who documented them at all times. Estrie was desperate to party and live a life free of obligations to Lilith and Sammael. Loukas, on the other hand, wanted a Stagnant life, but not at the expense of disappointing Lilith, Sammael or his friends.

"What do you say, you down?" Mordred asked.

Loukas knew he had no choice, if he refused, Lilith would be denied the meeting with the Faerie Queen. He wanted to do it anyway, the idea of spending some time with Mordred wasn't bad either.

"Should I invite Astaroth and Mania as well?"

Mordred pulled a disgusted face. "Definitely not," his eyes met Loukas'. "I mean, I don't think Astaroth would enjoy himself, not to mention that Lilith wants to speak with him. As for the girl, Mania, did you say? She is … troubled, the Stagnant world is not for her."

Loukas nodded. "Okay, I will let Estrie know."

"Fantastic, I'll return to Hell tonight, meet me in the foyer when the third moon is in the sky." Mordred stood up and placed his drink down. Loukas also rose and together they walked toward the door once again in silence. Mordred opened the door and stepped out into the glowing white corridor. He turned to face Loukas, his eyes alight brightly; he leant forward and pressed his lips against the other man's cheek before a swirling cloud of bright blue smoke spiralled around the Faerie and took him from Hell.

Loukas placed his hand against the side of his cheek and smiled, breathing heavily. He lowered his arm and set off to find Estrie and inform her that she had plans tonight.

Lilith had dismissed the group in the assembly hall shortly after Mordred and Loukas had left the room. Her anger with the Faerie had been clear, she had cursed him angrily and wished him ill for snubbing her and her hospitality. The Queen of Hell did not like being anyone's second choice, even in favour of one of her own children. After being sent angrily from the assembly hall, Astaroth had decided to explore the fortress which he was now to call home for the foreseeable future.

It was a huge palace and the majority of it looked exactly the same, each corridor was the exact same length and had the same glowing white walls lit with evenly spaced torches illuminated by bright flames. Astaroth assumed the structure was so similar across its entirety in case of an attack; no one new to the fortress would be able to navigate it. As he made his way around the building and through the corridors, Astaroth thought he saw something out of the corner of his eye, a shadow, and he felt a breeze run across his back, he turned various times trying to catch a glimpse of whatever was stalking him. He assumed it was likely one of Lilith's Demons, angry that their mother had brought home strangers that had the same scent as both Stagnants and Demons. Every time he turned, he saw nothing but the shimmering white corridor behind him.

After time spent wandering around and going into various rooms, including a dusty, dark ballroom of immense size that had clearly not been used in thousands of years, Astaroth found his way back to the corridor on which his door was located, he identified the door to his chamber by a small X he had scratched into the black wood before he had gone to find Estrie. He placed a hand on the door and pushed, the door swung open silently with ease and the blue-eyed Cambion made his way inside.

"It's about time you found your way." A man was seated on one of the black sofas in the centre of the room with his body facing toward the door.

"I have been waiting for quite a while." His voice was like ice, cutting and cold. The man was as pale as snow and his deep-sunken eyes were the same dark glowing crimson as the suit he was wearing. His hair was a dirty white and it hung loosely just above his shoulders, he was gaunt and looked as though he had not slept or eaten in weeks.

"And you are?" Astaroth said. He had narrowed his eyes and knitted his eyebrows menacingly and stood with his back straight and his head held high. He didn't like the man, not just because he had no idea who he was or why he was in his bed chamber, but there was a deep-rooted evil to him. Astaroth could sense an anger stuck to the man's very essence; he knew Lilith was evil, even he was evil to some extent, but that was for a purpose, for the good of others. The evil in this man was different; it was selfish, pure unmitigated rage. Chaos.

"I am surprised you don't already know the answer to that, after all; you are a visitor in my kingdom." As the man spoke, he locked his red eyes with Astaroth's cyan ones in an aggressive stare which neither dared to break.

"No? You have no idea?"

Astaroth shook his head slowly so as not to break eye contact.

"This realm belongs to Lilith."

The man let out a high-pitched laugh as he stood and approached Astaroth. He was quite tall. Lilith had to look up when speaking with him and he towered over Astaroth.

"That is incorrect. Hell is, or rather, it was mine. That was until Lilith forced my brothers and I to sign over our realms, give up our thrones and crown her Queen. I am the rightful ruler of Hell, no Stagnant knows Lilith's name, but everyone knows my name, everyone knows I am the true sovereign of this realm. I am Lucifer Morningstar. I am Satan." His voice remained cold and high but grew louder as he spoke.

Astaroth stepped back and bumped into the closed door behind him. This explained why he felt uneasy in the presence of the man, he was not just evil, he was evil incarnate. Astaroth had heard stories of Lucifer and his terrible power, but Lilith had said he hadn't been seen in Hell since her coronation and years before time had been recorded. His fame had only grown because of the power he had to control and tempt Stagnants.

"Why are you here?" Astaroth asked. His voice shook a little, but he stood his ground.

"A number of reasons. I wanted to see Lilith's newest toys and I have found you disappointing at best, the first version of you, Cain, was much more interesting to watch."

Lucifer paused for a moment before continuing, he bit his lip but continued making eye contact; he enjoyed watching Astaroth as he recoiled upon hearing about Cain.

"I also wanted to offer you my help. Like you, I do not want the Arcadian Laws being passed, the Seraphic Laws are too restricting as it is, but you cannot take down the Angels alone. To do that you are going to need a great and extremely dark power; one that Lilith and Sammael cannot give you, but I can."

"For a price, I assume?" Astaroth knew better than to trust Lucifer or to make any kind of deal with him, but he was curious as to what the Devil could possibly want from him in return.

"Of course," Lucifer stepped back from Astaroth and took a seat once again as he gestured for Astaroth to sit on the opposing sofa. Astaroth did as the Prince of Hell requested and placed himself on the soft, black seat with his back straight. He watched as Lucifer tapped the coffee table between them and a roll of bone white paper appeared in a flash of crimson light.

"Read the contract." Lucifer nodded at the paper.

Astaroth leaned forward and picked it up, his eyes scanned the paper, for a moment it was completely black and then slowly but surely the writing began to appear in a thick red liquid; Astaroth assumed it was red ink and not blood, but he wasn't one hundred percent sure. He read through the contract and squinted in order to see the small print at the very bottom of the page before placing it back on the table and pushing it toward Lucifer.

"You want my soul?" He had heard of selling one's soul to the Devil, it was against the Seraphic Laws, but he had never thought of it as literal; he couldn't even begin to imagine how that would be done. It sounded painful.

"I do. The soul of the strongest half Alium, half Stagnant being who also has the blood of Lilith in their veins would be very useful to me. If you give me your soul, I will give you the same powers I have given to many great evils, Grigori Rasputin for example."

"Grigori Rasputin was poisoned, stabbed, shot at close range and drowned." Astaroth said.

"Exactly, he was not taken down easily," Lucifer was a salesman, but not good enough.

I think I am going to decline your offer." Astaroth said. He flinched slightly when Lucifer's eyes flashed white angrily before he took a deep breath and returned to their normal red. "My soul and I are actually very attached."

"You have no hope of winning unless you accept my offer. Without the power that only I can give you,

you will never be able to defeat the Angels and save your friends."

Astaroth shot up violently as he narrowed his eyes at Lucifer once again. "Save my friends? Is that a threat?" His friends were his family, and he would let no harm come to any of them; he loved them, although he would never admit that out loud.

"Not at all, but for beings like me the future is not that difficult to make out. Eventually, you will be forced to accept my offer, but it will be too late to save everyone."

Astaroth felt a breeze as he started to respond to Lucifer, but he was already gone. Lucifer did not seem to have used magic to leave the room, but he was definitely gone.

"So, let me get this right," Mahina said. She and her siblings had taken Nakir to their home after he had come down from Heaven and told them of their Celestial descent.

"As we speak, Angels in Heaven or some other paradise realm are creating new laws to govern Alium species because they pose a threat to the humans that you call Stagnants. These laws were delayed because the other Angels wanted to include laws incorporating half Demon, half human creatures called Cambions, and they couldn't do that until they turned eighteen and posed a threat to Angels and Stagnants. Now, you want us, Stagnants with the blood of Celestials, to infiltrate their group whenever we can and spy on them before they attempt an attack on Heaven to put a stop to the Arcadian Laws. Did I miss anything?" she asked sarcastically.

Nakir shook his head. "All of that is correct." He looked around the conservatory, a large room made of glass where they were seated. It was Nakir's favourite part of the house so far, it reminded him of Heaven where all of the buildings were made of crystal or glass, unlike the horrible stone that made one feel entrapped. The room was furnished with two white leather sofas being used by Moroccan and Mariah, and Nakir was seated on a matching chair which was pointed toward a large black screen; he knew this to be a television.

"How do you know it's definitely the Cambions?" Moroccan asked. The Angel had explained that he and his brother had raised the four half-Demons and how they were powerful but seemed harmless. He had said that one day his brother, Adriel, had gone to Earth to check on them and never returned to Heaven. He had gone down himself and found Adriel dead and the

Cambions missing. Moroccan held issue with this, there was no proof that the Cambions had doe anything to Adriel, there wasn't even any proof that they were still alive.

"There is not any solid evidence as of yet, but very few others could have killed Adriel, he was one of the Seraphic Army's finest soldiers. I suppose we will find out whether the half-breeds have any involvement with the Demonic plot to stop the passing of the new laws when you infiltrate them."

Nakir seemed to trail off at the end of his sentence, he was growing weary of mortals, they were boring.

"How are we supposed to join and spy on them if we don't even know where they are?" Moroccan asked.

Nakir looked ready to respond when Mariah jumped in. "Never mind about that! What will we get for doing this? I assume we will receive a reward?" She ignored the angry look shooting from her sister's shining eyes. Mariah had wanted to ask this question as the Angel had explained the plan.

"You mean other than the chance to avenge your parents?" Nakir had told the two of them that the Queen of Hell, Lilith, had been aware of her mother's Angelic heritage and knew she could pose a threat in the future and so she had sent a Demon to kill the Musa family. Demons, being stupid but dangerous creatures, had killed Chidiebube and Ginika, and reported back claiming they had killed the entire family, forgetting about Mahina, Moroccan and Mariah. They were the perfect secret weapon, and this was their chance to get revenge.

"And save both the Alium and Stagnant worlds?"

By stopping the Cambions, they would stop the Laws from being rewritten and Alium members would still have to follow rules that protected the Stagnants. This really was a mission to save everyone from the wrath of Demons and angered Alium.

Mariah rolled her eyes and sighed. "Yes, other than that?"

"You will also be given a seat each on the Seraphic Council and, with a single wish, you can have fame, riches, anything your heart desires." Nakir said.

He would never understand the lure of greed and materialism, it was such a typically Stagnant concept. He assumed they believed it was their legacy on Earth; most would not be remembered by the masses, but their little trinkets could be passed down through generations.

"Could we have our parents back?" Moroccan asked as he looked over at Nakir, his silver eyes wide with hope. They narrowed again as he lowered his head when Nakir shook his head.

"As is stated in the Seraphic Laws, necromancy is strictly forbidden for anyone to use. It is a perversion of all that is natural, souls are to remain in the afterlife and it would be an even greater crime to raise a body without a soul."

Nakir spoke diplomatically, it was an Angel's prerogative to inform and dissuade any deviations from the law. He watched as the siblings made eye contact for a moment before looking down into their laps. He felt sorry for them briefly, but his attention was quickly grabbed by a glowing white light in the form of a dove which had appeared in the centre of the room.

Tomorrow evening an Alium gathering is to be held in Highgate cemetery. It has been called by Sammael and has been labelled as crucial for every wronged Alium that can make it in time.

The message was delivered in a deep voice into the minds of each being in the room. Once it had finished the message, the glowing dove disappeared from view.

Nakir looked at Mahina, Mariah and Moroccan. He had been hoping for a little more time to prepare them, but things never went to plan when Demons were involved.

"It is time to ready yourselves, your mission is about to begin."

Chapter 5

Estrie was excited. Loukas had wasted no time
after Mordred left. He had gone straight to his sister's
chambers and told her that they had both been invited
out into the mortal world. She had never been in the
presence of Stagnants before, but she was desperate to
see them. She didn't think they could be very different to
her, all she wanted was a good time, free of
responsibility and duty. She was excited for Loukas as
well, she knew her brother hated his Demonic side, so it
was going to be nice for him to forget about it and cut
loose for even a short while. Estrie had also seen her

brother's eyes light up when talking about the Faerie. She was hoping this escape would be good for the two of them tonight and let them have a bit of time together.

She rolled slowly off her bed and wandered through the surrounding curtains. She was still in the same clothes she had created before, but she planned to wear a different outfit when they went out with Mordred. Estrie made her way out onto her balcony and traced her hand along the smooth white stone wall before her as she looked out onto the vista of Pandemonium. She wasn't impressed with the view. She liked pretty things and Hell was far from that, it was nothing more than a red wasteland of death and destruction, not much to look at; luckily, she hadn't gone out for the view. Estrie had gone out to check the sky and as she suspected, two of Hell's glowing red moons were at their peak and the third was almost there. It was time to change.

Estrie tapped her shoulder and slowly the black clothing began to peel off and dissolve into the air, revealing her tan skin. She did not expose anything for as soon as the fabric covering her disappeared, it was replaced by a chain of shining silver metal that hung from her neck, it covered her chest and hung between her legs as a dress but left her back and midriff visible. Her hands glittered with a number of silver rings and her shoes transformed into a pair of high, silver stilettos.

Her eyelids were slowly coated in silver shadow. A small bag appeared, hanging from her shoulder by a smaller chain as she brushed her hair over to one side of her head, and with that she was ready to go.

She made her way back into her bedchamber and continued through into her sitting area. Estrie disliked the way that the room looked, boring and far too plain. Of course, Lilith had been the one to decorate. It wasn't like Estrie wasn't grateful to Lilith for giving her powers and great abilities, but she hated the fact that she was expected to view her as a mother. Lilith hadn't been around for anything, not their first words or their first steps; nothing. At least Sammael had actually been present, not to mention the fact that Lilith only wanted Estrie and the others because they were useful to her.

The Cambion shook her head slightly and sat down on the edge of the glass coffee table, she looked over both of her shoulders to check she was alone before lifting one of the bottom cushions of the black sofa. She dropped it back down again after pulling out a large rectangle with a black screen, a phone she had summoned for herself a few years ago after hearing Sammael complain about Stagnants and their reliance on the things. She had found it fun to have. Then she had discovered things called apps, and an even better application known as a camera. Estrie had found that not only was a phone good for looking at herself, but she had been able to communicate and see the lives led by Stagnants. Since making that discovery, she had wanted to go into the Stagnant world. Of course, she had to keep the phone hidden from Sammael, and now Lilith. Demons didn't appreciate the genius of Stagnant technology, not that it mattered, Hell didn't have very good reception; much to Estrie's disgust. She slipped the phone into the bag hanging by her side and got back to her feet. With one final brush down of necklace chains, Estrie made her way out of her chamber to meet Loukas and Mordred in the Foyer.

"Oh good, you've both arrived."

Mordred hadn't been waiting long. He had arrived a little early and had spent his time waiting in the foyer of the fortress trying to look at anything but the massive statue of the nude Lilith in the centre of the room. He was pleased to see Loukas and Estrie making their way down the two staircases on either side of the room, both looking divine and ready for a fun night in the world of Stagnants.

"I hope you haven't been waiting long?" Loukas said as he reached the bottom of the stairs. He stood before Mordred awkwardly as he played with one of the chains dangling from the edge of his cropped hoodie; it seemed that, like his sister, Loukas was not overly fond of the clothing picked by Lilith.

"No, not long, the third moon hasn't yet reached its peak," Mordred paused and smiled as Estrie walked over to him and brushed her lips gently across his cheek as though they had known one another for years. "But, if you're both ready."

"I am more than ready," Estrie said. She was desperate to go, to get away from Hell and Lilith and everything else tainted with the Alium.

"As am I. Where exactly are we going?" Loukas was as excited as Estrie, but unlike her, he was not one for spontaneity, he liked to know where he was going so he could plan for each eventuality.

"Well, I hope you are both ready for a good, albeit wild, time tonight, for I am going to get you into the magnificent and opulent Café de Paris in London." Mordred said excitedly.

Estrie clapped her hands, she had seen some of the well-known Stagnants on her phone go to the Café de Paris, she knew it was a stunning place that was going to be packed with Stagnants.

"Well then, shall we get going? If Lilith catches us, she'll put a stop to the fun before it's even begun."

"She never has been one for a good time," Mordred said as he made his way through the fortress to a room neither Estrie nor Loukas had visited before. It was completely bare, apart from the one wall that was rippling and glowing with bright blue magic. There was a vacuum-like energy reaching from the wall as if trying to drag in all beings within the room. It was Hell's portal. Each of the eight realms had only one portal, stationed within its capital, that connected it to all other realms, pocket dimensions and the Stagnant world.

"Have you ever used a portal before?" Mordred asked.

Both siblings shook their heads.

"No," Loukas said. "Sammael brought us here."

For a moment Loukas wondered how Sammael had managed that, the laws stated that to enter a realm one must use the Portal of the realm, but then he recalled a further clause he had once read allowing any natural inhabitant of that realm to teleport to and from that world at their will. So a Demon could come and go between Hell and Earth whenever they chose, but would have to use the Portal in Hell to gain entry to Faerie or Álfheimr.

"They're quite simple," Mordred explained, his white hair being tousled by the pulling winds of the portal. "Just think of the realm you wish to be in. When traveling to Earth, you must also think of the specific location since there is no capital for your destination. So simply walk into the Portal thinking Earth and Café De Paris. Understand?"

Both siblings nodded and followed the Faerie Prince as he strode confidently into the portal.

Lilith knew what was happening, she knew that the Faerie had taken two of her children from Hell, she was aware of everything that happened in her realm. She didn't care much; it was the price that had to be paid in order to gain a meeting with the Queen of the Faeries and they needed the Faeries on their side to have a hope of winning the upcoming war. The only thing that bothered Lilith about the situation was that neither Loukas nor Estrie had informed her of what they were going to do. If they were keeping this a secret from her, what other deceptions were they hiding? She thought perhaps she should close the portal behind them and prevent their return.

She pushed the thought from her mind, she had other things to worry about at the moment, including something she had seen when hugging Astaroth for the first time. The Queen of Hell had been excited to meet Astaroth, she rarely felt such emotions anymore. Sammael had told her that Astaroth was powerful and a good asset to have in their arsenal against Heaven. She planned to give him a strong embrace to show she loved him and his power, but what she had seen when she hugged him had shaken and distracted her throughout the rest of their meeting.

The mother of Demons was seated on a throne in a large room of white, it wasn't *the* throne, the one that gave life and power to Hell and all of its denizens. That throne was hidden from prying eyes for whoever sat there could take control from Lilith and become the sovereign of Hell. There was nothing more in the room, just the black throne in the centre of a sea of white and Lilith liked the simplicity of it. It was very Stagnant to have clutter and mess. In the end, everything would return to dust, except for herself, of course. She sat in the large empty room, the black of her hair, eyes and jumpsuit melting into the throne and clashing against the glowing stone. She was awaiting Astaroth's arrival. She had sent one of her Demons to go and collect him. The silence of the big empty room was broken by a knocking on the large arched doorway facing the throne.

"Enter." Lilith called.

The door swung outwards and Astaroth entered. Like Lilith, he stood out against the bright white of the room like a walking shadow. He walked to the foot of Lilith's throne and dropped to one knee in a bow.

"Mother."

"Get off your knees," Lilith commanded. Astaroth stood and she was unsure whether this was her ichor controlling him as it had Cain, or if Astaroth would just do whatever she asked because she was the only maternal figure he had ever known. As he got back to his feet, Lilith noticed that in the white light of the room, he had small flecks of cherry red in his ink black hair; a link to his birth mother. She turned her head from him until he was fully back on his feet and his hair looked more like hers once again.

"What can I do for you?" Astaroth asked.

"I do not need you to do anything. Take a seat,"

Lilith gestured with her hand and a smaller chair of black appeared before her.

Astaroth did as Lilith requested.

"I have something I need to speak with you about, Astaroth. When I first embraced you, here in Hell, I was given a vision, most likely from Chaos. It is too hard to explain the details of the vision for Chaos works in mysterious ways, but I can tell you what it meant. Like most Alium, you are very difficult to kill, but it is possible; however, it seems that only one set of beings can kill you - the Kasai. A Kasai is a being in any Alium species that somehow, mysteriously, has Heavenly Fire attached to one's soul; you are a Kukan, an Alium being with darkness lining your soul. I am surprised Sammael did not pick up on this, but I digress. Both of these, Kukan and Kasai Alium, are very rare and are the natural enemies of one another. Although I could not see which specific Kasai is destined to kill you, I was able to tell that it is someone closely linked to you. Be careful and remember, you can trust no one but me."

It was clear in Lilith's tone that she was concerned, she did not enjoy being blind when usually she was omniscient.

Astaroth recalled Sammael teaching them about Kukan and Kasai and a whole host of Alium beings that had specific things attached to their souls. There had once been a race of deities and Angels from Japan that had been called Kitsune. Within this Pantheon there were thirteen types of Kitsune who had control over elements. When the Kitsunes came down to Earth and mated with Alium, they created new beings of each species, each with a lining on their soul. There were those such as Tengoku, whose souls were lined with celestial light, Seishin with vitality, Umi with the ocean and the sea, Chikyu with Earth and Kasai lined with fire. Their descendants all turned out to fit the Angel's expectations and held similar ideals to the original Kitsunes and would try to snuff out the darkness.

Then there were the ones who had no leaning to either side of the moral compass: Kawa, with their souls lined with the magic of rivers, Yama with mountains, Mori with the forests and the woods, Jikan were lined with time and Ongaku whose souls were lined with sweet melodies.

The majority of these different Kitsune never mated and slowly faded from existence. Finally, there were the descendants whose souls were affected by the magic and it corrupted them: Kaze with wind, Sanda tainted by thunder and the most malevolent of them all, Kukan whose soul was lined with darkness. Very few descendants of Kitsunes were left, and the original deities were believed to be extinct. It was surprising that Astaroth was a descendant of a Kukan Kitsune when his mother was a Stagnant. Somehow, years and years in the past, a Kitsune must have tainted her bloodline; it explained why he was so powerful compared to the other Cambions.

As he recalled all of this information and registered what Lilith had just told him, Astaroth's mind wandered back to his conversation with Lucifer. He had intended to bring it up with Lilith and she had just presented him with the perfect opportunity.

"If this is a battle of souls, would it make sense to sell mine? That way I would be free of the Kukan influence and the Kasai Alium would be no threat to me."

Lilith shook her head; strands of her long black hair fell into her face.

"No, that would make you more vulnerable. At the moment, only one; very rare set of Alium can kill you." She paused for a moment and brushed the hair back behind her ears as she looked upon her favoured son, her brows knitted and shark eyes narrow. "Sell your soul? To whom, may I ask, would you be selling it to?"

"Actually, mother, that is something I wish to discuss with you." Astaroth watched as Lilith leaned further forward in her seat, he could see her fangs poking out between the gap in her mouth and the clear rage across her face; she knew what he was going to say before he spoke.

"After we left the assembly hall earlier today, I returned to my chambers where a guest was awaiting me. Lucifer Morningstar. He offered to buy my soul in return for a power that would help us win against the Angels and he claimed it would allow me to save my friends, whatever that means."

Lilith snarled. "That bastard!" She stood up angrily as if to go somewhere but sat back down again almost instantly.

"You are not to sell your soul to Lucifer under any circumstances! Your soul is a powerful one, it is a mixture of Stagnant, Alium, and Fallen Angel blood, as well as being infused with my ichor and now you have the power of a Kukan Kitsune. When Lucifer buys a soul, he gives new power to the seller, but he absorbs the power within the soul. If he were to have yours, he would gain immense strength and would attempt to win back control of Hell. The magic he would give you is not worth the price. You would lose all emotions, you would not care if you saved your friends or not."

She stopped again, tapping her nails anxiously on the side of the wooden throne and turning her head every few seconds. "What else did he say to you?"

Astaroth did not like how agitated Lilith seemed. He had been told that she always remained calm, that nothing flustered her; this was far from the way the Queen of Hell had been described.

"Not much else, he referenced Cain and how you used him until you grew bored and then cast him aside and how you would do the same to us. The Angel said the same thing when we escaped; that is what provoked the attack."

"That is not true!" Lilith hissed. "I love you; I love the others; you are *my* children. Together we will defeat the Angels, together we will rewrite the Laws; I will *never* grow bored with you. As for Cain, I never cared for Cain, unlike you, he was just a means to an end."

Lilith knew that as she spoke she seemed distracted, but she couldn't help it; Lucifer being back in Hell was cause for concern, she could not let him get back in power; he cared nothing for the rights of the Alium, only himself and his revenge on her for usurping him.

"Whatever you do, Astaroth, do *not* listen to Lucifer and do *not* sell your soul." Lilith said. Astaroth nodded and smiled. She did not smile back.

"You may go."

Astaroth rose from his seat and bowed once again to Lilith before turning and making his way out the door, still thinking about Lucifer's words and the new information that his soul was lined with darkness.

Café de Paris was a nightclub established in 1924 by Faeries as a way for them to convene in the Stagnant world and have a place to party. It allowed them to mix with mortals and tempt them with Faerie foods, drinks and revelry which would ultimately end in the Stagnants traveling back to the Faerie land and being kept as slaves for eternity. It was eventually shut down by the Seraphic Council for breaking the Seraphic Laws and endangering the lives of Stagnants. After a number of years and a Stagnant war, the Faeries reopened Café de Paris. They followed the Laws of the Seraphic Council and allowed all Alium and Stagnants entry as long as they were all aware of the rules for their specific species.

Estrie had been thrilled when Mordred had managed to get their group to skip the queue outside, she had seen famous Stagnants do the same thing on her phone. As the doors to Café de Paris opened, Estrie was hit by a wave of hot air and the sound of loud electronic dance music blasting through the club. She was stunned when they entered the club, feeling as though she had stepped back in time to the twenties. The club was decorated in a luxurious baroque style, adorned with gold detailing and a great deal of red velvet. A golden chandelier hung from the high ceiling above the dance floor, which was flooded with hundreds of Stagnants, Faeries, Warlocks and even Vampires. People were scattered around the club: on the stairs, in the various bars and the numerous chic rooms and balconies above the dance floor. The decadence of Café de Paris was exhilarating.

Mordred led Loukas and Estrie up one of the glittering staircases and then onto their own private royal balcony located on the mezzanine. The floor was covered in a gorgeous royal blue handmade rug with an ornate symbol of the Café de Paris woven into the centre. There were a number of seats and pouffes decorated in gold, crimson and blue velvet and like the rest of the club, the balcony was held up by gorgeous French pillars and was furnished in regal gilt. The Faerie male made his way to the centre of the balcony where a set of tables held glasses and multiple bottles of wine being cooled in ice buckets; he picked up the most expensive bottle he could see and popped the cork, it was loud enough to be heard over the sound of the music playing below them, as was the cheer Estrie gave as she was handed a glass.

"Welcome to Café de Paris," Mordred said. raising a full glass and handing another to Loukas. "A place where the Stagnant and Alium worlds are one." They tapped the glasses together before each taking a sip of the wine.

Estrie walked over to the edge of the balcony and ran her hands along the gilded railing as she looked out at the people dancing below her.

"I love this place," she said in a gleeful sigh. That was no lie, Estrie adored the Café de Paris, even though she had only been there for a short while, she felt comfortable, accepted; happy. She had an inkling that this feeling was only going to be amplified as the evening went on, as she mixed with Stagnants and had more of the wonderful wine. As her brown eyes scanned the crowd, she noticed a group of Stagnants at a bar at the side of the dance floor, she knew they were Stagnants, they just radiated a different energy to Alium. The group were dancing, laughing and cheering gleefully as they waited for their drinks. One of the men in the group caught Estrie's gaze and smiled. She smiled back and giggled to herself when he beckoned her over with a wave, she held up her forefinger in response and swung round to face her brother and their host with a wide smile.

"Not that I don't want to spend time with the two of you," Estrie began, "but I am going to make my way to the dance floor. I came here to experience Stagnant life and that is what I intend to do."

"Yes, you go, Estrie, have a good time," Mordred said with a smile. He was happy that she was so excited, he knew she would enjoy it and he also knew she would want to mingle which would give him some extra time alone with Loukas who would most definitely not want to mingle.

Estrie turned her body more toward Loukas as she flicked her hair dramatically and brushed down her chain dress. "Do I look okay?"

Loukas looked his sister up and down before making a face.

"I don't know why you bothered wearing clothes,"

Estrie scrunched her face up angrily and opened her mouth to scold her brother when Mordred jumped in. "You look stunning, Estrie, now go and enjoy yourself." He flashed his glowing teeth at her in a smile, she grinned back as she passed him and began making her way down the steps to the dance floor.

"You should be nice to her; she has the same insecurities you do; she just hides them in a different way."

"I suppose so," Loukas responded as he sipped his wine. He looked over the top of his glass to see Mordred staring at him, the white of his open shirt seemed blue in the hue of the vibrant lights scattered around the club.

"What? Have I spilled something?" He glanced down at his cropped hoodie, the chains tapping lightly against his tan stomach providing a little bit of cold in the boiling room. When he raised his head again, Mordred was chuckling. "Seriously, what is it?"

"You're not having a good time, are you?" Mordred said. He didn't need his telepathy to see that Loukas was uncomfortable, he was not the clubbing type. Mordred imagined that he would prefer a picnic in a field or enjoying a coffee in an actual café.

"Honestly, not really. This is very much Estrie's scene, but not mine. I appreciate the gesture though, I have always wanted to see how Stagnants live and now I have - I'm not disappointed, I'm sure it's fun." Loukas smiled weakly.

Mordred chuckled again, he found it cute that Loukas was trying to act like he could be happy in this world of drinking and dancing.

"Don't worry, this is only one aspect of Stagnant life, we can easily explore other avenues another day. I actually own a nice little manor in the country, it's quiet and secluded, and it's not too far from a Stagnant village; you are more than welcome there anytime you wish."

"Oh, you want to spend more time with us?" Loukas asked.

"Well, Estrie is wild, even for me. I actually want to spend more time with you."

"With me? Why?"

Mordred wasn't completely sure why he was so intrigued by the green-eyed Cambion. His mind was fascinating and with his visage he would not have looked out of place in the Faerie courts; but neither of those points were the reason. There was something more to him, something deeper, something that excited Mordred and made him nervous, emotions he had not felt for a long time. Sometimes he worried that immortals froze, that their emotions subsided, and they became empty voids. Loukas gave him hope that this was not the case.

Unsure of what to say, Mordred drank the rest of his wine very quickly and placed his glass on the table. He took Loukas' glass from him and placed it next to his own. Taking a deep breath, Mordred stepped closer to Loukas. He could feel the Cambion's breath on his face and the heat exuding from his body. He noticed that a lock of Loukas' dark hair was hanging in his face, he tucked it back into place with a gentle stroke. For a moment, they stared into each other's eyes and to Mordred's surprise, Loukas made the first move. He grabbed the Faerie by the face and pressed their lips together. They remained locked for a moment before Loukas pulled back, his face flushed and a nervous smile was on his lips. They both rushed back into the kiss, where the previous one had been soft and gentle, this one was stronger and more passionate, both of them were breathing heavily, their hands running along the other's back and in their hair. They clashed, Mordred the glowing white of Angels, Loukas with the black of Demons; and yet in that moment they were one. Their kissing continued and Mordred walked backwards, pulled Loukas with him.The two fell down in the throes of passion onto the row of velvet crimson pouffes.

"Can I buy you a drink?" another man offered.

Since she had gone down onto the dance floor, Estrie had been approached by numerous men who thought that buying her a drink was going to get her to kiss them; or more. She had met the man who had waved her down from the balcony and he had introduced her to his group. She had spent a while with them, dancing and drinking and talking. She had immense fun. When they had to leave, she had been invited to go to the next club with them, but she knew she couldn't leave Loukas and Mordred and so she had politely declined. After that, man after man had approached her; she had accepted some of their offers of a drink, but she noticed a pattern of them getting annoyed whenever she rejected more than just the drink and had taken to paying for her own. Despite the constant harassment, she was still having a great time.

"Can I just have the money instead?" she turned to smile at the man before her as she continued to dance. He was tall, which she liked, but he was also a redhead.

She had no issue with this, other than the fact that Mania also had red hair.

The man laughed. "Come on," he encouraged. "Why don't we go see a movie sometime?"

"I've already seen it." Estrie said, her tone aggressive. Her eyes flashed from brown to red momentarily, the man jumped back a little before walking away quickly. Unaware of the colour of her eyes, Estrie turned back to face the same way as the crowd. She threw her arms in the air with a full glass in one hand and jumped to the beat of the music, as did the majority of other people around her. Wine splashed everywhere and the lights of the club sparkled from the gilded adornments and luminous white pillars. Her hair bounced as the chains on her dress jumped along with her, She had never felt so free. The music slowed and she began rocking to the melody, she cheered happily along with the crowd, as she raised the glass to her lips once again.

After dancing for a while, which according to Stagnants was bouncing and occasionally dropping to the ground, Estrie felt a tap on her shoulder. Thinking it was Loukas or Mordred, she turned, her partially wine coated hair flying through the air. There was someone behind her, but it was not her brother or the Faerie; she was a woman, a Stagnant evidently. Like most Alium, Estrie could easily pick up on the energies of other species be they supernatural or not. The woman was shorter than Estrie, her thin, brown hair was hanging down her back, almost touching her waist. The short red dress she was wearing could hardly keep hold of her emaciated body and the darkness of the fabric made her seem paler than she was; she looked unwell.

"Yes?" Estrie pulled a face when looking at the woman, her eyes were sunken deep in her face and her lips were thin, almost to the point of being invisible. The raven haired Cambion didn't want to talk to anyone. She was having fun on her own and didn't need people to help her, she was enjoying the Stagnant world and could definitely see herself making a life there.

"Hello," the woman's voice was coarse and raspy, she coughed loudly. "I was going to ask if you wanted something to help you have a good time; but clearly you've already taken something." She was looking directly into Estrie's eyes.

"What do you mean?" Estrie said as she tried to catch a glimpse of herself in one of the wall mirrors, but they were too far away for her to see. "I'm already enjoying myself, but if you have something to further my enjoyment, then please, do share."

The woman looked at Estrie hesitantly for a moment, she couldn't stop looking at the other woman's eyes. They were a bright red, and they seemed to leap and dance. Like flames.

"Okay, come with me." The brunette said.

Estrie smiled and began following the girl in red. She wondered what on earth the woman was going to give to her to aid her enjoyment of the evening. The energy and the alcohol had already done a great job with that. It had made Estrie feel a little out of control, and she had accidentally set a couple of things on fire without meaning to; but she felt great. They ended up leaving the Café de Paris, much to Estrie's dismay, and walked down Coventry street. As soon as the air hit Estrie's face she felt instantly worse, her head felt light and she stumbled a little, catching herself on the wall.

"Are you sure you want more stuff?" the raspy-voiced woman asked.

"I haven't had anything yet!" Estrie snapped. Her eyes grew brighter again without her knowledge and she was confused when the woman recoiled before continuing to lead the way.

The two of them turned onto a backstreet of the west end, well concealed from the naked eye. The walls surrounding them were dirty and dark, the ground was slimy and covered in what Estrie hoped was mud; the only light provided in the dark street was the soft illumination of the cold moon. There were various people walking up and down the street, the majority of them had their faces covered with masks and hoods, they clearly did not want to be identified. Estrie and the woman began slowing their pace as they reached the dead end where a man was waiting for them; the lower half of his face was covered by a thick black mask and the top of his head was covered by the hood of his dark sweatshirt. All Estrie could see were his eyes, they were thin and a deep brown with unusually small pupils. He looked like someone she would associate with Lilith.

"What does she want?" the man asked the woman in the red dress. Although his question was simple, his tone was angry.

"Just give her E, I think she's already had something." The woman responded before breaking into another loud and crackly coughing fit.

Estrie had reached her limit with this woman, first she had interrupted her good time, then she dragged her out of the club into the cold, and she continued to accuse her of having whatever Stagnant concoction was going to make her happy. She grabbed the woman's thin wrist to get her attention.

"I told you, I haven't had anything!"

The woman screamed and Estrie let go immediately, she had left a bright red handprint on the woman but not from gripping her too tightly. This handprint was blistering, as though her hand had been alight when she grabbed the wrist.

"I am so sorry. I - I don't know how that ..."

Estrie trailed off as she looked down at her palm in horror, she had always had great control over her power, nothing like this had happened before.

The man stepped forward to inspect the other woman's wrist. He shook an angry arm at Estrie and began to shout at her to go before he did something he regretted; clearly the woman meant something to him. Estrie would have liked to have seen him try to attack her. He would be lucky to get close enough to her before she turned him into nothing more than a pillar of salt.

She turned and began running back down the street as quickly as her heels would allow. Estrie was hoping to find her way back to the Café de Paris but she didn't know her way around the streets of London well enough and she hadn't been able to focus when walking with the woman in red. She assumed it was the alcohol that was affecting her, she hadn't been drunk before, but tonight she drank excessively. The alcohol must have clashed with her Alium blood, maybe Loukas was experiencing the same thing. As she went down each street trying to find the golden lights of Café de Paris, she got more and more anxious that she was never going to find her way back to her brother, and she wasn't powerful enough to transport herself to Hell. As she got more worked up, she could feel herself getting hotter and hotter, she stumbled into a door and fell into what she assumed was a bar, she couldn't be completely sure with her vision blurring slightly. She grabbed onto the wooden bar and felt magic flow from her, setting the mahogany alight with bright flames. She stumbled and fell onto her back when she heard shouting coming from the people around her. As she lay looking up, her vision began to blur more as the noises around her grew louder. First there was screaming, followed by the stamping of people running to safety and then nothing but the crackling of flames.

Estrie would never understand the full extent of what she had done, her brother would shield her from that. As she lay, surrounded by the fires and thick black smoke of her own creation, she felt relieved and happy; even if she was going to die, she had been able to live her dream of spending a night in the Stagnant world. Apart from the pushy men and weird thin women, she had enjoyed herself. With this thought, her eyes closed and for Estrie, all went silent.

Chapter 6

Lilith had been waiting in the foyer for a number of hours. After her conversation with Astaroth, she had decided to wait where she could see Estrie and Loukas sneaking back inside. As she waited, she was able to run through the contents of the conversation with her son. Lucifer was back which meant trouble was brewing. She had never met a more callous and unfeeling creature such as the Fallen Angel. He had been beautiful once, the most beautiful of all Angels and Demons, but his pride had overtaken him, destroyed him and made him a monster. His pride had been damaged once again when Lilith had taken control of Hell from him. That had been centuries ago, but she knew he had never recovered from his loss and his silence only meant that he was biding his time. Lucifer could not forget what he could not forgive, and for him, that was any wrong done to him. Lilith considered rallying the Princes of Hell to tell them of Lucifer's return. She knew some would like to see him back in power, but the majority would not. Most were loyal to their Queen.

There were seven Princes of Hell and each presided over a dark aspect of life that had been labelled the Seven Deadly Sins. The first was Lucifer, the light-bringer, Demon of Pride and leader of the riot against Heaven. Then there was Mammon, Lilith's least favourite brother, the Demon of Greed, responsible for Stagnant obsession with money and material objects. Azazel was the Demon of Wrath, he infused the Stagnant world with anger, brought wars and adored chaos and destruction. Closest with Azazel was Asmodeus, the Demon of Lust who struck the hearts of men with feelings of dangerously strong passion and desire. The Demon of Sloth was Belphegor, responsible for Stagnants growing weak, lazy and susceptible to possession from his children who did not have bodies of their own. The sin of Gluttony was overseen by Beelzebub. He worked closely with Mammon and corrupted the hearts of men with desire for more. The seventh prince was Leviathan, the Demon of Envy, he infiltrated the minds of all beings and filled them with jealousy and bitterness. The Princes each had their own plain and usually remained there.

The Lords of Hell, like Sammael, oversaw various aspects in Hell and remained close to the side of Lilith. Like Lilith, all Greater Demons, be they Princes or Lords, had immense power and could not be killed, but they could be injured for long periods of time and needed time to recover. They were forever warring for control of the other realms, but none would dare challenge Lilith for hers. Although they had been Angels, she had been a Stagnant, a Witch and a Demon; she knew more about feeling and causing pain and suffering than all of them combined. Lilith decided it was probably a good idea to alert the Princes and tell them that if any of them even considered betraying her to Lucifer, she would personally hunt them down and feed them to the Hellhounds.

The Queen of Hell was also very concerned with the business surrounding Astaroth and the Kasai, she had believed all descendants of Kitsune to be extinct and yet there were apparently still two alive. Astaroth, a Kukan, was one and the mysterious Kasai destined to kill him was the other.. In all of her years alive, and they included *every year*, Lilith had never had a vision be wrong, nor had she known of any Kukan to survive against a Kasai.

Her train of thought was broken instantly when she felt three pulses run through her realm. They had used the portal to enter. She made her way through the foyer to the door of the Portal room. As she entered, she saw Mordred, his white shirt and hair stained black with what looked like ash. Next to Mordred was Loukas, his eyes were wide and watery, and he too was stained with soot and carried the smell of fire. In his arms was an unconscious Estrie, her hair was hanging over his arms and her eyes were closed, but she was still alive, Lilith could both see and hear her breathing. She was not in a good way - something strange was happening to Estrie.

"What the hell happened?" Lilith demanded.

"I took them to the Café de Paris. We -" Mordred paused and looked over at Loukas, whose eyes were fixed on his sister.

"We lost track of Estrie in the crowd, it turned out that she left the club, we don't know if she was with anyone or if she left alone, but she ended up in a bar a short way from the club. Clearly, she had too much to drink, and it triggered something within her, and she lost control of her magic. She burnt down the bar accidentally and passed out. When we found her, she was fully submerged in flames, but didn't have a burn on her. The same can't be said for the girl we found in the back room, she was dead and burnt beyond recognition-"

CONNOR IRVING

"But we can't tell her that!" Loukas interjected. "Estrie would never recover if she knew she had murdered an innocent Stagnant." He chose his words carefully; it was only Stagnants she wouldn't want to kill, unlike Loukas who didn't want to kill anything mortal or Alium.

Lilith waved a dismissive hand at Loukas, she didn't care about the death of a Stagnant, but if he didn't want Estrie to know, she wouldn't tell her. The Queen of Hell was more bothered by what Mordred had said.

"She was completely unconscious and there were flames all over her, but she received no injury?"

"Yes," Mordred confirmed.

"Was there any magic protecting her?"

"No, she was too far gone for that, and no other Alium were around at the time." Mordred said.

"The idiot, he missed two of them!" Lilith muttered angrily to herself. She meant Sammael, of course. He had missed the lining of darkness on Astaroth's soul that made him a Kukan and now, she was fairly sure that he had missed a lining on Estrie's soul, a lining of fire. From what she was being told, it seemed that Estrie was a Kasai. It made sense, at least it did to Lilith; the girl did have a dreadful attitude.

Lilith turned her eyes to Loukas, "Take her to her chamber and station a Necrotic outside her door."

Loukas nodded and began to make his way past Lilith to Estrie's room. A Necrotic was a creature known to Stagnants as Zombies, beings brought back to life by Necromancy without a soul; they had no personality or free will, they returned only to serve whoever raised them. Necrotics were illegal under the Seraphic Laws, but Lilith had dozens of them, as did the majority of Alium who possessed such dark magic.

Mordred started to follow Loukas but was stopped by Lilith's hand on his ash-covered chest. Had this been anyone else, he would have warned them against touching him in such a commanding way; but he and Lilith had been friends for years.

"Not you. It is time you go back to Faerie. I trust almost getting my daughter killed warrants us an audience with your Queen tomorrow?" Lilith said bitterly. Although she was not particularly fond of how Estrie acted, or the fact that she was a potential Kasai, Estrie was still her daughter.

"I shall let the Queen know to expect you." Mordred said as he stepped back so that Lilith's hand fell off of his chest. Before the Faerie could say another word, Lilith flicked her wrist and he was surrounded by a pillar of black cloud, when it cleared, Mordred had vanished from Hell.

Lilith shook her head in an irritated fashion as she began to make her way to Estrie's chambers. She was determined to discover if her suspicions were correct, that Estrie was a Kasai as well as a Cambion. If she was, the mother of Demons had a hard decision to make. Was she to banish Estrie to keep Astaroth safe? Or was she to risk keeping Estrie with her and hope she didn't end up killing Astaroth? She shook her head again; nothing was ever simple for a woman, turned Witch, turned Demon.

The Queen of Hell waited by Estrie's bed as she slept. Once she had sent Mordred back to Faerie, Lilith had gone to her daughter's chamber. The Necrotic, a pitiful ugly creature, had bowed to her and allowed her entry. All in Hell knew Lilith and if they didn't, they could still sense the power she exuded. When in the room, Lilith had sent Loukas from his sister's side, it was late and the Cambions were expected to be awake early the next day to visit potential allies. Unlike them, Lilith did not need sleep. Loukas left after a little persuasion and Lilith was left alone with the unconscious Estrie. She had taken the seat from the vanity table facing the bed and placed it next to Estrie's bedside cabinet. It was uncomfortable, but someone had to keep an eye on the girl, her magic was out of control and the alcohol wasn't going to help. Lilith believed that the alcohol had awakened the beast inside her daughter, and it was going to be a struggle trying to contain it.

The shark-like voids of her eyes watched Estrie for a while as she slept, her breathing was heavy and laboured and she moved restlessly as she attempted to push her covers off. The fire, especially one as hot as Heavenly fire, as Lilith suspected, running through one's veins and across one's soul was definitely going to make her far too warm. The Demon rose to lean across Estrie, removing the bed covers to cool her. The Cambion shook a little before her breathing grew quieter and her movements became less erratic.

"Oh Estrie, what am I going to do with you?" Lilith said as she ran a hand through Estrie's long, black hair; it was strikingly similar to her own. The mother of Demons sighed, she did care for Estrie though the feeling was not reciprocated, but if she was a Kasai, she was a danger and threatened the entire mission.

Lilith knew how to test Estrie to see if she was a Kasai, as suspected, and she knew that she had no choice but to try it. The Queen of Hell sat back down and flicked her wrist. A small silver dagger appeared in her hand; she wasn't sure what realm she had summoned it from, but like everything, it had to arrive from somewhere. Very few beings could actually create something from nothing, and Lilith was not one of them. With her free hand, Lilith reached over and raised Estrie's arm. She drew the thin blade down the length of her daughters' arm and watched as her tan skin slowly separated and her blood began to spill. For a moment it seemed like her blood was natural, a thick red liquid, but

118

quickly it began to glow a bright red and the sound of crackling could be heard loud and clear from both the blood running down her arm and from the open cut on her forearm. Slowly the wound closed and healed itself. Lilith waved her hand and the crackling blood faded from existence as did the silver knife in her hand. She placed Estrie's arm back by her side and sank back into the chair with another sigh.

The mother of Demons knew now that she had three options. Estrie was dangerous, she had no control of herself and there was nothing to suggest that she was going to be able to keep her magic contained. She was either going to have to attempt to draw the Heavenly fire from Estrie's soul or she was going to have to banish her for good. If neither of those worked and Estrie was still a danger, the Queen of Hell was going to have to do what was necessary; she would have to kill her daughter.

Mania hadn't slept much that night. She had first heard Estrie and Loukas sneaking down the corridor and then she had managed to doze lightly before being awakened by Lilith stalking into Estrie's room.

The red-headed Cambion wasn't sure what was happening with Loukas, Estrie and Lilith, and she didn't really care, but after she had been awakened, she hadn't been able to get back to sleep and her head had started hurting again. The headaches hadn't happened often since they had escaped the prison. The visions had come back that night as well, which scared her. Mania had a multitude of issues ranging from not wanting to be with anyone ever to having delusional thoughts which often led to terrifying visions. The one she had that night was a mild hallucination of voices echoing around her chamber telling her to do things and not to trust those who cared for her. She was quite used to this kind of thing and nothing would ever scare her as much as the last vision she had suffered in the church prison. She remembered seeing herself, as though her soul had left her body. Mania had watched and followed herself through the different rooms of the prison and in each one, either Astaroth, Loukas or Estrie were lying in a pool of their own blood - all dead. When the vision had ended, she was in a completely different room from where she had started. She broke down in tears, unable to comprehend that what she had just seen wasn't real. Even when her brother, Astaroth, came into the room and ran to her side in an attempt to comfort her as she cried with her head in her hands; she still did not believe that they were not all dead. After hours of her crying and screaming in grief and fear, Mania had been convinced to walk back through the prison and she was able to see that Loukas and Estrie were fine and that everything she had seen was false.

After that episode, she spoke to Sammael. He had attempted to find the cause of her visions. She hoped they were not prophetic and had been pleased when he had discovered they were not. The Lord of Hell did find that Mania's visions were actually part of a mortal illness of the mind known as schizophrenia. That meant that sometimes she was completely fine, but at times she would hear a voice from nowhere or would dissociate from reality, causing hallucinations which she was unable to distinguish from the real world. Sammael had told her of Stagnant drugs that would potentially help her, but he didn't want to give them to her as mortal medicine often affected and sometimes diluted Alium blood and magic. Mania asked her father if there was any form of magic that could help her suppress the hallucinations and voices.

He had laughed and said *"If there were, do you not think Witches and Warlocks would have made a fortune from it yet? No, Alium magic does not work on Stagnant illness, mental or otherwise."* Mania had lived with it since then, the hallucinations coming in waves, the voices ever present.

For the rest of the evening, Mania stood on her balcony and looked out at the vista of Pandemonium. Hell was silent most of the time, except for the odd screech of a Demon. It made her wonder what the other seven Alium realms were like. She had read of Heaven, the realm of gods and Angels and its capital, Olympus, with its glittering towers of crystal. She read about Alfheimr, the land of Elves, whose capital Álfheim was filled with the most magnificent artworks and sculptures. They sounded far more pleasant than Hell, land of Demons or The Underworld, Land of the Punished whose cities were filled with the screaming of tortured souls. Mania thought she would prefer Acuran, the realm of Monsters. There she could have visited Ṭirākaṉ, the city of Dragons and seen the beautiful creatures up close. However, in Acuran, she would have to be careful not to step too closely to Iṟakkāta, the undead city, to avoid being ripped apart by Manananggal Vampires, vicious winged creatures cursed by the gods in the early days with an insatiable lust for blood. They had the ability to separate their upper and lower halves to fly through the air and feast on their victims. They were far more dangerous than the Ambrogian Vampires like Amber Alarie.

The three red moons of Pandemonium had now disappeared from the sky. Mania knew it was morning in Hell, time for her to get ready before meeting Lilith and the others in the assembly hall so they could be assigned a specific Alium group to visit and persuade to join the cause. Mania pushed through the black curtains into her bed chamber as she yawned and rubbed her eyes. Not sleeping wasn't really an issue for her anymore, she was always tired, but she could still function. She didn't even bother checking her wardrobe for something to wear, although she didn't see eye to eye with Estrie often, she completely agreed on her standpoint when it came to Lilith's clothing choices for them. The dresses were truly disgusting. Instead, Mania stood before her full-length mirror across from her bed and flicked her wrist. A cloud of bright red magic spiralled around her in an upwards motion before collapsing and revealing that she was no longer in her thin black nightgown. Now she was wearing a soft red t-shirt under a leather jacket with her cherry hair running down her back. Her legs were covered in tight black jeans and a pair of dark red heeled boots appeared on her feet. She shook her head while running her hands through her hair; it was longer than she had thought, and with one final glance at herself in the mirror she set off to the assembly hall, praying she would get there without being intercepted by anyone.

Mania's wish was granted, she managed to find her way to the assembly hall without seeing or speaking to anyone. Ske had heard Loukas' door opening as she was making her way down the corridor and so she had done a little trot to the end of the hallway and made a sharp turn before he came out. It wasn't that she didn't like Loukas, the only person she disliked was Estrie, but that didn't mean she actually wanted to be around them, or worse, to speak to them. When she arrived at the Hall, three people were already there, seated around the table of black wood: Lilith, Sammael and Amber. None of them were speaking, nor did they acknowledge Mania as she entered the room. She didn't mind at all and silently took a seat. They waited for a short time until Astaroth and Loukas arrived. They also maintained silence as they walked in and took their seats. Mania noticed that Astaroth's eyes were surrounded by dark shadows; he hadn't slept either. As for Loukas, his face was red and puffy, and his hair was a ruffled mess, he had evidently been crying and likely hadn't slept.

"Good," Lilith said slowly. "We're all here,"

"Estrie has not yet graced us with her presence," Astaroth said before he was shot a withering look from Loukas and closed his mouth. Mania had never seen Loukas look at anyone so sternly, especially not Astaroth. They were like brothers.

"Nor will she be. Estrie is still asleep and will be accompanying me later as I visit Faerie." Lilith pushed a lock of hair out of her face and moved swiftly on.

"I am sending each of you to visit a particular sector of Alium, you are to take the gifts that I have provided and when you are with them, it is your mission to persuade them to join this quest. Convince them that it is in their best interests to fight against the Angels, some will be easier to convince than others. Once you have persuaded them to join us, you are then to invite them to a gathering tonight at Highgate Cemetery. This gathering will be the members of the Alium who have not yet agreed to join us. They will be there as an incentive, to show our growing numbers. After that, everyone at the gathering will be invited back here to attend a function, a ball where they will mingle, dance and form a basis of trust before the big attack. It is absolutely vital that you get all of these Alium members to commit to our fight, without them we will likely lose."

Lilith's black eyes were wide open, and she spoke with energy. She had been planning this for years and finally her goals were nearing fruition.

"What if they do not cooperate?" Astaroth asked. "What if they refuse to join us?"

"Then you are to kill anyone in the room, we cannot risk having them tell the Seraphic Council. The Angels may know some of our plan, but they do not know it all. I will not have our mission compromised!"

Lilith snarled at the thought of her plan being foiled, she had worked too hard, given up too much and allowed Sammael to do as he wished for too long, if it fell through now, at the final hurdle, it would all be in vain.

Mania was less interested than Astaroth, which wasn't rare. She was very studious but that was because it kept her mind clear. Astaroth had a natural talent and interest when it came to all things Alium.

"So, where are we being sent?" she asked.

"As you know, I am going to Faerie with Estrie. As for the rest of you… "

Lilith flicked her wrist and a small brown box appeared before each of the Cambions at the table, inside were the gifts they were expected to give their chosen Alium species.

"Astaroth, you are traveling to The Underworld;s capital city, Irkalla, the spirit world created by the Mesopotamian Pantheon. It is a most sacred space and home to the Wraiths. In that box there are coins collected from the pockets of the dead which allow them to exit Irkalla; such things are heavily sought after in the spirit world.

"Loukas, I am sending you to Namur in Belgium, to the Chateau Miranda, home to the Queen and some courtiers of the most powerful Vampire clan, the Aurum. Amber will be accompanying you; she wants to see her people once again before revealing herself. No one will recognise her; most think she is a myth and the Elders will not be present. As a gift, you will present them with that box, do not drop it. It is filled with glass vials of Angel Ichor collected after the death of Adriel. To Vampires, Angel Ichor is a drug with effects that are similar to the effects that ecstasy has on Stagnants."

"And finally, Mania, I am sending you to the Tver region of Russia. There you are going to be meeting with Lycaon, the very first Maledictus werewolf, and the rest of his pack. If my sources are reliable, there are some newer Lycanthropes in his pack and they are struggling with controlling their shifts from human to wolf, in that box are talismans for them to wear which will help them to maintain control when they change and will also give the pack the ability to tap into their wolf-like powers while remaining in a human form."

"You must all be careful. These creatures are dangerous and some of them are manipulative. Watch your backs, but do not let these contacts slip through your fingers."

When Lilith finished speaking, each Cambion reached for the box before them. They picked them up and left the hall, ready to go through Hell's portals and be transported to the destinations Lilith had designated.

Russia was freezing. Mania had been expecting the cold when Lilith said she was going to the Tver region, but she had not been prepared for how cold it actually was; the leather jacket was not nearly enough to provide any warmth. Using one hand, Mania tapped the top of her black leather jacket, while keeping the small brown box of talismans in her other hand. The jacket shimmered in a red light before growing longer so that it almost reached her feet. The skirt of the coat, the collar, the wrists and the inside of the jacket were now all lined with a soft, black fur and she instantly felt a little warmer. How did Stagnants cope without magic?

Her wide auburn eyes scanned her surroundings. She was in a deep forest surrounded by tall trees of almost black bark and dark jade leaves, everything around her was coated in a thick layer of shining white snow and the air was thin causing Mania to take deep breaths. She didn't like the air being so thin, it made her head feel light and dizzy which made it easier for the voices to get louder. As soon as she had this thought, they streamed into her head violently, each voice fighting to be heard.

You'll never find them.

You're going to die out here in the cold.

Why would the wolves want to speak to you? They'd much rather talk to us, we're the interesting ones.

Mania put her hands on the side of her head. "Shut up," she muttered to herself. "You're just in my head, you aren't real."

She jumped as she thought she saw a figure walk in front of her, a hallucination she told herself. She jumped again as she felt something brush against her back; she turned to see what it was, but nothing was there. She continued to press her hands against her head as she muttered to herself that none of it was real; she raised her head in the hope that she could ignore the voices and the visions and find the pack of Lycaon. She opened her eyes and screamed when she saw a bag coming toward her head; she had no time to react, no time to think of an incantation, she had no choice but to let herself be taken. Mania felt a violent thud on the back of her head and everything went black.

Chapter 7

Mahina, Mariah and Moroccan Musa had received a great deal of information in the time they had been with the Angel Nakir. They considered most of it unbelievable, but they could not deny what they had seen; after all, seeing is believing. The Angel had given them all of the necessary information they were going to need, and he had taught the siblings how to cast some simple spells to help them get by once they had infiltrated the camp of Lilith and her Cambions.

Now, Mahina, Mariah, Moroccan and Nakir were once again seated in the conservatory at the back of the

Musa's home, the sun was shining brightly outside, heating the room so that it was almost uncomfortably warm for the two Angels. The white sofas and chair were stained black, burnt from when Moroccan had attempted a fire spell that had been too strong; although this showed a lack of control and a clear lack of skill; Moroccan was showing potential and was going to make for a spectacular magic user.

Nakir was seated in the chair with Mariah on the sofa to his left, Moroccan on the one at his right and Mahina stood between the two, rolling her eyes at her siblings who were deep in conversation. Some of it was relevant to what they were readying to do, but the majority was idle chat about how they couldn't believe what was happening and some conspiracy theories they had about the Alium world; nothing of interest to Nakir. The Angel's wings were tucked up against his back and he was placed at the very edge of the seat being careful not to get any of the ash on his silver armour. At his feet was a small leather satchel decorated with silver embroidery.

"I have gifts for the three of you," Nakir interrupted. Moroccan and Mariah fell silent almost instantly as they turned their heads in a simultaneous motion to look at the Angel. He heard Mahina chuckle as he bent down and picked up the leather satchel, he opened it and began to place the contents on the table between them. A mirror, a set of rings, a book bound in grey and gold, and a horn of brown, white and black wood.

Nakir picked up the mirror first, the front was glass, and the back was the same startling blue as the waters of the Maldives, decorated with ornate patterns and a glistening blue gem in the centre.

"This is the Yata no Kagami. Long ago, when the Ancient Japanese people discovered Angels whom they worshipped as gods, they came across Amaterasu, a powerful Angel linked closely to the sun. Amaterasu hid in a cave after being tricked by her brother, Susanoo, and she refused to leave the cave.

Another of the Japanese Pantheon, Ishikoridome, created this mirror - Yata no Kagami - and used it to capture some of the sun's light to lure Amaterasu back out into the world. Since then, it has been enchanted by the Angel-gods of every Pantheon and when someone holds it and uses the name of Ishikoridome they are connected to another mirror in Olympus where the Seraphic Council resides. You are being given this mirror so that you have an easy way to return to us. even when in Hell."

Nakir placed Yata no Kagami on the table. Next, he picked up the curved horn. The different streaks of colour created a marbled look of brown, black and white.

"This is Gjallarhorn. It once belonged to the Norse Angel Heimdall who would blow the horn if Asgard or Vanaheim, the homes of the Norse Angels, were to prepare for an attack. Now that all of cities of the Paradise realms, Olympus, Asgard, Vanaheim, The Otherworld, Jannah, Avalon, Aaru and Takamaghara are linked together, Heimdall no longer needs to watch for attackers and so, we are giving you Gjallarhorn. If you are ever in immediate and mortal danger, blow on the horn and you will be immediately transported to the side of Eir, the Norse Angel-goddess of protection, wherever she is."

Next Nakir reached for the book bound in grey and decorated with golden thread.

"Hecate is the Angel of Magic, once believed to be a goddess by the Ancient Greeks. She wrote down all of her spells in this book, which she entitled the Grimoire of Caelum. You are to take this with you but keep it hidden from Lilith and the Cambions Use it to study and practice your Seraphic magic."

The Angel picked up the three rings from the table. They were slim circles of silver adorned with a small black jewel set in the top. From their appearance and the energy radiating from the rings, it was easy to sense that they were not of Seraphic descent.

"These rings were once one called the Andvaranaut which belonged to the Norse dwarf Andvari. The one ring was taken by the Angel-god Loki who was not aware of the ring's curse. He knew only of the blessing it carried that helped the wearer find gold. When the Seraphic Council obtained the ring, they separated it into three separate pieces. This diminished the curse and also diminished its blessing. Then Metis, the Angel of Thought, blessed the rings so the wearer would have their thoughts blocked by all telepaths. We are aware that Lilith has some gifted telepaths on her side so the rings will protect you from them. They will be invisible to anyone but the wearers, however, they will only work so long as the wearer is of sound mind. Should you get overly emotional, or lose control of yourself, they will become visible and your thoughts will be vulnerable." The rings clinked loudly as Nakir placed them back on the table.

He then raised the leather satchel in his bronze hands. "This is your final gift, one from the Angel-goddess of wisdom from the Greek Pantheon, Athena. She once gave this satchel to the hero Perseus as a receptacle for the head of Medusa. It will hide all magical items including itself from anyone but the carrier."

He began to pack away all of the gifts except the rings. He gestured for the Musas to place the rings on their respective fingers. The Angel watched as they put on the separated Andvaranaut, he knew that as wearers they could still see them, but to his eyes, their hands were bare of any jewellery.

"Remember, remain focused and of sound mind. If you stand any chance of surviving your time with the Cambions you must stay on track and you must convince them that you are one of them. Speaking of that, stand up and let's make you look less homeless and more like hellions."

Mahina, Moroccan and Mariah stood up, looking somewhat offended by Nakir's comments about their appearance. Granted they had stopped caring about how they looked after their parents' deaths and had taken to shopping at charity shops because they couldn't afford much more. Nakir had said that Lilith liked to think of herself as classy and regal, she was always dressed to impress, and she expected anyone in her surrounding entourage to do the same. She was more likely to accept the Musa siblings into her ranks if they met her high standards for appearance. Her retinue was quite exclusive, even when she was desperate for help.

Nakir studied the three Angel descendants. His expression was pinched as he thought about how to style them. He understood why some mortals got paid for such a task - it was quite difficult. He twisted his hands quickly and watched as they were surrounded by pillars of spiralling bright white smoke, it twisted quickly and rose high above the siblings before dropping down to the ground and disappearing, leaving Mahina, Mariah and Moroccan dressed very differently.

Moroccan had been wearing a plain hoodie and a pair of tracksuit bottoms. Now, he was dressed formally in a shirt of white, with a blazer and trousers made from a heavy silver fabric which matched his eyes and hair. Nakir had based the look on something he had once seen Sammael wear.

He dressed Mariah and Mahina in matching dresses of silver satin that clung tightly to their bodies. The dresses shone brightly against their dark skin, like the reflection of the moon over a lake. The three similar outfits created a striking effect.

"And now we wait for the gathering tonight." Nakir said. He watched as Mahina, Mariah and Moroccan looked down at their clothing, admiring their appearances. They seemed happy with the new fashions and Nakir decided to let this feeling last for now. It was going to be a while before they were feeling happy again.

Irkalla was the capital city of the Underworld realm and the Mesopotamian Shadow World. It was the home of the Wraiths, the spirits of dead Stagnants who could see through the veil and were kept partially alive by talismans in their tombs and graves, allowing them to form a body of shadows and walk among the living Stagnants but seen only by members of the Alium. The Wraiths survived on dust and, unlike other spirits, Wraiths were neither punished or rewarded for their time on Earth, instead they lived a shadow of their old lives. They were ruled by their petrifying Queen, Ereshkigal, and their hostage king, Nergal; the darkest of Mesopotamian gods; these beings were not Angels as they had come long before. They did not have the same status as a God, but they were a part of something in between, a council of terrible and powerful beings called the Magnorum. Ereshkigal and Nergal resided in the Palace of Ganzir at the very centre of Irkalla, and that was where Astaroth had emerged.

The palace was very much like the rest of the realm. Dead. It was made up of lofty towers of black that never seemed to stop growing taller and taller. It stood on dead grey ground covered in cracks. A thin layer of ash seemed to cover everything and made Irkalla look like an old black and white photograph.

Astaroth had not yet seen a Wraith but he could sense them in the distance, the souls of the dead exuded a very distinct energy that no other Alium did. It was a sense of illness and decay, one that made Astaroth feel uneasy and nauseous; he did not like being in this realm, he did not like being surrounded by death even if he now knew he could only be killed by a Kasai.

Astaroth felt a movement behind him and heard a crunch on the dead grey ground. He whirled around with one hand holding the box of coins clutched tightly to his chest and his other hand stretched out ready to attack whatever appeared ready to assault him. He knew there were Demons in Irkalla; Lamashtu, for instance, who had been thrown from the Garden of the Gods because of her appetite for young Stagnants. He saw that it was not a Demon, but instead a woman stood before him, a goddess of Mesopotamia and one of the Magnorum and he lowered his hand. She was very tall with dead flowers decorating her long hair which almost touched her knees, her skin was deathly pale and the lighting of Irkalla made her skin and hair look as grey as the ground beneath her bare feet. The only colour visible on the woman was the gold of her eyes and the golden sheet wrapped around her body, but even that was cold and fading.

"Welcome, mortal," her voice was little more than a whisper and yet it seemed to echo around Astaroth as if she had shouted. "I am Geshtinanna, scribe of Irkalla; what is your name?"

Astaroth had read of Geshtinanna before, it was her duty to write the name of the dead in her book so that Ereshkigal and Nergal knew how many Wraiths were in their realm. However, if Geshtinanna wrote the name of a mortal in the book; they would be forced to stay, and their essence would be consumed by the Wraiths, which allowed them access to the Stagnant world for a brief time.

"That is not of concern to you." Astaroth said. He heard Geshtinanna growl angrily although her grey lips did not seem to move.

"I am here to speak with the King and Queen of Irkalla, and I come bearing gifts." Astaroth opened the box given to him by Lilith to allow Geshtinanna a peek at the coins that had been taken from the pockets of the dead.

Geshtinanna gasped loudly. Coins such as those were widely sought after by Wraiths, but they were rare since Irkalla did not have many living visitors. The coins could be used by Wraiths to enter the Stagnant world for as long as they desired. She knew the Queen and King would want to have these coins. She could sense great power from the Cambion and knew she would not be able to take them from him. Her only option was to allow him an audience with the rulers of Irkalla.

"Very well, mortal, if you will follow me." She turned and began walking toward the palace of Ganzir, her feet barely touching the ground as if she were floating. They reached the entrance to the palace, a large black hole leading into even blacker darkness. Geshtinanna gestured for Astaroth to enter with a pale hand.

"I'm not going in first," he said. Astaroth wasn't a coward, but he wasn't stupid either; he knew that the Wraiths desired these coins, and he didn't put murder past them in order to get them.

"I am forbidden to enter Ganzir, you have no choice, you must go in alone, mortal."

Astaroth glared at Geshtinanna. He was a Cambion, he was Alium - a mortal was a Stagnant and he was better than any Stagnant.

"Will you stop calling me mortal, my name is-" he caught himself before he revealed his name to Geshtinanna. He heard her giggle but again he saw no movement in her face. He shook his head angrily, he was a son of Lilith, a son of Sammael; he was destined to save the Alium from the Angels; destined for fame, glory, kleos and aristea; how could he have almost been tricked into giving his name away so easily? Astaroth took a deep breath and shook his head again before pushing past Geshtinanna and heading straight for the endless cavern of darkness that was the palace of Ganzir. The castle of death.

Mania opened her garnet eyes and sat up quickly as she looked around the room. Her surroundings were very different from the snowy woods of the Tver region of Russia. She was in a large circular room with a high ceiling held up by tall columns of stone coated in thick green moss. It was lit by a candle chandelier hanging from the ceiling and the floor was littered with richly coloured materials, satins and silks of crimson, saffron and sapphire; in the centre of the floor, directly beneath the chandelier was a pit of fire heating the room. Mania was seated on a raised part of the floor by one of the bumpy grey walls. She was covered by a thick red fabric that, like her hair, was wet from the snow that had melted when she had been brought in unconscious.

"Oh good, you are awake." She heard the man's voice before she saw him, low and gruff, almost like a growl. Mania looked to her left and saw that there was an archway leading to another part of wherever she was being kept. In the arch stood a tall man, his skin dark and his brown hair touching his shoulders and he was draped in robes of dark blue. At first Mania thought he was an Angel, his eyes looked gold, but upon a deeper inspection she saw that they were not gilded, but were a luminous yellow the colour of lemons. He was a Maledictus Werewolf, a mortal cursed by the gods in the old days with the uncontrollable ability to shift into a wolf on a full moon. They were the most common Werewolves now. The Natus Wolves, those born with the ability to shift, were almost extinct due to hunting in the sixteenth century. The third and final type of wolf came from Witches and Warlocks with very little power who enchanted pelts of dead wolves to wear and transform into a wolf. They were known as Pellis Wolves and very few magic users had any desire to practice such magic anymore.

"Where am I?" Mania asked, looking around. Now that she knew she was in the company of a Werewolf she recognised the signs that she was in a Werewolf den. There were clumps of fur on the fabric and fangs were scattered across the floor, probably from pups. There was no furniture or clothing. Wolves didn't need such Stagnant objects, not when they could change at will.

"Worry not, you are still in Russia. Sammael told us you would be coming today, but we cannot have anyone knowing the whereabouts of our den. The risk is too great." The man replied. He had an accent, but not one Mania could place; clearly, he was used to speaking an older dialect from a lost world.

"And who are you?" Mania got to her feet and met the man in the centre of the room, she had never been in the presence of a Werewolf and was eager to examine him.

"I am the leader of this pack, in fact, all Wolves bow to me. I am Lycaon."

Mania had heard of Lycaon before in her studies. He had once been the king of an ancient Greek kingdom called Arcadia. That was the accent Mania hadn't been able to place. He invited the Angels of the Greek Pantheon, his gods, to dine with him in order to test them and their omniscience. Lycaon slaughtered his own son, Nyctimus, and served his flesh to the twelve Olympians. Even before they ate anything, the gods knew that the meat before them belonged to a Stagnant. Disgusted and angered by Lycaon's horrendous acts, Zeus, the king of the Olympians, cursed him so that upon each full moon Lycaon would suffer a torment like no other. Every bone in his body would break and reshape, his nails would be forced out and replaced with claws and his teeth were replaced with fangs. His skin would be covered in fur and he would be overtaken by a desire to hunt in the form of a wolf. Lycaon became the first Werewolf and his son, Nyctimus, was resurrected. Lycaon truly was a monster like no other.

"What is your name, Cambion?" Lycaon asked.

"I am Mania, daughter of Sammael and Lilith." Mania's voice shook, she was scared. Lycaon had murdered his own son as a test, and now she was alone with him with no one to help her if he attacked. "Where is your pack?"

"I sent them out while you are here, many of them are nervous around mortals, even those half Alium." Lycaon said as he sniffed the air and she flinched. "You have no need to fear me, demon blood is not appetizing to Wolves."

Lycaon moved swiftly behind her and sniffed her neck, he chuckled again when he felt her shaking. He moved away from her and dropped down to the floor.

"Please, take a seat and tell me why you have been sent to me."

You can't trust him. The minute you sit with him, he will tear out your throat. The voice in Mania's mind said to her. She knew not to trust the voices, or act on anything they said; but they knew how to tap into her fears, how to manipulate her desires. *You must act first. Kill him before he kills you as he killed his son.*

"Be quiet!" Mania snapped. "Leave me be!" It took her a moment before she realised that she had spoken out loud. She looked to Lycaon who had narrowed his yellow eyes and knitted his brow.

"To whom do you speak?" Lycaon questioned.

"I have … it doesn't matter. I must tell you why I am here,"

Lycaon sniffed the air again, he caught the scent of fear from Mania once again and there was something new, something he had only smelt on Stagnants before. An illness stemming from the brain, one that could not be repaired since the root could not be replaced.

"I sense that we are more similar than you think, Mania. Wolves too have voices in their heads, ones willing us to hunt and to run and to shift."

Mania shook her head and walked back over to where she had awakened. "I am not here to discuss myself!"

She did not like talking about her mind, her visions or the voices; Estrie had always been cruel about it and although they never said it, she knew Loukas and Astaroth viewed her as weak; a liability. Mania dug through the fabrics she had been under and found the small wooden box given to her by Lilith for Lycaon. She turned back to the Wolf King and took a seat across from him as she slid the box over to the leader.

"A gift from Lilith, talismans for your young and those who cannot control when they shift."

Most Werewolves learned to control their shifting in their teen years, children struggled and even some adult Wolves often lost control. Talismans such as the ones in the box were blessed by the moon and repressed full transformations in favour of allowing the wearer to tap into certain Wolf abilities like their super speed and strength.

Lycaon opened the box and drew out one of the talismans, a necklace adorned with a glowing crescent moon pendant exuding the power of the moon. Useful gifts indeed!

"And what payment is required in return for these?"

"As all of the Alium are aware, the Angels are planning to announce new laws, ones that will be unforgivingly restrictive for our people. Lilith has sent me to ask you to join our cause, to help us fight against the Angels. More will be explained tonight at Highgate Cemetery by Lilith herself, there will be all manner of Alium there, but Lilith hopes to have you by her side to show the power of her growing army in order to convince other Alium to join us."

"By "fight against the Angels", do you mean we will be waging war on the cities of Heaven?"

"I do, we will march on Vanaheim, Asgard, Olympus and Heaven, others if necessary."

"Olympus? Do you plan to destroy the Olympian Angels?" Lycaon seemed to be getting more and more excited.

"We plan to take down any Celestial being who gets in our way."

Lycaon grinned, showing Mania his large white fangs for the first time. She recoiled, but the Wolf King did not see.

"So, I would have the chance to avenge myself?" Lycaon muttered to himself in glee. He turned his glowing yellow eyes to Mania. "If Lilith can give me assurance that *I* can kill Zeus, then my Wolves and I will join your cause."

Mania smiled back at Lycaon nervously as she got to her feet; she did not like the sight of his fangs, nor did she like what he had said. She was not like a Werewolf, she was in control of the voices; or at least she hoped she was.

"Come to the gathering tonight and to the ball in Hell after; you can discuss your terms with Lilith there."

Lycaon followed Mania as she stood. "I'll be there."

"One last thing," Mania said. "Is there any chance of the remaining Natus or Pellis Wolves joining us?"

Lycaon snarled. "I will ask Ashina about the Natus Wolves," he referred to the leader of the Natus pack. "But I'll be damned if I will work with the Pellis!"

It was then that Mania remembered the rivalry between Maledictus and Pellis wolves; those cursed were angry at those who wished for such a punishment.

"My apologies, I forgot the history of your kind."

Lycaon did not respond to her apology. "If you don't mind, I am going to have to put that bag on your head again; none but the pack may know the precise location of our den." Lycaon brandished the thick brown sack in his hands.

147

Mania sighed heavily and nodded. "If you must." She bowed her head as the first Werewolf slipped the sack onto her head and she was sent into darkness once again.

Astaroth didn't have to walk through the palace to find the captive King and maleficent Queen of Irkalla for as soon as the Cambion entered the void-like entrance of Ganzir there was a whooshing noise and a powerful wind as he felt the ground move under his feet. After a couple of moments in pitch black, the area around Astaroth illuminated slightly to reveal a room exactly the same black, white and grey as the realm outside. This room, a throne room, unsettled Astaroth more than the rest of Irkalla. The energies it radiated were more than illness, more than death; they were entrapment and violence. Astaroth felt as though he would never leave, as if all resistance to fate and death would be futile.

There were two black thrones in the centre of the room rising from the ground like solidified shadows. Seated on the thrones were two beings, they were far from Stagnant looking, but Astaroth could at least tell that one was male, and the other was female: the King and Queen of Irkalla.

The Queen was the Mesopotamian goddess, the darkest of the Magnorum, Ereshkigal. According to legend, she had once been welcome in the home of the Magnorum, the Garden of the Gods, and she had been kidnapped by the original ruler of Irkalla, the dragon Kurnugia. He had tried to force her into marriage, but she refused and fought against the dragon. By the time the Magnorum water god, Enki, had arrived in Irkalla to rescue her, Ereshkigal had killed Kurnugia and taken over his realm as the Queen. When she first arrived in Irkalla, she had been a beautiful goddess. As soon as she had been crowned Queen her skin had melted away and her bones had decayed to the same grey as the realm. She became a clothed skeleton with dead black hair falling to her waist and thick grey wings, similar to Kurnugia's wings, had sprouted from her back. Rumours of her power spread across the world and she quickly became the feared leader of the Wraiths, those souls of Stagnants who could see through the veil and were kept alive by necromantic talismans that Ereshkigal claimed as soon as their bodies died. If she missed them by even a second, she had no right to claim them.

The King of the realm was second only to his wife. He, too, was a Magnorum member, the Mesopotamian god of war and destruction; Nergal. He had not wanted to marry Ereshkigal, he had actually been visiting Irkalla in order to request something of the goddess and she had fallen for him instantly. She stationed two of her Wraiths at each of the seven gates of Irkalla so that he could never leave. When the other members of the Magnorum learned of Nergal's capture they immediately charged Irkalla and fought their way into the palace of Ganzir, but once again they were too late, the two were married and like Ereshkigal, Nergal had become a walking grey skeleton with leathery wings and curly black hair bouncing off of his shoulders.

Standing before the two of them, Astaroth could understand why they were so respected and feared in the Alium world. Very few beings would ever speak of the Magnorum or their members, even fewer would dare go to the Garden of the Gods or Irkalla where bad things happened. The Mesopotamian Pantheon was the most powerful and dangerous of all pantheons. The Cambion bowed before the two royals, it was only then that he noticed his hands and his black suit had morphed into the same shade as the rest of Irkalla and he looked dead. Astaroth shuddered at the thought of death before rising again to face the ruler of Irkalla; they couldn't hurt him, none but a Kasai could do that and as far as he was aware, the dead could not also be Kasai.

"So, you are the son of Lilith," Ereshkigal began, her voice like the rest of her and her realm, dead and desolate. "Somehow, I expected more."

"My Lady, my Lord," Astaroth decided to rise above any comments made by the goddess or her husband, he needed to keep them on Lilith's side. Insulting such proud beings was not the right way to go about that.

"A gift from Lilith." He held out the box in his now grey hands.

King Nergal waved his hand, and the box flew from Astaroth and into his dead palm. He opened the box with his grey bone fingers and gasped before showing them to his wife and looking back at the Cambion.

"Tell the Queen of Hell we appreciate this gesture, but we will not help her." Like his wife, Nergal had a voice that unnerved his addressee. They both had an ability to make one fear death with but a word.

"But you do not know what we ask of you," Astaroth said.

"Actually, we do." Ereshkigal responded, an air of superiority in her tone. "We know of the Angels' plan to create the Arcadian Laws and we know that Lilith wishes to wage war on Heaven to put a stop to this. We have no interest in entering a war with the Celestial world."

"I would have thought a war would interest you, especially you, King Nergal, god of war." Astaroth wasn't going to leave without a yes. They had already accepted the bribe offered by Lilith; they were at least going to listen to the plan. He was sure that once they understood the plot and were given a sufficient reason, the leaders of Irkalla would see sense.

"Besides, do you know what you risk by not helping us?"

Ereshkigal moved her head in a way Astaroth assumed meant she would be rolling her eyes if she had any.

"No, tell us, Cambion, what do we risk?"

"If you do not help us put a stop to these new laws, the Angels will close all seven gates of Irkalla. You will not be able to claim more souls and you will be trapped here with no new souls and no visitors for the rest of time. Eventually, as tombs collapse and wars are fought in the Stagnant world, the talismans keeping your people alive will be crushed and the only remaining beings in Irkalla will be the two of you." Astaroth made sure to be precise, he did not want them being confused about what allowing the Angels to win would cost them.

Ereshkigal and Nergal didn't move for a moment, they didn't breathe, they didn't speak. It was uncomfortably quiet for Astaroth who stood before the two clothed skeletons.

Then the Queen spoke. "You are good with your words, Cambion, Lilith should be proud. We will consider joining your group, is that all?" Despite her words of encouragement, Ereshkigal sounded disgusted and angry.

"There is a meeting tonight at Highgate cemetery followed by a ball in Hell, you are both invited as are your people - those coins are from the pockets of the deceased, they will allow your Wraiths to walk on earth and in Hell. Hopefully, we will see you there."

"I will be there, as will some of my people," Ereshkigal said. "Nergal, however, will not attend. He is unable to leave Irkalla." Astaroth knew exactly what that meant; if he ever escaped, he would never return.

"We will see you at Highgate, Cambion." She waved her bony hand and Astaroth was scooped up and taken from Irkalla by a spiralling pillar of grey cloud.

Chapter 8

Estrie woke with a blistering headache. She felt as though there was a tiny heart beating in her head and that every noise she heard was causing it to have a heart attack. Never before had she felt so ill, granted being half-Alium and blessed by Lilith's ichor, she had never had to suffer from Stagnant illnesses before; but it seemed that even magic could not stop a hangover. Not only was her head banging violently, but her stomach was also churning, and her skin felt like it was on fire. She sat up, groaning with each individual movement, and pushed the soft silk covers from her body before slipping off the bed and onto her feet. As she walked, or stumbled, over to the vanity table, she tried to think back to the night before but she didn't recall much. Estrie remembered going to the Café de Paris with Mordred and Loukas, she remembered leaving them on the balcony to talk to a group of Stagnants. The last thing she remembered was turning around to see a little woman in a red dress trying to talk to her; but after that, everything was a blur. She placed her hands at the edge of the black wooden desk as she looked at herself in the mirror. She had never looked worse. Her makeup from the previous night hadn't been removed, so silver glitter and lipstick were smudged across her face and her skin looked hard, dry and dehydrated. Her hair was knotted and parts of it were stuck up from the way she had been laying as she slept. It was her eyes that confused Estrie the most, they had gone from being a dark brown to a deep scarlet and she couldn't tell if it was the hangover or if this colour change was being caused by dancing flames behind her pupils.

She knew that she was late for whatever Lilith had been planning, but surely it can't have been that important if they'd let her sleep instead of forcing her to go along. Estrie decided it would be best to go and check the assembly hall, just in case they were still waiting for her.

Shaking her head, Estrie clicked her fingers, and a cloud of red mist began spinning around her. By the time it dispersed, Estrie's hair had been straightened and washed, her face had been cleared of makeup and her body had been bathed before the magic had changed her clothing. She no longer resembled a hungover mess in a thin nightgown. Now she looked powerful in a black body suit that revealed her arms, sides and hips. She wore black leather pants and a pair of heeled ankle boots, decorated with small silver studs. She knew she looked good, but she still felt horrendous as she made her way out of her chamber, wobbling as she went.

When Estrie arrived at the double doors of the assembly hall, she took a deep breath, steadying herself to be berated for her tardiness. She pushed both doors and they swung open with a loud whooshing noise. Estrie slowly made her way into the room; if she moved much quicker, she feared she would be sick; an experience she had never suffered and never wished to. Luckily for Estrie, only Lilith was waiting for her. She could deal with Lilith.

"Good afternoon," Lilith said smarmily from her seat at the round table. "You saw fit to wake then?"

Estrie wasn't in the mood for Lilith's sarcasm. "If you wanted me awake for whatever you were planning, you would have awakened me."

"Don't you take that tone with me; I am your mother."

"You are not my mother!" Estrie hissed. She hated that Lilith viewed herself as the mother of Estrie and the other Cambions.

Lilith's shark-like eyes narrowed, and her brows knitted as she took a deep breath.

"What?" her icy voice was little more than a whisper.

"You are not my mother, nor are you Loukas' or Mania's or Astaroth's." Estrie's eyes seemed to get brighter as she spoke, as did the flames on the candle chandelier above the table. "A mother cares for their children, raises them, feeds them and clothes them. You - you abandoned us and left us prisoner to the Angels. A mother is meant to love, and you are incapable of love, the only reason you want us is for your plan. You are only the mother of Demons, and we … we are mortal. I know your legend, Lilith, you could never be a mother to us, even if you wanted to be."

The legend Estrie spoke of was thousands of years old. When Lilith had first been kicked out of Eden, God had cursed her so that she could never have a mortal child and if she did manage to get pregnant with a Stagnant child, it would die upon birth. That was why Lilith had turned to the Fallen Angels and become their

Queen. Estrie was being cruel, and she knew it, but Lilith was not her mother, nor would she ever be.

Lilith bared her fangs and snarled. The Queen of Hell had been planning to sit with Estrie before going to Faerie, she was going to talk to her about the fire lining her soul, about how she could pose a danger to Astaroth. Lilith was going to offer to teach Estrie how to control the Kasai within, but now she knew Estrie could not be contained.

"How dare you! I was going to try and help you, but you have shown me how you feel. As soon as we return from Faerie, I want you gone."

Estrie's eyes flashed a brighter red and one of the candle flames above grew hotter and melted the wax instantly so that it splattered next to Lilith; both women recoiled a little as the hot wax poured across the table.

"What do you mean you were going to try and help me?"

Lilith looked up from the wax and glared at Estrie; the girl was completely unaware that she had caused the flame to intensify.

"You are a Kasai; your soul is lined with fire and you cannot control it."

"So what?"

"Astaroth is a Kukan, his soul is lined with darkness and shadow. A Kukan can only be killed by a

Kasai. You are a danger to him, and I want you gone before you cause him any harm."

"I would never harm Astaroth!" Estrie snapped. "How could you even think that?"

Even if she was angry, Estrie would never purposefully harm Astaroth, he was like a brother to her. If she was going to hurt anyone it would Mania, but even then, she would need a very good reason. Estrie slammed her hands on the table angrily, her eyes flashed again uncontrollably, and the rest of the candles above melted and leaked across the black table staining parts of it white with wax.

"That's the issue with you Kasai, you can't keep your emotions in check." Lilith said as a spiralling pillar of green cloud appeared behind her with a weak pulling force emerging from it. She had been waiting for this portal from Faerie to arrive since she would only be allowed to enter the realm with explicit permission from the Queen. This portal was her permission. The Mother of Demons stood as she waved her hand and a large brown chest banged onto the table before Estrie, containing gifts for the Faeries.

"You have until tonight to tell me if you are going to leave as I have requested. If you do not, I will take matters into my own hands. Now, grab that chest and follow me through the portal, we are going to parlay with the Faerie Queen."

Estrie glared at Lilith, angry that she was so nonchalant about casting her aside when she had been spouting love and motherly protection only moments before. The Cambion stood and took the chest before her by the thin metal handles at either side, she lifted it and dropped it back down almost instantly, breathing heavily.

"You want me to carry this? It's so heavy."

"*It's so heavy,*" Lilith mimicked. "The Egyptians carried huge blocks of sandstone to build the pyramids."

Estrie rolled her eyes.

"Fine, get me a thousand Hebrews and I'll try lifting it again."

"You have magic, use it and follow me."

Lilith sighed again, she never thought anyone would be able to get under her skin as well as Estrie could. The Queen of Hell made her way around her seat and straight into the spinning portal of green magic.

Estrie stood still for a moment as she thought about what Lilith had just told her. She was one of the only beings that could kill Astaroth, but she never would, would she? Not on purpose, but what if she wasn't in control. She shook her head. Lilith had managed to manipulate her thoughts and Estrie wasn't going to let that happen; she wasn't leaving without a fight. Estrie flicked her wrist and the chest lifted into the air and flew just in front of her. It moved forward as she did, and she

and the chest disappeared into the spinning portal to
Faerie just before it slammed shut and disappeared from
the assembly hall.

When Amber left the Vampire community to go
into hiding, the Aurum, the powerful clan that were now
the leaders of the Vampire world, had just been on the
rise and had no palace or power. Most of them didn't
even know what they were, nor could they control
themselves. After Amber disappeared and was labelled
dead or a myth, the number of Vampires joining the
Aurum grew, each new Vampire turned would join in
hopes of gaining power and the favour of the Elders.
Amber's oldest friends believed her dead. Although she
had not been around, Amber Alarie had kept tabs on all
Vampires. She knew that, although the Elders oversaw
all Vampires and that the Aurum acted as a governing
body, it was ruled over by Ophelia, a Vampire. Vampires
who did not join the Aurum either became outcasts
hunted by Ophelia's minions, or they joined a rival
Vampire clan ruled over by Ophelia's older brother,
Orpheo. This clan, named the Argentum, was less

powerful and had fewer members. Now that she was ready to return, Amber was planning to unite the two factions and rule as Queen of what she would name the Palladium. When Amber had disappeared into Hell, escaping the bloody chaos, the Vampire community was centreed in Bordeaux, France. Since then, they had moved to Spain, Germany, Italy; and across the majority of the European nations, Now they were settled in their current environment, Celles, the province of Namur in Belgium.

Amber and Loukas were now standing outside the ruins of the former Chateau Miranda, a castle built of grey stone in 1866 by Edward Milner for a Count and his family. It was taken by Ophelia and the Aurum shortly after and the Vampires lived in the chateau throughout revolutions and wars. Eventually, Stagnants believed the chateau to be deserted as mortals never saw Vampires until it was too late, so they called for the castle to be demolished. Ophelia appealed to the Witches and Warlocks of Belgium to help protect Chateau Miranda. They cast their spells and created a new part of the Veil to surround the castle so that it was hidden from the eyes of all Stagnants. There was one condition that came with this spell, The chateau would only remain hidden so long as nothing about it changed, there could be no extensions and no repairs made lest it disrupt the spell. Now Chateau Miranda looked desolate and parts of it destroyed and the Vampires of the Aurum could do nothing about it. But the Stagnants believed it was demolished, thus it was safe for the Vampires to reside there.

As the two made their way up the long gravel drive, they were able to see how badly the chateau looked, the grey stone was cracked, parts of the black tile roof had collapsed and the clock at the top of one of the centre towers had stopped working completely. Amber didn't understand why the Vampires hadn't moved to a new base, but then again, there were hundreds of them here and they were hidden from Stagnants, making it a perfect hunting ground. They reached the large arched door and before they could knock, it opened. Loukas and Amber looked at each other cautiously, both knew how sneaky Vampires could be.

The Vampires they had come to see today were Ambrogian, the most common type of Vampire. The stagnants wrote about them in romance novels. Amber and Loukas were glad to see the Ambrogians.

There were three other types of vampires. The Mananaggal, expert winged hunters with the ability to separate their top and bottom halves and whose lust for blood was second to none. Empousa Vampires, an all-female group of winged unkillable beings with one bronze and one donkey leg created by the Angel-goddess Hecate. Due to their hostility, those two groups had been trapped in Acuran, the realm of monsters and in Iṛakkāta, the city of the undead. The final group of Vampires were the Vetala, the most peaceful of the Vampire species who survived purely off of animal blood. They had been created by the Angel-goddess Kali. They resided high in the Gangkhar Puensum, a mountain in Bhutan unclimbable by Stagnants.

"Bonjour," Amber called as if she thought perhaps hearing the tongue of their native land might soften any Vampires nearby. She entered a large parlour. The ceiling of the room was a royal blue, lined with white, and deeply cracked. Straight to her left and her right were sets of stairs coated in rubble and crumbled grey stones and straight ahead was another door, this one brown and almost hanging off of its hinges.

"Qui es-tu?" a sultry voice sounded at the top of the stairway to the right of Loukas and Amber. It had come from a woman who looked quite young, no older than sixteen years. She had pale skin that was almost colourless and looked as if it were made of marble. Her eyes were bright blue, and her long blonde hair was tied up regally atop her head with not a lock out of place. She was in a dress of baby pink satin that hung loosely on her body, yet still showed off her figure. She wore a golden brooch with a sapphire in the centre attached to her dress. She looked majestic among the ruins of the stairway. Her appearance was incongruous in the ravaged setting.

"Une ambassade de l'enfer. Sammael a envoyé un mot pour nous attendre." Amber responded. She recognised the woman before her, she had definitely seen her before, but she couldn't remember where exactly. All Amber could recall about the woman was that they had met under negative circumstances, but she had met many people in times of tragedy, and she couldn't remember them all.

"I'm sorry," Loukas interrupted before the blonde woman could respond any further to Amber. "Not all of us present speak French, so can we switch to English?"

He sighed heavily. The sooner they got this meeting done, the sooner he could return to Estrie's side. He didn't like her being alone with Lilith. Estrie knew how to push their mother's buttons, and Lilith had a horrendous temper; one wrong move from his sister, and Lilith could snap and tell her she had killed someone.

"My apologies, Cambion," the blonde woman said, her thick French accent remaining.

"Loukas," he introduced himself with a smile.

"I am Ophelia, Queen of the Aurum." She smiled back and flashed two long sharp fangs at Loukas and Amber. "I didn't expect you quite so early, I would have tidied up."

Loukas could not decipher whether or not the Vampire was being sarcastic or not. He smiled back politely and nodded.

"Is there somewhere we might speak?" He had expected Amber to do most of the talking. These were her people after all, but for some bizarre reason she had gone silent, and her eyes had narrowed with distrust when looking at Ophelia.

Ophelia made her way elegantly down the steps at a leisurely pace as she wove her way around the debris of broken stone and pieces of the collapsed roof.

"Of course. I think all of my subjects will have gathered now," she walked past Loukas and Amber and looked the other Vampire up and down. She was much smaller than Amber, but, it seemed, just as fierce.

"I took the liberty of inviting my brother, the leader of the Argentum clan, Orpheo. We agreed you would want to talk to the leaders of all Vampires and not just one - that would be bad politics."

"Indeed, it would, we appreciate the gesture." Loukas said. Vampires could be fickle, and their emotions easily changed. Being polite was the best way to keep them on one's side.

Ophelia smiled once again before placing a pale hand on the wooden door, hanging off of its hinges. She pushed gently and it opened with a loud, uncomfortable creaking. Ophelia made her way into the next room with

Amber and Loukas just behind her. The room was very similar to the throne room of the fortress in Pandemonium. This room showed far more destruction with parts of the ceiling painted bright red and the majority of it cracked and scattered across the ground, the grey walls were broken; and the stained glass windows were shattered in an inward direction and boarded up with thick planks of wood. There was a rusty chandelier hanging loosely from the ceiling and covered in candles, lighting the room; despite many Aurum Vampires having enchanted jewellery which allowed them to walk in the sun, some would not and so all windows had been covered to prevent any sunlight intruding into the room. In the centre stood an empty throne until Ophelia walked over and took her seat. On one side of the room there was a large group of Vampires in gold, and on the other side was a group wearing silver - the colours of the Aurum and Argentum.

When Ophelia was seated, a man from the Argentum moved to her side. He was the taller of the two but there was no mistaking that they were siblings. His eyes were the same bright blue, his skin was pale and hard, and his hair was the same blonde and touching his shoulders. He was Orpheo, brother of Ophelia and leader of the Argentum. His bright eyes looked past Loukas and landed on Amber, instantly he was taken back thousands of years, a memory from his human years.

He had just turned eighteen and had seen a woman sneaking out of her home in the middle of the night. Concerned for her safety due to recent reports of animal attacks, he had left his house to follow and protect her, if necessary. At one point he lost track of her in the woods and was left wandering around alone with only the moon lighting his path.

Then he felt it, a strong arm wrapped around his chest and something growling in his ear. He tried to fight against the crushing weight of the arm, but the unknown being was incredibly strong. In one final desperate attempt to break out from its grip, Orpheo opened his mouth and sank his teeth into the cold, pale flesh of the arm gripping his shoulder. He bit hard enough to draw blood. The blood was bitter and icy cold as it ran into his mouth and down his throat. Even through this attack, the creature did not release him, but attacked again, sinking two long fangs deep into his neck. Orpheo screamed for help as he felt his blood being drawn from his body, but he was too deep in the woods for anyone to hear him. As the creature continued to feed on him, Orpheo felt weak and tired, then he was dropped to the ground. He clawed his way onto his knees and saw the creature that had attacked him for the first time, a woman with dark brown eyes and big brown hair, her face covered with his blood. After seeing her, his vision went blurry and Orpheo lost consciousness.

When he had awakened, Orpheo was back in his bed in his home. He examined his neck in a mirror and could see no signs of an attack and so he wrote the previous night off as a bad dream and had opened his curtains. He drew back the thick fabric and cried out as his skin was instantly burned when the sun's rays touched his face. He dropped to the floor and felt his burns healing immediately as his sixteen-year-old sister, Ophelia, burst into his room at the sound of the commotion. The minute he saw her, the scent of her blood triggered a strong sensation and Orpheo knew something bad was going to happen. He yelled at her to get out, but she didn't listen and moved closer to him. He attacked her in the same way he had been attacked by the woman the night before. She bit him as she tried to escape and took in some of his blood. In his frenzy, he drained her entirely and she died in his arms.

Orpheo spent the rest of the day inside, crying over his sister and mourning his old life; somehow, he had died and returned a monster. Although he was terrified of himself, his overriding emotion was hunger, a hunger for more blood. When night came, Orpheo realised he was free to go out and he took to the streets killing and feeding on anyone he passed. It was this same night that he saw the woman again, the woman that had attacked him; she was walking along the blood-stained street crying over all of the dead bodies around her and then she saw him and charged. She clawed at Orpheo and sank her fangs into him time and time again before twisting his head violently, hearing his neck snap and he dropped to the ground; once again she thought she had killed him.

A few hours later Orpheo woke again and to his surprise, Ophelia stood next to him, her face covered in blood. Together the two of them began turning more people into their kind and then they were found by the Elders. Together they came up with rules and laws for these creatures and even created a name for their species - Vampires. Slowly the Aurum and Argentum came into being and Orpheo never saw the woman who changed him again. He never told his sister his story.

If Amber Alarie recognised him, her face betrayed no sign of it, but Orpheo recognised her and knew that this was going to be his chance at revenge, but he was going to have to wait and play the game slowly. If Amber didn't yet recognise him, he was going to make sure she didn't until it was too late.

"Welcome," Ophelia began. She knew that her visitors would see it as odd that she, a girl who looked sixteen, had so much power; but they had no idea the horrors she had seen and the things she had to endure to become as powerful as she was now.

"The majority of us here are aware of your cause, we know of the Arcadian Laws, we know the Angels want to restrict and oppress us further; but we Vampires must look out for ourselves. We cannot fight against the Angels for nothing, if we were to lose it would mean further punishment and further restrictions. What can Lilith promise us to convince us we will be safe, that we will win?"

Amber still wasn't speaking and Loukas thought he could see worry in her eyes; he knew he would have to convince the Vampires to join them in the approaching battle for control.

"The punishment you will face for standing against the Angels will not be too far from the restrictions the Seraphic Council wish to impose on you now, whether you fight and lose, or just accept the laws, you are going to be oppressed. However, if you fight with us, whether we win or lose, you will be revered as heroes and legends. We also offer you these."

Loukas opened the wooden box in his hands and a shining white light lit the room even more.

"Vials filled with Angelic Ichor, drugs to your kind."

Orpheo said nothing, his face unreadable, his eyes fixed on Amber, but Ophelia smiled as she clapped loudly.

"Very well done, Cambion. Lilith has a true diplomat on her hands. Very well, you shall have the support of the Vampires, both Aurum and Argentum."

She stood and took the box from Loukas' hands before walking past them to lead the Cambion and the Vampire out of Chateau Miranda. Orpheo continued to glare at Amber with rage-filled eyes and his heart seething with the desire for revenge.

The realm of the Faeries was split in two, one side was Unseelie, a dead realm for darker Faeries who worshipped the evil Fomorrian gods rather than the gods of the Tuatha Dé Danann who had seats on the Seraphic Council. The realm held four of the eight Faerie cities and although technically under the control of the Faerie Queen, a dark Lord by the name of Donn garnered more respect there than she. The second half of

Faerie housing the more affluent creatures and palaces within its four cities was known as Seelie. The Seelie realm was beautiful and home to the Faeries who worshipped the Tuatha Dé Danann, and the Queen who ruled over all of Faerie.

It was in the Seelie half of Faerie that Lilith and her daughter appeared. Behind them stood a great structure of white stone, the Ládir Fortress in the city of Cathair Róidiam. It had been built on the edge of the Scrios Forest as the first defence lest any Unseelie break through the magic, keeping them from stepping a foot over the border.

Cathair Róidiam was a great distance from Lilith and Estrie's desired destination. The capital, Cathair Órga, was more than a day's ride in the mortal world, but Faerie was not the land of Stagnants and time did not work in the same manner. Lilith knew that what would have been a long ride on horseback would be but a few hours walk in the realm of Seelies.

Seelie was a land that often reminded Lilith of her time in Eden, back in the first days of creation, before her life had been ruined by Eve. The ground was covered in bright green grass and flowers of vibrant colours.There were trees laden with colourful fruits and orchids and the trees were surrounded by Dryads, the tree Faeries who tended the land with their magic and danced in Faerie revels. There were lakes of crystal-clear water scattered around the land providing places for Naiads, the water Faeries, to play, dance and cast their spells. The entire realm was lit beautifully by the sky, a mixture of swirling green, blue, pink and yellow lights made entirely of the same substances that produced the Northern Lights, also known as the aurora borealis.

Lilith and Estrie began their journey in silence, traveling down hidden roads and paths, avoiding being seen by Seelie knights in the towns and cities. For hours they walked, admiring the beautiful white buildings of Cathair Róidiam, its walls glistening with the iridescent glow of the sky. Their venture took them past the shimmering city of glass, Cathair Gloine, where Estrie had smiled at the sight of Faerie children giggling and playing with the dryads of the trees. Lilith had scowled as a piece of mud thrown by one of the children almost hit her dress.

The Queen of Hell looked so out of place in Faerie, she radiated ruin and destruction, the land itself could sense this; as she walked across the grass, flowers leaned out of her way, only to move back once she had passed. The Naiads and Dryads jumped back into the lakes and trees as they saw her approach. It didn't bother Lilith that she scared the native creatures of this land, she had never been particularly fond of Faeries.

Next they passed Cathair Platanam, an area Lilith said that it was best to avoid, for it was here that all

Seelie weapons were made. Each blade, every arrow and spear were handcrafted from enchanted gold. The enchanted gold was the only metal Faeries could touch without being scalded. The weapons were crafted by the Sorracht an Óir, the Sorority of Gold, a select set of Faeries priestesses permitted to know the deepest secrets of enchanted gold and how to mould such material into weapons lighter than air and stronger than diamond. If any but a member of the Sorracht an Óir witnessed or discovered such secrets, they would be hunted and killed.

Once they were successfully past Cathair Platanam without being spotted by the Sorority of Gold or their guards, the two women reached their final hurdle. The Gate of Cosaint at the border of Faeries capital, Cathair Órga. It was a large, sharp gate of intricately winding gold which spanned the length of the capital, guarding the great gilded palace and all her inhabitants. The Faerie Queen's castle was visible in the distance through the gaps in the gate. It was a huge structure of shining gold - quite a materialistic building for such a natural realm and thus was the fickle nature of Faeries.

"How do you know the Faerie Queen?" Estrie broke the silence. As much as she didn't want to speak with the woman trying to banish her from her friends, Estrie also didn't want to be alone with her thoughts. She didn't know when she was going to lose control and she feared she might possibly harm someone.

"When you spoke of her before it was with disdain... why?"

Still walking, Lilith rolled her eyes and said: "A very long time ago, there was a prophecy foretelling that one day the Queen of Demons, the Queen of Faeries and the Queen of Witches would join together to defeat a common enemy. Just after the battle of Camlann in 537 AD, this common enemy surfaced and, as was foretold, the three of us - the Faerie, Witch and myself joined together and put a stop to their plan. We each ended up sharing our essence with the other two ... I took a piece of the essence of both the Faerie and the Witch into my being and gave them each a part of mine. Since then, we have been linked and we must remain linked to keep this evil at bay. Although we worked together, none of us liked each other and after our battle was over the Witch Queen attempted to take over Hell. I called for the help of the Faerie Queen, but she said she wanted no part in the war. I managed to stop the Witch and trapped her in a prison realm. Killing her would have destroyed our link, and I never forgave the Faerie Queene for leaving me to fight the battle alone."

Estrie was somehow surprised, she knew Lilith had a past, but she never imagined it to be so interesting. One part of Lilith's story woke something in Estrie's mind, something about the date was very familiar.

"537 AD? The battle of Camlann? Why do these dates sound so familiar?"

Lilith sighed. "Did Sammael teach you nothing of Alium history? The battle of Camlann was the battle in which King Arthur died."

"And the Faerie Queen?"

"King Arthur's half-sister, the most powerful Faerie to ever exist, Morgana le Fay."

Estrie let out an excited squeal. Morgana le Fay had been underestimated and oppressed her entire life, she had fought against the laws trying to ban her religion, the worship of the Tuatha Dé Danann, and eventually she had succeeded. She arranged for King Arthur to be killed, she destroyed all Faeries older than herself and she took control of Faerie and Camelot. Morgana le Fay was Estrie's second favorite role model; her first being Medea, of course.

"I wouldn't be so excited, she's a lot less impressive in person."

"So, who is the Witch Queen?" Estrie asked eagerly, maybe it was Medea; she had been a powerful Witch, but not as powerful as her Aunt Circe, maybe it was Circe.

"That does not matter, no one will ever meet her again."

Estrie didn't ask any more questions about the Witch Queen, clearly it was a trigger story for Lilith. Instead, the two watched the gate and waited in silence for a few moments. There was a figure approaching in the distance, a man with messy blonde hair and dark green eyes. Both women recognised Mordred instantly. He was dressed far more formally than he had when visiting Hell and when he took Estrie and her brother for an evening in the Stagnant world. His chest was covered in a golden breastplate and a cape of rose gold ran from his shoulders to the floor.

"Mordred." Lilith greeted him through the fence.

"Mordred," Estrie muttered to herself in revelation. Of course, that's who he was. How had she not put those pieces together until now? Mordred was the nephew of Morgana le Fay, his mother had Morgause and King Arthur killed. Morgana had partially raised him, and it was he who had killed Arthur, thus granting Morgana the power to become Queen of Camelot and Faerie. This made him a Prince of Faerie and having seen him do magic, Estrie knew that Mordred was Unseelie. He worshipped the darker Celtic gods and, unlike Seelie magic, his did not require an enchantment, but sometimes it was unpredictable, and the effects were always darker.

"Come on in." Mordred waved a hand covered in a rose-gold glove and the twisting trellises of gold unwound and created an archway for the two to pass through. Lilith travelled through first, followed by Estrie. Estrie was unsure why the Prince was eyeing her with confusion and pity.

Mordred led them to the entrance of the shining palace of gold. Bronze strips in the shape of twisted vines and branches were wrapped around the spires and towers of the great building, and the light from the sky bounced off the gold to create a magnificent colourful shadow across the ground before it. From what could be seen, the windows were just empty arches as was the main entrance, an empty arc of shimmering gold.

The Demon Queen and her Cambion daughter smiled back at Mordred as they made their way through the archway and into the palace. As they followed the Unseelie Prince through the corridors of gold and bronze, Estrie looked around in awe, the place was beautiful. It was nothing like Hell, if only she was the 'daughter' of the Faerie Queen, then she wouldn't have to live in a desolate wasteland of death and torture. The three of them came to a stop outside another archway, Mordred waved his hand, and the edges of the arc began to glow bright green again before the colour was stripped away and flew past them, removing the barrier of protection from the entryway.

Mordred led them into the room, it was a large semi-circle with three walls and an open balcony looking out onto Faerie. The walls were gilded and cast an auriferous glow across the white marble floor. The majority of the room was empty except for a large bed protruding from one of the curved walls, the headboard and legs were gilt and twisted into the shapes of trellises and flowers, and it was covered in sheets of glistening white silk rippling with the swirling shadows of gold from the walls and the ever-changing lights of the aurora borealis shining in from the balcony. There was a woman sprawled elegantly on the bed, her bright red hair running across the white silk like blood. A dress of golden satin clung to her body and her head was adorned with a headdress of gilt leaves. Her lips were the colour of plums and her eyes were lit with the same lights as the sky of Faerie. She was stunning.

"Lilith, I was wondering when you were going to show up." The woman said, her voice as smooth as silk. She slid slowly off the bed and began making her way over to the golden railing of the balcony. She placed her back on the rails and spread her arms across the top as she smiled at Lilith and Estrie. As she posed, she seemed to exude an ethereal glow.

"Well, here I am, Morgana," Lilith responded coldly. "And I come bearing gifts, I know how much you like presents."

"Ooh, goodie," Morgana clapped her hands together as she walked closer to Lilith, Estrie and Mordred.

"What have you brought me?" she said to Lilith who made a dismissive gesture toward Estrie. Morgana turned her gaze to Estrie and the chest immediately.

"An honour to meet you, my Lady," Estrie bowed as low as her leather trousers would allow. The heavy wooden chest floated before the Faerie Queen.

Estrie was quite obviously star-struck. She had read about Morgana for years and had admired her greatly, although she had imagined her a little differently. There was something even more impressive about the real Faerie Queen. She exuded mystery, strength, and power, but not in a threatening manner. The aura she exuded was subtle enough that it was understandable why King Arthur and so many others underestimated her, but it was also clear how she had conquered them so easily.

"Yes, I'm sure it is," Morgana flicked her wrist and took control of the floating chest, she sent it over to her bed and followed, saying nothing more to Estrie. The Queen of Faerie gasped as she opened the box before giggling and looking at Lilith.

"You have either done something very bad or want something very big if you're returning these."

She drew out a small, jagged dagger of gold from the chest. Since Faeries couldn't use any metal but gold, the army of Faerie had once owned a large collection of enchanted golden weapons, The gold-crafted weapons helped to boost their powers and made it almost impossible for them to lose any battle they fought. Those weapons included legendary weapons such as Excalibur, Clarent, Arash's bow and Ogmios' whip. After Morgana had left Lilith to fight against the Witch Queen alone, Lilith had gone to Faerie and stolen the enchanted blades, knowing that Morgana would never risk the lives of her many subjects to reclaim the weapons. It was these blades, bows, arrows, whips, and others, that Lilith was returning to Morgana as a bribe.

Lilith clenched her fists at her side, she hated Morgana, but she needed the Faeries in her army. They were an old and powerful race, making them potent allies and skilled warriors.

"You are correct, Morgana, I am here to request something of you."

"This will be interesting," Morgana ran a hand through her red hair as she placed the dagger back in the chest and closed it. As the chest floated to the floor, the Faerie Queen crawled back onto her bed and looked at Lilith, superiority and amusement glistening in her eyes.

"Ask away."

Lilith took a deep breath and unclenched her fists.

"The Seraphic Council is planning to create a new set of Laws to replace the Seraphic Laws, they are close to finalising them and then they will be ready to release and govern all Alium by these laws. This would have happened a number of years ago, but thanks to my husband's unfaithfulness, they were forced to wait until my Cambions," she gestured to Estrie, "were of age so they could add laws to govern them. As I said, the Arcadian Laws will affect every Alium, including the Faeries; I have had a sneak peak of what the laws entail and for your kind it involves a ban on any Stagnants entering Faerie and a rule that all Faerie - be they Seelie or Unseelie - royalty, gentry and nobility - will have to carry a piece of iron or another power-dampening metal on them at all times. They are oppressive and I will not stand for them. We, my Cambions and myself, are holding a gathering tonight at Highgate cemetery where we will be informing all other Alium of our cause and explaining how we intend to put a stop to the passing of these laws, after that we will host a ball in Hell for all new allies to mingle. We have come to ask for your support in the upcoming battle and at the gathering tonight. The Faeries are well respected in all communities and I know if we are seen to have your support, others will join."

"How interesting! You seem to have asked me to join your cause and to attend your meeting and party without actually inviting me." Morgana chuckled and played with a snake-shaped ring on her forefinger.

"Need I remind you that you didn't help me in a war once before and lost some of your people's most sacred possessions. Do you really want to make that same mistake again?" Lilith growled angrily. This was exactly why she disliked Faeries, they were manipulative, at least when a Demon wanted something they said it outright and killed if they didn't get the response they desired.

"Lilith." Mordred said, his tone low, his one word a warning. As a Prince of Faerie, he had a duty to protect his Queen; as the nephew of Morgana, he had a duty to protect his aunt.

Morgana raised a hand to Mordred in thanks and dismissal.

"It's okay, Mordred, the Demon Queen is clearly very passionate about her cause. I respect that." She turned her attention back to Lilith.

"Okay Lilith, I'm not promising anything, but I will show my support at your gathering and ball tonight. I will make my final decision on whether I will take part in your war once I have seen the rest of your army and heard your plan. Is that good enough?"

"It is." Lilith said. "We shall see you there."

Before Lilith could finish her sentence, the Queen of Faerie twisted her wrist and Lilith and Estrie were engulfed by a spinning pillar of golden cloud, removing them from Faerie.

Chapter 9

Astaroth was the first to return to Pandemonium after his success with the Wraiths. He was a little shaken by his visit to Irkalla, he knew that not all souls ended up as Wraiths, but it didn't look like much fun for those whose souls were claimed by Nergal and Ereshkigal.

His arrival was closely followed by the return of Loukas and Amber. Loukas, although still concerned about Estrie, was eager to tell his best friend about his skill as an ambassador with the Vampires, and he seemed even happier when he was congratulated by Astaroth. Loukas was accustomed to being overlooked in favour of Astaroth so any praise made him both surprised and happy.

Amber, on the other hand, did not seem like her usual self, she was quiet and contemplative, rather than loud and self-involved. Clearly something was bothering her, but Astaroth didn't know her well enough, nor did he really care about her concerns.

Next back in Hell were Estrie and Lilith, both seemed a little deflated despite their victory with the Faerie Queen. Lilith was upset because she hated to make compromises and had no desire to work with Morgana. Estrie, despite being impressed by the Queen of Faerie, had been dismissed and almost ignored. Perhaps it was true what they said - you should never meet your heroes.

They waited for Mania to come back from Russia, but she never appeared on her own so Lilith tracked her down and teleported her back to Pandemonium. With her dark red hair covered in snow, she seemed distracted and worried as she played with the belt of her coat obsessively. She announced that she had managed to secure the loyalty of the Wolves but had forgotten the magic required to transport herself back to Hell and so had been wandering around the forest of the Tver region trying to find a warm place to wait until someone found her. Despite her story, Astaroth knew there was something else wrong with his sister, something she was hiding, but he wasn't going to press her about it in front of everyone.

Once they were all back in Hell, they made their way to the assembly hall at the request of Lilith. Sammael was already in his seat awaiting their arrival and grinned at them when they came in. They seated themselves around the table, with Lilith in the large throne-like seat, Amber to her left and Sammael to her right. Astaroth took the seat next to Sammael, the father of the Cambions, and Mania sat next to her brother. Loukas took his seat by the side of Amber and Estrie sat next to him.

"Welcome back, I trust you were all successful?" Sammael inquired, his voice like gravel. "You all secured the alliances?"

"*I* dealt with the Vampires, Father." Loukas's eyes sparked with excitement and his mouth was in a wide smile. His smile faltered at Sammael's next words.

"Astaroth, did you get the Wraiths on our side?" the Demon Lord asked.

Astaroth looked over at Loukas apologetically, it was quite unfair how both Sammael and Lilith favoured him and hardly took notice of Loukas.

"I did, their Queen and her entourage will be at the gathering and party tonight."

"As will Lycaon and a few of his pack and potentially some of the Natus Wolves." Mania added, "they were most thankful for the talismans."

"Very good," Sammael nodded at both Mania and Astaroth, pride in his eyes. "And the two of you, Lilith, Estrie."

Lilith shot a dark look at her husband. "I don't answer to you, Sammael, don't forget that!"

Lilith was often calm, but she had seen Morgana smile when she mentioned Sammael and his cheating; soon all Alium would know that she wasn't enough for her husband, that he had actually resorted to taking pleasure from Stagnants over her. Sammael recoiled at her words and looked to Estrie for his answer.

"Yes, the Faerie Queen will be coming tonight." Estrie responded, still a little despondent after her meeting with Morgana. It wasn't just that, Estrie thought. Lilith's words were still playing in her mind, she had until the meeting tonight to decide whether she was going to leave, or fight against Lilith. Even thinking about it made her stomach churn and her blood boil - literally, for the more emotional Estrie became, the hotter the fires in her blood raged.

Sammael smiled once again around the table, his teeth in a shining white row. "Very good. I have received confirmation that representatives of the Sirens, Witches, Warlocks, and many individual beings will be coming to our meeting tonight, though many of them do not know what it is about."

Lilith looked at Sammael out of the corner of her eye, she couldn't bring herself to look fully at him. She had a feeling that she was not going to forgive him as easily as she had anticipated. In reality, he had done exactly what Adam had done. He had become bored and picked up a new toy.

"Good, we should be able to amass a great army to add to the Demon hoards. Well, it is midday in London now, Highgate isn't closed to Stagnants until later this evening, go and do as you wish until tonight but make sure you are back here around five o'clock in Stagnant time."

The Cambions and Amber stood and began making their way to the door of the assembly hall, but they all stopped for a moment as Lilith thought of a further point and called after them.

"And I want you all in red, it is my ceremonial colour."

After that, Astaroth, Loukas, Estrie, Mania and Amber cleared out of the room, leaving Lilith and Sammael alone in the assembly hall.

Both knew that a conversation was needed, but neither actually wanted to speak. They sat in uncomfortable silence looking toward the door as it slammed shut behind the group. It was odd for Lilith and Sammael to feel this way, to feel any way really; after so many years of being alive, neither had much use for emotions unless they were completely necessary, but it seemed that having the Cambions had awakened feelings inside both Demons; not all of them positive. Lilith had thought that this was potentially a good thing, after all, indifference was the worst feeling, wasn't it?

Sammael coughed awkwardly, clearing his throat as he readied to speak. "Lilith, what is wrong?"

"I'll start with the most recent issue, shall I?" she hissed. "How, in the name of Gaap, did you miss that two of our Cambions are Kitsune descendants?"

"What?" Sammael asked. He had seen all four Cambions do magic, none of them had shown signs of Kitsune blood within them; there had been no uncontrollable fires, or black holes, lightning storms, nothing. "You must be mistaken."

"I am not. When I first hugged Astaroth I was given a premonition of him being killed by a Kasai - a fire Kitsune - and I sensed the darkness lining his soul; Astaroth is a Kukan. I worried that I wouldn't find the Kasai destined to kill him because they are so rare. Then Mordred took Loukas and Estrie out into the Stagnant world, where Estrie lost control and burnt down a building, killing someone. At first, I thought she had likely gotten too drunk, and her powers had lost control, so I did a test. I cut her arm and she *bled fire*. When I confronted her about it, she lost control again, so I issued an ultimatum." Lilith paused for a moment and took a deep breath. She didn't need to breathe, but it helped keep her calm.

"How, Sammael, how did you miss that?"

"I don't know, maybe I was busy raising them, while you sat down here plotting!" Sammael yelled at Lilith and instantly knew he had crossed a line. "Lilith, I'm… "

"How dare you! I wanted to raise them, but the minute I end up on Earth, the Angels are alerted. I will be taking a risk with tonight's gathering, but we should be fine, they won't want to face that many Alium, but that is beside the point. Don't you dare throw that back in my face, this is about *you* and *your failures.* I could have killed those children, but no, I allowed them to live; the progeny of your lechery!"

"Is that what this is about?" Sammael asked, his tone back to normal. "Me and the Stagnants?"

"Isn't that what it's always about?" Lilith demanded. "The fact that you can't keep your hands off those disgusting mortals?"

"I know you're upset," he said.

Lilith's nostrils flared angrily as she whirled around to face him. "Upset? You think I'm upset?"

She wasn't shouting, but her tone was hostile enough for Sammael to get the message.

"No, I am angry, I am ashamed, I am embarrassed; but nothing you - or any man - can do will ever upset me!"

She had suffered at the hands of men her entire life: abused by Adam, cursed by God, used by Lucifer; and now, Sammael had humiliated her.

"We can move past this, we've done it before,"

"Yes, you are right, Sammael, we have done this before, that is the issue! You promised last time that it would be the *last time*, and at least you didn't have any children out of it! Now I have constant reminders of your infidelity, constant reminders that I am not enough for you!"

"You are enough for me, and the Cambions, they're yours too; just because you didn't birth them doesn't mean you aren't their mother," Sammael's voice remained steady and at his normal volume; he could see how distraught Lilith was getting and he knew that whether he reacted calmly or got angry the result was going to be the same.

"They do not view me as their mother," Lilith sighed. Estrie's words had affected her, not that she had shown the disrespectful girl that, but she wasn't wrong, a mother did help their child grow, she was there to feed, clothe and teach them, and Lilith had done none of these things.

"But that is not the point! In a matter of hours, I am going to have to stand before all of our potential allies and tell them that *my husband* preferred Stagnants over me. Do you know how difficult that is going to be for me?"

"Lilith, I'm so… "

"No," Lilith interrupted and stood from her seat. "You do not get to apologise again, Sammael. No amount of grovelling is going to get me to move past this any quicker, if ever. A few billion years, Sammael, we had a good run,"

Sammael looked to Lilith from his seat, his green eyes wide. "What do you mean?"

"Despite everything people like Lucifer said about Demons being unable to love, despite my own view of 'who needs a heart if hearts can be broken', despite everyone telling me that you, like all Demons, would not be happy with your lot; I trusted you. I laid everything on the line, I shared my life with you from the moment I met you, to the death of my son, to the rise of the modern world, and you, you have thrown all of that away for a cheap thrill with two Stagnant sluts!"

She wasn't crying, and she wasn't shouting, but Lilith's emotions were raw, and her words cut through Sammael with a vengeance.

"Lilith, what are you saying?"

The Queen of Hell flicked her long black hair off of her shoulder so that it ran down her back as she made her way toward the doors of the assembly hall and pulled one open. She turned momentarily to face Sammael.

"As soon as this battle is over, I am going to summon the Princes of Hell and we are getting a divorce. I want you out of Pandemonium and I want you out of my life."

With that, Lilith stormed out of the assembly hall, slamming the door behind her, leaving Sammael as alone as he had made her feel.

"Mania," Astaroth called. He had been trying to get his sister's attention since they had left the assembly hall, but she walked faster than he did. and she refused to turn around and wait for him. Astaroth knew there was something troubling his sister and he wasn't going to allow her to suffer alone for that always ended badly.

"Mania, wait!" he shouted a little louder as he saw her reaching for the door to her chambers.

Mania paused, her hand hovering above the handle, as his voice hit her ears. She turned to look at her brother, her auburn eyes catching his deep blue ones.

"What is it, Astaroth?" He was not a bad brother, and he was definitely her favourite of the other Cambions, but she needed some time to be alone.

"We need to talk," Astaroth knew that if he went straight to the point, she would refuse to speak with him. He needed to lure her in and approach the situation calmly; Mania was the emotional one, he was the level-headed one.

"Please?" Astaroth said as Mania narrowed her eyes in a suspicious manner.

"Fine," Mania sighed as she pushed down on the silver handle of her door. "Come on in."

The siblings entered Mania's chambers, hers were exactly like all of the others. Once you got over the shock of being in Hell, and the awe of the Demons, the multiple moons, the destroyed buildings of Heaven and Lilith's magnificent fortress, Pandemonium was actually quite dull.

Mania and Astaroth sat down on opposing sofas, it was clear that they came from the same mother and father, both had the exact same skin tone, and both had the same slightly hooked nose, even their hair was similar, although Mania's was a dark red and Astaroth's was almost pitch black, in the right light, you could see flecks of cherry in his thick locks. The only visual thing that really set them apart were their eyes, the brownish red of Mania and the blue of Astaroth. The two, although they looked alike, were quite different. Astaroth was a natural leader, he was strong and confident, and although he didn't mention it, Mania knew that he had a desire to impress not just Lilith, but the world, he wanted power and fame; but of course, this was disguised as a loyalty to the cause. As for Mania, she just wanted to be left alone, she loved her brother and cared for friends, but she didn't need them, and she knew they didn't need her; in fact, she believed herself to be a liability in their eyes.

"Okay, Astaroth, what do you want?" Mania wasn't one for small talk and the sooner she completed the conversation, the sooner her brother would leave her alone.

Astaroth chuckled at the direct nature of his sister. Even as a child she didn't mince her words.

"Something is bothering you, what is it?"

"I don't know what you mean. I'm fine." She knew that her blunt response wasn't going to help her convince him, but she had never been able to feign her emotions; they ruled her, not the other way around.

"Mania," Astaroth sighed and turned his head to the side, as though trying to decipher the puzzle that was his sister. "You forgot the route to get back to Hell, that's not like you, you have a great memory."

"It was cold, I was tired; I was up all night because of ,,," She stopped for a moment. Should she tell him that the hallucinations were coming back?

Don't tell him.

He'll think you're even crazier than he already does.

If you tell him about your Stagnant disease being back, he'll tell Lilith and she hates Stagnants.

"Mania!" Astaroth shouted, he had been trying to get her attention for a few moments, but she had been staring blankly at him, her eyes wide open as she scratched at the skin on her palms.

Mania blinked as her brother shouted her name and snapped her back to reality.

"Sorry, what?" she asked meekly, her head was pounding violently."Why were you up all night?" he asked slowly and softly.

Mania shook her head. "Yes, I was up all night because of the racket Loukas, Estrie and Lilith were making."

"Oh yes, I'd forgotten about that." Astaroth had heard some commotion the other night, and he had seen Loukas' face the next morning. He had looked worried and sad. Astaroth had meant to ask about that, but he had his sister to worry about now.

"That doesn't explain your condition upon returning from Russia, you looked scared, and you were hardly concentrating. Please, tell me what's wrong."

Mania could hear the rare sound of concern in her brother's voice. She knew he wasn't going to leave until she gave him an answer, and she found it impossible to lie to anyone, but she especially could never lie to Astaroth.

The voices in her head were right. Schizophrenia was a Stagnant mental illness. Lilith would have no issue with the illness itself, she would probably have attempted to help her; but the fact that it came from her Stagnant side, that was the issue. Alium didn't suffer from such illnesses, which meant it had something to do with her mother whom Lilith hated, even having never met her.

Mania stood up, and unstuck parts of her hair from her face that were wet from the melting snow. She removed her coat and dropped it onto the sofa before sitting next to her brother and taking a long, deep breath.

"The hallucinations have come back. Not as bad as before, but they're becoming more frequent. In Russia, I met Lycaon, I gave him the talismans that help the wolves control their two sides and I asked if they would help me. Of course, the answer was no, and I…"

Mania choked on her words for a moment, her eyes glistening with tears. She blinked and quickly wiped away the streaming tears.

Astaroth, much to their surprise, wrapped an arm around his sister's shoulder and squeezed her into a hug. He hated seeing her like this. Mania was emotional, but she was strong; whenever she cried it was never over unimportant issues.

"Go on, finish what you were saying." He encouraged as she wiped her face on his blazer.

"I realised that I am going to be this way forever, nothing is going to help me." More tears streaked down her cheeks as she buried her face in Astaroth's blazer, her whole body shaking with the force of her feelings.

Astaroth said no more, he had nothing he could say no matter how desperately he wanted to comfort Mania, but he couldn't, he didn't understand what she was going through. He knew he had to keep this hidden from Lilith and from the others; he was not going to let his sister be ostracized. Although he would never say it out loud, he loved Mania, and he would do anything to protect her.

"Yes?" Estrie was standing in her doorway, looking at Loukas. He had knocked on the door only a few moments after she had gotten back to her chamber, pulled her phone out and made herself a drink. Of course, the knocking had startled her so, as she scrambled to hide her phone in case Lilith was her visitor, her drink spilled all over her pants. Fortunately, they were leather, so the liquid didn't soak through to her legs, it just slid off onto the floor.

"Can I help you?" she was breathing a little heavier than normal, she didn't like moving as quickly as she had to hide the phone.

"Are you okay?" Loukas asked as he looked his sister up and down. Estrie seemed both startled and wet.

Estrie rolled her eyes and grabbed Loukas by the lapel of his silver jacket.

"Get in here," she demanded as she pulled him into her chamber and closed the door.

"Do you want a drink?" Estrie asked as she walked over to a sofa and sat down. Loukas didn't respond, instead he was looking around, although the room was exactly the same as his, something seemed off. The air was thick with magic and it seemed to be coming from the lamps, though the flames weren't particularly bright. Estrie coughed loudly, grabbing his attention.

"I said do you want a drink?"

"Yeah sure," Loukas replied. He went to sit down on the seat opposite from Estrie.

"Not there!" Estrie shrieked.

Loukas stopped mid-way down. He looked behind him at the black sofa, there didn't seem to be anything wrong with the seat.

"Why not?" Loukas asked but got no response. The green eyed Cambion turned his back to Estrie and lifted up the large sofa-cushion. On the stone bed of the dark sofa was a large rectangle of black, a Stagnant device that Loukas knew Estrie had, but thought she had left in the church-prison. He picked it up and turned back to his sister.

"Really, Est?"

"What? Did you expect me to leave it?" Estrie responded incredulously. That phone was as much a part of her as her hair; and she couldn't live without her hair or her phone.

Loukas chuckled and handed it over to Estrie who placed it on the table next to two large wine glasses filled with a sparkling pale liquid. She pushed one over to Loukas who picked it up and took a sip.

"How are you feeling, after last night?" Loukas asked.

He didn't know what Estrie remembered, but considering she wasn't beating herself up, he assumed she had no memory of the fire or accidentally killing a Stagnant.

Estrie lowered her glass from her dark red lips and said, "I don't remember much past dancing and drinking in the crowd."

Estrie giggled a little at the thought; oh, how she had loved the Stagnant world.

"This morning, I felt horrendous, and I looked it. Of course, Lilith and her bombshell didn't help, but I feel fine now. Morgana was a bit disappointing, but still impressive, and my headache has completely gone."

Good. She had no memory of the dark turn that the night took.

"At least you're feeling okay now. What was this bombshell you mentioned?"

Estrie made confused eye contact with her brother, she had assumed Lilith had already informed the others that she was expecting her to leave.

"You mean you don't know?"

"Don't know what?" Loukas asked, getting increasingly concerned. What had Lilith said?

"I am a Kasai, you know one of those fire things we learned about."

"A descendant of a Kitsune with fire lining their soul." Loukas confirmed and gestured for Estrie to continue.

"And Astaroth is a Kukan, his soul is lined with darkness. According to Lilith, Kukan and Kasia are mortal enemies and Astaroth can only be killed by a Kasai. Of course, being the presumptuous bitch she is, our *dear mother* has decided that I am the most likely threat to Astaroth's life, and she has given me an ultimatum. I either leave of my own accord after the gathering tonight, or I stay and fight against Lilith."

Despite the gravity of the situation, Estrie seemed rather nonchalant about it, but Loukas knew his sister well enough to recognise the slight inflections in her voice as she forced herself to show no emotions.

Loukas took another sip of his drink. He knew he was going to have to deal with this situation carefully, he could see the worry behind Estrie's red, dancing eyes. Loukas wanted his sister to be happy, but not if it meant she would be leaving him, she was the only person who truly understood him, who loved both the Demon and Stagnant parts of him; the only person he could trust and not doubt.

"And have you decided what you're going to do?" he kept his voice as steady as Estrie was keeping hers, neither sibling dealt with other's emotions very well.

Estrie placed her glass back on the table and looked to her brother with her bright solemn eyes. It had taken her a while to come to a conclusion. She had really only made up her mind when Loukas knocked on her door and she had believed it to be Lilith expecting a decision.

"I am going to leave." she said. Estrie quickly continued before her brother could try to change her mind.

"This isn't an easy choice for me, but there is no way I can fight Lilith.

I don't like her, but there is no denying her power. I am going to join the Stagnant world, my magic will help me, but I will mostly live as a human;"

Loukas felt he had listened long enough.

"And what about me? What about Astaroth and Mania? You're just going to leave us? We are your family."

He was speaking and breathing quickly, but he kept his volume in check, riling Estrie up would get him nowhere.

"I'm not dying, Loukas, we can still see each other, it will just have to be in secret, like when we went to Café de Paris the other night."

Estrie hadn't quite convinced herself that this was true, but it was worth telling Loukas.

"And as for Astaroth and Mania, she'll be glad to be rid of me and he will hardly notice I'm gone."

"Est," Loukas' voice broke. "Please,"

He had no idea what he wanted to say. Too many emotions and thoughts were running through his mind.

He quickly wiped a tear from his eye before it could run down his cheek. He did not need his body to reveal his emotions.

"Loukas, enough!"

Estrie directed her words like a blunt knife into her brother's chest. Seeing Loukas cry had raised Estrie's walls immediately, she would not be vulnerable, she would not show weakness, not to her brother, not to anyone.

"I cannot control myself, whether I want to or not, I could hurt Astaroth. Either way, I will make an enemy of *Lilith*."

She spat the Demon Queen's name as if it were venom. She hated the woman that claimed to be Mother of the Cambions. She hated the woman who was banishing her from her brother and her father. She hated the demon who was casting her from the world she knew.

"You won't cope out there on your own." Loukas said. "Alone in the Stagnant world, you will be cold and in the dark-"

"I am not afraid of the dark, but I am afraid of what the fires of my soul will reveal." Estrie said honestly. She was not trying to be dramatic. Not much in life scared her, but from what Lilith had said, she was a danger to everyone she loved.

"I need to leave the Alium world before I do some damage."

"It's too late for that!" Loukas snapped before he slammed a hand over his mouth. What had he just said?

"What?" Estrie demanded.

"Nothing."

How could he have been so stupid? How could he have let that slip? His one goal had been to protect Estrie from the truth of the events at Café de Paris, and there he was, giving her hints of the damage she had done.

Estrie stood up, her red eyes leaping angrily and the flames in the lamps getting brighter.

"Loukas, what do you mean 'it's too late for that'?"

Loukas shot to his feet. "Nothing, I - I have to go and get ready for the gathering. Don't forget to wear red."

With Estrie trailing after him, Loukas walked at an inhuman speed to the door which he flung open and slammed shut in her face. He felt the flames of the lamps getting hotter and hotter as he fled.

Chapter 10

Estrie arrived before Lilith and the other Cambions.
She wanted a little time to herself before she had to
witness the building of an army where she would not be
a participant. She stood at the entrance to Highgate
Cemetery, the chosen venue for the Alium gathering.
The entrance was impressive, a large, gothic structure of
sharp angles, made up of brown stone and glass.

It was early evening now, the sun just setting
casting a bright orange hue across the entrance. The
surrounding area and the cemetery itself were empty. It
was only open to Stagnants at specified times of the day

and even when it was open, the Stagnants had to pay an entrance fee, which Estrie did not understand. Why would anyone pay to see a brick structure or a monument of stone? Then again, sentimentality had never been one of Estrie's strongest traits. On the other hand, she wouldn't have said no to an expensive family heirloom if it was offered.

It was the beginning of summer in the Stagnant world and so, despite the setting sun, the air was warm. Estrie was thankful for the warmth for she had complied with Lilith's request to dress in red, but it was not clothing that would win Lilith's approval. Thin scarlet fabric wrapped around her neck and ran down her chest in the pattern of sparse flowers and was joined to a very short skirt of the same sheer fabric. Her arms and legs were mostly bare. Her hair was tied up tightly in a high ponytail and her outfit was completed with a pair of almost impossibly high red heels. If she fell, not only would she flash everyone around, but she would require a good deal of assistance to rise again.

As she looked out into the illuminated landscape of London, admiring the architecture of the old buildings and impressed by the newer skyscrapers, Estrie thought about Loukas' comment, wondering what he meant. How was it too late for her to do some serious damage? Had she done something she couldn't remember? There was a large chunk of the night out with Loukas and

Mordred missing from her memory. If that was the case, if she had destroyed something or harmed another being … if she had done anything like that; she had no choice but to leave.

If she lived in the Stagnant world, if she tried to live like a human, her powers would be suppressed. She would forget how to tap into them as witches and warlocks sometimes did. Perhaps she would be a happy woman then. If she didn't have access to her magic, she wouldn't be a danger to anyone. She could fall in love, have fun, get a job and eventually die of old age knowing she had done all she could to care for and protect those she loved, including her brother, even if it meant leaving and never seeing him again. If she had doubted herself before, she had no doubts now. Leaving Hell and leaving the other Cambions was the right thing to do, even if that meant Lilith would win.

"Lilith told me," a low, gravelly, male voice said from behind Estrie.

She knew who it was before she turned and saw Sammael. The father of the Cambions looked dashing, the red velvet of his suit in bright contrast to the green of his eyes. His dark hair was combed slickly back across his head and he carried an ebony cane, adorned with a shining red jewel at the top.

"I know that you're a Kasai, that the fires of Heaven run through your veins and along your soul. I know that Lilith has given you an ultimatum, but I am here to tell you that you do not have to choose."

"What do you mean?" Estrie asked. "Lilith has changed her mind?"

This didn't seem likely, but perhaps she had, perhaps she wasn't as evil as Estrie believed.

Sammael shook his head in a manner that made Estrie think he was responding to not only her words, but her thoughts as well. So Lilith had not changed her mind and she was as evil as Estrie thought.

"No, but that doesn't matter. You are my daughter by blood and Lilith's by magic, it is up to me to decide what happens to you and I am telling you that you will forever be welcome among my children."

"What would Lilith say about this?"

"Does it matter?"

"Well, she is your wife," Estrie pointed out in a low, sarcastic voice that almost made Sammael laugh.

"Not for much longer." Sammael said. His words were solemn, but his tone seemed more jovial than Estrie expected.

"Lilith is filing for the Princes of Hell to divorce us once the battle is done."

"Oh, I'm sorry."

Estrie wasn't sure what she was supposed to say. She had never been given news like this before. She had thought such things as marital discord would be above such beings, but it seemed that even Demons suffered trouble in paradise. Or trouble in Hell, as would be more fitting.

"But that is even more reason for me to go."

"How so?" Sammael asked.

"If I stay it will only cause more issues between the two of you. If I go, not only will I protect Astaroth, but I may be able to prevent a civil war in Hell."

"The civil war has been a long time coming, though I will not be part of it; it will likely be a war of the Princes for the hand of Lilith," Sammael said.

"If the reason you are leaving is so that you do not hurt or kill Astaroth, I may have a solution."

Estrie's eyes widened at the words of her father, her skin and hair glowing like her eyes in the amber light of the setting sun.

"What solution? It is a problem with my soul, how can you fix it?"

"It is not a problem, and it does not need fixing, but if it will get you to stay, I will attempt it."

"Attempt what?" She was willing to try anything if it meant she was no longer a danger and could stay with her brother. As much as life in the Stagnant world was appealing, Estrie knew that giving up her magic would not be as easy as she wanted it to be. Being alone, without Loukas, wasn't much of a life after he had been such a constant fixture in her life since birth.

"I once knew two siblings, a Witch and a Warlock; both were Kasai, and both were out of control. They sought the help of a powerful Egyptian Angel whose name was Sekhmet, and she was a goddess of fire in the Egyptian Pantheon. They told her of their problem and the Angel-goddess agreed to help them learn to manage their powers.

Using the power of her father, Ra, an Angel-god of the sun, she constructed a puissant ritual in which she drew power from the celestial body and extracted the fire from each sibling's soul. She planned to send the flames up to the sun and rid them of the Kasai magic forever.

For one sibling, the Witch, it worked well and she was free of any fire on her soul. She retained their magic, and she was able to control herself. As for the other sibling, the Warlock, Sekhmet was unable to draw the fire from his soul completely. Instead she angered it and the fire took complete control of the Warlock. He lost himself and became a vessel for the Kasai. The Heavenly fire controlled the Warlock like a puppet and turned him against any Alium he saw. The brother became a killing machine until he had murdered one thousand Alium, then the fires recognised that the vessel itself was a Warlock, an Alium. He was killed by his own fire, burned from the inside out.

"Over time more and more deities, Angels and even Demons have attempted the ritual. Some have gone the way of the Witch, but more have followed the path of the Warlock. If you feel that you want to try this, I am willing to attempt the ritual, but I cannot promise it will be successful."

"I want to do it." Estrie said without a moment's thought.

"Are you sure?

"Yes, I want you to try to draw the fire out of me."

Estrie could see no downside. If it worked, she would be able to stay with her friends and her family. If it failed then she would leave the Alium world, and would not be in danger of killing. The fires wouldn't turn on her as they had the others; or at least she hoped this was the way it worked.

Sammael nodded and smiled at Estrie. "Very well, the magic here is strongest in the Catacombs, we will go there."

Sammael turned and made his way into Highgate Cemetery. Estrie followed quickly, her stomach filled with nerves and hope. This was her chance to ensure protection for her loved ones.

"Where are they?" Lilith hissed angrily. She was inquiring about Estrie and Sammael who had not arrived in the House at Highgate Cemetery as she expected.

The house was situated in the heart of the cemetery and did not reflect its surroundings in the slightest. It was constructed entirely of floor to ceiling windows which flooded every room with natural light.

Lilith, Astaroth, Mania, Loukas and Amber were waiting in a room of windows that reflected the glowing bright orange of the sky onto the floor and onto the white and silver furniture. It was a large reception room which opened out onto one of the three terrace balconies decorated with unique topiary in the shape of tombstones and obelisks like the ones in the graveyards below. The Queen of Hell had recently procured the house after its previous owners had fled, claiming that the structure was haunted. They weren't wrong, but the Wraiths that occasionally visited were not malevolent in the slightest.

"I am sure they won't be long, Mother."

Loukas attempted to assure Lilith, but he wasn't entirely convinced himself. Estrie didn't care about Lilith's commands and would likely turn up whenever she felt like it, and as for Sammael; it didn't take a genius to figure out he and Lilith were having problems.

"Well, we can't wait for them forever, we have a growing group of Alium outside and various Alium leaders on their way to stand with us and show their support."

Lilith had no intention of standing in the dirty woods surrounded by graves and dead bodies. No, she intended to address the summoned Alium from the house terrace with her Cambions and newest allies by her side.

"I say we start without them." Amber said as she checked her reflection in one of the window-walls. Like everyone else, the Vampire had dressed in red, but in her eyes, she was dressed better than the rest of them. Amber wore a red leather dress that covered one pale arm and left the other arm bare. Her shining brown hair was hanging loose down her back and she looked quite tall in the metallic gold heels. Although she wasn't showing it, Amber was quite nervous about the gathering and the ball. Orpheo was going to be there, Orpheo the first human she had ever turned, the boy she had thought she left dead. If he recognised her, he had hidden it well.

"That might actually be the best option, there are a large number of Vampires and Werewolves down there and I doubt they'll play nicely for very long without their leaders," Astaroth said.

"Yes, you're right, Astaroth," Lilith responded as she adjusted one of the flared pant legs of her velvet jumpsuit. Lilith continued just as Amber began to complain that it had actually been her idea.

"Sammael knows the way here, I'm sure he will collect Estrie if he sees her. He's always had an ability to pick up women."

After a short wait, Orpheo and Ophelia Lenoir, the leaders of the opposing Vampire clans, the Aurum and Argentum, materialised behind Mania who jumped as they gave their greetings. Ophelia looked elegant in a shimmering red cocktail dress, her hair glowing almost white in the light of the glass room. Orpheo looked just as regal as his sister in a blazer of crimson, his hair just a shade darker than Ophelia's. The Vampires helped themselves to a drink from a silver drinks cabinet in the corner of the room.

Despite common folklore, Vampires could consume Stagnant food and drink, but they *needed* blood to sustain their life force.

The Wraith Queen appeared next with Ereshkigal arriving soon after. She came alone, her husband Nergal remaining a prisoner of Irkalla. The decaying bone of her entirety seemed darker in the mortal world than it had in the spirit realm, her dark hair clashing against the ripped red cloth hanging from her bones. Around her neck was a black chain holding a coin that allowed her to move freely around the Stagnant world. It was most likely one of the coins Astaroth had brought from the pocket of a dead man.

Next came the leader of the Wolves from the forest of Tver. Lycaon didn't wear much more than the red cloth around him serving as a robe. Usually, he spent most of his time as a wolf, it was easier than having to constantly deal with the stupidity of humans. As soon as he entered the room, his yellow eyes scanned everyone present, he snarled as he caught both sight and scent of the Vampires and made sure to stay on the opposite side of the room away from them. He was probably going to have to work with them, but that didn't mean he had to like it.

The final beings to arrive were the emissaries from Faerie. Few fairies had much respect for the time and schedules of others. There were three people that materialised from this realm. First came a Faerie whose face and body were completely covered in armour of shining gold, they carried a glistening blade the same colour as their armour; it was instantly recognisable as one of the enchanted blades returned by Lilith. The second to arrive was Mordred, for the first time in a while he was dressed to impress, rather than to seduce. His arms and chest were covered in a shirt of red chiffon that he wore with formal black trousers. He was still as handsome as ever; the beauty of Faeries was greater than all others, with the rare individual exception. The third and final creature to emerge from the portal was Morgana le Fay, the Faerie Queen herself. As was to be expected she looked ethereal in a ballgown of crimson silk, her fiery red hair woven with glistening rubies and adorned with a silver tiara. As she stepped out of the spinning cloud of black, it slammed shut behind her and she brushed a stray lock of hair back into place with a red glove glistening with silver rings.

"Oh, Lilith, what a poor turn out." Morgana said as she pursed her lips pitifully.

"This isn't it, Morgana, everyone here is to stand with me as support while I address the rest of the Alium *outside*." Lilith responded smoothly. She was not going to let the Faerie Queen get under her skin, not tonight.

"Where is the red-eyed girl? The one that grovelled before me pathetically. I liked her." Morgana asked before giggling and gasping with a smile on her red lips.

"And where, oh where, is Sammael? Are they together? He always has had a wandering eye."

"We have no idea where they are," Lilith said bluntly as she waved her hand and opened the door to one of the terraces.

"Now come on, we have kept our guests waiting long enough; I don't want them getting annoyed before we begin."

The Queen of Hell marched quickly from the room and out onto the terrace, leading the others past the decorative tombstones and to the edge of the balcony where she rested her hands on the thin black rail and was met by the cheers and applause of hundreds of Alium before her, all ready to listen to the Mother of Demons and her plan to take down Heaven.

Sammael had taken Estrie to the catacombs in the west of Highgate Cemetery, on the other side of the graveyard where Lilith was holding her gathering. He knew better than to alert his soon-to-be ex-wife of such plans, she would try and put a stop to it. Once Lilith decided on something, such as Estrie being banished, she was unlikely to change her mind. However, she could hardly send her daughter away if she no longer presented a threat.

They were currently walking between a circular island of grey stone and a curved set of crypts of dark cobblestone and closed black doors. Above them, the sun had almost set, and the majority of the curved corridor was covered in shadow with only the fireball in

Sammael's palm lighting the way. The Demon Lord and the Cambion came to a stop at the last of the closed black doors. The outside was exactly like all of the other crypts, made of grey cobblestone with a triangular pediment crowning the top. It was illuminated by the orange flames in Sammael's hand. He pushed open the door and extinguished his fireball as he led Estrie into the crypt.

That particular crypt had been created by a Warlock years before in case any Alium needed to perform a powerful spell quickly and privately. It was, of course, hidden from Stagnants. The inside was illuminated by a flaming torch on each of the three walls. The crypt was bare, other than the three torches and a large block of grey stone in the centre of the room.

"If you would lay on the altar," Sammael directed with a hand. Estrie did as her father requested and sat herself elegantly on the slab before kicking her legs up and dropping onto her back, her dress spilling across the stone like blood, her hair like ink.

"Okay, you are going to have to keep very still and close your eyes. When you are relaxed, I am going to put you to sleep and tap into the fires of your soul. When they come alight, I will draw them out. We will not know if the ritual has worked until you awaken. Are you sure you still want to do this?"

Estrie closed her eyes and relaxed her shoulders. "I have to."

Sammael knew she was right, this was their only option, if they didn't do it then Estrie would have to leave anyway, if the spell succeeded, she would be able to stay; the option of the ritual failing wasn't even worth thinking about for either of them.

"Very well." Sammael said.

The ritual was a complex and powerful one that was going to require a great deal of energy. Sammael waved his hand and put Estrie to sleep and decided to take a moment before doing the spell; he was going to have to be fully prepared and have a clear mind. He took a few deep breaths and looked down at his slumbering daughter, he hadn't noticed how like her mother she was; not Lilith, but her biological mother. Astłik was her name, a descendant of Armenian royalty, when living she had been stunning, her skin tone and hair colour the exact same as Estrie's. Appearance was the only thing they shared however. Astłik had been quite shy and often attempted to conceal her face to avoid attention from the men that wanted her and the women that wanted to be her. Estrie was much feistier than her mother; an attribute Sammael was happy to say came from him. He hadn't thought of Astłik since her death, but now that he did; he felt something he hadn't felt in a very long time - guilt. She died because of Sammael. No

Stagnant woman had the ability to survive birthing the children of Demons. He had inadvertently killed her and he had not cared at that time. His lack of concern was Lilith's doing. Over the centuries she had molded him to be like her - thoughtless, uncaring and heartless. It was due to Lilith's influence that he was so closed off to his feelings and emotions. But now it wouldn't be long until he was free.

After a few moments of silent reminiscing and deep breathing, Sammael decided he was ready to attempt the ritual, he was ready to free his daughter from the raging wildfire within her. He stood behind her head and crouched as he placed a forefinger on each side of her head. He closed his eyes as he began his chant.

"*Ra, Angelus ex solis, Deus, exaudi orationem meam. Sekhmet ad hauriendam ignes ab hoc corpore suo et liberabo Kasai de execratione maledicta congessit. Hoc volo, sic fiat semper.*"

As Sammael chanted, the fires within Estrie began to surface, first her veins became more prominent, branches of dancing flames beneath her copper skin.

"*Ra, Angelus ex solis, Deus, exaudi orationem meam. Sekhmet ad hauriendam ignes ab hoc corpore suo et liberabo Kasai de execratione maledicta congessit. Hoc volo, sic fiat semper.*"

He chanted again a little louder this time. More veins appeared, running up her neck and across her face, releasing more fire from her palms. The escaping fire hurtled into the torches on the walls at either side of the crypt. The streams of bright Heavenly fire continued pouring from the Cambion as her body convulsed for a few moments. The convulsions suddenly stopped suddenly and Estrie dropped limply back onto the slab with a thud.

Sammael, now safe from the flames shooting out of his daughter, straightened his back and neck and adjusted the cuffs of his scarlet blazer. He was sweating and despite not needing to breathe, his chest was rising and falling rapidly. The ritual he had just completed would have been easier had he been sharing the load with someone; it had depleted a great deal of his energy. Sammael knew it would take a few moments for Estrie to awaken. He hoped that she would no longer be a vessel for the Kasai. As he watched in silence, she gave a sigh and opened her eyes. There was no sign of the fire. Sammael noted that her eyes were once again a deep brown without a hint of the uncontrollable red from the internal flames. Estrie sat up and adjusted the red strap of her dress as she looked around, her face unreadable.

"Estrie, are you okay?" Sammael asked. Estrie turned her head to Sammael, her individual motions almost robotic.

"Never better."

She swung her legs down from the altar and rose to her feet. The moment her heels connected with the ground, her whole body jolted, as though it had been struck with a bolt of lightning. She blinked and between one beat of her heart and the next, the brown of her eyes became as red as blood once again.

"Estrie … " Sammael stepped forward slowly, concern on his face. Before he could continue his sentence, Estrie flicked her wrist, and the Lord of Hell was launched off of his feet and thrown violently into the wall behind him. His head collided with the cobblestone and he slumped to the ground, his vision blurring slightly. It took a heavy blow to knock out a Demon of such calibre, but somehow the Kasai in Estrie had the power. The last thing Sammael saw before his eyes closed, plunging him into darkness, was Estrie, her skin rippling with the dancing fires in her veins. She waved her hand and drew the fires of the torches toward her. Three streams of flames flew to her and she consumed them through her nostrils and mouth.

With that, Estrie flicked her hair over her shoulder and strutted out of the crypt, slamming the door shut behind her.

Mahina, Mariah and Moroccan were surrounded. Nakir had transported them to the edges of Highgate Cemetery shortly before the arrival of the other Alium so the silver-haired siblings had been able to secure their places in the crowd before it grew too large. They had taken a place near the front but set slightly back so as not to draw too much attention to themselves. Shortly after, hundreds of creatures arrived by portals and different entryways around the graveyard. Mariah and Moroccan could safely identify a few of the beings, such as the Werewolves, most of them had wild hair and all of them had the same neon yellow eyes. The Vampires were easily identifiable as most of them arrived when the area beneath the House in Highgate was cloaked in darkness, and the Faeries were unable to disguise their beauty from anyone. Other than that, however, the three siblings struggled to identify the different species. They were only sure that they were surrounded by Alium.

The clapping and the cheering began at the back of the crowd where they were the first to catch a glimpse of the small group on the terrace. The wave of cheers and applause grew closer and closer to Mahina, Mariah and Moroccan. Mariah looked up at the balcony emerging from the great glass house. She gasped as she saw the group, three vampires, two women with flaming hair, a man with eyes like emeralds, one with eyes like the ocean; a being covered in gold, a man with hair the

226

colour of snow, a werewolf with bright yellow eyes and a gorgeous but terrifying woman with eyes like the night sky. From stories alone, she was recognisable as the Queen of Hell, Lilith. All but the gilded soldier were awash in brilliant red. Without tearing her eyes from the group on the balcony, Mariah took her hand and pointed out the group to her siblings.

"Thank you, thank you." Lilith's icy voice washed over the crowd as she held up a hand, grateful for the warm welcome. She must have been using an enchantment to carry her voice to the entire gathering. After a few moments of more howling, clapping and cheering from the crowd, the noise died down. Lilith smiled, flashing her fangs quickly.

"Welcome, all of you. I appreciate you coming on such short notice, but of course, we had to be careful not to alert the Angels."

Mariah was surprised by the surge of booing, jeering and hissing noises made by the groups around her at the mere mention of the warriors of Heaven. It was clear to her that one wrong move from the siblings; any slight example of Seraphic blood or power, and they would be in grave danger. Mariah took a deep breath as she tried to control her shaking, she hadn't expected to be so scared. Nakir hadn't explained how terrifying some of the Alium were. She jumped as a Drakaina. a woman with the lower half of a snake came near. She

227

nearly screamed when she felt something warm slide into her hand and between her fingers. She looked down and saw her brother's onyx hand in hers and Mariah breathed a great sigh of relief. It was odd that Moroccan would do such a thing, he hadn't even hugged her in years. Yet it was comforting to know he cared and she guessed her little brother probably needed comforting just as much as she did. Of course, he would never admit it, not to her anyway. She looked up at Mahina, who was surprisingly tall compared to her siblings, and received a reassuring smile in response.

"Yes, yes, we all hate the Angels." Lilith said as the crowd settled once again. "And that is exactly why I have gathered you all here this evening. Years ago, I discovered that the Angels wanted to dispel the Seraphic Laws in favour of a new set called the Arcadian Laws. I saw a plan for these new rules, and they were barbaric: they called for suppression of magic, for Faeries to carry iron, they limited Werewolf breeding and so much more. They were an abhorrent oppression of all Alium."

"Thankfully, *I* was able to delay the passing of these laws for a number of years with the discovery of a new species of Alium, a species that is half Stagnant and half Demon - the Cambions. Of course, the Angels wanted to include the Cambions in the Arcadian laws, but this was not legal, only Alium species with at least one member aged eighteen or above, can be included in the laws and so, the Seraphic Council decided to wait until they came of age. On their eighteenth birthday, Heaven sent an Angel to take them to one of the Paradise realms where they would be tested and tried. This was a mere formality so they could rule the Cambions as Alium and write them into the Arcadian Laws. Upon the arrival of the Angel, the Cambions slaughtered him and escaped their prison and came to me in Hell; it is thanks to this that the passing of the Arcadian Laws is still not possible as the Angels have no proof of what the Cambions did and so they cannot yet class them as Alium."

"I stand here now with my strongest allies - the Queen of Faerie, Ereshkigal, the first Werewolf, Lycaon; the leaders of the Aurum and Argentum clans and my Cambions. We propose that now, as the Angels search for their proof, as they search for a reason to pass the Arcadian Laws, we march on the Paradise realms until we reach Heaven. Once at the centre, we will trap God and we will take control. As Alium we will write our own laws, and the Angels will be at our mercy!"

As Lilith finished, more cries and cheers erupted from the crowd followed by wave after wave of applause. Mariah looked from her brother to her sister, their chrome eyes meeting with the same thought; they had to let the Angels know. The Seraphic Council needed to know that it was the Cambions that had murdered Adriel, they needed to finalise the Arcadian Laws and they needed to ready all of the Paradise realms for battle.

Mariah looked back up to the balcony to see Lilith looking out proudly at the reaction she had provoked. She saw a look of relief on the faces of the ones Mariah assumed to be the Cambions. She saw the looks of superiority from the Faerie Queen, the leaders of the Aurum and Argentum, Lycaon and the Wraith Queen. They knew that even the mention of their names had helped to sway any hesitant parties in the crowd. Mariah's attention was diverted to a man who looked almost identical to one of the Cambions, his hair slick and black, his eyes emerald green and he was wearing a suit of crushed red velvet. The man stumbled forward, placing his head by Lilith's ear and whispering something. A worried look flashed across Lilith's face, a look that was not noticed by the clapping and whooping Alium, but Mariah was watching.

The Queen of Hell placed her clasped hands on her stomach and took a deep breath.

"I know that this is all a lot of information to take in all at once, so I welcome all of you to think about your decision and mix with my allies and other potential allies at the ball in Hell."

Lilith flicked her wrists and spinning red pillars of cloud appeared at various points around the cemetery.

"These portals will take you straight there. I look forward to talking to many of you later this evening."

For a moment, Mariah thought that Lilith's dark voids met her silver eyes. The part-Angel averted her eyes as Lilith and those around her disappeared in their own personal clouds of magic in order to welcome their guests to Hell and to deal with whatever crisis the dark-haired man had just brought to Lilith.

Chapter 11

The ballroom hadn't been used in centuries, the last time anyone had danced on the floor, marvelled at the great white columns, or ventured out onto the balcony to look out at the vista of Pandemonium had been after Lilith and Sammael's wedding, and that had been around 7000 BC. Since then, the room had been left in darkness with the great chandelier unlit. The pillars had cracked due to the lack of maintenance and the once heavy black fabric of the curtains separating the ballroom from the balcony had become thin and wispy. Everything had been covered in a thick layer of dust.

Sensibly, Lilith had inspected the ballroom shortly before leaving for the gathering at Highgate. She set her Necrotic slaves to work cleaning and preparing it for the party later that night. Now, as the Queen of Hell arrived in the ballroom a little later than everyone else, she was impressed with the work the slaves had done in such a short period of time; the entire room gleamed, and the chandelier was casting a bright light that reflected in the shining white walls. The curtains had been replaced by a new set of thick red drapes tied back by ropes of silver. The drapes opened the room to the balcony. The pillars, unfortunately, were still cracked and looked ready to crumble.

All manner of beings were scattered across the dance floor. As expected there were Demons, Vampires, Faeries, Wraiths and Werewolves. They were joined by Witches, Warlocks, Dracaena, Dökkálfar and Svartalfar. In the corner of the room clustered a small group of Alium members playing instruments and singing. Lilith assumed they were Sirens, due to the hypnotic qualities of their music.

Lilith scanned the room as she entered. She was slightly late to the party since she had spent time scouring the Fortress for Estrie. Sammael had arrived after her during the gathering and informed her that Estrie had lost control and disappeared. Lilith was increasingly concerned. If Estrie was out of control, it was all too likely that the Kasai would take her to begin hunting its natural enemy, Astaroth, the Kukan. Thankfully there seemed to be no sign of Estrie anywhere in Hell, but that didn't ease Lilith's worries. Being missing was only giving Estrie more time to plan an attack. Nevertheless, the Queen of Hell had a party to host and she needed to make sure that every Alium present was going to join the cause.

"This is a wonderful gathering, Lilith, Hell is not quite what I expected." Lilith recognised the woman in front of her as Aurelia Acantha. A Witch in her early fifties dressed in the most fashionable Stagnant clothes. She was the Colchian representative from the Maleficias, a group of three Witches who set the rules and regulations for all Witching Covens. There were two other women beside her. They were her companions within the Maleficias. Leonora Casimir was the Coxani Witch. The Mangkukulam witch was Vilma Eztli.

Colchian, Coxani and Magukukulam were the three orders of Witches. The Colchian order members were the most powerful Witches descended from the Royal House of Ancient Colchis and the Sun Titan, Helios. They received their power from the sun.

Coxani members, the second order, were descended from Vadoma, a powerful Seer and they were skilled in the art of Fortune telling and travelled the world cursing those who disrespected them on their travels. The Coxani drew their magic from the Earth.

The third and final order of the Mangkukulam were considered the most dangerous. They originated in the Philippines and used their own special brand of magic known as Kulam, widely compared to voodoo.

These three Witches were women that Lilith needed to impress in order to insure the support of all the Witches.

"Many people say that," Lilith responded with a tight smile on her face. "What is it that you were expecting?"

Aurelia looked at Lilith with grey eyes, her face scrunched up in a puzzled expression. She chuckled.

"Je ne sais pas!" Aurelia exclaimed. That was one of the things Lilith did not like about the Witch; she was far too eccentric. "I don't actually know."

Lilith forced a laugh. "Yes, most people say that as well." She looked over Aurelia's shoulder and caught the eyes of Astaroth. The Cambion must have understood the look in his mother's eyes as he came over instantly.

"Hello," he grinned at the three Witches who giggled as Lilith rolled her eyes. "I do hope we can count on the Witches' support in the upcoming battle."

Leonora twisted a lock of her dark hair around her finger slowly as she smiled.

"Why don't we get a drink and discuss it." Leonora linked her arm with Astaroth's and began leading him toward a table covered in drinks near the singing Sirens and the other Witches followed suit. Lilith breathed a sigh of relief. The Maleficias would make brilliant allies and were notably powerful, but they were unpredictable.

The Queen of Hell composed herself and began making her way around the room, greeting her guests, including Sybaris, the Queen of the Dracaena and Malekith, the King of the . She even spotted and greeted a number of the Princes of Hell, all of whom had invited themselves. The evening was off to a good start and Lilith hoped it would remain that way.

Loukas was uncomfortable. Being in a room surrounded by Alium was far more awkward and unnatural to him than being surrounded by party animals at the Café de Paris. At least they had been human and were not reminders of his Demonic blood. Besides, at that party, Mordred had been there to … distract him. Now the Faerie Prince was too busy fawning over Morgana le Fay to pay attention to Loukas.

The Cambion wasn't too sure what his role at this ball was meant to be. Was he expected to talk and win over new allies as Astaroth seemed to be doing with the Witches, was he meant to be circling the floor greeting people but not actually saying anything like Lilith, or was he meant to be out searching across the different plains of Hell and other various realms for his sister. Loukas knew something was wrong with Estrie, he had heard her name mentioned between Sammael and Lilith on the balcony of the House in Highgate, but the cheers and applause from the crowd had been too loud and had prevented Loukas from hearing what was happening with Estrie.Now she was missing and he was frantically worried. The last time she had been alone, his sister had lost control and accidentally killed someone.

"Hello," Loukas' attention was grabbed by three beings he hadn't noticed before him, they spoke in melodic unison. Two of them were identical women, they looked exactly the same from their black-blue hair to the navy dresses they wore. The third being stood between them, a man, his hair the same colour as theirs and his suit the same navy material as their gowns. Their eyes were all a deep, glowing pink, shining brightly against the paleness of their complexions.

"How can I help you?" Loukas' dark green eyes bounced between them all, their beauty captivating. He found himself wishing for them to speak more.

"We were hoping," the male began, his voice low and hypnotic, like the soothing patter of raindrops on a glass panel. "that you would thank Lilith for us."

"For what?" Loukas asked quickly. He didn't want to do much talking, he desperately wanted them to carry on.

"For letting our siblings sing, very few would trust our kind enough for that." The man said as he gestured to the corner of the room where beautiful beings played small instruments of what looked like stone as they sang a heavenly chorus.

Loukas followed his finger to the singers and realised why he was so captivated with the beings in front of him and why he desired them to keep on singing.

"Oh, you're Sirens."

"Seirenes, yes." One of the women said using the old dialect and name of her species.

"I thought… " Loukas began.

The other female Siren cut him off, her voice full of disdain. "That we would have the bodies of chickens?" She spoke of how Sirens had been depicted in the tales of Mythology.

"Or that we would have the lower halves of fish?" again she spoke of the misconception made by Stagnants that Sirens and Mermaids were one and the same.

"Umm, yes. Sorry." Loukas responded, bowing his head awkwardly. He hated causing offence, and he despised confrontation. He hoped that by apologising the conversation would end and he would be left alone to will the party to end quicker.

"No need to apologise, clearly you've never met a Siren, it's understandable you'd have misconceptions."

The male Siren, also known as a Triton, said with a smile. He received withering looks from his sisters, but he paid them no attention. "We do not have the lower half of fishes for we are a completely different species to Mermaids; they are much more vicious and cannot leave the ocean. As for the idea that we would have the bodies of birds, that comes from one particular myth which is true, but unfinished. In short, all Sirens were once beautiful beings, and we even had a member on the Seraphic Council. The Angel-goddess Demeter enlisted the help of three of our ancestors and gave them the bodies of birds to help find her daughter, Persephone, the current Queen of the Greek Underworld. They failed their task and so Demeter left them as half-birds. From that point on the Sirens and the Angels have never fought on the same side. As for our ancestors, they became the most famous of our kind and birthed more hybrids on an Island. The Sirens who kept human shape were, from that point on, no longer written about by Stagnants."

"Yes, yes," a female Siren said sharply. "Thank you for explaining our entire history." She turned her pink eyes back to Loukas, they were filled with a deep anger, not toward the Cambion in particular, but the world.

"You, thank Lilith for letting our brethren sing and tell her we will fight by her side, she need only send a portal for us. Now, back to the Sirenuse we go."

She spoke of the group of islands that were home to the Sirens and were hidden from Stagnants. She and her sister turned, making their way toward the door of the ballroom.

"You guys go ahead" the Triton called after his sisters, not breaking eye contact with Loukas. They both turned, rage splashed across their faces; evidently, they weren't used to their brother not doing as they commanded.

"I'm gonna stay a while."

"Whatever." His sisters snarled in unison. They strutted away, their heeled shoes tapping against the floor simultaneously as they headed to the door.

"I apologise for Nerissa and Daryah; my sisters don't like being away from home unless absolutely necessary. I'm Theron, by the way." The Triton said with a smile.

Loukas could smell the scent of the sea coming from Theron, most people, Stagnants at least, would associate such a scent with the beach, and fun days in the sun; Loukas, however, was reminded of a book he had read in the Prison as a child. It had held information on dangerous, slumbering creatures that could awaken and wreak havoc at any moment. It had been the Kraken that frightened Loukas the most. After reading that even a faint splash near its waters could awaken the Kraken, the Cambion had sworn to never go near or into the sea.

He didn't want to be responsible for the deaths of thousands of innocents; he was struggling with the idea of slaughtering the Angels in the war, and they were far from innocent despite what their scriptures claimed.

"And you are?" Theron's enchanting voice drew Loukas from his own mind and back to reality gently.

"Loukas." A man's voice sounded from behind Loukas, one it took him a minute to place. Before he had a chance to respond to Theron or the other voice, he felt someone hug him from behind and press their lips on his cheek for a moment before slipping round and standing directly in between the Cambion and the Siren. It was Mordred, his hair the same glowing white as the walls of the ballroom, his eyes the same blue as the clothing of the Sirens, he looked a mismatch of colours in his deep red suit, yet still managed to pull it off; this was the beauty of Faeries, they could look good in anything.

"Mordred, hi," Loukas said as he placed his hands on the Faerie's shoulder directing him to stand slightly to the right of his previous position.

"This is Theron, a Triton. Theron, this is Mordred, a Faerie,"

"A Prince of Faerie." Mordred said proudly. He narrowed his eyes at Theron before smiling at Loukas sweetly.

"And Theron, I am Loukas. It's lovely to meet you." Loukas brushed over Mordred's comment and smiled at the Triton.

"Is it?" Mordred muttered.

"Mordred!" Loukas hissed. "Yes, it is."

"Sublime, I'm sure." Theron responded, his hypnotic voice less like the tapping of rain and more like waves crashing against a rock in a storm. "My sisters were right. I do need to return home. Thank Lilith for us, and I'll see you on the battlefield." With that the Triton followed the lead of Nerissa and Daryah and headed for the exit.

Loukas whirled on Theron. "What the Hell was that?" he demanded.

"What?" Mordred asked. "He was flirting with you."

"He was not. And even if he was, so what?"

"What do you mean so what? I can't have someone flirting with my boyfriend. Imagine how... " Mordred was cut short.

"Boyfriend?" Loukas said, his eyes wide. "When was this decided?"

"I'm fairly sure *we* decided it, at Café de Paris, when we... " he was cut off once again.

"That doesn't mean we're in a relationship, does it?" Loukas knew he was gay, he knew he wanted a boyfriend, but that was a desire. He hadn't expected that it would ever happen. He was part Demon and Lilith and Sammael had proven that Demons couldn't love, who could love something that couldn't return the affection?

"I don't know. I thought so, but if you're not ready for that, you don't owe me anything. I just thought... " Once again Mordred's sentence was stopped, though not by another response from Loukas. Instead, he was silenced now by the Cambion as he grabbed Mordred's head and began to kiss him passionately as the two spent a moment to take the other in, their touch, their taste, the smell of their surroundings.

It was Loukas who broke away, smiling widely. "Follow me." He began making his way toward the exit at a jog, periodically looking behind to see if Mordred was following. As was expected, the Faerie prince was indeed only a few steps behind him.

Moroccan hadn't left Mariah's side for the entire evening, not just because he could sense how anxious she was, but because he himself was terrified of the supernatural creatures surrounding them. Mahina, however, seemed to have no problem and had ditched her siblings the moment she could to talk to a passing Faerie.

Moroccan had noted that many Alium looked human, like the Vampires, Faerie's and Werewolves, but each had a visual sign that they were far from Stagnants, be it their eyes, their fangs, or their ethereal beauty. Of course, there were those who would never be able to fit into the Stagnant world in any way, the Dracaena with their snake bodies, and the Wraiths with their skeletal appearances. It was an unnerving experience to be responsible for spying on beings that would attack at the first sign of espionage.

As Moroccan's silver eyes ran around the room cautiously, a creature hobbled past him, its skin white as a sheet covered in purple veins and large patches of black, dying flesh. Behind its eyes there was no life, it walked slowly and was covered in loosely fitting grey clothing. Moroccan had an idea of what the creature was from Nakir's descriptions. The Angel had tried to prepare the siblings for anything they were likely to meet but learning about them and actually seeing them were very different situations.

"Is that a… " Moroccan began looking at his sister.

"A Necrotic?" Mariah finished for her brother. "Yes. A resurrected body with no soul used as a slave by stronger Alium. They're basically Zombies, and they eat brains, so don't worry; you're safe."

Moroccan chuckled as he glanced at his sister out of the corner of his eyes. She had never been able to pull off a joke, and she stumbled over her words more when she was nervous.

"So, what are we meant to be doing? Mingling?"

"I assume so, but I have no idea how to begin a conversation with these creatures." Mariah said.

There was clear disdain in her voice, Moroccan wondered if she felt just like he did, there was a subconscious hatred within him directed at everything from the setting of the Ball to the Alium members surrounding them; he assumed it was the remnants of Angel blood in his genes, or maybe it was because he knew certain members in this very room were responsible for making him an orphan.

"I would advise not calling them '*creatures*'," a smooth voice said from behind Moroccan and Mariah. The two turned to see a tall woman before them, her skin smooth and bronze, her hair long and lustrous and her eyes black as ink. Lilith.

"They might take offence to that; I know I would."

"Our apologies," Mariah curtsied slightly. "This is a wonderful gathering; your fortress is impressive."

"I know." Lilith said before swiftly moving on, clearly, she hadn't approached the Gibborim siblings for small talk.

"Who are you?"

"I am Mariah, and this is my brother, Moroccan." Mariah said.

"And what are you, species-wise? Your minds are blocked to me which makes you powerful, yet I cannot sense Alium blood in your veins, only Stagnant."

Moroccan smiled nervously, both he and Mariah knew that their minds were blocked to all telepathy thanks to the split Andvaranaut rings invisible to the eyes of all but the wearers. As for what species they were, Nakir hadn't given them any indication of what to pretend to be.

"Changelings." Moroccan burst out with the name of the first humanoid Alium creature often found in the Stagnant world he could think of.

"You're Changelings?" Lilith asked sceptically. Changelings were Faerie children left in the place of a kidnapped Stagnant child to cause mischief and horror for the Stagnant parents. Very few ever survived past childhood.

"We are," Mariah said weakly. "It took us a long time to discover who we are and what we can do, but we were raised by Stagnants in the mortal world. It was only around a year ago that we discovered we had magic, and from there we researched and found that we are, in fact, Changelings."

Moroccan smiled once again as Mariah spoke. His sister may have been dreadful at telling jokes, but she was a skilled liar.

"How interesting," Lilith did not sound convinced. "And I trust that this new army has your support?"

"Of course," Moroccan said, nodding his head almost violently and receiving a disapproving look from both Mariah and Lilith.

"Fantastic," Lilith was speaking slowly, her eyes bouncing between the two siblings as if trying to figure them out. "I shall have to introduce you to the Faerie Queen, Morgana, later. Perhaps she will allow you to join Faerie society."

"We would love that, thank you." Mariah said curtsying again.

"Yes," Lilith drawled. "Well, I must attend to my other guests, but please; after the ball, do stay in Hell; you will be a welcome pair within our ranks." With that,

Lilith began making her way around the ballroom once again.

"That went well, I think." Moroccan said, turning to his sister who was taking a deep breath and exhaling slowly.

"What?" Mariah responded. "How did that go well? She was definitely suspicious of us."

"She asked us to stay in Hell," Moroccan said defensively, why was his sister always so negative? "I doubt she's inviting everyone here to stay; it's her way of bringing us into her inner circle."

"I suppose so." Mariah continued with her heavy breathing, one hand on her chest, the other running through her silver hair. "We'll have to inform the council soon, let's wait for the party to die down a little first."

"I think we should split up, talk to more Alium separately. We look suspicious standing together all the time," Moroccan suggested. He believed what he was saying, but mostly he just wanted to escape from his sister's negativity for a while.

"I agree." Mariah said. "Let's reconvene later."

The Gibborim siblings separated and began making their way around the ballroom in separate directions with Mariah heading toward a small group of Vampires and Moroccan walking into a group discussion between a set of Witches and Werewolves.

Mahina felt guilty for leaving her siblings, but she needed a break, unlike them she was not excited by their new situation. She had been happy in their old life, she had finally gotten them into a routine and their lives seemed to have been improving. And now, they had been ripped from their world and forced into another of gods and monsters where the most harrowing part of their lives, the death of their parents, lay front and centre. It was emotional manipulation, Mahina had thought Angels would be above such things, but it seemed the complete opposite, from what she had seen and heard so far the Demons were less manipulative than Heaven's warriors.

"What are you thinking about?" A heavily accented woman's voice snapped Mahina back to reality. The woman was shorter than the Gibborim and was dressed in skirts of vibrant colours decorated with golden coins and beads.

"Nothing much." Mahina responded. She wasn't sure how to address the woman before her, she was a mesmerising beauty with pale green eyes and chestnut skin.

The woman chuckled. "That's not true, I could see in your eyes that you were deep in thought, lost to the world." She placed a hand covered in many golden rings on Mahinas arm. "But, I won't pry."

A look of confusion ran across the woman's face.

"What is it?" Mahina asked.

"I am a Coxani Witch, their elected Queen, Rhoda."

Despite Leonora Casimir being the Coxani representative on the Maleficias, the traveling Witches were known to elect a Queen each year. For the previous four years that title had been given to Rhoda Ubelhor.

"With just a touch I can usually see into a person's future." She withdrew her hand from Mahinas arm. "But yours is hidden to me. When I touched you I saw nothing."

Mahinas heart was beating fast in her chest, she worried Rhoda might hear it.

"Oh? What does that mean?" She kept her voice as steady as possible.

Rhoda smiled through dark lips. "It means that you're special, and that I would like to get to know you."

Mahina smiled back and laughed lightly. She was so very confused, was the Witch hitting on her or just being friendly? Mahina hadn't thought about anything like that in over five years, it was an entirely new experience to her. Not that it mattered. She wasn't here to make friends, or anything more, she had been enlisted to stop people like the Coxani Queen.

She was going to respond when out of the corner of her eye, Mahina saw Lilith walking away from Mariah and Moroccan, both looking quite frightened before slowly walking away in opposite directions.

"It was lovely meeting you," Mahina said. "But if you'll excuse me, I believe my siblings need me."

Rhoda nodded, the glittering head ornament woven through her thick black hair jingling lightly.

"Of course," she said. "I will be remaining in Hell for the duration of this war, at Lilith's request. If the desire to see me again happens to run through your mind, my room is in the east wing." The Witch winked before moving off to join a conversation between a Vampire and Drakaina.

Mahinas mouth curved up in a smile, so she had been hitting on her! She shook her head, her siblings needed her. Mahina turned and began walking toward Moroccan who was nervously trying to talk to a rather scary looking Unseelie Lord.

Astaroth wanted to escape, no, he *had* to escape. He had been stuck with the leader of the Maleficias, Aurelia Acantha, since she had latched onto him when he had freed Lilith from Aurelia's attention. Her companions had slowly disappeared after a short conversation with him, but Aurelia had kept him engaged in small talk.The

Witch had had a lot to drink. Her tongue had become very loose, as had her hands, and she had made it clear that she found Astaroth very attractive. The Cambion had attempted to engage passers-by in conversation hoping they would help him escape from the Witch, a few had smiled politely and quickly moved past the two of them, more had avoided any and all eye contact upon seeing Aurelia's inebriated state, and Mania had just laughed when she had seen the look of helplessness in her brothers' eyes.

"I have a lovely summer home in Venice," Aurelia slurred. She was still linked with Astaroth, his arm was the only thing preventing her from falling to the floor. "You are more than welcome to visit." The Witch attempted to wink but instead ended up doing one long, heavy and aggressive blink.

Astaroth made a noise in acknowledgement and looked around the room, desperate to catch someone's eye. "So, Aurelia, can we count on you and the Witches to join our army?" It was worth a try.

Aurelia opened her brown eyes from her attempted wink and looked up at Astaroth. "Explain the situation to me again, I've forgotten." She giggled.

The blue-eyed Cambion rolled his eyes, he had explained it to her several times now and each time he hadn't gotten a straight answer. "The Angels are making new laws." He spoke loudly and slowly hoping to get through to her. "These laws are oppressive- I mean these laws are bad. We want the Witches to fight against the Angels. Will you do that?"

Aurelia began nodding as he spoke, her head flopping backwards and forwards at an increasing speed. As he stopped, so did she.

"No." she said firmly.

"What?"

"No." she said again.

"What do you mean 'no'?" Astaroth tried to retrieve his arm from the Witch, but her grip was tight, it seemed that even drunk she knew that falling was a bad idea.

Aurelia began blinking rapidly. "I mean no. I will not put my Witches in danger, none of us will."

"But you will let the Angels control and demean them?"

"I don't know what that means?" Aurelia slurred slowly as she stumbled slightly in her heels.

"Kiss me." She said loudly.

"What about the Warlocks?" Astaroth asked, dodging Aurelia's lips. "Have you heard from the Medeis?"

He spoke of the council of Warlocks, three representatives of the three specifications of Warlocks. Like the Witches, the most powerful were the Colchian Warlocks, followed by the Hyperborean Warlocks, descendants of Abaris the Hyperborean. They were skilled in the arts of healing magic and potion making. The third and final Warlock type were the Solomon Warlocks, their skills lay within the crafts of exorcisms and protection. As descendants of King Solomon, they were in charge of protecting the most powerful magical artifacts, such as the Seals of Solomon holding the Horsemen of the Apocalypse at bay. The Medeis was made up of Absyrtus Nukpana the Colchian, Hecataeus Jabez the Hyperborean, and Menelik Gaukel the Solomon Warlock.

Aurelia hiccuped and chuckled. "Why would you want them? They're practically powerless."

Astaroth knew she was exaggerating, but he also knew that Warlocks were far less powerful than Witches. The magic of the Warlocks required the use of a staff. They couldn't hope to reach the same levels of power as their female counterparts.

"Besides, they won't join you once they've heard the decision of the Maleficias."

Astaroth groaned loudly. Of all the people Lilith could have left him with she chose a fifty-year-old drunk cougar witch who had no intention of helping them … why? He took a deep breath before attempting to explain why the Witches needed to join the cause when a loud bang sounded from the centre of the room, shaking the ground. Everyone wobbled where they stood, and all conversation halted. Astaroth's blue eyes ran around the room. He saw Lilith glaring at the space the noise came from as she began walking toward it cautiously. He pulled his arm free from Delia who slumped against the pillar behind her and slowly slid to the floor.

"Astaroth," Lilith called over. "Keep back." The Demon Queen sounded worried.

Astaroth did as he was told and remained further back, it seemed that Lilith knew what had caused the noise and the quake and it was of great concern to her. Angels perhaps? But it was impossible for them to enter Hell, Lilith had raised a force field blocking Angels from entering Hell thousands of years ago; whatever threat had interrupted the ball was not seraphic in origin.

Everyone watched as Lilith circled the space in the middle of the room, her arms outstretched feeling for magical energies that would direct her to the culprit, her eyes narrowed in worry and anger. She lowered her arms and turned to face Astaroth. As the Queen of Hell began to speak, another loud noise sounded, this time accompanied by an explosion of white hot fire; it struck Lilith's back and launched her onto the floor, landing at the feet of Astaroth who helped her to her feet. Such a blow would have scalded, if not killed, a Stagnant. Luckily, Lilith was powerful enough for it to barely tan her back. She patted down the ash-stained shoulders of her red dress and turned back to face the direction she had been thrown from.

The fire had not disappeared, instead it was a large collection of leaping white flames almost reaching the ceiling of the ballroom causing the walls and pillars to glow brighter. No one attempted to approach the fire, instead they stood a safe distance back and watched silently as the flames began to intertwine and spiral, spitting out the occasional violent ember onto the ground. The spinning fires got faster and faster before shooting out in all directions, almost hitting various guests around the ballroom before extinguishing and revealing a person in the centre of the room. A woman. She was dressed in a pair of black leather pants and a tight red top revealing her midriff and a pair of black high heels. Her hand was on her hip, covered in glistening golden jewellery, and her dark hair was tied up tightly on the top of her head in a high ponytail running down over her bare shoulder and ending near her waist. Her dark red lips were pursed tightly, and her bright red eyes were fixed on Lilith, flickering angrily.

It was Estrie.

Chapter 12

Astaroth was surprised to see Estrie, he assumed she would boycott the entire gathering, including the ball, just to spite the desires of Lilith. Then again, she had always been dramatic and enjoyed creating drama and her entrance was likely to do just that. There was something different about Estrie now, something he couldn't quite put his finger on; she had always been confident, but this was different. It was a dangerous kind of confidence. Her aura had changed as well, her power was radiating from her in an aggressive and bright way;

she was stronger than she had been only hours before when Astaroth had seen her last.

"How the hell did you get in here?" Lilith demanded as she glared at Estrie and moved to stand in front of Astaroth. "I placed Necrotics at every entrance." As the Demon spoke, Astaroth wondered what she meant, why had she not wanted Estrie at the ball when she had been so irritated when she had not attended the gathering at Highgate?

"I know," Estrie drawled. There was a crackling beneath her voice, the violent sizzle of flames. "They put up a struggle, but the dead don't like fire."

"Why are you here?" Mania had made her way next to Lilith, her brown-red eyes narrowed toward the raven haired Cambion.

"I am here to say my goodbyes to you all." Estrie responded, her voice calm but a clear rage resonated through her.

"Goodbye?" Astaroth said. He attempted to move past Lilith, but the Queen of Hell pushed out an arm to keep him back. "Where are you going? Why are you going?"

Estrie pursed her lips again and took a deep breath when Astaroth addressed her. "Did Lilith not tell you?"

"Tell me what?" Astaroth said. No one answered. "Tell me what?" he asked again, louder this time.

Estrie scoffed and gestured to Lilith. "Go on then, *mother*, tell him."

Lilith scowled at Estrie and turned to her favoured son. "Astaroth," she sighed. "I had hoped to save you from this, but Estrie is a Kasai, and a dangerous one at that. I believe she is the one destined to kill you."

Astaroth's eyes widened. Lilith had said that she could sense the Kasai prophesied to kill him was close, but he had never imagined that it would be someone so close to him, someone he had grown up with, whom he viewed as a sister. No, surely not; Estrie had always been rebellious, but her sense of loyalty was stronger.

"Mother, you must be joking. Estrie may be a little chaotic sometimes, a little unruly, but 'dangerous?' I don't think so."

"She is dangerous!" the Demon Queen hissed. She spun back around.

"There, I told him, now go." She commanded; her shark eyes narrowed at the Kasai.

"I will go, Lilith, I will; once you tell me why I'm dangerous, to my memory I have done nothing but overpower Sammael to prove such an accusation." Estrie said, the flames under her skin pulsing, dancing and pushing against her flesh in elegant patterns.

"Just know that you pose more of a threat to everyone, not just Astaroth, than you think." Lilith responded, her head high and her arm still outstretched before Astaroth.

"Tell me, Lilith." Estrie's tone lowered and the crackling beneath her voice grew louder. "You're clearly hiding something."

"Leave, now." Lilith stretched out her other arm and thin layers of black magic began pouring from her palms and running around her fingers.

"Tell me!" Estrie yelled as she launched a fireball from her hand. The flaming orb shot forward on a direct course, not to Lilith, but behind her to Astaroth.

Lilith cried out and twisted her wrists creating a thin veil of magic before herself and her son, the ball of fire collided with the force field and extinguished immediately.

"Fine, Estrie, you want to know why you're so dangerous. You killed someone!"

A chorus of gasps ran around the room.

"She did what?" Astaroth demanded.

Estrie stumbled back slightly, the flames in her eyes dimming slightly.

"What?"

"Loukas begged me not to tell you, but if it will get you to leave then I have no choice but to confess. When you and Loukas and Mordred went out, you had far too much to drink, and this awoke the Kasai within you; mentally you were weak, and the Kasai was able to take control as it is doing now. You left the club and you burnt down a building, everyone escaped but one girl. She was trapped and died."

Estrie shook her head as a steaming tear ran from her eye and down her cheek.

"You're lying. You are lying, Lilith, admit it!"

"I'm not lying, Estrie. You have a large portion of that night missing from your memory do you not? That is from when you lost control and you killed that girl."

"Mother, stop it." Astaroth whispered in Lilith's ear. He could see Estrie was beginning to panic, the fires in her eyes were brightening again and the flames beneath her skin were pulsating and writhing aggressively as she cried.

Lilith dismissed Astaroth with a wave. "That is why you have to go, you pose a great danger to everyone. Do you want to murder more people?"

"Mother," Astaroth began as Estrie began breathing heavily, and her skin began to glow slightly.

"You killed that girl, Estrie, you slaughtered an innocent. You are a murderer and now you have to leave!" Lilith grew louder and louder as she spoke.

"Stop!" Estrie yelled, her eyes and the fire in her veins were glowing the same gold as the jewellery scattered across her body. She had ceased crying and was now angry, the Kasai had once again taking total control. Estrie began strutting toward Lilith from the centre of the room.

"Dangerous, am I? A threat? A killer? A *murderer*? Let's see how dangerous I can be, shall we, Lilith."

Lilith raised her arms ready to fend off any magical attack from the Cambion. The Queen of Hell cried out as Estrie grabbed her wrist with a white-hot hand and dragged her with ease from Astaroth and onto the floor behind her.

"Estrie … " Astaroth didn't get to say anything other than her name before Estrie slipped a small golden blade out from her waist band and plunged it into Astaroth's chest. As he yelled out, Estrie muttered something in a language similar to the crackling of a fire and suddenly the blade erupted into flames of white and began to melt inside Astaroth who screamed in agony before collapsing and clattering to the floor with a thud.

"What have you done!" Lilith cried, still on the floor clutching her now blistering wrist.

Mania tried to move toward her brother but found her movements restricted, she cast her eyes over to Estrie who had an arm outstretched, evidently, she was in some kind of telekinetic hold created by the Kasai traitor. Mania's eyes ran around the room, it seemed that everyone in the room was in the same situation, unable to move; a prisoner to the will of Estrie.

"This is on you, Lilith, Astaroth was the price you had to pay to get me to leave. Yes, he will die, no Kukan can survive Kasai fire, but don't worry; you won't ever have to see me again. Good luck with your quest. As for the rest of you, beware, this is what becomes of Lilith's allies; think twice before joining her."

And with that, Estrie was swallowed by a spiralling pillar of fire. When it died down, she was gone and her hold on everyone in the ballroom was ended.

"Did no one think to do anything?" Lilith yelled as she got to her feet, still clutching her wrist; the blistering had not subsided and it was a fiery red. The Queen of Hell moved to kneel beside Astaroth. She looked down at him, unable to hide the fear and worry painted across her face.

"You two," Lilith pointed at Mariah and Moroccan. "Take Astaroth to the infirmary. One of the Necrotics outside will show you the way. As for the rest of you who do not reside here, begone, I will call on you when I need you."

No one spoke or made any movement as Lilith got back to her feet. "Now!" she bellowed, her angry voice echoing around the ballroom. Instantly, the Gibborim twins moved forward to carry Astaroth's unconscious body to the infirmary and various Alium disappeared in colourful clouds of magic and portals.

"You all stood there and watched it happen!" Lilith yelled. She had summoned her Cambions and other Alium allies to the great hall of her palace. They were all huddled in a group before the Queen who was seated on her throne; the red of their clothes like blood on snow in the otherwise white room.

"And you two, where the Hell were you?" She addressed Loukas and Mordred who both put their heads down.

"Is my brother okay?" Mania asked, looking at the floor.

"Are you being serious?" Lilith demanded. "Is he okay? No! Astaroth is fighting for his life!"

"Can we do anything to help him?" Mania asked, her voice shaking. "A spell? An energy transfer?"

The Queen of Hell shook her head. "Astaroth will either defeat the Kasai fire, or he will die. I fear it will more likely be the latter, no Kukan has ever survived a Kasai attack." Her tone was solemn, her face like marble.

A small cough came from among the group, it came from Morgana le fay. "Are you sure there is nothing you can do, Lilith? Nothing at all?"

Lilith narrowed her shark eyes at the Faerie Queen. She knew exactly what Morgana was going to say and, in her mind, it was not up for discussion.

"Morgana," she growled.

"I'm merely asking." Morgana replied. "I just thought that in all your years, you may have come across a being who has the power to harness and control any fire, including that of a Kasai."

"We are all still here, you know!" Mania snapped: her eyes wide. "So, stop playing whatever game this is. Lilith, I mean Mother, if you know of someone who can help Astaroth, please call on them." It was clear in her tone that this was less than a plea and more of a demand.

Lilith snarled, she could normally keep her emotions in check with ease. Most of the time she felt nothing at all, but the worry she felt for Astaroth mixed with the anger toward Morgana and now Mania spitting out commands, it was becoming increasingly difficult to remain calm and neutral. It was a good thing Sammael was keeping quiet, one word from him was likely to send her over the edge.

"There is one person," Morgana began, the edges of her mouth turned up in a smirk.

"Morgana, silence!" Lilith stood from her throne, in her anger she seemed to cast a faint layer of darkness across all she touched.

"There is one person, yes, but I refuse to beg for her help, not after all she has done."

"So you'd willingly let Astaroth die in order to save face?" Mania asked incredulously.

"You know nothing of what you're talking about, Mania, keep quiet." Lilith responded harshly. The Demon Queen wasn't fond of the rebellious streak her children were beginning to show, first Estrie, then Loukas, and now Mania.

"She may know nothing of it, Lilith, but I do." Morgana said, the air of amusement in her voice had disappeared. "You know *she* can help you, and you know that you *need* Astaroth to have any hope of winning. Even I could sense his power and potential; you need him to lead your army, all Alium will follow him, even those who will not listen to you."

Lilith shook her head, she hated it when Morgana made sense.

"Fine, I will go and degrade myself, but I cannot promise any results. I do not have the best of relationships with *her*."

Mania let go a sigh of relief. "Who is she?"

"Her name is Pasiphaë, you may have heard of her when Sammael taught you Alium history, if he did that right." Lilith had not forgotten that it was her soon to be ex-husband's fault Estrie had lost control and ruined her evening, nor had she let go of the resentment she had been holding toward him.

"Sammael, stay, the rest of you are free to go."

Upon her dismissal, Mania, Loukas, Mordred, Morgana and Amber hurried from the hall.

266

The two Demons remained silent for a moment, looking at each other; they had not had a one-to-one conversation since Lilith announced she wanted a divorce. Lilith's nostrils flared as she moved forward from her throne, she stopped when she was facing consort.

"You *stupid bastard*." She hissed as she swung her arm round, there was a loud cracking noise as Lilith's palm collided with Sammael's cheek. "What were you thinking, doing that ritual on Estrie the night of the gathering?"

"I thought it might free her of the Kasai, that she might be able to stay if she posed no threat." Sammael said as he clutched his cheek.

"Had that ritual had any chance of working, *I* would have done it! Besides, it requires the blessing of a sun deity, Sammael, and even then, the rate of success is minimal, you know this; how were you so blind as to what would happen?"

"I don't know, Lilith, okay?" Sammael sighed "I was angry at you, and she looked so much like her mother and-"

"'Her mother?'" Lilith said, her tone as cold ice. Of all the stupid things Sammael could have said, this was possibly the worst. "So, you still hold a torch for the dead Stagnant?"

"Don't twist my words, Lilith, you know that's not what I was saying."

"You know, Sammael, just when I think you can't make a situation any worse, or irritate me any further, you somehow find a way."

"Well don't fret about it, you'll be free of me soon." Sammael snarled. "Now why did you keep me behind, Lilith? Was it to slap and berate me, or is there something you need?"

"I need you to accompany me on my visit to Pasiphaë, after all these years of being imprisoned, she's likely to harbour many negative emotions toward me. Having you there will likely be a deterrent to her in case of a planned attack. And if she's foolish enough to attack anyway, it's better to have two sets of Demon magic than one."

"I won't be coming." Sammael said bluntly.

Lilith looked at Sammael out of the corner of her eye. He hadn't out right refused her like this before. "And why not?"

"I would be no help at all." The Lord of Hell rubbed his brow and sighed. "Since Estrie overpowered me and knocked me unconscious, my magic has stopped working."

"What?"

"My magic has stopped working; I can't even cast simple spells. I think Estrie may have either blocked it somehow or taken it for herself."

"That would explain how she managed to freeze everyone in the ballroom and how she burned me with such ease." Lilith clutched her wrist at the thought, she had been wondering how the Kasai had managed to do that.

"You don't seem to care."

"That's because I don't. Once I loved you, Sammael, then you ruined us, and I kept you around because you were useful. Without your magic, what are you?"

Lilith knew she was being cruel, but she was also telling the truth, without his magic Sammael could do nothing for her; he was a liability, if anything.

"You may remain in Pandemonium until our divorce, but after that you will no longer be welcome anywhere in Hell. Without your magic you are nothing more than an immortal Stagnant, the Earth will be more suited to your needs."

Sammael gasped, Lilith knew he never expected her to be so cruel. "Lilith, please, Hell is my home. I was sent here long before you; I helped you gain control."

"And *I* am in control which is why I can banish you from Hell. Now, leave me, I have to mentally and physically prepare before I see Pasiphaë again."

Sammael said nothing more, he knew better, instead he bowed his head slightly before turning and exiting the hall in silence.

The Queen of Hell sighed heavily, she felt as though the life she had fought to build was crumbling around her. Her marriage was a failure, her son was dying, and she was powerless to help him, and she now had to grovel at the feet of a woman she had despised for thousands of years. Never before had Lilith considered giving up on anything, but she had doubts about her plan. She had concerns that the rebellious nature of her children or the distrust between each Alium species was going to allow the Angels to exploit their weaknesses and turn them against each other. Was giving up on the entire thing the best thing to do? Would it be better to let Astaroth die and use that as an excuse to call off all plans? Maybe. It would save lives, save her from being judged and ruined by God and the Angels again.

No. If she gave up, then every single Alium would suffer. Whether she wanted to or not, Lilith knew that she *had* to keep fighting, she had to do whatever she could to save Astaroth so that together they could stop the Arcadian Laws from being passed. It wasn't about her; it was about the rights of Alium everywhere.

Lilith pushed her shoulders back and raised her head high. She clicked her fingers and immediately her deep red dress was replaced by an elegant black jumpsuit, heels and silver belt. If she was going to beg an enemy to help her, she was going to look good doing it. Once ready, the Queen of Demons flicked her wrists and was swept up by a swirling pillar of black cloud and, once it had dispersed, the hall was empty.

Chapter 13

Thousands of years ago, the Titan-Angel of the sun,
Helios, fell in love with the sea nymph, Perseis. Together they
had four powerful children, Perses, Aeetes, Circe and Pasiphaë.
All of these children were unique to other immortals, for they
did not have a set jurisdiction, they could bend anything in the
mortal world to their will; they called this power Pharmakeia,
or Witchcraft. When the Olympian Council discovered what
these children could do they wanted to imprison them in order
to stop any spread of this power, but by this point, Aeetes and
Perses had Kingdoms of their own which they could not leave
without rulers and Pasiphaë had married a mortal son of Zeus,

King Minos of Crete. Because of this, these three children of Helios were allowed to remain free, with keen supervision from the god-Angels, but Circe had no husband nor a Kingdom and so she was trapped on an island called Aeaea.

All of the children of Helios and Perseis went on to have their own adventures, but Pasiphaë's experience was the most gruesome and gruelling of the four. After her marriage to Minos, Pasiphaë learned that he was hubristic and vain; two Stagnant elements despised by all god-Angels. When the mortals began to dispute Minos' right to the throne of Crete, he and Pasiphaë prayed to Poseidon, the god-Angel of the ocean, to provide proof that Minos was the rightful King. Poseidon sent from the sea a magnificent white bull as proof of Minos' right to rule and requested that Minos then sacrifice the bull as thanks to all Olympian Angels. Minos promised he would do as Poseidon requested, but instead he sacrificed a lesser bull due to the magnificent nature of the one from the sea. Pasiphaë begged her husband not to try to trick the Olympians, but he dismissed her pleas and went through with his plan.

Poseidon was not fooled. At the sacrifice of the lesser bull, Poseidon emerged from the ocean and swore an oath on the river Styx that he would make sure Crete paid for her King's insolence and hubris. Unbeknownst to all, Poseidon had decided that the catalyst for this would be Pasiphaë, he had cursed her in a most inhumane way; he had placed inside her a deep lust for the white bull of the ocean.

Pasiphaë summoned the inventor Daedalus to her and commanded him to make for her a suit in the shape of a realistic heifer. As he was a prisoner, Daedalus had no choice, he created the suit for her and left it in the pen with the white bull. That night, Pasiphae snuck out of Knossos palace to the stables, she climbed into the heifer suit and she mated with the sacred bull; after which the curse of Poseidon was removed from her, leaving her feeling dirty and ashamed.

She returned to the palace in the hopes that nothing would come of the evening and that her secret would be kept forever. In this wish, Pasiphaë greatly underestimated the Olympians and their desire for retribution. A few weeks later, Pasiphaë began showing signs of pregnancy, she prayed and prayed to the Olympians to make sure her child was normal, but their cruelty knew no bounds. After a few months, Pasiphaë birthed a monstrous creature with the head and legs of a white bull and the torso of a human. It was half bull and half man. She named it Asterion, but it became better known by the name given to it by Minos. The Minotaur. A symbol of strength and fear throughout Crete and all of Greece.

As for Pasiphaë, word spread of her gross misconduct and she became a pariah, she lost the respect of her people, her slaves and even her other children would not look her in the eye. Minos kicked her from their bed and forbade her from leaving Knossos palace; he called her a disgrace and an abomination, despite all blame for this misfortune being on him. He shunned Pasiphaë but made use of the Minotaur by having him play a key role in his revenge against Athens for the death of his first son. But worst of all, Minos took other women to his bed and made no secret of it. This was the most painful of humiliations for Pasiphaë, she was a goddess, and she was being embarrassed by a mortal. It was this which drove her into action. She cursed Minos so that whenever he reached a climax in his sexual activities, he would release scorpions into his partners, and they would die.

Knowing that was the best revenge she was going to get, Pasiphaë waited. Over time a hero slayed the Minotaur, her children all left Crete to escape the torment and ridicule of their parents. During a trip to hunt down the escaped Daedalus, Minos died.

She had then planned to return to the halls of her father or perhaps to go and live with Circe on Aeaea, but she was approached by a woman who called herself Lilith, Queen of Hell. Lilith explained a prophecy which stated the two of them, with another powerful Queen, Morgana le Fay, had to join forces to defeat a being more powerful and evil than any of them. Pasiphaë sceptically agreed and began working with Lilith and Morgana to defeat the great evil threatening the world. Together they destroyed this darkness by each taking a portion of the others essences and channelling all three magics - Demon, Faerie and Witch - together.

Despite having shared their essence and working together, Pasiphaë had grown to love the power and sought a new kingdom for herself, Hell. She marched through the eight *cities of the realm, slaughtering any Demon who dared stood in her way; but in the end, the might of Lilith was too great. Pasiphaë was trapped in Hell for a long time as Lilith created a prison world modelled after her old home in Crete, Knossos Carcerem. Lilith sent her there with no way of escape, but over time this prison was discovered by many more who needed to trap or hide something they did not wish the outside world to know about. These prisoners were mostly children. Pasiphaë became a mother to these rejects just as she had mothered the Minotaur. Her favourite beings that were often brought to her prison realm were magical children whose parents were terrified of them or didn't want them. There weren't many but she kept them close and personally raised them.*

Lilith arrived in a pillar of spinning black clouds. This land was a prison world that lay somewhere between the eight Alium realms and the teleportation and portal laws did not apply here; anyone could teleport in and out of the realm unless imprisoned there. Knossos Carcerem was the name of the realm, it wasn't a horrible prison; she and Morgana had done the best they could to make it as comfortable as possible for her. The sky was always bright blue and the sun from which she drew her power, as a daughter of Helios and sun-goddess, was forever shining. Her home was an exact replica of Knossos palace, glorious stone pillars and columns of bright colours were scattered among beautiful murals and wall hangings decorated with the sacred Labrys and fantastically carved pediments. The palace stood atop a great hill surrounded below by a forest of oak, chestnut, pine, cypress, and evergreen plane trees allowing for animals and wanderers to be sheltered from the ever-beating sun. The forest opened out onto beaches of wondrous golden sands and the entire realm was surrounded by an endless turquoise sea.

Lilith emerged at the bottom of the hill before the palace, it was not possible for anyone but Pasiphaë to teleport directly into Knossos palace despite it being her prison, the Witch had found ways to control a few basic elements of the land. It was a grand structure of bright colour; definitely one to be admired and Lilith couldn't help but feel a little pride at the fact she had helped create it. Lilith shook her head, she didn't have time to admire her own architecture, her son was dying and the only person who could help him was at the top of the hill.

"Lilith," a voice said from beside her. Lilith turned her head and saw a woman standing next to her, not Pasiphaë, but still one she knew.

"Invidia."

Her response was cold, she had met Invidia a number of times and despised her, she was one of the children Pasiphaë had raised from birth, Lilith only knew this because she had been the one to bring her to Knossos Carcerem originally.

Invidia laughed. She was shorter than Lilith with silver hair and shining blue eyes, her face was angled with pointed cheekbones and a sharp jawline. She had evidently visited the Stagnant world recently, something Pasiphaë would not likely be happy about, as she was dressed in blue skinny jeans, black ankle boots, a white blouse and a black and silver leather jacket.

"Why are you here?" her voice was gravelly yet calming.

"I'm here to see Pasiphaë, not that it is any of your concern."

"It's my concern if you're here on business surrounding my family."

Lilith scoffed. "You don't have a family, that's why you are here."

"We may not be close, I bet my siblings don't even know I exist, but we are tied by blood. That makes us family."

"You are correct, none of them are aware you exist, and I intend to keep it that way."

"What about my father? Does he know of me?"

"No, you are the one secret I have been able to keep from Sammael." Lilith snarled. Invidia was the first product of Sammael's infidelity with the same mortal that had birthed Astaroth and Mania; Lilith regretted not killing the mother after the birth of Invidia. The Demon Queen had found the baby waiting in Pandemonium with a note explaining who it was and who had fathered it. The Queen of Hell had immediately sent the child to Knossos Carcerem and had never mentioned her to Sammael. She had hoped that it would never happen again, but only five years later, Astaroth, Mania, Loukas and Estrie were born.

Of course, as an act of revenge, Pasiphaë had told Invidia who she was and who her father was and since then, each time Lilith visited Knossos Carcerem, Invidia bombarded her with countless questions about the family she had never met. Lilith knew that despite her innocent curiosity, Invidia was hiding a violent rage and an aggressive jealousy toward her siblings for being raised by Sammael and chosen by Lilith when she had been cast away to a land of rejects.

"If you'll excuse me, I have to see Pasiphaë." Lilith said and began making her way up the hill. Invidia had delayed her enough, and she didn't have time to waste.

"You still haven't told me why you're here." Invidia called.

"Ugh," Lilith groaned loudly. "One of your brothers is dying, and Pasiphaë is the only person who can save his life." She continued walking.

"What?"

It was difficult to tell whether Invidia was in a state of shock or glee. She began to follow Lilith quickly up the hill.

Mahina and her siblings had been sent from the ballroom in quite an aggressive manner, they had barely been able to see or hear what had happened. They had been frozen by Estrie, who they had previously assumed to be on the Demon's side, and by the time they saw the injuries sustained by Astaroth, Lilith had banished all guests from the ballroom. Mahina was quite thankful that she didn't have to remain in the ballroom, or go with the Cambions to the infirmary, she didn't cope well with chaos and she had dealt with more than enough for one night.

"We should tell the Angels." Moroccan said to his sisters.

The Musas made their way down the glowing white corridor in which their rooms were stationed and turned as Mariah opened one of the arched black doors and they entered.

"Now?" Mahina asked. She had been hoping for a chance to lay down and relax, even for just five minutes.

"Yes, now." Moroccan said. As his sisters took a seat on one of the black sofas, Moroccan made his way around them and lifted a thick brown bag, the Satchel of Perseus, one of the gifts from Nakir. He reached into the bag and pulled out a small mirror with blue backing. The Yata No Kagami, a powerful object once used to lure the Japanese Angel-goddess of the sun, Amaterasu, back to the Heavens. Now it was used as a way of contacting Olympus from anyone of the eight Alium realms. Moroccan took a seat between his two sisters, looking from one to the other.

"Ishikoridome." Mahina's eyes flashed gold as she uttered the enchantment. The glass of the mirror rippled for a second before becoming smooth once again. Where the reflection of the Musas had been, an Angel could now be seen, not Nakir, a female and an Olympian recognisable by her crystal like wings. Unlike most Angels her eyes were not gold against her bronze skin, but instead her irises were lit with a multitude of vibrant colours. Her hair was tied in a number of colourful braids behind her head and a dress of glittering rose gold hung from her shoulders.

"We wish to speak with Nakir,' Mariah said.

"Nakir is occupied." The Olympian Angel said. "I am Iris, goddess of Rainbows and messenger to the Olympian Angels. Why have you contacted us?"

"Seriously," Mahina rolled her eyes. "We've reached Heaven's voicemail?."

Mariah shot her sister a hostile look. "We have news of the Cambions,"

"Proceed," Iris said. "I shall make sure the Seraphic Council hears what you have to say."

"Nakir was right," Moroccan began. "The Cambions are here in Hell. Lilith is massing an army, she has the Faeries, Wraiths, Vampires and Werewolves on her side so far, maybe more, and the leaders of these species are being housed here in Pandemonium so that you can't reach them. However, we do have good news; Astaroth, the most powerful of the Cambions, is injured, maybe mortally so."

Iris said nothing for a moment, she remained completely still as she took in the information being thrown her way. The Angel-goddess jumped slightly when Mahina tapped the screen aggressively to ask if she'd frozen.

"This isn't a phone, I cannot freeze." Iris hissed. "Do you know when Lilith is planning her attack?"

Mariah shook her head. "We do not, my siblings and I have only just been brought into Lilith's circle. She seemed intrigued by us."

Iris made a grunting noise in response. "Keep us updated." With that, Iris waved a bronze hand. The mirror rippled once again and the reflection of the three siblings returned.

Moroccan got up and placed the mirror back in the Satchel of Perseus.

"What was that?" Mariah demanded, her silver eyes narrowed at Mahina.

"What do you mean?" Mahina responded.

"'*Seriously, we've reached Heavens voicemail?.*'"

Mariah tapped on the glass table before them aggressively as she mocked Mahina's words and actions.

"Oh, relax," Mahina said. "Did you not think it ridiculous? We have been given what is literally the most important job in the world and we can't even get through to the man who enlisted us!"

"The *Angel* who enlisted us," Mariah corrected. "And you're right, it is the most important job in the world, so why don't you treat it as such and focus instead of being sarcastic with the soldiers of Heaven and flirting with Witches."

Mahina's eyes widened and her nostrils flared as she got to her feet.

"How dare you talk to me like that! For years I have done everything for

you and your brother, and now I have to help the entire world?"

"No!" Mariah shouted back as she stood. "You don't get to throw that at us this time, this is greater than any of us! You aren't our superior when it comes to this, you are our equal."

"Mariah, Mahina, please ... " Moroccan began.

"Shut up, Moroccan!" Mahina yelled. She flinched as her brother recoiled, that was the first time she had ever shouted at him, he had always been so quiet that she worried shouting at him could shatter his confidence. Mariah, however, had always been the opposite, she loved an argument and would try any method to get a rise from her sister. Mahina sank back down, placing a hand on her forehead, her silver hair running over her dark hand like a stream of stars in the night sky.

"I'm sorry. Please, both of you, just leave me alone for a while."

She sighed. She just needed a break. Whenever she had felt like this at home, Mahina had locked herself away in her room and read a book for a few hours.There was something about getting lost in a world other than her own that comforted her. At least, it had when a world of gods, monsters and magic had seemed completely unreal. Now it was her life and it was far from comforting.

Without another word, her two younger siblings made their way from the room, Moroccan, moving quickly without looking in Mahina's direction; and Mariah slowly, glaring at her sister, her glittering eyes dark with disdain. When she heard the door to her chamber close, Mahina got to her feet once again and retrieved the Satchel of Perseus from the floor behind the sofa. She opened it and pulled out a thick, leather bound book, the Grimoire of Caelum, the Angel had called it, a book of all seraphic magic written by the Angel-goddess of magic, Hecate. It wasn't quite a fantasy novel, but it was the next best thing to distract her, and Mahina thought there could be no harm in a bit of light study into her newfound powers. She undid the silver buckle on the book and opened it, immediately she was met with a glowing white light emerging from the pages. It hit her like a tidal wave and she screamed as her head was launched back, the powerful light still forcing itself onto her as her eyes closed and her arms went limp.

By the time Lilith reached the top of the hill and the foot of Pasiphaë's palace, a great structure of red, blue and yellow pillars, she was ready to murder Invidia. The eldest daughter of Sammael was far too curious, she had spent the entire walk up the hill asking the Demon what felt like hundreds of questions about her siblings and father and when Lilith had answered those, Invidia had presented a hundred more.

"So, what's Mania's star sign?" Invidia asked. Lilith had noticed that the girl seemed to have more questions about Astaroth and Mania, her full blood siblings, than Loukas and Estrie. It made sense, blood calls to blood.

"Mania and Astaroth are both Leo's. Estrie and Loukas are Geminis." Lilith responded with a great sigh.

Invidia made what seemed to be a disappointed humming noise. "July or August Leo's?"

"By the eight cities of Hell, do you ever shut up!" Lilith hissed. "My son is dying and your warden is the one and only woman who can help him. I don't have time to answer your idle questions about siblings who don't know anything about you and would likely hate you if they did."

The Queen of Hell made her way past two sets of Labrys' on facing red walls and through a crimson archway which served as an entrance.

Invidia flinched at Lilith's words and followed her into the palace, her bright blue eyes narrowed at the Demon Queen.

"He's not your child!"

Lilith turned to face the girl, her shark eyes wide with a burning rage. "What did you just say?"

"I said, Astaroth is not your child." Despite Liliths anger, Invidia stood strong and kept her voice clear.

The Queen of Hell clenched her fists. She had had far too many people telling her that the Cambions were not her children. They had her blood running through them, she loved them as though she gave birth to them, she'd do anything for any of them, except Estrie, of course, but she had been dealt with.

"Listen, you jealous psycho, just because no one wanted you does not mean… "

A small ball of fire shot from behind Lilith and exploded next to Lilith's feet, cutting off her sentence and scorching the floor. The raven-haired Demon whirled to see where it had come from.

"Hold your tongue, Lilith." A woman had emerged from another archway on the other side of the empty entryway, her arm stretched out and dripping in glistening jewellery. She was tall and tan, her eyes a bright gold and hair a glowing blonde. She was in a form-fitting black jumpsuit and a pair of lance-like high heeled boots.

"Pasiphaë." Lilith greeted the Witch as Invidia ran to the side of her warden.

"Why are you here? It's been thousands of years, why have you chosen now to finally visit me? Is it just to insult those in my care?"

Although she spoke in English, Pasiphaë had not lost her Minoan accent. There was clear hatred in her golden eyes as she looked upon Lilith. Maybe the saying wasn't true, maybe time didn't heal all wounds.

Lilith took a deep breath, she hated Pasiphaë and had sworn to herself that she would never set eyes on the Witch again after she had trapped her in Knossos Carcerem; and now, here she was, ready to beg the golden-eyed Minotaur mother to save her son.

"I am here to ask your help, Pasiphaë," Lilith said.

The Witch let loose a harsh, high pitched cackle before her face fell back to its stony visage.

"You must be joking. You trapped me here for over a thousand years and now you're requesting my aid?"

"I am prepared to… "

Lilith began but was silenced as Pasiphaë raised her hand which was decorated in numerous gold rings.

"If you're planning a proposal, then I suggest we do this properly. I shall grant you a formal audience. Follow me."

Lilith was led through the bright corridors of the Knossos Palace replica. They passed various ornate murals on the walls depicting Pasiphaë's story: Poseidon summoning of the white bull from the sea. Minos' faking the sacrifice of the bull and the god of love, Eros, shooting the Witch with his arrows. There was one which showed Pasiphaë threatening Daedalus, followed by another of her clambering into a cow suit. The most nightmarish and graphic one of all was of Pasiphaë mating with the bull, a look of abject horror on her face as Eros' magic wore off and she realised what she was doing. Walking past it, the corner of Lilith's mouth curled up, she remembered creating the murals, another punishment for the Witch, and now, another reason for Pasiphaë to deny the Demon any help.

The three women turned right through an archway of royal blue, a labrys hanging high above. They entered a large room filled with chattering people of all ages. Lilith assumed these were the wards of Pasiphaë, the abandoned Alium children sent to her realm for her to raise. There was a dais at the far side of the room which Pasiphaë and Invidia made their way up to via a set of deep blue steps. Invidia gestured for Lilith to wait at the bottom. The Witch took a seat on a U-shaped throne in the centre of the dais and Invidia stood behind her warden. As Pasiphaë sat, all fell silent and dozens of eyes turned to her. Lilith thought how easy it would be for her to push Pasiphaë out of the palace through one of the gaps between the azure pillars behind her.

"Lilith, Queen of Hell," Invidia began. "Queen Pasiphaë of Knossos Carcerem has granted you an audience; why have you come to her realm?"

Lilith stopped herself from scoffing. She had already answered this question and she found this whole farce ridiculous, but then again, the members of this realm were trapped, this was probably the most excitement they'd had in decades.

"The Seraphic Council has recently been discovered to be plotting a serious action. They plan to release a new set of laws that restricts and oppresses all Alium beings. They want to limit the magic of the Witches and Warlocks, the breeding of Werewolves and feeding of Vampires and so on. Since discovering this some years ago, I have amassed a great army of Alium members led by my three Cambions - Loukas, Mania and the strongest of them all, Astaroth.

Astaroth is special, not only does he have infernal blood, Stagnant blood and my blood running through his veins, he is also a Kukan, a descendant of the shadow Kitsunes. In short, he is practically invulnerable, except, of course, to the descendants of the fire Kitsunes, the Kasai. I personally believed the Kasai to be nearly extinct and thought that meant no harm could befall my boy. Alas, I was wrong on both counts and we discovered a Kasai among our ranks. She lost control and has managed to harm Astaroth. Even as we speak, her fires attack his very soul. And so, I am here to ask for your help.

"Pasiphaë, please, I beg you. Save my son. He's the only chance we have."

The Witch looked at Lilith for a moment in complete silence before she slowly clapped her hands together, the slapping of her flesh and clinking of her rings echoing across the hall.

"A very well rehearsed speech, Lilith. But, unfortunately I cannot help you."

A smug smile appeared on the Witch's face as Invidia's stony look faltered at her warden's words.

Lilith let loose a low snarl, baring her fangs. She composed herself as all eyes turned on her.

"Don't lie to me, Pasiphaë, you're an Angel-goddess of the sun and Queen of Witches; flames run through your very essence. I have seen you save people from Kasai before. So what you mean by you cannot, is that you will not."

Pasiphaë nodded. "Yes, I suppose you're right, I will not help you. Why would I? You trapped me here for hundreds of thousands of years and you surrounded me with memorabilia of the most horrifying time in my life; in what world would I help you?"

"In one where you care about your kind, the Witches are going to suffer heavily from these new laws, Pasiphaë, if Astaroth is not saved."

Pasiphaë waved a dismissive hand. "I care not for mortal Witches, they bore me. And as for these new laws, they can hardly strip me of my rights more than you have."

Lilith took a deep breath and closed her eyes for a second. She was going to have to swallow her pride for what she was about to do, but it was for Astaroth, her favoured son.

"If you help me, Pasiphaë, I shall set you free for six months."

Pasiphaë cackled again, louder than before. A chorus of laughs echoed from her wards.

"Your son's life is only worth six months of my freedom? I want complete freedom, for me and for my wards. You created this realm, no matter who trapped them here, you have the power to free them all." The Witch bartered, her glowing eyes lingering expectantly on Lilith.

"You must be joking," Lilith scoffed. If she let Pasiphaë and all of her apprentices free for the rest of time she knew the Witch would try and take Hell for herself once again and with the help of a small army, she might very well manage it. "Four months of every year." Lilith offered.

"Ten."

"Five"

"Eight."

"Six," Lilith said. "That is my final offer. For six months of every year beginning in January, you and your wards may return to the real world. But, if you try anything, taking over my world, resisting return to

Knossos Carcerem, anything; I will bring you straight back and let this land crumble with you in it."

Pasiphaë gritted her teeth and scowled. "Very well, six months it is."

She waved her hand and two beings, clearly siblings, made their way through the crowd. They were both tall with cream-coloured, pale skin and long white hair; their eyes were frosty and a cold wind seemed to follow them as they neared the front of the crowd. Their appearance was quite the opposite of Pasiphaë.

"Lilith, meet Talvi and Skadi, the unwanted children of the Norse Angel-god, Ullr. They're both Cryokinetic and I have trained them in the arts of battling fire magic, including that of Kasai. They shall accompany you to Hell to heal your son and remain with you for the duration of the war. Think of them as a gift."

Talvi and Skadi said nothing as they bowed to Pasiphaë and then to Lilith before the Queen of Demons flicked her wrist and the three of them were picked up by swirling clouds of thick black magic. By the time the smoke cleared, Lilith and the two cryokinetics were gone from Knossos Carcerem.

Chapter 14

Astaroth opened his eyes to three women standing over him. He sat up and instantly knew he was in the Underworld, the realm of the punished. He was not, however, in the capital, Irkalla, which had been a land of pure greys and whites. This city had hints of colour, dark green grass, red hues in the greyish sky. There were tall, bushy trees scattered in small groves, each growing a small, purplish fruit - pomegranates. He could hear no screams, but could see souls, glowing ghost-like beings floating around in the distance, their faces blank and vacant. It seemed to Astaroth that he had awakened in the city of Asphodel, home to the souls who had not been so cruel *in life that they deserved punishment within the cities of Timoria or Helheim; but also not heroic enough to be welcomed into the realm of Paradise, land of the liberated. There was a strange smell to the world, a sickly sweet scent that stung the back of Astaroth's throat.*

The Cambion looked down at his hands, instead of the grey they had been when in Irkalla, they had now turned a transparent black, it seemed his body had not travelled with him to Asphodel, only his soul which, unlike the others in this city, was lined with shadows and darkness.

"Welcome, Cambion," said one of the women. She, like the others beside her, was not a soul. She had a body of pale skin covered in black and bronze fabrics, and her deep red hair held a tall bronze crown.

From descriptions he had read, Astaroth knew exactly who she was.

"Lady Persephone."

He nodded politely as he greeted her. Persephone was an Angel-goddess of the Underworld and like this realm's king, Nergal, she had been kidnapped and trapped in the Underworld by a powerful being claiming to love her. In Persephone's case, the captor was Hades, an Angel-god of the Greek Pantheon who presided over the souls of Asphodel and Timoria. Unlike Nergal, however, Persephone was free to return to her mother in Olympus for six months of the year.

"May I introduce my daughters," Persephone gestured to her left to a shorter woman whose skin was separated down

the middle so that one half of her was pitch black and the other was a glowing white.

"This is Melinöe, goddess of ghosts and bringer of nightmares."

Astaroth nodded to Melinöe whose lip curled at the sight of him. Persephone now gestured to the second woman at her right who was almost identical to her mother, with the same pale skin and red hair. The only difference was that this daughter of Persephone had thick, black wings sprouting from her back.

"And this is Macaria, goddess of blessed death."

"Why am I here?" Astaroth asked. "Am I dead?"

"Not yet," Macaria's voice was surprisingly calming for such an intimidating goddess. "Your body is currently under attack and it seems that your friends have been able to freeze your body for the time being. This left your soul susceptible to me and any psychopomp who wished to lure you to them."

Astaroth made a puzzled face as he finally got to his feet.

"And why would you want to lure me here?" He almost jumped as a soul floated past, a glowing shadow of a person. He scowled as Macarias lip curled up in a smirk.

"Our mother has wanted to talk to you for some time." Melinöe said.

"About what?" Astaroth sighed. He was beginning to get impatient, he couldn't stand game playing and that's precisely what these goddesses were doing.

"Your plot," Persephone responded. "To put a stop to the passing of the Arcadian Laws."

"I know not of what you speak." Astaroth said. These were Angels, they had a loyalty to Heaven he reminded himself, if he confessed then it gave them reason to keep his soul trapped.

Persephone chuckled. "Don't lie to me, Cambion. I am, as are all Angels, aware that Lilith has returned, that you have helped her amass an army including but not limited to the Faeries, Vampires and Werewolves; and that you plan to lead an attack on Heaven." There was a smug gleam in Persephone's golden eyes.

"How do you… "

"As Angels, we are privy to the knowledge of the Seraphic Council, but, as goddesses of the Underworld we are not permitted to know how they get their information. All we know is that it came from within your ranks."

Astaroth's brow furrowed. "So we have a spy." He muttered to himself before turning his eyes back to the goddesses. "Why tell me this? Surely it's better for the Angels to have this knowledge to themselves?"

"It likely is," Persephone said. "But we do not support the Angels." She smiled as a look of confusion ran across the Cambion's face.

"It is the Angels who keep me here for half of the year, who separate me from my mother and push me into the arms of a dirty, disgusting oaf."

She spoke of Hades. It seemed that despite the Stagnant romanticism of their story, the goddess still despised her captor.

"We want to offer you our help." Macaria said. With a beat of her wings she shot up into a tree and picked a pomegranate from one of the branches before lowering herself once again.

"The Seraphic Council closed the portal to Heaven which lies in Olympus. Without that you have no entry to Heaven. Our mother returns to Olympus for six months in a few days, when you are ready to attack, bite into this and she will know to open the portal." She handed the pomegranate to Astaroth.

"We do," Melinöe began. "ask for something in return."

Astaroth rolled his eyes. Was anything ever free. "And what would that be?"

"We want Hades. He kidnapped me, he forced my mother to be his Queen and to mother his children, only to then cast them aside the minute their brother, Zagreus, was born. He deserves to suffer." Persephone said, her eyes lit with intensity as she imagined the possibilities.

"Very well," Astaroth said. He knew that none of his party would decline such an offer, what was one Angel for the sake of an entry to the realm of gods and Angels?

"Hades shall be yours once the war is won."

Persephone and her daughters smiled. "Thank you for your cooperation, Cambion, but do not think this makes us

allies. I am doing what I must to ensure my revenge."
Persephone said.

Before Astaroth could speak, Macaria flapped her large,
obsidian wings. A great gust of wind shot forward from them
and struck Astaroth; instantly his shadowy soul was shattered
into thousands of tiny shards and blown out of Asphodel.

Astaroth's sapphire eyes shot open, his body jolted
into a sitting position as he let loose a low, hoarse cry
and gripped his side. To his surprise, the wound was
frozen, covered with a blue-white frost. Despite the cut
being sealed, the pain was blinding, he dropped down
onto his back once again as his friends rushed to the side
of his bed in the infirmary.

"Give him some room," Lilith commanded, but no
one seemed to pay her any mind. Loukas and Mania
hovered over their brother, worry lighting their eyes,
and Morgana Le Fay stood just behind them, admiring
the magic holding the Cambions wound together.

"Are you okay. brother?" Mania asked, tucking a
lock of cherry red hair behind her ear.

"I've been better," Astaroth grinned before wincing. "Help me sit up." At his request, Loukas took one shoulder and Mania the other and they slowly moved their brother so that his back rested on the metal board at the top of the bed.

Looking around the infirmary, a large room of stone littered with a number of uncomfortable looking beds and various tables covered in potions and spell books of healing magic, Astaroth saw two beings he didn't recognise as a member of their ranks, nor who visited Hell for the ball. They were a few years older and his opposite in almost every way from their snow white hair, to their unnaturally pale skin. Even looking at them, Astaroth felt a chill run down his spine, but given their frosty demeanour and the magical ice on his laceration, it was to be presumed that they had closed the knife wound left by Estrie.

"Astaroth," Lilith said with a smile, the relief clear on her face. "This is Skadi," the Demon gestured to one of the pale beings, her hair was braided delicately so that all of her frosty eyes could be seen. "And this is her sibling, Talvi." Talvi was taller than her sister, but her hair was longer and messier, covering most of her face.

"My thanks to you both." Astaroth could feel that, although he was still in immense pain, the Kasai fire had left his body. Estrie had not succeeded in her attack. He still couldn't believe what she had done, they had been raised together, spent every waking moment around one another for eighteen years, and she had tried to kill him. In some ways, this knowledge, this betrayal hurt more than the knife.

Talvi nodded. "You will need to rest for a few days, our magic is strong, but it will take a few days for it to fully flush out the Kasai fire." Their voices echoed quietly in a frosty tone.

"We thought we'd lost you," Loukas said, there were red marks under his eyes and his cheeks were puffier than usual. Had he been crying?

"For a moment, we couldn't sense your soul in your body."

Astaroth nodded and gripped his friend's arm, receiving a glowing smile in return.

"That is because my soul was not in my body, it was actually in The Underworld."

Lilith's ink-like eyes widened in fear and anger. She had almost lost her favoured son, and why? Because of that idiot Sammael.

"You died?" Astaroth shook his head and a wave of relief ran around the room.

"Not quite. When you froze my body to slow Estrie's magic, it allowed the angel-goddess, Macaria, to draw my soul to Asphodel."

"What would Macaria want from you?" Lilith asked.

"It was actually her mother who wished to see me."

"Persephone?" Mania questioned, an ecstatic smile on her face which made Astaroth chuckle and clasp his side again. His sister had always loved the tale of Hades and Persephone, a girl ripped from a land of gods to be with the man she loved and rule a land of death and destruction. It was a shame he was going to have to ruin it for her.

"Yes, Persephone. She told me that the Angels know of all our plans, of our army and of Lilith's return. It seems we have a mole."

Lilith cast an accusatory glare in Morgana's direction.

"Don't look at me like that," the Faerie hissed. "My people have just as much to lose as yours!"

The Queen of Hell flashed her fangs, most people would have jumped at the sight but the Queen of Faerie didn't even flinch, she had been on the bad side of Lilith before.

"If you betray me again, Morgana," Lilith began, clearly old wounds had not healed between the two, a powerful distrust was rooted at the base of their alliance.

"Persephone also told me that the Seraphic Council has closed Heaven's portal," Astaroth interrupted the two in an attempt to continue his tale.

"Closed the portal?" Loukas asked. He cast a worried glance to his mother. "How are we to attack Heaven if their portal is closed?"

Lilith began to pace. "That does present an issue," She said. "But I'm sure we can find another way into Heaven."

"Do you still have your contacts in Heaven? " Morgana asked. Lilith nodded and then shook her head.

"I have, they tell me things but they would never go as far as to reopen the portal. If they were caught they'd be killed instantly."

"Well, how about… "

Their suggestions went on for some time with Astaroth attempting to interject at every silence only for him to be spoken over with some ridiculous suggestion on how to get into Heaven without the portal.

"Will everyone just shut up and listen to me!" Astaroth raised his voice and then lowered it, wincing as he reached the end of his sentence and the small group around him fell silent.

Loukas placed an apologetic hand on his friend's shoulder. "Maybe we should discuss this later," he suggested. "You're supposed to be resting."

Astaroth shook his head, breathing heavily. Shouting had tired him out, and the pain seemed to be coming back stronger.

"No, I have more to tell you."

Lilith nodded. "Go ahead, Astaroth."

"Persephone returns to Olympus in a few days," Astaroth said. "She has offered to open the portal for us when we need it."

"For a price, I presume." Morgana received a withering look from Astaroth, not that she cared. Who was he to silence a Queen?

"That goddess doesn't do a thing for free."

"Her only request was that, at the end of the war, we give her Hades."

Mania smiled. "Aw, how sweet. She wants to save her husband from the punishment of his brothers."

Astaroth winced. "Actually, she wants him to kill him." He looked over to his sister who had taken to looking rather intensely at the ground.

Lilith pursed her lips for a moment. "A fair request, I assume that's all she asked for?"

"It was." Astaroth confirmed. He held out the small pomegranate in his hand that no one had yet noticed, the edges bruised from his grip on the purple fruit.

"Persephone gave me this, she said that I should bite into it to signal her to open Heaven's portal."

Lilith walked forward and took the fruit from Astaroth, inspecting it for Angelic spying tactics. Of course Persephone had her reasons for supporting the cause, but she was still an Angel, her father the chief of Olympus, she was not above suspicion.

"I'll place this in my vault until we are ready to attack."

"Now, I insist we let him rest." Loukas said. Mania mumbled in agreement.

"You're right," Lilith agreed. "Come on, everybody, out."

At Lilith's command, she, Morgana Le Fay, Loukas, Mania and the two new cryokinetics of the group, Talvi and Skadi, exited the infirmary. The minute he heard the double doors slam shut behind them, Astaroth dropped onto his back, his bright eyes closing as he dozed off into the realm of Morpheus.

Lilith's vault lay far beneath the fortress of Pandemonium, it was a large pentagonal room lit by torches of bright red flames, with smooth white walls and a black floor like a lake in the dead of night. The walls were lined with shelves covered in boxes and valuable magical objects that Lilith wanted no one else to have access to, a curved blade soaked in the blood of Eve, lay front and centre. It was her most prized possession. The Queen of Hell and Sammael were supposed to be the only people who knew the location of her vault; the entrance lay beneath the large statue of Lilith in the entry to the fortress.

The Demon stormed over to one of the shelves and opened a small brown box. She threw Persephone's pomegranate in the box and slammed it shut. She had never been so angry, Astaroth had almost died because of Sammael's idiocy. She had, of course, already berated him about the danger he had placed him in, it was the final straw in her decision to obtain a divorce. But that was nothing compared to the rage she felt now toward the Lord of Hell. She was sure that if she saw him, she would kill him, something she could now actually do due to his lack of power. That was another thing worrying the Queen of Hell, Estrie had managed to strip a Lord of Hell of his magic, she knew Kasai had great power, but she had never expected it to manifest in such a way.

"Trouble in paradise?" A high voice asked from behind Lilith, like nails down a chalkboard.

"Lucifer," Lilith snarled as she turned to face the Prince of Darkness. He stood before her, his crimson suit looking ludicrously oversized on his thin body. His pale skin and white hair were almost the same colour.

"What are you doing here?" She demanded, her black eyes meeting his scarlet ones in matching hostile glares.

Lucifer dragged his hand along one of the shelves. "So this is your vault," he said. "I've searched for this for quite some time. You chose a clever hiding place."

The Queen of Hell flashed her fangs. She had hoped Lucifer would never find this place, even when they had been friends, when she had carried his Demon spawn, she had never wanted him in her vault. Lucifer was powerful enough without access to the most powerful objects in all of Hell. "What are you doing here, Lucifer?" Lilith repeated.

"I'm here to make a deal, of course." Lucifer responded, removing his hand from the shelf and turning his dark red eyes back to the Demon.

Lilith rolled her eyes. Of course that was why he was here. Lucifer was also wanting something, at least this time she was prepared.

"I will not be giving you the soul of my son."

Lucifer's gaunt face dropped, losing any of its jovial charm. "Surely you must know it's for the best?"

"The answer is no, Lucifer." His presence unsettled her, Lucifer hadn't been spotted in Hell since she had been crowned Queen and usurped him as the realm's sovereign.

Lucifer sighed. "Oh, Lilith, Lilith, Lilith. Astaroth is powerful, that is true, but you in your infinite knowledge *must* know that there isn't a chance of you winning this war without the power I can give him."

"We don't need your power."

"On the contrary, dear, you desperately need my power. Already your son has almost been killed and one of your daughters has left your stand. Not to mention that somehow the Angels know your plans from an insider. Your plot is falling apart at the seams."

There was unchecked joy in Lucifer's eyes as he spoke, Lilith knew that there was nothing the Devil loved more than spelling out a brutal truth to someone who was already down; aside from making a deal, of course.

Lilith looked down at the ground for a moment, she knew Lucifer was right and she hated it. Yes Estrie had turned out to be a Kasai, and Astaroth had nearly died, but she was doing the best she could given the circumstances. And as for the moles in her ranks, she was going to deal with them personally when she found them, no one betrayed the Queen of Hell and lived to speak of it.

Looking back up with a cool expression, Lilith dismissed Lucifer's words with a swift movement of her hand.

"A momentary issue, Estrie is gone and Astaroth is healed."

"And when he is injured again?"

"That is most unlikely, Lucifer," Lilith said. "As you well know, only a Kasai can kill a Kukan, Kitsune descendants are extremely rare." There had hardly been any spotted in the last thousand years.

"And yet you have found two under your very nose." The joy had left Lucifer's crimson eyes, he was growing bored and when the Prince of Darkness grew bored, he got angry.

"Old magic is shifting again, Lilith, you must feel it. Once again it grows stronger and stronger. If you think these are the last Kitsune you will come across, you are sorely mistaken." His mouth fixed in a thin line, his cheeks shaking slightly as his jaw clamped.

Lilith couldn't deny it, she had felt a shift in the air, heard whispers of old gods and sensed magic darker than her own growing and spreading through the eight realms like a sickness.

"I make my offer again, Lilith." Lucifer's eyes were wide, almost popping out of his gaunt, papery face. "Give me Astaroth's soul and I will give him the power he needs to put a stop to the Arcadian Laws."

Lilith locked eyes with the devil for a moment. It was a shame that he had become this creature before her, a white husk obsessed with power and control. When they had first met, in the early days of the world, Lucifer had been one of the most beautiful beings she had ever seen, 'the light bringer' he had been known as, and he had certainly lived up to it, a shimmering angel of gold and white. After his fall, he had inspired her and his brothers with his great ambition, his plans to make Hell the greatest of all the eight realms. Now he was less than a shell of the great Angel he had been, completely consumed with the idea of taking Hell back from Lilith. It was disappointing, to say the least.

"No, Lucifer, I will not give you Astaroth's soul. We do not need your old magic and I refuse to aid you in stealing my kingdom."

Rage illuminated Lucifer's face.

"You will regret this, Lilith." He hissed.

Between one breath and the next, Lucifer disappeared, leaving no sign that he had ever been in Lilith's vault. The Queen of Hell closed her eyes and sighed heavily, it was not going to be easy to protect Astaroth from Lucifer while leading an army and hunting down the traitor in her midst, but she was going to have to do it. She rubbed her temples slowly before beginning a set of incantations to fortify her vault, she had to make sure Lucifer had no way of getting back in, there were too many valuable and powerful objects in there that she couldn't afford to let him take.

Chapter 15

Amber Alarie's chamber lay in one of the towers of Lilith's fortress in the west wing. Everything within the two rooms was decorated with artwork and furniture from her favourite period of time, Le Grand Siècle. It was the Great Century - the period between 1601 and 1715 when France was ruled by King Louis XIV, the sun king, and later by King Louis XII.

The bedroom was surprisingly bare for someone like Amber, then again, Vampires rarely slept and so putting a lot of effort into the room would have been a waste of time. The white walls had been painted with a delicate gold leaf pattern and the bed, which lay almost in the centre of the room, was covered in deep red covers below an ornate headboard. Beside the bed on either side stood two cream and gold lacquered nightstands, and across from the bed was an inlaid escritoire of mahogany which matched a large wardrobe with a carved frame top at the far end of the room.

Through the archway was the lounge, a large square room lit by candles in golden holders on walls which were painted with the same gold leaf as the bedroom. The floor was covered by a large Aubusson rug of white and red. In the centre of the rug was a baroque cream and gold leaf marble coffee table between two sofas of ivory damask with gold buttons lined with brass, mahogany and gold leaf. The walls were decorated in elaborate pieces of artwork, paintings of many of Amber's homes throughout the years and above a brilliant white and gold fireplace was a portrait of Amber herself which she had commissioned by Françoirs Boucher in 1723.

The Vampire was now seated next to an extravagant mahogany bureau on an armchair of cream fabric and deep brown wood. She was dressed in a sheer black robe trimmed with a mass of dark feathers, her brown hair running down one shoulder in a number of spiralled ringlets next to her lusterless face. Her brown eyes shot up from the thin pages of a book in her hands as she heard footsteps heading up the steps of the tower, whoever it was could only be heading to see her as her room was the only one in the tower. A knock sounded.

Amber sniffed the air, there was no scent. Whoever was outside her door was clearly dead, the deceased carried no smell.

"Enter." she got to her feet, placing the book down on the bureau beside her.

The door creaked and another Vampire entered, one Amber had expected a call from sooner. Orpheo Lenoir, leader of the Argentum, the second most powerful Ambrogian Vampire clan.

"Bonjour, Madam Alarie," he looked exactly as he had when she had first seen him, tall and slender with almost ashy skin and long, straight hair of a perfect mix of yellow and brown.

Amber looked the blonde man up and down, she had wondered if he recognised her and given the fact he had used her surname despite never having been given it, he clearly did.

"Monsieur Lenoir," Amber forced a smile. "How can I help you?"

Orpheo's bright blue eyes narrowed. "You don't remember me, do you?"

Amber tilted her head, she couldn't tell if this was a trick question. "Who's to say?" She evaded the question as best she could. "I've met many people in my life. It's clear you remember me though."

The blonde Vampire scoffed as he pulled at the lapels of his expensive, black suit. "Seriously, you don't remember me? You killed me!"

"I've killed many, I can't be expected to remember every one." it almost burned Amber's throat getting such a sentence out, she had made a point of learning and remembering the name of every person she had killed, whether they turned or not. "Besides, clearly I helped you."

"Excuse me?"

"Had I not killed you, you would have died in that desperate little town in your thirties after spending your life working in a shop, or as a blacksmith. Instead, you're the second most powerful Vampire on Earth."

"I was a child!" Orpheo snapped.

"In those times you were practically middle aged." Amber retorted. She wasn't wrong, what age had he been when she'd turned him, almost twenty? Most people died before forty in those days, he'd have lived no life at all.

"Now tell me, why are you here?"

Orpheo's shoulders tensed. "I don't know."

"You don't know?"

"No," he shook his head. "In truth, I had come here to kill you, to take my revenge," a small wooden stake dropped from the sleeve of his suit. "But what good will revenge do if you don't even know who I am?"

Amber's eyebrows arched. Her lie had saved her. Without thinking she wrapped a pale hand around Orpheos throat and lifted him from the ground. "You couldn't kill me if you tried." She dropped him.

Orpheo landed on his knees, blue eyes looking up at Amber through his hair. "Death is too good for you." He snarled as Amber smirked. "I am going to destroy you."

Amber laughed. "You don't have the strength."

"Not alone," Orpheo said as he got back to his feet. "But I know many you have killed and turned, the Rettslig, many other members of the Aurum and Argentum. When they find out who you are and that you're alive, Madam Alarie, they will all come for you."

Amber's eyes widened. Most of the beings she turned didn't even know what she looked like, she was a myth, a legend of the night, if she was exposed it would ruin all of her plans to retake Vampire civilization as her own kingdom. She flashed her fangs and readied to attack as another knock sounded at the door. She glared at Orpheo as he chuckled, even she knew that she couldn't kill an ambassador of the Argentum with someone standing right outside the door.

"Enter." Amber called. The arched door swung open and Mania walked in, her hair bouncing. The

Cambion's blood-like eyes scanned the room, her brow creased.

"Am I interrupting something?"

"No, not at all." Orpheo responded before Amber had even opened her mouth. "I was actually just leaving." He turned to Amber.

"Think about what I said."

And with that, Orpheo Lenoir pulled the edge of his suit coat down and exited the chamber of Amber Alarie who shot daggers at his back as he walked away.

"I hope you don't mind me visiting unannounced." Mania said, snapping the Vampire's attention back to her.

"Why are you here?" Amber asked boredly, she didn't have the time to be dealing with the red head, she needed to speak to Lilith as quickly as possible and get Orpheo Lenoir taken care of. Not to mention the fact that she didn't like being alone with Mania, the girl made her uncomfortable. She had a strange scent about her, an illness, not one of the blood, but of the mind; something Amber had only ever smelt on Stagnants before. She was unstable.

"I have a question about Vampirism."

"And you can't ask one of the other Vampires currently in Hell?" There were a couple of dozen at least, a mix of Argentum and Aurum members.

Mania shook her head. "I don't want to ask outside of Lilith's circle, not with the traitor still around. Besides, you're the first Ambrogian Vampire, I expect you know more about Vampirism than anyone."

Amber rolled her eyes. "Take a seat." The girl was right, Amber had made it her mission to know anything and everything about her kind.

The two women took seats on opposing sofas separated by the ornate cream and gold coffee table in the centre of the room. Amber could tell Mania was nervous, she could see small beads of sweat running down her face and hear her heart beating faster than usual. Not to mention that she couldn't stop playing with her hair.

"Get on with it then." Amber demanded, she didn't want to spend more time with Mania than she had to.

"I'm not sure where to start,"

"Try the beginning."

"Well, when I was born,"

"Not that far back!" Amber could think of nothing worse than having to sit through the girl's tedious life story.

Mania took a deep breath. "I see and hear things." She spoke quickly. "Things that aren't there. I have voices telling me to do things that I don't want to do, and occasionally I see visions of things that aren't happening."

Amber knew this, Sammael had once explained that as a child the girl had been found talking to herself or crouched and crying, convinced that the bodies of her dead friends were surrounding her.

"Okay?"

"They went away for a while, and now they're getting worse. They got so bad only a few days ago that I couldn't use my magic. I need them to go away."

Amber felt sorry for the Cambion as a tear rolled down her cheek and she rushed to wipe it away with the leather sleeve of her jacket.

"I don't see how this relates to Vampirism."

Mania sniffed. "Would turning me into a Vampire stop them? The voices and the visions?"

Amber shook her head. "Unfortunately not, when you become a Vampire, your body and mind are frozen in the exact same moment. Your illness would remain with you for the rest of time, mixed with your new lust for blood. You would be deemed a threat by the Seraphic Council and by the Rättslig, an order would be put out to kill you on sight."

Mania nodded in understanding. "So I must live the rest of my life with this illness, as a liability to my friends and family."

"There are always Stagnant medicines you could explore."

Mania scoffed. "And have Lilith look at me as even more of a burden?" She snapped before softening her voice. "I'm sorry, this isn't your fault."

"Nor is it yours," Amber said. "There is no one to blame because there is nothing to be accused of. You are not a burden or a liability, Mania, your illness may hinder you at times and yes, it may be difficult to live with, but you are strong and you are powerful. Nothing and no one will ever be able to take that from you."

Mania smiled as she got to her feet and wiped another set of tears from off of her face. "Thank you, Amber." She made her way toward the door.

"Mania," Amber called and the Cambion turned to face her, a hand resting on the door handle. "Your mental illness does not define you. You are not 'mentally ill Mania,' you are 'Mania, daughter of Lilith, princess of Hell and saviour of the Alium who battled Angels and her own Demons to save her people.' Never forget that."

With a final, weak smile, and an appreciative nod, Mania slipped through the door, closing it gently behind her.

Amber sighed heavily, that had been a lot to deal with in such a short space of time, and yet, she still wasn't finished. She had to find a way to stop Orpheo from exposing her and she knew the only way to do that was to make sure he was taken care of. She couldn't do it herself, it would raise far too much suspicion, but Lilith would have a plan. Amber was sure of that. She listened carefully until she was sure that Mania had made it to the bottom of the tower and was making her way through the fortress and then made her move toward the door. She was going to speak to the Demon Queen, have Orpheo Lenoir killed and take back control of her people once and for all.

Mahina opened her eyes with a groan as she heard the banging at her door. She sat up and spotted the Grimoire of Caelum on the floor beside the sofa, it must have fallen off of her after knocking her unconscious. The book had shown Mahina many things beyond her understanding, the power it exuded had been enough to incapacitate the Gibborim for what she assumed had been hours. She wished the Angels would have warned them before giving them the book as a gift and yet she was thankful, the Grimoire had given her a new wealth of knowledge, knowledge she had to share with her siblings as soon as possible for it would change their perspective.

There was more banging on her door. "Mahina," she heard Mariah's voice, far more gentle than her own. "Are you in there?"

Mahina got to her feet and opened the door, Mariah and Moroccan stood outside, both looking sheepish. She gestured for them to come in and with a quick glance to her left and right, Mahina shut the door.

"You're still in yesterday's clothes." Mariah pointed out as she picked up the Grimoire of Caelum from the floor and placed it on the coffee table in the centre of the room.

Mahina pulled a puzzled face. "Yesterday?" Had that booked knocked her out for twenty four hours? She looked over at her siblings who were no longer in their ball outfits.

Moroccan nodded. "Mariah and I wanted to apologise,"

"You don't have to," Mahina shook her head, her hair flying about her head in brilliant spirals. "I was tired and anxious, I should have listened to you both and been a lot more polite to the Angels. Even if they are lying to us."

Mariah looked up quickly. "They're what?"

"They're lying to us." Mahina confirmed. She couldn't wait to explain what the book had shown her.

"About what?" Moroccan asked as he took a seat on one of the black sofas. Mariah sat next to him.

"Everything," Mahina didn't know where to start. "The Demons, our power, our parents… "

"You mean they weren't killed?" Mariah asked.

"No, they definitely were killed," Mahina confirmed, her voice a little more upbeat than she had intended. "But they told us we couldn't bring them back, but we can!"

Mahina launched into a long spiel about how when she opened the Grimoire of Caelum she had been hit by a wave of powerful magic which had filled her brain with violent visions. She had seen Witches and Warlocks raising their loved ones and the Angels punishing them for it through curses and even death.

Moroccan, who had sat up straight at the first mention of their parents being resurrected brushed the book with his hand.

"So, with this book, we can bring our parents back?"

"No," Mahina said. "In my vision I saw the Witches and Warlocks using a different book,"

"One full of dark magic, I presume." Mariah interrupted, her chromatic eyes resting on Mahina with some scepticism.

"A mix," Mahina corrected. "But the Grimoire of Caelum has shown me a number of spells and enchantments that the Angels want to keep from us that they would imprison or even kill us for using."

"Then it must be dark magic." Mariah said again. "The Angels haven't lied to us, Mahina, they told us that magic such as Necromancy is illegal."

"Why give us a book which gives examples of it then?" Moroccan interjected.

Mahina smiled, she knew that by even mentioning resurrecting their parents that Moroccan would join her side. Despite Lilith being responsible for the death of their mum and dad, the Demon and her companions offered far more opportunities to the Musas than the Angels did. The Seraphic Council offered them a seat in their meetings and one wish which included limits and that was only if they helped them oppress an entire civilisation. However, the Alium offered them almost unlimited power and the opportunity to help all oppressed creatures get their rights back. To Mahina it seemed like a no-brainer whose side they should be on, it was going to be easy to convince Moroccan to join her, but Mariah was going to be a problem. The eldest of the three was going to have to be careful as she approached this situation.

"Does this have something to do with that Witch?" Mariah asked, folding her arms.

Mahina's eyes widened. "Excuse me?" Her sister had always known how to get a rise out of her.

"The Coxani Queen, Rhoda," Mariah said. "The one you were flirting with at the ball. Is she the reason for your sudden scepticism?"

"I was not flirting,"

"You were a little." Moroccan interjected. He sank back into his seat as Mahina shot him a withering look.

"But no, Rhoda has nothing to do with this. The Angels have been lying to us, they want to strip people of their rights and I believe it is time we reconsider where our loyalties lie."

Mariah stood. "Lilith killed our parents,"

"And the Angels are stopping us from returning them." Mahina argued.

"Think of Lilith," Mariah implored. "She fought against Heaven, she sought knowledge above her station and she was cast from Eden."

"And now look at her," Mahina retorted. "She's the Queen of Hell, she has the ability to alter reality with the click of her fingers and to end civilisations with a mere whisper."

Her sister shook her head as she scoffed. "You can't be serious, Mahina, you want us to join the Demons?"

"To be fair," Moroccan spoke sheepishly as he stood between his sisters. "We know basically nothing about this world apart from what the Angels told us and in our limited time here, I have found their reports of Lilith's evil and the danger of the Alium to be greatly exaggerated." He avoided looking at Mariah who was glaring daggers at him and instead opted to look at Mahina who was smiling, he smiled back.

"Exactly, the anger of the Alium is justified, and the Angels have clearly been manipulating us." Mahina said.

"I can't believe the two of you, but when you are seeing sense, you know where to find me." She reached for the Grimoire of Caelum but her ebony hand recoiled as a white blast of magic shot just past her. Looking up she saw Mahina with her hand outstretched, palm glowing.

"If you are not with us, Mariah, you are against us." Mahina said.

Moroccan gave his sister an incredulous look. "It's not like that…"

Mahina raised her hand and Moroccan's mouth was forced shut, the Grimoire had shown her a lot of new magic.

"And that, Mariah, means," Mahina continued as she lowered her arms. "that I cannot allow you to be near the Angel gifts. I can't risk you snitching on us to the Seraphic Council."

She could see the rage in her sister's eyes, but that didn't matter. Mahina planned to help the Alium and the only way she could do such a thing would be to have the Angels believe they still had control of their secret weapons. Mariah wasn't going to ruin that for her.

Mariah rolled her eyes, her nostrils flaring, mouth fixed in an angry line. "Whatever," she hissed as she forced her way past her siblings and out of Mahina's chamber for the second time in two days.

With their sister gone, Mahina took a deep breath and released Moroccan's mouth from her magical hold. He began to berate her for her words and actions but remained quiet as Mahina raised her eyebrows and narrowed her silver eyes.

"I trust you understand the importance of discretion. Now, more than ever. We can never let the Alium discover our heritage, they'd kill us before we had a chance to explain."

Moroccan nodded. "What of Mariah?"

Mahina shook her head. "We don't have to worry about her. Even if she decides to back the Angels, she wouldn't betray us to Lilith, she still loves us."

She walked over to her brother and brushed his face with her hand before taking a seat and sliding the Grimoire of Caelum in front of them both.

"Now, sit, you need to study." She opened the book which once more began radiating a powerful light and Moroccan took his seat next to her, pulling the book toward him.

Chapter 16

It had been over two days since Estrie had attacked Astaroth and disappeared from Hell. Since Astaroth had been saved Loukas had not left his bed. The first night he had been so saddened by his sister's betrayal that he hadn't been able to stop crying. She was his sister, the woman he had spent every single day of his life with and whom he would have done anything to protect. She had left without so much as a farewell. After that, his sadness had turned to anger and a deep-rooted bitterness. For years he had confided in Estrie, told her his darkest secrets and she reassured him that whether he hated himself or not, she would always love him and *always* be there for him. Now she had abandoned him at the time of his greatest need. In order to kill Angels and battle against Heaven, he was going to have to fully accept his Demonic half, something he had fought against since birth.

When he awoke that morning, something had changed in Loukas. He was still angry and still sad, but rather than thinking she had left, he found he was now thinking of her as dead.

Estrie didn't exist to him anymore.

She truly was gone.

The pain started in his chest and lifted to his throat as he choked back a powerful sob. Memories crashed into his mind, he and Estrie playing in the prison as children blissfully unaware of their incarceration, seeing her happy when they had finally broken free and even the glee in her face before their ill-fated night in the Stagnant world. The memories swirled in Loukas' brain and his head started to ache. He closed his emerald eyes, trying to separate the memories and soothe his throbbing mind and dull the empty ache in his chest. Instead they lingered, spinning around in his head faster and faster. Loukas tried to process the thoughts and the feelings to no avail, it didn't make any sense. How could she be gone? How could she have taken a part of him with her? He felt nothing and yet was hit by wave after wave of emotions causing a numbness throughout his body. He had all of his memories of Estrie within him and yet they disappeared as quickly as he recalled them. Just as quickly as she had disappeared.

He pulled the black covers of his bed tighter around him and allowed a single tear to run down his cheek, hitting the soft, silk pillow beneath his head. The bed was supposed to be comfortable, and Loukas often found it to be so, but now it felt lumpy, he was constantly tossing and turning trying to find the perfect position. Everything felt wrong without Estrie, the world was unbalanced.

"Loukas."

A man made his way through the black curtained arch separating the lounge from the bedroom. The Cambion recognised the voice immediately. He rolled over slowly, every bone in his body aching as he sat up and looked at Mordred, who now stood at the foot of his bed, his white hair ruffled and his blue eyes looking on him with pity. He really was very different from Morgana, though the family resemblance could be seen in the sharp angles of his face and high cheekbones.

"Are you okay?" He sat at the edge of the bed.

"Never better." Loukas' voice was dripping with sarcasm. "What do you want, Mordred?"

The Faerie Prince flinched slightly at the harshness of Loukas' words.

"I've come to check on you," he responded with a smile. "Estrie attacking your brother and leaving so suddenly must have been hard?"

Loukas' eyes narrowed, his anger was manifesting toward Mordred now instead of his sister. He knew it was wrong and yet he couldn't help it.

"Maybe things would have ended differently had you not been distracting me."

Mordred blinked. "What?"

"Had you just left me alone at the ball, maybe I could've talked Estrie down."

"I was trying to be romantic." Mordred had taken Loukas from the ballroom and out onto the balcony where he had opened up about all of his feelings toward the Cambion. Having only known him for such a short amount of time and rather than presuming them to be together, he had officially asked Loukas to be his boyfriend. Loukas had accepted, not that he was acting in such a way now.

"Romantic," Loukas scoffed. "You took me to a balcony in Hell. I live here."

He knew he was being harsh, Mordred had done nothing wrong, but he needed someone to blame. He supposed he could have blamed Lilith, or even Astaroth, but they were family and he needed them. They had to love him - blood calls to blood. But an outsider like Mordred could never grow to love him, he was a

Demon, who could ever have feelings for such a creature.

"I get that you're hurting, but you don't have to take it out on me." Mordred stood. "I'm your boyfriend-"

"My boyfriend," Loukas spat. "We've literally known each other for less than a month. I never should have accepted."

As he spoke he felt the sting of tears flooding his eyes, he held them back, no one was going to see him cry.

"Is that genuinely how you feel?" Mordred asked. Loukas knew exactly what Mordred was saying, Faeries were known for caring deeply and they were not a species known for giving second chances, if Loukas rejected him now, that would be it between them.

Loukas nodded, he had already lost his sister, he wasn't going to let anyone walk out on him ever again. "Just go, Mordred." It was getting harder and harder to hold back his tears.

Mordred's face hardened, the angles of his face and glistening eyes seemed more intimidating than beautiful in his anger.

"Worry not, Cambion, once this war is won, you won't ever have to see me again." He began to walk away.

"If you despise me," Loukas began and Mordred turned back to face him. "Just know, you cannot hate me more than I hate myself."

Mordred glowered before turning back and storming out of Loukas' bedchamber. The raven haired Cambion waited until he heard the lounge door slam shut before allowing the tears to stream down his face and chest. He let loose a hoarse sob and clawed at the bed sheets as he collapsed back down, wrapping the silk duvet around him tightly. He had lost Estrie and pushed away Mordred. Maybe what they said was true, he thought.

"Who needs enemies when you've got yourself?"

"Silence!" bellowed Enyo, the Angel-goddess of Bloodlust and War from the Greek Pantheon. Her words echoed off the walls of a great hall composed of four crystal walls. She stood at the top of a small set of steps, on a dais of glistening gemstone, looking down with hawkish eyes.

There were dozens of Angels with various gods and goddesses in the Hall muttering and arguing among themselves, but all fell silent at Enyo's command. The group before her were known as "The Concilium Pugnatum" or the War Council. It was a separate section of the Seraphic Council made up purely of the Angel-gods and goddesses of War from each Pantheon charged with planning and organising the strategy of battles before leading the armies of Heaven. They were all powerful and highly skilled when it came to the art of war, but they were not easy to keep in line because each believed themselves to be the superior deity and didn't like to listen to the others. Enyo was their leader, the only one that all accepted to be their superior, she surpassed them all in ambition, in battle and had a far more strategic mind than any of them. She had been listening to the lot of them arguing for hours and no plans had yet been laid out.

"We do not have time for this bickering," Enyo continued. "The Musa siblings have gone silent, that can only mean one of two things, they have been caught or they have switched sides. All we know is that Lilith and her Cambions have amassed a great army which means that it will not be long now until they attack. How long before the Arcadian Laws are to be passed?"

"Not long now," Montu, an Angel-god from the Egyptian Pantheon responded. "Just over a month, I believe."

Belonna nodded. She wished they could be passed earlier, the Alium would be far easier to control with these new laws, there would be no need to increase the defences around Heaven as they had already had to do.

"Their attack will be soon now," Vahagn Vishapakagh, the Angel-god of war from the Armenian Pantheon stepped forward from within the crowd of Angels. He had received the title of 'the Dragon Reaper' in the early days of the world when he had trapped all Dragons in Acuran. The Angel still had a set of scars across his face left by a Vēṭṭai Dragon's talons.

"A Caṇṭai Dragon has been taken from Acuran, reportedly by Lilith."

"What does that matter?" Ogun Onire, the Yoruba god of War asked. "The portal to Heaven is closed. Dragon or no Dragon, the Alium have no way of getting here to attack."

Belonna shook her head, her golden helmet wobbling. "Don't underestimate Lilith, if she wants to get here she'll find a way."

The Angel-goddess recalled a time, thousands of years ago, when Lilith had stormed Heaven shortly after making the transition from human to Demon; she had murdered dozens of Angels and had only been stopped by God Himself.

"So what do we do?" The Finnish Angel Tursas said.

"We prepare for war."

***

After a few days of being bedridden in the infirmary, Astaroth had finally been cleared of all Kasai fires and discharged by the Cryokinetic healers, Talvi and Skadi. Although his body was still in pain and the stab wound had only just closed fully, Astaroth was feeling almost back at full strength. He had wandered around the fortress looking for his family and friends, Mania seemed to have disappeared, as had Sammael. Astaroth had no desire to get to know any of the Alium members who had taken up residence within their ranks. He had spotted Lilith and had approached her but had been shooed away by Amber Alarie who was begging to interrupt the Demon's discussion with Morgana Le Fay. Astaroth had then decided to visit his brother, he hadn't seen him in a number of days. He knew it was a bad sign. Even as children, Loukas refused to leave his side if Astaroth had so much as a cough.

Loukas looked peaceful as he slept, Astaroth noticed, he always had. It was the only time he got to escape his self loathing, in dreams he could escape and be anything he wanted. Now, as he slept, Astaroth could see a faint smile on Loukas' face as his body twitched slightly and rolled on to his side, the silk sheets dancing gracefully around his body. The Cambion took a seat at the edge of his brother's bed. Amber had sent him to collect Loukas for a meeting, but he didn't want to wake his brother, not when he seemed to be at peace. As much as Astaroth had been hurt by Estrie's betrayal, he couldn't even imagine how hurt Loukas was feeling, Estrie had been his rock since birth. Loukas made a noise as he rolled onto his back. His eyes opened slowly as he yawned. "Astaroth?" He rubbed his eyes and squinted as they adjusted to the light.

Even in Loukas' first waking moments, Astaroth noted that all traces of peace had left his brother's face and had been replaced by pure anguish. New lines of grief and torment seemed to have been carved into Loukas' face, they made him look older and even more like Sammael. Even his eyes seemed to have darkened from emerald green to bottle green in the time since Estrie had left.

"Hey," Astaroth said with a small smile. He was doing all he could to hide the pity he felt for his brother, he knew how Loukas hated being pitied by anyone, but especially family and friends.

"I saw Mordred as I came up,"

Loukas sat up, his face moving uncomfortably at the mention of Mordred.

"Okay?"

Despite his blase response, Astaroth could tell Loukas was hiding his true emotions.

"He didn't look too good," Astaroth continued. "He was about half a bottle of Faerie brandy down when I left him."

"Okay?" Loukas said again. He wasn't giving up anything freely.

Astaroth wasn't used to having to drag information out of Loukas, they had always been close and his brother had always been honest and forthcoming. He clenched his fist into the bed sheets, he knew he had to be calm, Loukas was in pain, but Astaroth wasn't known for his patience.

"What happened there?"

Loukas shrugged. "We broke up."

"Oh," Astaroth was not only shocked by Loukas' new blunt approach, but also by the fact that he had been through a break up before Astaroth had even known about the relationship. Maybe they weren't as close as they had been, this war had put a lot of distance between the four Cambions, they all wanted different things. Astaroth knew that much and yet he couldn't help but feel a little guilty. Had he been neglecting his friendships?

"Well, I'm here for you." Astaroth smiled again.

Loukas didn't return the kind look, his face remained icy, his green eyes distant and almost hazy. Instead he got out of bed and strode through the black curtains to the balcony.

Astaroth followed and joined Loukas in looking out at the vista of Hell, miles and miles of emptiness before them. Of course, there were a few small white buildings leading to the fortress and the Demons running across the land and flying through the sky.

"Have you ever looked in the mirror," Loukas began without looking at his brother. "and were unable to see or find a single thing you like about yourself?"

Astaroth's thick eyebrows raised in surprise. He hadn't expected such a philosophical question from his brother. The Cambion thought about the question for a second.

"I can't say I have." Astaroth had always found his reflection to be quite appealing, and as for what was inside, he was powerful, strong and ambitious; what was to dislike?

"Then you can't be there for me." Loukas responded. "I have to wake up every single day hating myself. I have to go about my life knowing that half of me is a monster, and just because I don't act on the Demonic thoughts I have doesn't mean I don't have them. Estrie was the only person who understood that, and she left me. I am utterly alone."

Astaroth wanted to argue, to tell Loukas that his blood didn't matter, that he wasn't a monster and that he was not alone; but he knew that his words would have no effect on his brother.

"We share the same blood. Does that make me a monster?"

Loukas looked at Astaroth incredulously.

"No, of course not. You are the leader of a rebellion, you use your Demonic side out of necessity."

"As do you," Astaroth was quite surprised by Loukas' words. Did he really think that he was the only Cambion who had to stop themselves from acting on the darkest impulses of their Demon blood.

"I am not the leader of this rebellion, we are Lilith's generals. There have been times where I have had to stop myself from going out in the open just to rip out an Angel's throat, just for the fun of it. You are not alone in this."

The brothers locked eyes, they were so similar and yet so different. Loukas was both terrified of himself and desperate to prove himself, whereas Astaroth always seemed confident in whatever he did.

"And yet I feel as though I am," Loukas said solemnly. "Estrie was the one person who understood me, and she is gone. Until you hate yourself, Astaroth, you will never understand how I feel every single day."

He began to move toward the curtains to return to his chamber when Astaroth caught him by the wrist. Loukas looked up at Astaroth who pulled him forward and wrapped his arms around his brother in a tight hug. For a moment Loukas seemed unsure of what to do, he was about to pull away when Astaroth squeezed tighter. Loukas returned the embrace and buried his face in his brother's shoulder, allowing tears to flood down his face.

"For as long as I am alive," Astaroth said. He fluttered his sapphire eyes, blinking away the small sting of his own tears. "I will protect you, brother. For as long as I am alive, you will never be alone."

"Where are they?" Lilith hissed. She spoke of Astaroth and Loukas.The Demon Queen had called a meeting of her allies in the courtyard of her fortress rather than the council room for she had something to show them, a gift, and the recipient was yet to arrive.

The group consisted of Lilith, Morgana, Mania, Amber, The Lenoirs, the Musas, Lycaon and Ereshkigal.

All stood in the courtyard, a large circular area of white stone enclosed within a ring of the small, temple-like buildings which were littered around Hell. The air was clear today, rather than filled with the usual red mists. which made it the perfect day for a presentation.

There was a loud creak followed by a louder bang as the door of Lilith's fortress opened and closed and Loukas and Astaroth emerged.

"Our apologies, Mother," Astaroth said, his boots crunching against the red sands.

"It took me a moment to collect myself." Loukas finished. He pulled at the cuffs of his black velvet suit, one that matched Astaroth's suit.

Lilith shook her head, she could sense the sadness coming off of the two of them, especially Loukas, berating either of them in this instance would do no one any good.

"No matter, you're here now,"

"Does that mean we can get on with this?" Morgana asked. As a Faerie, a creature of nature, Hell's atmosphere did not quite agree with her, especially outside of the fortress walls.

Lilith cast the Faerie Queen a dark look before her face warmed again as Loukas and Astaroth stood at either side of Mania, she loved seeing her children together, there was no greater feeling for a mother.

"I have gathered you all here today to witness one of Hell's most sacred rituals. The presentation of Stygian Titles. It is time that my children, Astaroth, Loukas and Mania be crowned."

"That explains why you're all dressed up." Amber sounded bored already. She had been trying to get Lilith's attention, but the Queen of Hell had been busy trying to organise this 'surprise' for the Cambions.

Lilith looked down, she wasn't quite sure what the Vampire meant. She was in a sleeveless, velvet red dress with matching gloves running just past her elbows. She sighed, it wasn't easy being the sovereign of a realm, planning a rebellion against the most powerful army in the universe and remaining calm and sane. Thankfully for the Demon she had no need to respond. At that moment multiple pillars of black cloud spiralled in the centre of the courtyard, grabbing everyone's attention. The clouds dissipated revealing six men. Six of the Seven Princes of Hell.

"Gentlemen, perfect timing," Lilith approached the Princes who were all dressed in matching suits of crimson velvet. She embraced them all gently and air-kissed them all on each cheek. She turned back to the rest of the group.

"May I introduce the Principes Infernum - The Princes of Hell. Mammon, Asmodeus, Leviathan, Sathanas, Belphegor and Beelzebub," Only Lucifer was missing as was to be expected. Lilith had banned Lucifer from all formal events in Hell after he had tried to ruin her wedding to Sammael.

"Good day," said one of the Princes with a nod. His name was Asmodeus, the Demon of Lust, he was far taller than any Stagnant man with dark hair brushed into neat waves and entrancing purple eyes.

"Shall we proceed?" Another Prince with greasy looking silver hair and yellow, frog-like eyes asked.

"Why in such a hurry, Mammon?" Lilith addressed the Demon of Greed with slight disdain in her voice. Mammon did not respond but instead glared at Lilith and flashed a small set of fangs.

"Very well," Lilith sighed. The Princes of Hell had never been much fun. "Astaroth, Mania, Loukas go and stand in the centre of the courtyard."

At Liliths command, the three Cambions moved to the centre of the circle, standing in an uncomfortable line with all eyes on them. They were the perfect family portrait, the two dark haired brothers stood at either side of their sister whose hair was red and almost as dark as her dress, a rose between two thorns; a flame dancing in the shadows. Immediately the Princes of Hell moved into position, surrounding the Cambions in a circle before they began moving their hands in a complex routine and chanting in a language that no one recognised. As the Princes chanted, black magical energies began pouring from their palms and weaving its way through around their fingers. Their chorus grew louder and faster as the energies running around and through their fingers grew brighter. As the Princes of Hell reached the climax of their incantation, magic shot from their palms and struck the Cambions in the chest, the three bodies shook as the magic surged through them and exited through their feet into the red sands beneath them.

Lilith felt a change in the energy around her, three jolts in the fabric of Hell. She knew what was happening, the same had happened to her when she had been crowned Queen of Hell. She hadn't felt the change in atmosphere then because the realm had belonged to Lucifer until she had taken a seat on the Hidden Throne and the Stygian Crown had been placed on her head.

The Princes of Hell slowed their chanting and fell silent as the magic surging from their hands began to fade into nothing. Lilith began clapping, as did the rest of the group, while the Demon's shark-like eyes shot daggers at them.

"What just happened?" Mania muttered quietly to her brothers.

"No idea," Astaroth responded in the same hushed voice.

Lilith chuckled, did her children forget she had advanced hearing?

"The Princes have just connected the three of you to the realm. Where your magic was derived from your Alium blood, it is now tethered and taken from the realm. It will make your magic stronger, more powerful."

"It also means," Prince Asmodeus spoke again, "that you are able to receive official Titles now." He flicked his wrist and three small Demons with bumpy lilac skin and glowing purple eyes appeared carrying cushions of dark red fabric. They were the Asmodei, the children of Lillith and Asmodeus, whose purpose was to protect, collect and carry important objects for the nobility of Hell.

Lilith bent and picked up an object from the crimson cushion, a diadem of black metal and diamonds glistening like moonlight on water. She hovered it over Mania's cherry red hair for a moment.

"I crown you, before the Princes of Hell and in the name of the Chthonic deities, Mania, daughter to Sammael, a Duchess of Hell." She placed the tiara on Mania's head. The young woman beamed as the surrounding group began their applause.

The Queen of Hell turned and picked up a band of silver metal neatly decorated with a number of green and black gemstones and held it over Loukas' dark head.

"I crown you, before the Princes of Hell and in the name of the Chthonic deities, Loukas, son to Sammael, a Duke of Hell and Lord of the Red Sands."

She placed the crown on her son's head and once again the group applauded. Lilith hated having to refer to her children as the son or daughter of Sammael, they were hers, but the laws of Hell stated the name of a blood relative must be used in a coronation.

Finally, Lilith picked up another band of silver from the third and final cushion, this one adorned with gemstones of a black and deep blue. She suspended it above Astaroth's head, and smiled at him as his eyes met hers.

"I crown you, before the Princes of Hell and in the name of the Chthonic deities, Astaroth, son to Sammael, the Grand Duke of Hell and General of the Stygian Army."

She placed the crown on his head and a final burst of applause ran around the courtyard. Lilith had wanted to make Astaroth a Prince of Hell, but the other six had protested and so she settled for the position just below Prince and had managed to get them to sign over control of Hell's army.

"Well, that was thrilling" Morgana drawled. "Can we go back inside now? This air is making me itch."

Lilith rolled her eyes, at least the Musas looked intrigued. A little too intrigued perhaps. Lilith put the thought from her mind, she was still concerned with the traitor hidden among their ranks, but it surely wouldn't be three changelings.

"Not quite yet, Morgana, I have a couple more gifts to hand out."

Morgana sighed heavily, dropping her head in frustration so her face was covered by her hair like a curtain of fire.

"Mania, for you I have this," in Lilith's hand a dagger appeared. It was small and curved with a silver handle and a black blade.

"This is Carnwennan, a dagger which once belonged to an old friend of Morgana." Lilith, of course, meant King Arthur, Morgana's half-brother whom she had spent a lifetime trying to destroy. She received a withering look from the Faerie.

"It has the ability to shroud its user in darkness and was used to slice Orddu, The Very Black Witch, in half."

Lilith remembered when that had happened, it was a shame really for Orddu had been a skilled practitioner. It would have served Lilith better had it been Orddu's mother, known as 'The Very White Witch' Orwen that had been cut in half.

"Thank you, mother, I shall use it well." Mania said as she was handed Carnwennan. Lilith found there was something odd about Mania's smile, it was empty though her eyes were fixed almost hungrily on the blade.

Lilith moved on quickly. "Loukas, you may have heard that I referred to you as the Lord of the Red Sands in your coronation. Well, the red sands are a patch of land here in Hell which the Princes and I fought over for years until it became a no-man's land. Now, we have decided to gift it to you to do with as you wish."

Loukas smiled, though Lilith could see the clear disappointment in his eyes. She knew he didn't want to stay in Hell and she knew it was unlikely he would if they did win the war. He would want to go out into the Stagnant world and live his life, even if she was against such a thing. Lilith knew she was going to have to accept it, it was Loukas' life and not hers. She didn't want her son to be disappointed with his gift and so with a flick of her wrist she presented a small curved horn of black delicately decorated with small gems to resemble the constellations of the night sky to him.

"And this is Svefnthorn. If you are ever in battle and feel overwhelmed, blow this and whoever your adversaries are will instantly drift off into a deep sleep for a hundred years or so."

Lilith was happy to see that Loukas' face seemed to pick up a little at this gift. She knew he wouldn't want something he could use to kill like Mania's dagger, the idea of killing was abhorrent to him and so she had given him the next best thing; the ability to incapacitate an enemy without the need for murder.

Loukas thanked his mother and Lilith moved on to Astaroth's gift, the one she was most excited to present.

"Astaroth, as the new Grand Duke of Hell and General of the army, your present is a little different." The Queen of Hell let loose a powerful, blood curdling scream which seemed to echo for miles, bouncing off the red rock cliffs in the distance. The screech died down and everyone waited for a moment in complete silence.

Amber began to laugh as she clapped slowly. "Wow, now that… "

The Vampire's sarcastic remark was cut off as something in the distance repeated Lilith's horrendous roar and small rocks began to crumble down the cliff edge.

At first the top of the cliff seemed bare, and then two sets of talons appeared over the edge like scythes digging into the red rock. The talons were attached to two enormous feet covered in thick, black scales. A huge, black-blue head with bright yellow eyes appeared high above the creature's feet, it opened its mouth to reveal rows upon rows of dagger-like teeth and released another terrifying roar.

"Is that … " Astaroth's question was answered as a pair of scaly wings came into view. It was a Dragon. Its heavy wings were the same black-blue as the creatures hide and had spikes similar to its talons protruding from the end. The wings spread far and wide before beating and pushing the creature off the cliff and into the air. It began gliding toward the group, traveling easily through the air despite its size.

Morgana stepped forward, her eyes wide, fixed on the giant creature and her mouth hanging open.

"How did you get one? They reside only in… "

"Ṭirākaṉ," Lilith finished for her. Ṭirākaṉ was the capital city of Acuran, the realm of monsters. It was illegal for anyone, Angel or otherwise, to venture to Acuran and was even more so to bring something out of it, especially a Dragon, one of the most dangerous beasts in existence. They were made up of almost pure magic.

"It's not as though we've been following any of the previous rules." Lilith was pleased as she looked around the courtyard, this was exactly what she had been expecting, looks of wonder and fear. Mariah, in fact, looked terrified, but her siblings couldn't stop smiling.

The beast came down with a thud, the ground shook and the group was hit by a brazen gust of wind as the Dragon tucked away its wings behind two of its thick legs.

"Is that a Caṇṭai Dragon?" Astaroth asked as he made slow movements around the creature taking in all of its majestic beauty. Caṇṭai was one of the four types of Dragons bred by Warlocks in the early days, these were specifically for battle. The others were Vēṭṭai Dragons, bred for hunting purposes. The third type were the Kāvalar which were used a guardians for treasures and occasionally prisoners which was where the Stagnants had discovered their version of Dragons. And the fourth and final type of Dragon was the Kāṭṭu, these were the most dangerous of them all, untamable Dragons of pure energy left to roam Acuran by all who wished to remain in the land of the living.

Lilith nodded. "You can tell by these markings,"

Lilith brushed a hand over a set of swirls on the Dragon's scales that were a slightly lighter blue than the rest of its hide. The Demon Queen screeched again, this time the Dragon made no attempt to respond.

"Knife looks pretty crap now, doesn't it?" Amber muttered to Mania who looked down at the blade in her hand with new dissatisfaction.

Lilith glared at the Vampire before turning her eyes back to the Dragon.

"Astaroth, once you name her she will become yours, for as long as you show her respect she will allow you to ride her into battle." She stepped back from the Dragon and summoned her son forward.

Astaroth ran a hand over the scales of the Dragon before him, his sapphire eyes wide in awe. Lilith knew that although Sammael had taught the Cambions about Dragons, seeing one was an entirely different matter.

"Kirke," Astaroth said after admiring the dragon for a moment. "For her eyes are the same as a hawk."

The Dragon, Kirke, roared loudly before spreading her wings again, casting a blanket of shadows across the courtyard. A powerful gust of wind blew through the group as Kirke flapped her wings and took to the skies at a remarkably fast pace, she flew back over the cliff from which she had arrived and let loose another ground-shaking screech as she soared into the distance She would return when her owner needed her.

"Mother," Astaroth was grinning from ear to ear. "Thank you so much."

"Yes, thank you." Loukas echoed Despite his appreciation, Lilith couldn't help but feel slightly guilty, a piece of unused land in a realm he didn't want to be in and a magical horn seemed quite disappointing compared to a Dragon.

"Loukas, you spoke to the Sirens at the ball, didn't you?" Lilith asked.

The green eyed Cambion nodded. "I spoke to one of the Princes."

"Prince Theron." Lilith confirmed. She had seen the way Loukas had looked at the Triton during the ball, with a guilty desire, and how Mordred had interrupted them. The Demon had also heard of the 'break up' between her son and the Faerie Prince, so why not give him the chance to see the Triton again, that seemed like an adequate gift.

"Well, the Sirens have a couple of objects we need before we can finally mount our attack on the eight cities of Heaven, and since you have spoken to the Prince, I think it a good idea that you go to retrieve them."

Lilith explained that these objects were Lædingr and Dromi, the unbreakable chains used to bind the great Wolf Fenrir. Gleipnir, a fetter created by the Angel-gods of Asgard said to be as light and thin as silk, but as strong as creation. The final object was the Purple Red Gold Gourd created by the Angel-gods of the Chinese Pantheon; the Gourd was said to be able to suck any being, no matter how powerful they were, into it.

"Why do we need these?" Loukas questioned. Lilith could tell that he was trying to hide his excitement at the prospect of seeing the Siren Prince again, but it was definitely there, deep down.

"To trap God, of course." Morgana said loudly, she seemed to have been missing the attention. "God is a being of pure magic, chaos and energy, so therefore cannot be killed. Instead the only way we can hope to take down Heaven is by incapacitating the Almighty. The Gourd will suck Him in and should dampen his powers just enough so that Gleipnir, Dromi and Lædingr can be tied round and fastened; rendering Him powerless and trapping Him for eternity."

"Thank you for that long-winded explanation," Lilith drawled, receiving a sneer from Morgana in return.

"Loukas, take the portal to the Sirenuse and collect the objects. The rest of you, prepare for the arrival of the Alium. It's time to rally our troops."

Chapter 17

The Sirenuse was a pocket dimension, a world of turquoise waters and shimmering calcite and pearl towers that lay somewhere between the eight realms.

The land was home to no portal so any being, Siren or otherwise, could teleport in and out of the Sirenuse at will. That is exactly what Loukas had done. He wasn't entirely sure how to feel, he knew why Lilith had sent him and yet he wasn't sure if he even wanted to see Theron again. He had only met Triton once, and although he had found him to be attractive, there had been no instant connection, not like there had been with…

He shook his head, there was no need to continue this train of thought, there was a job to be done.

Loukas had emerged on a thin bridge surrounded by pools of what seemed to be glowing water filled with Mermaids and Nymphs. Kelpies and other aquatic beings were splashing through the gentle waves with a unique elegance. In the distance Loukas could see a number of spiralling, shell-like buildings whose pointed roofs seemed to pierce the grey, clouded skies.

He began to move forward when a long, thin, snake-like neck of green-blue scales with a fanged head shot up before him. Loukas barely had time to jump back before another streaked past him and tried to bite his arm. A bark sounded to his left and Loukas whirled to see a monstrous creature rising from the water. Its waist was girdled by the dripping heads of baying dogs, while six heads with triple rows of shark-like teeth attached to long snakey necks rose, snarling, from a wrinkled torso of blue flesh.

From his readings, Loukas knew exactly what this creature was, or rather who she was. Her name was Scylla, she had once been a beautiful Nymph whose beauty had brought her the attention of the sea god, Glaucus. Unfortunately for her, the Angel-goddess of Sorcery, Circe, desired Galucus for herself and in a fit of jealousy she had cursed Scylla and transformed her into the hideous beast which now floated before Loukas. He dodged another of Scylla's monstrous heads and blocked one more with a shield charm as he tried to remember more about the cursed Nymph. Then it came to him, Scylla had been placed on one side of the Messina Strait, and on the other side...

Loukas spun around quickly and looked over the other edge of the bridge and saw exactly what he had been expecting; the water had begun swirling as circular rows of spear-like teeth had begun to rise and spin in the waters. This was the sea monster Charybdis, the counterpart of Scylla housed on the other side of the Menissa strait. Those who were not killed by the dogs and heads of Scylla were forced into the rotating jaws of Charybdis.

The Cambion cried out and dropped to his knees on the bridge as one of Scylla's heads sank her fangs deep into his leg. Loukas sent a ball of green magic hurtling from his palm which slammed into the monster's head at point blank range, Scylla loosed a powerful scream as her jaw detached from his calf. He attempted to stand again but almost stumbled back over the edge and into the mouth of Charybdis. He raised his hands and created an orb of protection around himself, he felt the magical shield shake as Scylla's heads began banging into it, her fangs attempting to penetrate the magic and sink into the Cambion.

Despite his fears, Loukas couldn't help but be impressed by the security of the Sirenuse, if anyone could simply teleport into the home of the Sirens, it was likely a good idea to have a sound defence mechanism in place. That thought didn't particularly help him at this moment.

However, his reprieve came with the sudden outbreak of an enchanting melody. A Siren song. The beautiful sounds and lyrics washed over the shield and slowly dissolved Loukas' magic as Scylla and Charybdis withdrew to the depths of the waters surrounding the Sirenuse. Loukas turned to face the direction of the song as it died down and saw three beings dressed in regal blue making their way in his direction from the city, their pink eyes bright against their pale skin and their wet, blue-black hair sticking to their necks in delicate waves. Nerissa, Daryah and, of course, Theron; the Prince and Princesses of the Sirenuse.

"Loukas," Theron held out a helping hand to the Cambion who took it and gripped onto the Triton's shoulder to steady himself.

"Our apologies. Had you informed us you were visiting we would have been able to stand down our defences prior to your arrival."

"Why are you here, Cambion?" Nerissa, at least Loukas assumed it was Nerissa, questioned in a tone harsher than the coldest stream.

"I have been sent to collect some objects by Lilith." Loukas said.

"Of course." Daryah, the second sister replied with her equally chilling voice.

"You Demons always want something."

"He's a half-Demon," Theron corrected, receiving an appreciative smile from Loukas as his sisters rolled their pale pink eyes simultaneously.

Loukas released Theron's shoulder, his leg had only needed a moment to heal, at least his Demon blood gave him that advantage.

"We do not have long, I believe Lilith wishes to rally her army tonight."

"Then please," Nerissa said, an air of sarcasm echoing in her words. "Follow us."

She and her sister began to walk back up the path they had arrived from.

Theron cast an apologetic look to Loukas before the two men began to follow in the Siren's wake.

The Poison of God. Lord of Hell. Right hand to Hell's throne. Concubine of the Supreme Empress of Hell. These had all been titles belonging to Sammael. Now what was he? Who was he? He had lost his wife due to his infidelity, one of his children and his magic.

His name had once been carved in stone, his story told through the ages; now his name was but traced in the sand. ready to be washed away by the ever-thrashing sea of time. Sammael didn't even know if he was completely immortal as he had been or if he could now be killed like a Faerie or Vampire. Not only had he lost all of that in a few weeks, Lilith wanted him out of Hell once their divorce was finalised. She had always known how to kick someone while they were down.

He was angry, he could admit that. With Lilith for holding his infidelity against him in such a harsh way, with Estrie for betraying him even after he had tried to save her, but mostly angry with himself. How had he allowed himself to fall so far? He had cheated on his wife, the woman who upon all women were based, the stereotype of femininity, and then he had allowed his children to be taken and used as weapons in a bid to placate her. Even that hadn't worked.

Sammael was now in one of the spare chambers of the fortress. Lilith had demanded he move out of theirs. He wasn't sure what he was supposed to be doing, he had heard the roar of a Dragon outside which could only mean one thing, Lilith was preparing for war. Sammael wished he could help, but he could not, he was powerless, the fallen angel doubted he would even be welcome at the battle.

"That is correct," Lilith had entered the room wearing a suit of what looked like a thin, white material, but Sammael knew to be a fabric stronger than any armour, not that Lilith needed it. A dark red cape was draped over one of the Demon Queen's shoulders, her dark hair ran down the other like spilled ink. A Necrotic followed the Demon into the chambers.

"You will not be welcome at the battle, you serve no purpose to our cause anymore."

"Stay out of my head," Sammael hadn't even thought about the fact that he was now susceptible to magics such as telepathy, he couldn't prevent anyone from entering his mind anymore.

"Why? There's enough room for me there."

Sammael sneered. "I assume you've not just come here to insult me,"

"You're correct," Lilith moved further into the room and took a seat on one of the black sofas, she crossed one leg over the other and beckoned Sammael to place himself on the sofa facing her. He did so as the slave moved from the doorway and stood behind Lilith.

"Lucifer's back."

"In Hell?" Sammael asked. He hadn't seen his brother in thousands of years, why would he have returned now?

Lilith nodded. "And he's searching for a way to take back control of Hell. He has already tried to buy Astaroth's soul, and he has located my vault."

"Why come to me with this?" Sammael had no power, he couldn't stop Lucifer, he hadn't had that ability even before Estrie had taken his magic. Lucifer had always been the strongest of the Fallen Angels, only Lilith had ever overpowered him.

"Lucifer said, and I can feel that the old magic is shifting once again. He is growing stronger even without Astaroth's soul and I fear that, given enough time, Lucifer will find a way to take back my realm. I need a way to kill him and I thought you, being his brother and his closest companion when in Heaven, may know of such a way."

Sammael shook his head and gave Lilith a confused look. Surely she knew what he was going to tell her, she had been there as the old laws had been created.

"Lucifer is immortal in the same way you are; he cannot be killed."

"There must be a way of making him fade then?" Fading was the closest to death that pure immortals could get. It involved the very essence of a person being ripped apart by something incredibly powerful and it could take millions, if not billions, of years for the immortal's essence to piece together fully once again.

Lilith herself had once been a victim of fading, she had been stabbed with a blade that had been coated in the ichor of Asherah, the goddess of creation and wife of God. The Demon had been ripped apart by the polar opposition that had invaded her body. It had only taken Lilith a million years to fully form again, but it had been a harrowing experience for her.

Sammael thought for a moment, Lucifer had never faded before and so it was impossible to know if there was such a being or object that could cause such a thing. But it stood to reason that if Lilith could fade, so could the Lightbringer.

"There was one object," Sammael began, "that Lucifer feared. It has a number of names: The Holy Lance, The Spear of Destiny, the Spear of Longinus."

"The Spear used to pierce the side of Christ as he hung on the crucifix?" Lilith asked, a speculative look rippling through her dark eyes.

"It makes sense, the blood of the Nazarene rests on the blade. He was the antithesis of Lucifer as Asherah was to me." The mother of Demons rose from her seat and turned to the Necrotic behind her.

"Send a small hoard of Demons to Antioch, tell them they are not to return without the Spear of Longinus. They will know it when they find it." The Necrotic slave bowed and grunted before exiting the room.

"Is that wise?" Sammael asked. "Letting a portion of your army go as you prepare to go into war. Will you not need every last warrior?"

Lilith dismissed him. "What do you know of war?"

Sammael wondered if perhaps she had forgotten that he had once taken part in the biggest war of all, the original rebellion.

"I have Cambions, Faeries, Witches, Vampires, Wraiths, Werewolves and a Dragon at my disposal, not to mention a number of other Alium races, I believe I can spare a few Demons."

Sammael nodded, he knew better than to argue with Lilith, even if he did believe her to be wrong. The Lord of Hell believed that she his soon to be ex wife was making a grave mistake, not only in letting some of her army leave her side now, but by planning her attack so early. It was too rushed and she was greatly underestimating the size and skill of the Seraphic Army, but then again, what did he know of war?

An awkward silence followed, one that was thankfully disturbed by a knock on the door which was swiftly opened by Sammael. He was met, much to his distaste, by the eldest of all Ambrogian Vampires, Amber Alarie. The Demon and the Vampire had never seen eye to eye, he had heavily disliked the way she had commandeered Hell as her home, she was forever poking her nose into all the intimate details of his life with Lilith and he just knew that she had a hand in Lilith's decision to divorce him.

"Lilith's in here, isn't she?"

Amber pushed past Sammael and sauntered into the room. Her brown eyes fixed on Lilith as soon as she saw her.

"There you are, Lilith, I've been trying to talk to you for days. It's a good thing I heard you two talking, I knew you'd need rescuing from his dire conversation."

"A delight to see you as always, Amber." Sammael rolled his emerald eyes, but Amber had already turned back to the Demon Queen.

"I need Orpheo Lenoir killed." Amber said.

"Why?" Lilith asked. "I am not in the habit of killing my allies."

"He has threatened to expose me. Other than the Rättslig, who believe me dead, Orpheo is the only Vampire alive who recognises me. If he reveals my identity to the Vampires, they will turn on me, I will have no chance to take back my kingdom."

"That is of no concern to me," Lilith responded. "I apologise, Amber, but I cannot risk losing the support of the Vampires just to protect you."

"You are running that risk either way." Amber said. "If the Vampires find out who I am then they will know that it is you who has harboured me all of these years. You who hid their killer from them. If I am exposed by

Orpheo in such a way, rather than revealing my identity to the Vampire world as a legend rediscovered as I have planned, then you will not only lose the support of the Vampires, but you may very well face an uprising."

Sammael had to admit that despite his dislike for the Vampire, she certainly knew how to manipulate a situation to her advantage, she had always claimed to be a survivor and she was constantly proving this to be true.

"Very well," Lilith said in an unhappy tone. "I am sure I can arrange for some happy accident on the battlefield to befall Orpheo. But make no mistake, Amber, I do not like being manipulated." Without further words, Lilith left the room.

"Impressive," Sammael said with a nod of appreciation for the Vampires craft.

Amber scrunched up her face at Sammael. "Shut up." She said before promptly standing and exiting the chamber.

Loukas had been taken below the glistening city of the Sirenuse to a set of vast caves and caverns. It was damp under the city and there was a strong smell of salt in the air that stung the back of the Cambion's throat. His leg had healed, but Loukas was still sliding and struggling to remain upright on the slippery stone floor whereas the Sirens and the Triton had no issue walking barefoot. Then again his boots had no grip and their feet were slightly webbed. He felt uncomfortable underground, he knew that there was only a wall of jagged black rock between him and the home of all the deadly creatures of the deep blue sea. Loukas had always hated the water, ever since discovering the Kraken; and now he thought if such a being was to live anywhere it would be in the centre of all water-associated magic, with the Sirenuse. He shuddered at the thought.

"Are you okay?" Theron asked, his voice a whisper that still managed to bounce off of the arched walls.

"I'm fine." Loukas responded. The tapping and squelching of his boots on the hard, wet floor echoed through the cave. His eyes were squinted, straining in the dark where the only source of light was a small set of glowing stones in the walls and they struggled to break through the darkness.

"You've changed since we last met," Theron said, his pink eyes like taaffeite in the blackness. "You're angrier and more distant."

Loukas glared at the Triton for a moment.

"Don't presume to know me! We've met once." Even in the darkness, Loukas could see that Theron flinched, he was only trying to be kind. The Cambion's face softened.

"Sorry, after you left the ball, my sister attacked my brother and he almost died."

"But he's okay now?"

Loukas nodded. "Thankfully. But my sister is gone, she left without a goodbye."

His face hardened as he felt a sadness rising in his chest once again. Loukas clenched his fists and took a deep breath, it had taken him days to be able to get out of bed, to recover in any way from his sadness, he wasn't about to let himself fall back into that blanket of depression.

"I'm sorry." Theron said. "At least you have your boyfriend, Moron, was it?" He looked at Loukas with expectant eyes.

The Cambion knew exactly what the Triton was doing, it had nothing to do with Loukas' support system, but was instead about his personal life.

"Mordred and I rushed things."

"Which is code for you, in your anger, pushed him away, I presume."

Loukas shot him an incredulous look. "I… You… " He was completely lost for words.

"I am a Triton," Theron reminded him. "Our songs enchant the hearts of men, we know all about the desires of the soul."

The Cambion sighed, his emerald eyes met the Triton's carnation gaze.

"And what does my soul desire?"

"I guess we'll find out." Therons voice had returned to its hushed tone.

"If I can interrupt," Nerissa had dropped back and pushed her way between the two men. "We're here."

She gestured before her with a pale hand ending in long, sharp black nails.

Loukas' eyes followed her thin fingers to a large arched door of glowing white pearl. There was a strange energy surrounding the entryway, a song pouring from the cracks enticed the Cambion to come closer. He knew he probably shouldn't, a Siren's song rarely led to anything pleasant and yet he couldn't stop his feet from moving forward, his arm outstretched, reaching for the gilded handle. His eyes were fixed on the door, his ears enamoured by the beautiful sound, the song was less offensive than the one that had banished Scylla and Charybdis, more seductive and somehow more dangerous.

He was dragged out of the trance when he felt something wrap around his wrist. He jumped, worried that it was a tentacle of some monstrous creature that had found its way into the cave. The Cambion was relieved when he saw it was instead the pale hand of Theron pulling his arm away from the door.

"That door would kill you instantly should you touch it." Theron said. He smiled as he released Loukas' arm and moved forward himself. The Triton raised both arms as his sisters stood on either side of him and grasped his hands. They let loose a powerful song matching the beautiful melody of the entryway in perfect harmony. The door rumbled loudly as their song grew louder and slowly the pearl arch swung open and a loud scraping noise echoed through the cave.

The Sirens and the Triton entered the next room and beckoned Loukas to follow. The Cambion did as they said and entered a circular room of pearl walls lined with thin silver shelves which held a number of powerful aquatic objects. The Crown of Amphitrite, Queen of the seas and the Shell of Glaucus. Loukas even recognised the blade of the Japanese Angel-god of storms, Susanoo-No-Mikoto. The objects he had come for lay on a shelf to his left, two unbreakable glowing chains of silver known as Domi and Lædingr. They had been created by The Aesir, the Angel-gods of Asgard, to tie down the Great Wolf, Fenrir. When these chains hadn't been quite strong enough, the Aesir had created a third and final chain, a fetter by the name of Gleipnir. The fetter was said to be as thin and as light as silk, but as strong as creation itself and made from six impossible ingredients - the noise of a cat's footfall, a woman's beard, mountain roots, the sinews of a bear, a fish's breath, and the spittle of a bird. With the addition of Gleipnir, Fenrir had been successfully subdued. That was the third of four objects Loukas had been sent to collect. The fourth and final relic he had to recover was likely the most important, the Purple Red Gold Gourd. A powerful and curvaceous container created by the Angel-gods of the Chinese Pantheon with the power to suck in any being no matter how powerful they were.

"These are what Lilith requires?" Nerissa picked up Dromi and Lædingr with a heavy exhale, they were far heavier than they looked. Her sister, Daryah lifted Gleipnir and the Purple Red Gold Gourd, carefully positioning its ornate lid away from herself lest it open and suck the Siren into it.

"They are," Loukas said. He could feel the power rolling off the objects held by the Sirens, each was archaistic and embedded with deep potency.

"Thank you." He held out his hands ready to take them but to his surprise, the Sirens did not hand them over.

"We were charged with the protection of these sacred relics," Daryah said. "We will maintain our hold on them until we arrive in Hell."

"Very well," Loukas responded agreeably.

371

He had never transported himself back to Hell without the use of a portal, let alone move three other people with him, though he knew it was possible. A being with Demonic blood could teleport themselves and others to the realm of Demons without a portal.

"Shall we proceed to Pandemonium?"

Theron tilted his head in confusion. "Not just yet, we must collect the army of the Sirenuse first."

Loukas' brow raised as his eyes widened. "You mean, I'm going to have to transport an entire army to Hell without a portal?"

Suddenly it all felt very real, he was going to have to prove himself. Loukas was going to be expected to use his magic, to release his Demonic side and kill Angels as part of a great war. His chest felt tight and his breathing grew heavy, he felt Theron put a hand on his shoulder and looked at the Triton.

"You'll be okay, you can do this." Theron said with a comforting smile.

Loukas attempted to smile back, but his heart was beating too quickly and he was doing his best to hide that he was shaking.

"Let's go and collect your army." Loukas kept his voice steady, he needed to get moving so that he didn't pass out and embarrass himself.

The Sirens moved past him and through the cavern. Loukas followed quickly and was too preoccupied in his own thoughts to even notice the deafening bang as the pearl door slammed shut behind them. This was it. He was going to have to decide who he was. The man or the monster.

A Dragon! They had a freaking Dragon! And it was three times the size of an elephant. Mariah was in shock. Could the Angels win against an army of thousands and a Dragon? She had to tell them, the Gibborim had to tell the Seraphic Army about the great beast, and about how the Alium planned to use Persephone to get into Heaven and trap God. Thankfully, her treacherous siblings had remained with the Alium to learn more about the world. That left Mahina's chambers empty for Mariah to sneak into and warn the Seraphic Army.

Mariah made her way down the corridor which housed her siblings' chambers, her silver hair shimmering in the light of the torches hanging from the walls, her shadow dancing across the floor. She turned and opened Mahina's door with a quick glance down the corridor. All was clear. She entered.

Mariah wasn't fond of the decor in any of the rooms in Lilith's fortress, it was all far too plain with the symmetrical black sofas, the coffee table, the boring white walls. The only thing she did like was the fact that the brightness of the lamps scattered around the room were dictated to by her persuasion. In this instance the lights were dimmed greatly lest anyone walk by and see the glow from under the door. Mariah hated having to hide in such a way, it had been bearable before because she had her siblings on her side, but they had changed; the empty promise of power from the Demons had corrupted them and they couldn't see it.

She dropped to her knees and opened up the Kibisis, a satchel of brown leather once belonging to the hero Perseus who had slain the monster, Medusa. It had been a gift from the Angels. The interior was lined with a smooth blue fabric which opened into separate pockets.She slipped her hand into the smallest opening and withdrew a small mirror of silver and blue. The Yata No Kagami, the mirror once used to lure the Angel-goddess of the sun, Amaterasu, out from hiding and back to the Heavenly City of Takamagahara. It was now one of the Imperial Regalia which could be used to contact the realm of gods and Angels from any of the eight realms.

The spy ran a hand over the blue gem at the back of the mirror as she inspected herself in the reflection. Her appearance hadn't changed and yet, Mariah could see something different. In just a few short weeks she could see more strength in herself, her face had hardened and her eyes seemed to have grown brighter, almost as reflective as the mirror itself. She couldn't tell if she'd gotten prettier or simply more mature, either way she liked what she saw.

Her siblings had gone the opposite way. It was a strange feeling, knowing Mahina and Moroccan were no longer on her side, although they had always been different, they had always been together. Mariah had always fought with her brother and sister, but had anyone ever gone against them she would have backed them one hundred percent, and yet they no longer offered the same courtesy.

"Ishikoridome." Mariah uttered the sacred words and the glass of Yata No Kagami rippled as though a pebble had been dropped into a pool. As the glass settled once again, the Angel-goddess of Rainbows and messages, Iris looked back from within the reflection, her hair a mass of colourful swirls crowning her beautiful bronze face.

"Where are your siblings?" The goddess asked.

"Never mind about that." Mariah said. She couldn't quite bring herself to rat them out, the Angels would have them killed if they knew they had betrayed them.

She refused to be responsible for the death of her siblings.

"I have important news,"

Iris nodded, her vibrant chromatic eyes seemed filled with suspicion.

"Proceed,"

Mariah took a deep breath and readied to launch into all she knew about Persephone planning to betray them, that the Alium had Almighty trapping relics and there was a mighty Dragon among their ranks.

"We told you," Mariah's attention was ripped from the mirror as she heard Moroccan's voice and her heart sank. She looked up and saw Mahina and Moroccan standing on either side of Lilith, Astaroth and Morgana Le Fay. She hadn't even heard the door open.

"She works for the Angels."

Her breathing grew heavy as she realised that they had betrayed her. The mirror, Yata No Kagami, slipped from her hand and shattered on the smooth white floor.

Chapter 18

The room had grown brighter now, it seemed that someone else, likely Lilith, was now controlling the light of the lamps. Mariah's chest was rising and falling at a rapid rate and she saw the shards of broken glass from the mirror shatter across the floor before the harsh smashing noise hit her ears.

"So it's true," Lilith's black eyes burned into Mariah whose heart was in her mouth, her entire body shaking with fear. "You are a spy."

The conviction Mariah had previously, that she couldn't betray her siblings, washed away in an instant.

She was filled with two primary emotions, fear and anger.

"So are they!" she spluttered

"I know." Lilith said, much to Mariah's surprise. "They have already confessed to me, repented and pledged allegiance to me. I offer you the opportunity to do the same."

Mariah took a step back as she saw Morgana and Astaroth begin moving around the opposing sofas, broken glass crunching under foot, her hand wrapped so tightly around the strap of the satchel that her knuckles were growing lighter by the second. She couldn't decide who was more intimidating, the Cambion or the Faerie, Astaroth carried an air of danger and there was a darkness about his aura, but there was something sinister about Morgana hidden behind her glorious veneer. There was beauty in danger and danger in beauty.

"Join us, Mariah," Moroccan said in a monotonous voice. "The Alium community offers us more than the Angels ever could."

Mariah's brow creased as her lip quivered, her brother had been indoctrinated, brainwashed into believing what the Demons wanted. Although these were the Demon beliefs, Mariah could hear Mahina's words coming from Moroccan's mouth. If anyone had manipulated him, it was their sister.

Mariah shook her head. "Moroccan, what they tell you is a lie; think of what the Angels told us. These creatures killed our parents."

"And we can help you bring them back." Lilith said. "My people and I may have done many questionable things, but since starting this rebellion we have not lied once. The Angels seek to oppress us. The Angels seek to keep all power for themselves. The Angels have the ability to bring your parents back from the dead, but they prevent you from wishing for it."

"Spare me your well-rehearsed speech, Lilith." Mariah's voice shook, she could hardly believe she was standing against the Queen of Hell when she had barely even argued against a teacher in the Stagnant world.

"It is nothing I haven't heard before. You may be able to bring my parents back, but I know it will come at a price I don't want to pay. And as for the Angels oppressing Alium kind, maybe Vampires need to be restricted, maybe Demons need to be confined to Hell."

Lilith snarled at the words of the Gibborim. "Very well, you have made your choice. Astaroth, Morgana, seize her."

The newly crowned Grand Duke of Hell and Faerie Queen of legend moved forward again. Mariah raised her hands and let loose a defensive blast of white energy, it struck the floor in front of Morgana who laughed. Mariah whimpered, she didn't have much skill when it came to magic, during their training they had discovered that out of the three Musa siblings it was Moroccan who had the best magical ability, Mahina was most skilled with weapons and Mariah had fallen somewhere between the two.

"Mariah," Astaroth stepped forward again, there was nothing but amusement in his eyes. "There are two ways we can do this. You either come with us willingly, or we force you."

"Don't hurt her," Moroccan exclaimed. For a moment Mariah almost felt relieved that her brother cared, but he had been the one to turn her in, his care meant nothing.

"We won't," Morgana said as she passed over the burnt patch of ground where Mariah's magic had hit. "So long as she doesn't put up a fight."

Her jade eyes fixed on Mariah in a mixture between fascination and disgust.

Mariah assumed it was because the Faerie, like most others, had never seen a being such as Mariah and her siblings, Stagnants with the blood of celestials.

She tried to fire another blast, one more powerful than the last, but instead her palm illuminated with brilliant light before dying down only seconds later. She would have teleported from the room had she any idea how to achieve such a feat. Astaroth and Morgana were only an arms reach away from her now, her back against the white wall of the lounge with the curtain to the bed chamber on her right.

"If you take me, the Angels will know."

"By that point it will be too late, we will have taken Heaven." Lilith responded.

"Enough stalling, grab her now!" Lilith commanded.

With a scream, as her two pursuers lunged for her, Mariah bolted through the black curtain into her bedroom. She ran past her bed and flicked her wrist, willing her thick oak wardrobe to slam onto the floor before the archway. It did so and Mariah heaved a deep sigh of relief, her magic was completely useless. Her solace was but for a moment, a powerful blast shot through the air and shredded the wardrobe into splinters, Astaroth and Morgana entered the room followed by Lilith and her siblings.

Mariah stumbled back again through more dark curtains and onto the balcony overlooking the barren landscape that was Pandemonium. She heard the roar of a Dragon in the distant skies and the screech of Demons below. There was no escape as her pursuers emerged through the black drapery. Mariah pushed her back up against the corner of the balcony, then she remembered the Angel gifts in Kabisis. She fumbled with the bag, clawing her way through the leather satchel until she discovered what she was searching for.

A curved horn of ombre black, brown and white wood. Gjallarhorn. She remembered the words of Nakir: 'If you are ever in immediate and mortal danger, blow on the horn and you will be immediately transported to the side of Eir, the Norse Angel-goddess of protection.

She heard Lilith shouting for her capture and the footsteps for Astaroth and Morgana as they charged toward her. She raised Gjallarhorn to her lips and blew. A klaxon-like sound erupted from the horn as did a powerful surge of energy. It struck the group pursuing Mariah violently and they were thrown from their feet and slammed to the ground as Mariah was surrounded by a swirling pillar of cloud. When the cloud cleared, Mariah was no longer in Hell.

Lilith got to her feet with an infuriated scream. "She had Gjallarhorn! Why didn't you tell me?" She demanded of the Musas.

She would have simply killed the girl herself had she known, it may have gone against her promise to Moroccan and Mahina to not harm their sister if they pledged their allegiance, but it would have been a necessary evil. She was pleased, however, that the moles had come forth themselves and exposed the last one loyal to the Angels, or at least who she believed to be the last loyal Gibborim.

"I didn't even think… " Moroccan began, but he was cut off as Lilith's hand wrapped around his throat and lifted him from the ground.

"If I find out that this is a double bluff, I will feed you to the Hellhounds of Irae."

She dropped him with another growl of pure rage, Moroccan fell to his knees coughing at the feet of the Demon.

"Mother," Astaroth said. Lilith turned to face her son. "Mariah will be telling the Angels of our plans. If she tells them of Persephone before she opens the portal we have no way of getting to Heaven."

Lilith snarled. She knew things had been going too well. She had a full army, Loukas and the Sirens had returned with the chains and container that could trap God; they were assured victory, even if slightly rushed. But of course something had to ruin it, as Sammael had done their marriage, as Estrie had done with her perfect family, this girl, this Angel descendant now had the chance to tear apart her plans, moments away from the Demon's triumph. She would not let that happen.

The Queen of Hell clapped and a wave of thin, black magic shot from her in a great, expanding sphere.

"Allies," she called, her voice echoed through the sphere and ripped through the realms to the ears of Lilith's supporters.

"It is time. Rally your armies, make your way to Pandemonium and be ready to slaughter the warriors of Heaven in exchange for your freedom."

Lilith lowered her hands and the shadowy magic that had surrounded the Queen of Hell dissolved into the air. She moved over to the edge of the balcony, her hands gripping the white parapet as her eyes scanned the courtyard below. She could see the Princes and hordes of Hell beneath her, thousands of Demons mixed with the Sirens brought back by Loukas. Faerie warriors in their golden armour and Vampires who had remained in Pandemonium after the ball were littered about the courtyard in rows. The Demon smiled as she heard the doors of the fortress swing open beneath the balcony, a party of wolves taller than men shot forward howling into the skies of Hell, the Maledictus and Natus Wolves had arrived through the portal, hundreds of them.

"The Alium," Astaroth said as he took a place by Lilith's side. "They're rallying."

Lilith smiled again, her general was pleased with his army. The doors opened again and a host of black and white ghosts floated into the courtyard carrying blades of shadows. Wraiths, led by their Queen, Ereshkigal appeared. A group of rebel Witches and

Warlocks carrying their staffs emerged as did the many monsters of Acuran. Hecatonchires, creatures with fifty heads and a hundred heads, stormed into the courtyard followed by Dhampirs, Gigantes, Manananggal and Drakaina.

"What are they?" Mahina pointed in the distance at a group of what looked at first to be men riding large wolves. As they grew closer the wolves were revealed to be Hellhounds, hairless dogs larger than any other, with ripped flesh, exposed bone and eyes lit by the brightest of Hellfires. On their backs were six identical men whose skin was so pale it was almost green, bone ripped through their heads in the shape of crowns and their eyes were empty sockets.

"They are the Lords of Hell." Lilith said. They were slightly less powerful than the Princes but controlled most of Hell's armies. There was Apollyon, Demon of the Abyss; Oriens, Demon of Prophecy; Paimon, the Marquis of Hell; and the Demon of Secrets, Amaymon. They were accompanied by Egyn, Demon of Dragons, and Maggot, the Cardinal of Hell.

"Usually they reside on the outskirts of Hell's cities, but today they join us for war."

"And that?" Moroccan pointed at another being in the distance, Lilith could smell the fear on the boy.

The thing Moroccan pointed at was what looked to be a child with the same greenish skin and crown shaped bones as the Lords of Hell. He was in a chariot being pulled by a number of man-sized snakes, the Basilisks, and a wave of venomous serpents followed in his stead.

"That is the President of Hell, the commander of serpents and the leader of thirty Demon legions. That is Valac." Lilith said, her head raised proudly.

She hadn't expected so many of Hell's nobility to show their support, deep down she worried they might still endorse Lucifer. If she had any doubts about her position in Hell, this certainly washed them away; Valac did not support any cause he did not deem worthy.

The army was completed as Kirke appeared from behind the great red cliff, her amber eyes shining brightly against her black-blue scales. She circled the army, her wings creating powerful winds with each beat. Everyone's eyes were on the Dragon as she let loose an earth-shaking roar and began to hover just in front of the balcony.

Lilith looked over to Astaroth and gestured toward his Dragon. Lilith had to admit the beast was beautiful but terrifying, she could feel the raw magical energy coming off of her. The Queen of Hell watched as her son clambered over the parapet and jumped onto the back of Kirke, his hands gripping the silvery spikes protruding from her back. He climbed up so that he sat in the small gap between her neck and her wings, just high enough so that he could see, but not so precariously that he would fall. He looked so small compared to the Dragon, Lilith noted, and yet he would be so much harder to kill than the most powerful of legendary beasts. With another flap of her wings, Kirke shot forward, she circled the army again before landing behind the rows of soldiers and letting loose an ear-splitting roar.

The Queen of Hell.

The Mother of Demons.

The Maiden of Shadows.

These were all Lilith's titles, and now she was going to add one more. Liberator of the Oppressed.

She looked out at her army, thousands of warriors stood below her in rows and rows clutching blades, spears, arrows, and even whips. She saw the cryokinetic siblings, Talvi and Skadi, in the crowd in thin armour made of steaming ice. Amber Alarie was there along with Rhoda, the Coxani Queen. Loukas and Mania were dressed in thin grey-black armour made of the same material as Lilith's coat.

All looked ready to go to battle and all Lilith needed to do was give the command. This was what she had been preparing for over eighteen years. In her time - and in all time - Lilith had accomplished a great deal. She had Adam and Eve displaced from Eden, she had manipulated Cain into killing his brother, she had become the Queen of Hell; usurping The Lightbringer. But nothing came close to this accomplishment, saving an entire world from tyranny and oppression. This would return her to her rightful place back in the history books, her name would be remembered above all others, even above Eve. Lilith found it strange that even now, after all she had done with her incredibly long life, she still in many ways felt as though she was less than her replacement. Had Eve ever saved an entire race? No, of course she hadn't, no one had, she, Lilith, would be the first. She would be revered by all as a saviour.

"Warriors of Alium, my Stygian Army, I thank you for your punctuality." As Lilith spoke, her voice amplified across the courtyard beneath her, all eyes turned to her.

"Today is not just a victory for me, but for all Alium kind. The Heavens know that we are linked in our cause and that together we will not stop until our rights, our families and our allies are protected. We will not surrender until the eight realms are saved from the tyranny of the Seraphic Council, we will carry our struggle through the cities of Heaven laying waste to all who stand in our way until a new world, a new order, breaks out of the shadows and banishes the autocracy of the past."

The crowd cheered loudly, banging their blades and various weapons against their armour and shields. The Demon Queen smiled and lifted a hand, a small black cloud ran around it and when it dissipated a small purple fruit appeared in her palm. The pomegranate given to Astaroth by Persephone. She took the fruit to her lips and sank her fangs deep into the skin of the pomegranate, her mouth was filled with its juices as she chewed and swallowed. Almost instantly a pillar of cloud erupted in the centre of the courtyard, a hurricane of spinning, syphoning, white magic. A portal to Heaven. This portal was unlike one Lilith had come across before, usually a portal was a wall of pulsating magic, this seemed more like an overcharged teleportation spell. Although it followed the portal laws, it felt strange to her that Persephone was so willing to help bring about the fall of her family.

"Go forth," Lilith commanded. "March on Heaven, slaughter every Angel in your path, bring down the buildings of the Seraphic cities - the edifices of our despotism!"

At her instruction, the Stygian Army marched toward the tornado of Angelic magic. One by one each row of soldiers, Demons, Faeries, Vampires, Werewolves, Wraiths and all manner of other Alium were grabbed by the powerful winds surrounding the spinning cloud and sucked violently into the portal to the realm of gods and Angels. The Demon Queen dismissed Morgana, Mariah and Moroccan from the balcony and watched in amazement as her legions disappeared through the portal. Kirke shrieked loudly as she flapped her wings and rose from the ground, she hovered around the portal with Astaroth on her back, gripping the spikes protruding from her scales, watching as the warriors vanished from sight. One final harsh cry flew from Kirke's mouth as the Dragon shot forward into the spinning white cloud, the magic engulfed her and her rider before transporting them straight from Pandemonium to Heaven.

With Astaroth and his Dragon gone, Lilith saw that the courtyard was now empty of anyone and anything but the portal. With a wave of her hand, Lilith dematerialised and reappeared at the foot of the spinning cloud, the energy pouring from it and creating a bitter-sweet ambience for the Queen of Hell, Angel magic burnt her nostrils. She took a deep breath and stepped forward into the clutches of the hurtling air. As the Angelic energies hit her, Lilith felt as though she was being ripped apart from the inside. She had expected that this journey was not going to be a pleasant one for any Demon, but this was far worse than she had imagined. Usually going through a portal was similar to lying on a lake or river and allowing the gentle stream to guide you to your chosen direction. This however was comparable to being thrown into the most aggressive of sea storms. She was thrown from side to side without reprieve, when she thought a moment of rest was near, another whirlpool wrapped around her dragging her through the portal faster and harder than before. Her very essence was fighting for survival in the hurricane of celestial magic, the mother of Demons gave a scream as the portal rumbled, spitting her out and slamming closed behind her with a bang.

Chapter 19

"Cuṭar!" Astaroth commanded in ancient Tamil, the native language of any beast from Acuran. Kirke let loose a breath of hot, white fire as she shot through the air, her flames struck the Angels fighting on the ground as her horned wings impaled and beat the warriors in the skies.

The portal had released the Stygian Army in the city of Vanaheim, home to the Angel-gods and goddess of the Vanir; those Angels once worshipped as deities of nature by the Nordic peoples. Vanaheim was unlike any of the other cities of Heaven. Olympus, Asgard, Avalon,

Aaru, Takamagahara, Otherworld and Jannah were all cities of glowing towers and crystal palaces.

Vanaheim was far more natural. There were still incredible structures, palaces and obelisks, but these were made of glistening stone, surrounded by trees and encircled by trellises of colourful flowers and thick vines. It was a city that would not have looked out of place in Faerie, or in one of Lilith's tales about Eden. The sky was the only unnerving part of the city, like the rest of Heaven's skies it was a vast blanket of empty white light, it seemed as though it had no beginning and no end.

Hundreds, if not thousands of Angels had been awaiting the Stygian Army as they were expelled from the portal into Vanaheim. The battle had been instant with celestial and Alium blood being spilled almost immediately. It had been an even match, each side losing almost equal numbers until Astaroth had arrived on the back of his Dragon. As soon as they emerged, Kirke had wrapped her talons around hundreds of Angels at a time and burned hundreds more at Astaroth's command. No Angels had fled the battle, but fear ran through their ranks at the sight of a Dragon. Few had ever seen such a beast and their skill in battle had begun to falter. They quivered and ducked with each swoop of Kirke, their blades shook in their hands as she roared and their eyes closed momentarily as her fires ripped through their troops, hot and bright.

Astaroth pulled on Kirke's spike and the Dragon turned in his chosen direction. They circled the battle field, an almost empty field of emerald green grass and tall trees decorated in vibrant fruits and leaves of all colours. The Cambion pulled up and Kirke followed his command to sweep over an oncoming Angel. With a paw she kicked the Seraphic soldier, sending him hurtling down into the ground with such intense force his armour was shattered instantly and his own blade landed in his back. Astaroth noticed that there were a few tall buildings scattered on the outskirts of the fields that were not visible from the ground. They housed empty archways all around the circular buildings. The Cambion readied to turn Kirke back to the centre of the battle to continue roasting their enemies when he caught sight of something in one of the archways, a movement in the shadows, a grey feathered wing poking from the arch quickly tucking back where it could no longer be seen. Hidden Angels were waiting to ambush the Alium Army.

"Alikkavum!" Astaroth gave the order to destroy. Kirke shrieked and turned her amber eyes on the towers, her wings flapped and her giant body hurtled toward one of the circular buildings head first. She smashed through the grey stone, her mouth wide open. As she emerged on the other side, it was full of Angels. Those that were not killed by the thick, rectangular bricks were pierced by Kirke's dagger-like teeth before she shook them out of her mouth and let loose another blast of white hot flames, incinerating them all before they had a chance to hit the ground.

Before the son of Lilith had a chance to command Kirke into the next tower only a few metres away, a host of Angels shot from the archways. The same happened from all other towers surrounding the battlefield and Astaroth noticed that all of these Angels were female. Each wore heavy silver armour and carried shields and spears. They rose up from the ground with their great grey wings. Shimmering silver crowns ran across their foreheads and were tied into the back of their intricately braided brown hair.

"Valkyries," Astaroth growled. Of course they would be here. The Valkyries were an all-female portion of the Seraphic Army, they were the most fierce and skilled warriors of their kind and in the early days of creation they had been picked by Odin, the leader of the Norse Angel-gods, to be the ones in charge of deciding the fate of warriors and carrying the honourable dead to the city of Valhalla in Paradise, the realm of the liberated. There were only two dozen of them, if not less, and yet they were the deadliest of the Seraphic Army and were led by Jophiel, the Beauty of God, and the Angel who carried the flaming sword.

The majority of the Valkyries flew immediately to the sides of their brothers and sisters to assist in the battle with the Stygian Army, but a small portion of them remained close to Astaroth and his Dragon. They formed a small line before Kirke, their shields raised and spears pointed.

"Cuṭar!" Astaroth commanded and Kirke roared as flames shot from her throat. The white hot fire launched at the Valkyries but bounced off their shining shields without causing them any distress. Unlike most of their siblings, Valkyries had seen and faced more than Dragons in their time.

The Cambion's nostrils flared and his bright eyes widened in anger.

"Kolla," he growled. Kill.

Kirke charged forward through the air, her mouth open wide, her talons clawing at the Valkyries who avoided her with ease.

One of the Angels threw her spear, it shot through the air and sank deep into Kirke's hide, narrowly missing Astaroth's leg. The Dragon howled as her rider yanked the spear out of her shimmering scales and she released another burst of fire, the Valkyrie before her had no time to throw up her shield and was caught by the flames. The Angel screamed as her bronze flesh melted and her skeleton dropped to the ground, her bones shattering instantly.

With a snarl, Astaroth hurled the Spear back at his attacker, the pointed silver edge ripped through her armour, her stomach and then her spine before protruding out of the other side of her silver breastplate. The Valkyrie wrapped her hand around the wooden shaft and looked to her sisters with fear and tears in her golden eyes. Between one blink of an eye and another, the warrior Angel went from a powerful woman to a thousand granules of salt falling through the to the floor.

A truly biblical punishment.

One only the Almighty alone had unleashed on His enemies.

Their blades clashed with a spark. The two women grunted as they wrestled for control, Mahina's blade atop Mariah's blade in an attempt to force it from her sister's hand. The older sister wielded a fourteenth century Estoc sword, a long, thin blade double the size of Mariah's seventeenth century Hanger blade.

"What do you plan to do?" Mariah asked, jumping back from her sister's blade. "Kill me?"

"I don't have to kill you," Mahina grunted as she slammed her sword down onto Mariah's weapon. "I just have to incapacitate you."

Of course, she wasn't going to kill her sister, just because they were now on opposing sides didn't mean they had to be enemies. Mahina only wanted to disarm her sister and knock her unconscious, if she did that then she could get Mariah away from the battle to protect her. The safety of her siblings was still of utmost importance to Mahina, that was exactly the reason she had forced Lilith into promising Mariah's safety if she and Moroccan confessed and swore allegiance to the Stygian Army.

Whether or not Mariah was trying to kill her was unclear.

The younger Musa slashed her blade through the air and nipped Mahina across the cheek. She raised her hand to her face and when she took it away, her ebony fingertips were coated in blood. Mahina's silver eyes widened, her hand shaking as she looked at Mariah.

"You bitch!" She hadn't expected Mariah to be quite so vicious in her attack.

"You traitor!" Mariah retorted.

The two women jumped as an Angel shot between them, wings expanded and a wolf with glowing yellow eyes pounced on his chest, knocking the Angel out from between Mariah and Mahina. They began circling one another, blades raised.

"Traitor," Mahina scoffed. "I have chosen my side logically after I learned all the necessary information. You have been indoctrinated and manipulated by those who claim their moral compasses point north! Sometimes, the bad guys, the villains, whatever you want to call us, are not the ones doing 'bad' things! They are those who seek to control and manipulate others to serve their purpose!"

"And you haven't just described Lilith?"

"No!" Mahina yelled. For a moment it was as though Mahina and Mariah were the only beings in Vanaheim. The battle surrounding them washed away into white noise and a series of speedy blurs.

"Lilith has not manipulated me. She has shown me that the Angels do not deal in whole truths, they tell you only what they need you to know. Lilith and the Alium, they hide nothing, no matter how ugly things may get. That is why I chose them! Brutal honesty is needed in war."

Mariah narrowed her eyes and swung her blade at Mahina again. Her sister parried the blow and, using her free hand, created a small blast of magic which caught the bottom of Mariah's boot, unbalancing her and sending her to the ground when she dropped her sword with a clatter. Mahina pointed her blade at her sister.

Mahina wasn't quite sure what she was supposed to do now, if she took her blade away then Mariah would attempt to fight her further, but she couldn't hold her there forever, eventually some Vampire or Demon, or even Lilith, would spot them and wonder what was happening and if Mahina didn't kill her sister, they certainly would. Even now she could see Werewolves beginning to circle the two of them. Even the occasional Demon looked over in their direction, sniffing the air and growling in delight. Mahina wondered for a moment how they were smelling the Angelic essence within them so easily, Nakir had told the three siblings that it was barely traceable after so many years. Then she felt it again, a small drop of her blood escaping from the small laceration on her cheek. Anger rose in the eldest Gibborim, like bile in her chest, after all she had done for her brother and her sister, after all she had given up - going to university, finding the man or woman of her dreams, living her own unique life - Mariah had the audacity to attack her. Mahina's brow creased as she flicked her blade upwards, the sharp tip of metal slid across Mariah's face as her sister etched a matching line in her cheek, releasing a surge of crimson blood.

Mahina's anger died down as quickly as it rose when a Demon with cerulean, scaled skin and milky white eyes growled and jumped, landing next to Mariah; a clawed hand reaching toward her. Mahina flourished her blade and forced it deep into the Demon's chest. It squealed as a wave of magic shot down the blade and deep into the creature, corroding it from the inside out until it was left as a steaming body of ash which collapsed as the Gibborim removed her blade and placed it back on her sister's chest in one swift motion.

The eldest Musa did wonder why none of the surrounding Angels had attempted to rescue Mariah, she was their secret weapon, their spy, and yet there seemed to be no protection for her. Perhaps they were so assured of their success that their mole no longer mattered to them. If Mariah died. would it be considered collateral damage? If that were the case then it was proof of what Mahina had been trying to explain, the Angels had been using the Musas.

"If you're going to kill me, Mahina, then do it." Mariah spat. Mahina was hurt by the look in her sister's silver eyes. During her time caring for her siblings they had shot her glares of distaste and anger, but this, this was something new. Loathing. Did Mariah really hate her now? Had her opinion of Mahina changed so quickly? Mahina didn't give Mariah the satisfaction of seeing her words affect her in any way, though they cut through her more painfully than Mariah's sword. She would never kill her own sister after she had already lost so much. Even if they were on separate sides, Mahina would never wish her sister any ill will, even if this was a sentiment her sister did not seem to share.

She began to lightly draw the tip of her blade across Mariah's clavicle and around the back of her neck as she, Mahina, moved to stand behind her. She took a deep breath and removed the sword from Mariah's neck before spinning it around and striking the back of her sister's head with the ornate black handle. Mariah gave a light grunt and a thud followed as her unconscious body dropped into the long grass.

Mahina took a deep breath before raising her sword again and running into the middle of the battle once again. It was down to the Angels to save Mariah now, her sister was still breathing, if they did not, then it would be all the proof Mahina needed that she was doing the right thing in supporting the Stygian army.

Morgana Le Fay hadn't taken part in a war in thousands of years, not since the battle of Camlann in which her half brother, King Arthur, had been killed by her nephew, Mordred and secured her place as Queen of both the mystical realm of Faerie and the great Kingdom of Camelot. Despite her long break from conflict, the Faerie Queen moved with more elegance and grace than any other warrior on the battlefield.

She carried two thin blades of gold and swung them around herself as though she were dancing, her body bending to the rhythm of war, slicing through the

Angels and avoiding their attacks with ease. Like her people, Morgana wore armour of rose gold. Unlike the other Faeries, the Queen's armour was not heavy, but was made of an almost unbreakable, yet strangely thin, material. Her copper-rose hair was tied at the back of her head in an ornate braid and a tiara of pink bronze snuggled her forehead. Despite her clear skill, two Faerie guards followed in their Queen's path, with tall spears in their grasp and their heads covered in helmets of rose gold.

A Valkyrie landed before Morgana, her spear pointed toward the Queen of Faerie. Morgana winced slightly at the sight of the Angel's silver armour and the cold metal tip of her weapon, but this did not deter the Faerie from launching her attack first. She lunged forward with one of her blades, her blow blocked by the Valkyries spear with a clatter as the two metals collided. The Valkyrie grunted as she knocked Morgana's blade up and struck the Queen across the face with the hard handle, making her let out an angry yelp. Morgana shook her head and, with a scream, brought down her other blade, slicing the spear of the Valkyrie in half, splinters spraying across the battlefield. The Angel threw the lower half of the broken spear through the air. Morgana ducked so that it flew over her head and sank deep into the black armour of a Wraith hovering behind her. The phantom let loose a deep howl as it dissipated into the shadows, its obsidian blade dropping to the ground.

The Faerie Queen shot back up and surged forward once again, her golden blade sped through the air like a ray of sunlight. The Valkyrie blocked the attack with the second half of her spear and jerked it slightly, the silver head slipping under the cuff of Morgana's armour and nipping her wrist. The Faerie screamed and recoiled from the Angel, taking but a moment to inspect her wrist, it stung like ice and venom as bubbling rose-red blood spurted from her flesh. Cold metal had such an effect on her kind, as though it would do anything to expel the life-giving liquid from its host. She looked up only a moment too late and was met by the silver boot of her adversary slamming into her stomach with great force. Morgana stumbled backwards and doubled over, landing on her knees. Her multi-colored eyes narrowed as the Valkyrie spun the half spear in her hands and raised it, ready to impale and end the Queen of Faerie once and for all. Morgana let loose a scream and jumped to her feet, she swiped her gilded blade violently at the celestial warrior and knocked the spear from her hand before puncturing the Valkyrie's silver breastplate with the second blade. She pushed hard and grunted as the weapon audibly cracked the armour and sank into the Angel's chest. The Valkyrie bawled as the knife dug through her flesh and fell to her back, bringing Morgana to her knees straddling the warrior of Heaven. The flame-haired Faerie yanked her knife from the Angel's chest before placing both daggers at the throat of the Valkyrie in a crossed pattern. The Angel whimpered but did not cry nor beg for mercy as the light refracted from the weapons and danced across her face like a golden sea.

Morgana's lip curled as she drew the daggers apart, slicing through the neck of her opponent. The Valkyrie coughed and sputtered violently as the wounds opened on her throat, joining in the middle. Ichor spilled from both her gullet and mouth as aureate as the knives that had drawn it from her. With one final croak, the Valkyries body jerked and the light left her eyes. She was dead.

Morgana sheathed her blades at her sides and got to her feet, wiping the blood from her wrist. She knew she would have to let it heal by itself. Faerie magic could not heal wounds inflicted by cold metals like the silver head of the Valkyrie's spear. The Queen of the Faeries brushed down her armoured coat with a grimace. The Angel had bled on her.

With a heavy sigh, Morgana Le Fay began to move into the battle, ready to face her next Angel. To her surprise no one had not attacked her yet nor had one attempted to rescue the Valkyrie. It seemed that the Stygian Army was winning, they had moved with great ease across Vanaheim and although there were numerous Alium bodies scattered around the battlefield, the bodies of thousands of Angels were littered in the grass, impaled, beheaded and burned. She watched for a moment and saw Lilith ripping apart Angels with her magic, Amber Alarie feasting on Seraphic blood and her own nephew, Mordred, swinging his twin blades almost as elegantly as she had. The light shining off his weapons turned his pale skin and whiter hair as golden as the palace in Cathair Órga, the capital city of the Seelie half of Faerie.

Her kaleidoscopic eyes scanned the battlefield and then she saw Mordred stalking through the crowd, weaving his way between fights and dodging blasts of magic with ease, despite his wizened appearance. His amber eyes shot from the corpse of an Angel and pierced Morgana like a spear to the chest and she was instantly transported back in time.

512 AD: 25 years before the Battle of Camlann.

The man appeared in the clearing holding a staff of white oak, his face cloaked by a red velvet hood. His long white beard and withered hands were the only visible proof of his age.

The clearing was a barren circle of grass in the centre of ten tall grey stones under the light of the moon on the outskirts of the Brocéliande Forest, just outside of Camelot.

"You came," Morgana Le Fay stepped out from behind one of the stones, her dress the same red velvet as the old man's cloak, her deep red hair tied and decorated with chains of gold and glistening red stones.

"At your request, Lady Morgana." The old man dropped his hood, revealing a face covered in so many lines that Morgana often wondered if they had been carved there. His eyes were orange and glowing brightly in the night like owl eyes..

"How may I help you?"

"You can back down," Morgana said. "You can allow me my revenge." Morgana had been married to Sir Urien, a Knight of the Round Table and close friend of her half-brother, King Arthur. Although she had loved him, Morgana had grown bored and had found herself seeking comfort in the arms of Sir Guiomar; the cousin of Arthur's wife, Queen Guinevere. The two had begun an affair and for a short while, they were happy. That continued until the Queen of Camelot had caught them, she had publicly shamed Morgana and Guiomar had been banished from the Kingdom, leaving without so much as a goodbye. Morgana became a pariah in the eyes of the Lords *and Ladies of the Court and even the common folk. In her anger she had sworn revenge on the Queen.*

Morgana had spent months slipping love potions into the wines of Guinevere and Arthur's best friend, Sir Lancelot. The two had begun a sordid and secretive affair, they believed no one knew of their trysts. Morgana had been preparing to expose them. She knew if Arthur discovered the affair, then Guinevere would be shamed by all, banished from Camelot, if not publicly executed.

She had been on her way to expose Lancelot and Guinevere when the old man had pulled her aside. He had threatened that if she told the King of his wife's indiscretion, he would tell the court of her Faerie blood. She would be burned at the stake for such a thing. Camelot was not a land that welcomed those with magic. And so her plan had fallen through, at least for that time period.

That night, Morgana sent the elderly man a message requesting that he meet her at the clearing. And now, here they were.

The old man chuckled hoarsely. "Arthur is the Once and Future King, which makes Guinevere the Once and Future Queen. I will not let you jeopardise that."

"I will not ask again," Morgana said and was taken aback as the elderly man laughed again, loudly this time. She was not used to him showing such emotion, he was usually quiet and docile.

"Do not threaten me, Morgana, your power is nothing compared to mine."

Morgana's lip curled at his words, she knew them to be true. The old man was a Faerie, he had been the one to train Morgana as a youth in the Seelie world. Despite Camelot's hatred of magic, he was welcomed by the King and the court for he had helped Arthur discover the sword in the stone, and thus had practically given him the throne. He could expose Morgana, but she didn't have the option of doing the same.

She had no need to threaten him further as suddenly a glowing white rope of magic wrapped around his arms, binding them to his sides and ripping the staff from his grip. The old man let loose a hoarse moan as the rope tightened and another woman emerged from the shadows behind him, her hair glowing as white as the moon above them. Morgana recognised her instantly as her sister, Morgause. She hadn't seen her sister in years and this was one of the times she had least expected her to arrive. What did she want?

"Morgana," Morgause called. "Do something, I can't hold him for long." She yanked on the glowing rope as the old man struggled and gasped as it grew tighter.

Morgana began waving and spinning her hands in balletic movements, her long red sleeves fluttering in the cool breeze. She muttered prayers to her gods, the Tuatha De Danann; to Taranis, the God of Clouds and to Nuada, the God of Wind. Magic flowed from her palms and clouds drew down from the Heavens to form a great white palace with towers and

turrets before them and the winds rumbled, dragging the old
man into the castle of clouds as he called out in protest. The
sky shook and a powerful gale ran around the stone circle,
raising the palace and the elderly Faerie up into the Heavens
until he could no longer be seen.

Morgana sighed and lowered her hands, the winds died
down as her spell was completed. She wiped her brow in relief.
He was gone. She would never see him again. Or at least she
hoped she wouldn't, for if that man, that Faerie, ever found
Morgans Le Fay, he would surely kill her for her plans and her
actions. She prayed to all the gods and goddesses of the Tuatha
De Danann that never again would she lay eyes on the Faerie,
the sorcerer of legend.

Merlin.

The Faerie Queen was ripped back to reality by the
roaring of Kirke as she flew overhead with Astaroth on
her back. Morgana felt the blood leave her face, she
blanched as her eyes met Merlin's hawkish gaze.

The aged Faerie turned his body to face hers, raised
his white staff, and began running toward her; white
beard and red cloak billowing around him. As he headed
for the Queen he struck Demons and oncoming

Vampires out of his path, they exploded in blasts of bright red magic and by the look on his face, he expected Morgana Le Fay to meet the same fate, though maybe not quite so easily.

Morgana did not have time to wonder how Merlin had escaped his prison of clouds, he was coming for her and he was coming at a surprising speed. She drew her blades once again, but knew that even if it did come down to a one-on-one battle, she could not defeat him. The guise of an elderly man may have fooled many, but Morgana had grown up watching him perform impressive feats of magic, and defeating even the most skilled of Arthur's Round Table in combat. Morgana's hands stopped hovering over her blades and she took a deep breath before turning and running back through the crowd.

"Faeries, retreat!" She called as she fled. She grabbed a Vampire and threw him behind her into the path of her pursuer.

"Retreat! Retreat, Faeries, retreat!" As a Queen she could not leave the battlefield until she knew her people had heard her command. And yet none seemed to have done so, none but Mordred.

"Retreat!" Mordred called, gazing at his aunt. "Warriors of the Fey realm, retreat!"

At Mordred's call, Morgana saw a number of colourful blasts of magic from various points on the battlefield. Her people were doing as the royals had commanded, they were leaving the war. Morgana believed in the cause, and she knew that should Lilith and her children be successful then she would have to pay for having the Faeries abandon them, but that punishment would be nothing compared to the one Merlin intended to bestow on Morgana and her people.

The last thing Morgana Le Fay saw, before being swept away by a pillar of multicoloured cloud, was Mordred, running toward Merlin, his twin blades drawn and ready to protect his Queen and his people.

Astaroth kept a tight grip on one of Kirke's great silver spikes protruding from her back as he leaned over her side hoping for a better glimpse at what was happening below. He could see a number of colourful clouds emerging on the battlefield. The spells of transmutation died down quickly. Were members of the army fleeing? Surely not, they were but a few metres away from the bridge connecting Vanaheim and the next city of Heaven, Asgard, home to the second half of the Nordic Angel-gods and goddesses, and the seat of the Concilium Pugnatum, the war department of the Seraphic Council.

Astaroth could have flown there to begin burning buildings and incinerating the Angels who were brave or stupid enough to stand against a Dragon and a Cambion with the ability to turn celestials to salt, but he knew that it was unwise to enter a war zone alone.

Upon closer inspection, Astaroth noted that it was the Faeries who were fleeing. It did not surprise him that Morgana would have her troops pull out of the war; she had betrayed Lilith before, but he was curious as to why she had done so now, when they were so close to success. Astaroth pushed down on Kirke's spike and the Dragon followed his instruction and flew closer to the ground, hovering just above the battle, her wings casting a dark blanket across the soldiers. Other than the bodies of the deceased Seelie and Unseelie warriors, the Cambion could see but one of their kind still on the battlefield. Mordred. He seemed to be battling an old man, an old man who could move just as well, if not better and faster, than the Faerie Prince.

Mordred seemed to be handling himself well enough and so Astaroth pushed on his Dragon's spike and turned their attention elsewhere. He gave the command for Kirke to release her fire when he saw a collection of Angels approaching a group of Werewolves. Her flames melted their armour and their flesh and left them a mixture of ash and melted metal sinking into the soil of Vanaheim. Apart from incinerating minor threats which most of the Stygian Army could handle on their own, if required, the battle in Vanaheim was won. Kirke and Astaroth needed only to watch for now. There were but fifty Angels left on the battlefield now, and though Astaroth knew there would still be thousands left in the other seven cities, he did not doubt that his army of thousands could overpower them with ease.

The Cambion noted that the Princes, Lords and President of Hell had all grouped together, their horned crowns and pale flesh covered in the golden ichor of Angels. They no longer rode their Hellhounds. Astaroth had seen a couple of them pouncing on Seraphic warriors and ripping their throats out, and a couple more he had seen as fatalities of war. It surprised the Grand Duke of Hell that none of the nobility below him seemed to be carrying weapons; they had been relying solely on their magic throughout the battle, something Astaroth never would have done. Even Lilith carried a blade.

As he watched, a group of seven Valkyries slammed down around the Princes, Lords and President. None carried blades, but instead each held a portion of a long silver and red chain. Astaroth knew what it was immediately. The chain of Prometheus which had once been used to tie the Titan, Prometheus, to a rock for a millenia for the crime of giving Stagnants the ability to create fire. The Demon Azazel had been banished to the ancient Alium prison of Dudael for helping Prometheus do such a thing, but Prometheus, being a Titan, having the ichor of the Angels in his veins, had been tied to a rock and his liver had been torn out daily by an Eagle and painfully regrown.

The chain of Prometheus was enchanted to block any and all magic possessed by whomever was bound within it. As the nobility of Hell attempted to blast the Valkyrie warriors with spells of fire and of lightning, the spells reverberated. The Valkyries grew closer and closer and before Astaroth fully understood what was happening, the Valkyries had rounded up Hell's aristocracy and wrapped the chain of Prometheus around them multiple times. They were trapped. Astaroth gave the command for Kirke to fly forward, to attack the Valkyries, but by the time the Dragon had flapped her great wings, the warriors of Heaven had disappeared in a flash of brilliant light and they had taken the Princes, Lords and President of Hell with them.

Astaroth muttered a curse under his breath. How had his reaction time been so slow? The Valkyries' plan had been clear from the moment they had arrived. The Angels knew that they were losing and were collecting bargaining chips. Lilith cared for the Princes, and the Lords and President were the key to her success as Queen of Hell. By taking them away, they took away symbols of Lilith's power. Astaroth turned as he heard the shriek of a Wraith, and saw as the Valkyries once again disappeared in flashes of bright light, this time with Ereshkigal wrapped up by their chain. They appeared again and again taking more and more members of the army. Orpheo, the grandson of Lycaon; Arcas and even one of the Coxani Witches had been grabbed.

Then it hit him. If they were taking away symbols of power and strength, then they were not going to take him to hurt Lilith, they already had the Demon nobility. No, they would take something from him as well, something, or more likely someone, to disorient the Grand Duke of Hell, the general of the Stygian Army; and they had two choices. Mania or Loukas.

He barely had any time to think, he pulled on Kirke's spike and she turned back around as he scanned the battlefield and picked out Mania. She stood beside Lilith, battling one of the last remaining Angels. Surely the Valkyries wouldn't risk going for her when she was beside the Demon Queen. That left Loukas. His vision shot around the crowds of Alium and then he spotted him, his emerald-eyed brother stood with Mordred to his left and the Siren Prince, Theron, to his right, with a collection of Angel corpses surrounding them.

Astaroth took a breath, perhaps the Valkyries weren't after his siblings. In the same moment, as though they had been reading his thoughts, the Valkyries appeared in a line before the three men. Loukas, Theron and Mordred raised their blades to battle the Valkyries.

Astaroth rose to his feet, unsteady on Kirke's bumpy back, keeping a hand on one of the large spikes protruding from her scales. He didn't look down, if he had he wouldn't have been able to bring himself to do what he had to. With a deep inhalation, Astaroth drew a long silver blade from his side and jumped from Kirke's back. It wasn't a long fall, and Astaroth landed comfortably on his feet before charging along the ground, he sliced an Angel's neck as they attempted to stand in his way before he made it to the three men and the Valkyries. There were fewer of the female warriors than before, some lay dead at the feet of the men, others in the grass of the battlefield slaughtered as they tried to take down the enemy. Each still held a portion of the Chain of Prometheus which had now been separated into separate pieces.

The Cambion cared nothing for the two Princes, Theron and Mordred, they were winning their battles. But Loukas, who was already weighed down with Dromi, Lædingr and Gleipnir, was not faring as well. The Valkyrie was stabbing at him with her blade repeatedly and each time he was narrowly parrying her blow with his own heavy sword. Loukas cried out as the Valkyrie slammed down her spear once again, knocking his blade from his hand and slamming him to the floor.

She swung her portion of the shimmering red and silver chain to take the emerald-eyed boy hostage when Astaroth ran his sword through her back as hard as he could. The Valkyrie gasped as the blade pierced her back, her intestines, her stomach and finally the other side of her armour. She whimpered for a moment as the Cambion forced the blade upwards and before her eyes could close, she exploded into thousands of tiny white granules. Once again he had unintentionally transformed an Angel into salt. He offered a hand to Loukas, who was now staring at him in disbelief, covered in a spray of golden ichor, his hair littered with small particles of white rock.

Loukas took his hand, but as Astaroth pulled his brother to his feet, he shot past him with a cry and into Mordred. The Faerie Prince was knocked out of the way and Loukas fell into the arms of an attacking Valkyrie. She immediately tied the chain of Prometheus around him and disappeared in a flash of light before Astaroth could make another move.

Chapter 20

Lilith screamed as she punched a narrow blade into the skull of an oncoming Angel, the last of the Vanaheim army. The Angel gave a dull grunt and clattered to the ground, the blade embedded in his temple. The Queen of Hell ran a hand through her hair and adjusted the red cape hanging from her shoulder, it was torn and covered in golden ichor. Her black, void-like eyes ran around the battlefield. She knew the Faeries, at the command of Morgana, were gone. Morgana would pay for that later. Lilith was surprised at the number of Alium who had been slaughtered in the fight. Not as many as the Angel fatalities, but just under half of the Stygian Army lay dead in the long grass. As well as the bodies, the mother of Demons observed that a number of her allies were missing, surely they hadn't fled, especially those like Ereshkigal who seemed to have left her army without a leader. The Princes of Hell were gone too, as were the Lords and Valac. She whirled around to see that Mania was behind her, covered in ichor, but she couldn't spot Loukas anywhere.

Panic flooded the Demon. "Astaroth!" She called. She repeated herself, her voice shaking when her favoured son did not respond. Was he a body hidden in the scorched grass? Had the Angels taken him? Had there been a Kasai present unbeknownst to Lilith?

"Astaroth!"

"Over here!"

Lilith and Mania ran to the call of Mordred to find the Faerie Prince covered in cuts and his silky hair was matted with red blood and golden ichor. Beside Mordred, on his knees, his raven head in his hands, was Astaroth. His blade was cast to his side and his shoulders were rocking as tears streamed down his face.

"Thank Tartarus you're alive," Lilith dropped to her son's side. "Come now, Astaroth, we have a war to win." The Queen of Hell attempted to pull her son to his feet, but was shaken off.

Lilith scowled. Clearly he was upset about something, but he was a general and the Grand Duke of Hell. He couldn't show weakness, not in front of the troops. She needed him to stand and fight, the Angels of the Aesir would lead their attack in Vanaheim if the Stygian Army did not first move on Asgard.

"Astaroth, pick up your sword and get to your feet." Lilith commanded, she could feel the eyes of the army on her and her son.

"Rushed," Astaroth mumbled as he shook his head, more tears streaming down his face.

"This attack was too rushed and now they have Loukas. They have my brother, my best friend! I promised to protect him."

Lilith's brow creased. She understood friendship, she herself had had friends over the years, but none she would have cried over. Such strong affiliation was foreign to her. The Demon wondered if perhaps she would have ever cried like this if Sammael had been taken from her in the old days. She shook her head, they didn't have time for this.

"Then we must go and save him," Lilith and her son locked eyes, hers empty and dry, his were filled to the brim with salty teardrops. "Each moment you remain here, crying over his capture, is another moment the Angels will be torturing him for information on how to stop us."

Lilith rose fully once again and turned to the Stygian Army facing her, scattered across the battlefield and covered in blood and cuts.

"Many of our closest allies have been taken," Lilith's voice was projected throughout the battle front.

"The Angels hope this will discourage and deter us from our attack, but I implore you, let this fuel your passion! Use your anger at the capture and the deaths of your friends, families and rulers to power through this war. March now on Asgard and move forward through all the cities of Heaven, bring the Angels of the Aesir to their knees, destroy all you can and once we have control of the Heavens, we will demand the return of those close to us!"

Once again Lilith's words were met by thunderous applause and the banging of weapons against metal. The Queen of Hell certainly knew how to inspire a crowd.

"Mother," Lilith looked to Mania as she spoke, the dried blood in her dark red hair was barely noticeable. "Loukas had Dromi, Lædingr and Gleipnir." She spoke of the three chains they had planned to use in order to subdue and trap the Almighty. Lilith swore under her breath.

"Amber!" At Lilith's call, the Vampire appeared next to her, a blast of cold wind sweeping the air as a result of her vampiric speed. Amber was dressed similarly to Lilith, her marble skin protected by a thin, but strong, grey coat. There was a black leather sack wrapped around her shoulder and neck which made Lilith smile.

"Good, the Gourd is safe. We can still capture God, but it will take a great deal of magic to keep Him trapped in there without the chains." She had charged Amber with protecting the Purple Red Gold Gourd that had the ability to suck in and trap the Almighty, and the Vampire had not let her down.

Amber pursed her lips, the edges of her fangs pressing into the deep red of her lower lip. "Is that wise, Lilith? We have already lost so many. Should this fail, we will all be killed."

"We will not fail." Lilith glared at the Vampire, she knew Amber wanted to retreat now that Orpheo had been taken by the Angels. It was the perfect time for her to retake the Vampire world, not that there would be much of a world left for her to rule if they abandoned the cause now. If they did not finish their battle, the Angels would only pass the Arcadian Laws and hunt down the offending Alium.

"I have the powers of Hell in my hands and my son has a soul of shadows, the Seraphic Army has no hope of standing against us."

"I can turn them to salt." Astaroth had gotten to his feet, his eyes red and puffy from crying. Lilith was pleased to see that he seemed to have collected himself, even if it may have just been on the outside, she could smell his inner pain.

"You can do what?" Lilith asked.

Astaroth picked up his sword and sheathed it with a grunt.

"When I stab them, the Angels turn to salt."

Lilith looked at her son in awe. She had noticed small, white granules scattered across the grass in tall piles, but hadn't even considered that it could be salt. If what Astaroth claimed was true then he possessed a power that no mortal ever had. A power only God had used before, when turning sinners such as the wife of Lot, Ado, to salt when she looked back at Sodom. It was a perversion of the Almighty's power, and although Lilith knew Astaroth was powerful, she had never expected he would achieve such miraculous feats.

"Amber, give Mania the Gourd." Lilith said. The Vampire took the leather bag from around her neck and handed it to the Cambion. Both women gave the Demon looks of confusion.

"Astaroth, you are to cover your sister and protect the Gourd as we go through Heaven. Let no Angel near them."

Astaroth nodded, his face expressionless though his mother could see the pain and worry for his brother's safety trying to break through.

"We shall take Kirke."

He moved off, taking his sister with him to the Dragon laying on the outskirts of the battlefield, her glowing eyes scanning her surroundings, allowing nothing to pass her by unchecked.

Lilith once again addressed the members of the Stygian Army.

"Alium, take up arms," she commanded. "March on Asgard, break down the doors of Valaskjálf and destroy the High seat of Hliðskjálf!"

Lilith spoke of the great palace of Asgard, home to the Aesir and to the High Seat, Hliðskjálf, a throne from which one could watch over five of the eight realms - the realms of Underworld, Acuran, Alfheimr and Chaos. Heaven could already be seen by those inhabiting it whereas Hell and Faerie had forces blocking the sight of Hliðskjálf.

The army of Alium warriors retrieved their weapons and with one last look at their fallen brethren, they headed to the bridge connecting the two cities of Heaven. Many looked up as they were shadowed by the screeching Kirke passing overhead.

The Angel-gods of the Aesir attacked as soon as the first warrior crossed the threshold between Vanaheim and Asgard in a display that few had ever before seen. Hundreds of Angels in glowing armour carrying blades and spears shot forth from the silver roof of Valaskjálf, a great palace made up of hundreds of tall thin towers reaching high into the never ending sky of Heaven. The celestial warriors flew at unmatched speeds and landed before the palace of precious metals at the centre of Asgard.

Moroccan would have been impressed had he not been consumed by rage and confusion. He had watched as his sisters had fought one another and had witnessed Mahina leaving an unconscious, defenceless Mariah in the middle of a battlefield surrounded by Demons, Vampires and Wraiths. Thankfully he had seen an Angel swoop to the ground not long after and collect Mariah, flying her off into the distance at a supernatural speed. Although she had been saved, Mahina's actions impelled Moroccan into new levels of anger and a bewilderment he had never experienced before. Had his sister really changed so much just by reading a book? Had she really gone from such pure devotion to family, to no longer caring if her own sister lived or died? If that was the case, if her mind had been so easily shifted, Moroccan couldn't help but wonder if he had made the right decision by remaining with Mahina and betraying Mariah.

His train of thought was cut short by an Angel landing before him. She was formidable in armour of white and gold, her crystal-like wings giving her away for what she was, an Olympian Angel, the highest rank of Heaven. Not only was she an Olympian, but a golden winged crown wrapped around her ash-blonde hair showed that she was one of the Aesir. Her name was Frigg and her golden eyes glared at the treacherous Gibborim before her.

Moroccan decided against attacking her first, as he had throughout the battle, so far he had only killed Angels who would have taken his life. The Musa was not completely sure which side he wanted to be on. If he murdered an Angel, a being of supposed pure good, he would be forced to remain with the Alium whether his views on the Angels and their manipulations changed or not. To his surprise, the Angel did not attack him. Instead she held out her palm toward the Gibborim, he looked upon it in confusion and jumped back as the skin in the centre peeled open slowly to reveal an eye the same colour as an amethyst. Moroccan averted his eyes.

"Look." She commanded, her voice seemed to echo as she spoke.

Moroccan complied and looked into the purple iris in the Angel's palm. A pulse of violet energy erupted from the eye and struck Moroccan. Visions exploded in his mind.

Mariah lying dead at his feet, covered in scars and her own blood.

Mahina sat upon a throne of skulls with a blade in her hand.

Angels falling from the sky.

Finally the images in his head slowed, Moroccan saw himself in a vast, rocky wasteland surrounded by the ruins of broken temples. Bodies were scattered around him, those of Vampires, Werewolves and Faeries, Witches, Demons and Wraiths. He could pick out a handful of faces, Loukas, Amber, even Lilith, and yet most of the Fallen were blurred to him, nameless, faceless casualties of war. Collateral damage. There was a figure before him, again faceless and blurred, covered in shadows and surrounded by blood. The figure looked to be a man who drew his blade and pointed it at Moroccan, he stepped forward, his shadowed foot splattering a thick pool of blood further across the dirty floor of rubble. As the figure drew closer, Moroccan raised his arms and pointed his palms up to the skies, his eyes flashed with white. Immediately the never ending sky of Heaven was illuminated by a violent but brilliant crimson light and heavy orbs of dancing fire began to rain down. He watched as the fiery spheres ripped through the surrounding Alium and Seraphic warriors, some were set ablaze and killed instantly, reduced to charred bones in a similar fashion to the victims of Kirke. However some managed to survive without so much as an ash on their armour. The flames seemed to simply pass through them as a hand would pass through smoke. Moroccan twisted his wrists and the raging drops of fire bent with them, one by one dozens of them shot through the air, a stream of thick smoke trailing behind them, and plummeted into the shadowy figure. Despite the bright light of the fire hitting him, the figure remained shrouded from Moroccan's sight. With each hit the figure slowed in the approach but yet he did not stop, not until one final orb of blazing, white hot, fire shot through the crimson sky like a falling star, cutting through the air until it punched itself deep into the figure's chest. He dropped his long black blade to the ground with a clatter as he fell to his knees. For a moment it seemed that the figure was going to speak when the fire erupted from within and ripped the creature apart to leave nothing but a charred circle of grass where he had been kneeling almost a second ago.

Moroccan was pulled back to reality as the Angel-goddess before him closed her hand. The noise of the battle around him, the clashing of blades, the roar of Demons and the flapping of wings, was enough to make him wince, and yet it did not sting as much as the stench of Celestial and Demonic ichor which covered the threshold between the bridge and Asgard. From what he could see, the members of the Seraphic Army seemed to be doing a far better job at holding back the Alium forces than the Angels of Vanaheim.

Frigg looked at Moroccan, her golden eyes emotionless, her mouth fixed in a straight line. Despite her silence, Moroccan knew what the Angel-goddess wanted to say, that he was not to make her regret showing him such visions. Despite their vague nature, Moroccan knew what he had seen, he knew he held a great power and potentially an even greater destiny. All he had to do was take it.

The archers had arrived, led by Satet, the formidable Angel-goddess of Archery from the Egyptian Pantheon. She and hundreds of other Angels had appeared on the silver balconies of Valaskjálf, covered from head to toe in gilded armour, bows in arms and shining silver arrows emerging from the quivers on their backs. At Satet's command the Angels nocked their arrows into their bows, drew back their arms and set them loose. As they shot through the air each was illuminated with an azure flame and heading straight for Kirke and the Cambions on her back.

For a moment, Astaroth was worried, should the arrows pierce the Dragon in the right places, the left and right sides of her chest which housed her hearts, they would crash and would likely die instantly. Although he was a Kukan, a practically unkillable being of shadows, Dragons were creatures of pure magical energy, an explosion of their magic would be set free upon one's death and it would almost certainly kill Astaroth and his sister. His worries subsided when Mania, his ever studious sibling, informed him that she had once read that the hide of a Dragon could only be pierced by arrows and spears made from the hide of the first Vēṭṭai Dragon; Xiuhcoatl, and one of those had not been seen in centuries. It was rumoured that they didn't even exist, that Xiuhcoatl was still alive, but he was old and weak and remained slumbering in a hidden cave somewhere in the capital of Acuran, Ṭirākaṉ.

The great winged beast shot through the sky, flaming arrows flicking off of her great blue-black body as though they were toothpicks. She shrieked as she soared through the air, her wings casting a shadow that could cover entire cities in the Stagnant world. Kirke let loose a stream of fire as a group of Angels flew toward her and sent their burnt skeletons and melted armour to the battlefield below. As she shot forward, Astaroth stood on her back catching the arrows as they hurtled over her boulder-like head. He caught the arrows, still alight and spun them round quickly and launched them back at their attackers. They zoomed through the air, blue and silver like ice and plunged through the armour of the Angels as though it was as soft as wet clay. With a grunt and a cry, the winged warriors melted into pillars of salt atop the balcony. Despite the immediate panic Astaroth could sense among the archers of Heaven, none lowered their bows, instead they continued to fire more and more arrows.

Astaroth flicked his wrist as one of the Angels' long silver arrows headed for his face, his hand struck the metal with ease and cast it to his side. Unfortunately for the Grand Duke of Hell, the arrows were now coming in far too quickly for him to be able to return them, and so he had taken only to blocking them, some with magic, some with brute force. Astaroth watched as the host of distant Angels listened to yet another command from Satet. There was an immediate flash of silver as they nocked another set of arrows into their bows and sped them into the air. These projected far faster than previous attacks and a number of arrows slipped over Kirke's great head and hurtled past the Kukan before he had a chance to raise his magical shield of protection which sent the rest of the shining, sharp missiles ricocheting to either side of him.

His shield was lowered suddenly as a blood curdling scream sounded behind him. A scream that pulled Astaroth's heart into his mouth and filled him with instant dread and fear. He knew immediately what had happened and forced himself to turn around. He let loose a hoarse cry when he saw the hilt of a silver arrow sticking out of Mania's crimson armour, her garnet-like eyes brimming with a thick layer of tears. A drop rolled down Mania's cheek and with one final gasp she stumbled backwards, catching her foot on one of Kirkes spikes, and fell from the back of the great beast. Astaroth let loose a violent yell as his sister plummeted from the Dragon's back, her body limp and flaming hair spinning around her head.

As he yelled, Astaroth dropped to his knees, landing with his weight pressed against one of the thick spikes protruding from Kirke's back. The Dragon took this as a signal to begin to fly down at immense speed. She struck the earth in the centre of the battlefield, creating a crater in the marblelike surface of Asgard. Astaroth continued to yell as Kirke hit the ground and rolled, flipping him onto his back, surrounded by the rubble of the battle in Asgard.

Had a beating heart still sat in the chest of Lilith, it would have ceased its pulsing as she saw the Dragon, carrying two of her children and the most important object of the Stygian Army, crashing to the ground. She feared that perhaps the Angels had managed to kill Kirke and that in a few moments Astaroth, Mania and all of her hopes and dreams would be blown up by a powerful explosion of the pure magical energies of which Dragons were made.

Lilith closed her eyes as a shockwave of debris and dirty white dust ran from the shattered ground and spread across the battlefield. She felt chunks of the hard ground of Asgard and small granules of salt that had once been Angels hit her face and her armoured body. As it stopped, the Queen of Hell opened her eyes and, to her surprise, the rubble and dirt was suspended in the air, floating as though the gravity of Heaven ceased to exist. As she looked around the battlefield she noticed that the battles had slowed, although the war had not stopped. Angel and Alium alike were confused at the rocks which remained motionless in the air.

The mother of Demons gasped as there was a sudden change in the magical energies around her, she heard a blood curdling cry gush from the centre of the crater where the Dragon had fallen and a wave of shadowy magic erupted in a great sphere and ran quickly across Asgard. In the blink of an eye the magic struck the rocks in the air and the warriors of Heaven and instantly they were reduced to nothing but small white grains of salt.

Lilith recalled what Lucifer had said when he had ambushed her in the vault beneath her fortress - he had said that old magic was shifting again, ancient powers were once more awakening and returning to the world. It seemed now that such magic had appeared in her favoured son, Astaroth.

The Grand Duke of Hell let loose another horrific yell, filled with pain and torment; once again a sphere of magic as thin and transparent as shadows emerged from the crater and ran across the battlefield. Lilith gave a cry of disbelief and protest as the shadows washed over a small collective of Angels and Vampires and both the celestials and Alium beings melted into pillars of salt on the floor.

What was he doing?

Lilith began running forward toward the hole in the centre of the warzone. She barged her way through the crowds of Alium and plunged blades into oncoming Angels without a thought. All of the Demon's grace and decorum had abandoned her, her long dark hair was strewn across her face, her thin armour stained gold with the blood of gods and Angels. As she charged toward her son, she and all other warriors were struck by another blast of his shadow magic. Many were reduced to salt and even the Queen of Hell felt a sharp sting as the magic passed over her, but she did not stop.

Lilith froze as she reached the salt-covered edge of the pit. Kirke was awake and uninjured though it seemed there was no need for her fire and claws. The magical madness blasting from Astaroth with each heavy scream was more than enough to keep both enemies and allies at bay. He was on his knees, sobbing and wailing, a sound worse than any Banshee that Lilith had ever come across. His back was to her but Lilith could see what, or rather who, was in his arms.

Mania. Her red hair ran over her brother's arm like a river of blood, her crimson armoured legs and hands decorated in sparkling golden rings protruded from behind Astaroth who was clinging tightly to her body. Both were shaking as he sobbed and the Purple Red Gold Gourd lay only an arms-length away.

The Demon wasn't sure how to feel. Of course she was sad at the death of her daughter, but she had faced the death of a child before. It was Astaroth's reaction which drew the most concern from Lilith. She had seen his pain as Loukas was taken, the fact that Mania was dead was obviously going to hit him harder, but this - this was extreme. He had lost control of his power, as Estrie had, and now the Kukan seemed to be controlling him, using shadow magic and the perverse miracle Astaroth could perform to destroy not only the Seraphic, but also the Stygian Army.

"Astaroth," Lilith moved no closer, she could sense the raw and dangerous power rolling from her son and knew that if he felt threatened then his Kukan magic could be turned against her; not that she could be diminished to salt as easily as the Angels. She watched as his back tensed but his arms eased, releasing Mania's body from his tight grip, allowing her to roll onto the dirty white floor of the crater as another blast of shadow magic shot around them and destroyed more surrounding Angels and Alium.

Lilith gave a sharp gasp as her favoured son turned to face her, his face warped. Where his mouth was usually a thin line of pink, it was now wide, stretched beyond imagination, his usual sapphire eyes had lost all colour and now resembled the shark-like nature of Lilith's. His face was blanched white, also having lost any previous colour. The Kukan shadows that lined his soul had not only taken control of his power, but also his body.

"This attack was rushed!" Astaroth growled, a harsh echo seemed to whisper his words moments after he spoke. "My brother is a prisoner, and my sister is dead." Another painful wail shot from his crater-like mouth and another orb of dark magic erupted throughout Asgard. Lilith followed its trail with her eyes and watched as it tore through a pack of werewolves and a number of the Aesir and Olympian Angels and demolished them instantly, leaving nothing but small piles of salt on the hard ground.

"Astaroth, pull yourself together!" Lilith commanded him sharply.

Although the Demon was pleased with the destruction of the Seraphic Army that her son was causing, he was greatly diminishing the numbers of the Stygian Army. If they lost many more there would be no chance of reaching Olympus, no chance of trapping God and no chance of putting a stop to the Arcadian Laws. She considered trying to talk Astaroth into fighting the battle in memory of Mania, the way she had convinced him to fight to win back Loukas and the Princes, but she knew that this loss of control would not be so easily contained. She had only one option.

As her son's wide mouth rippled in his effort to howl with another destructive scream, Lilith shot forward with Demonic speed. She grabbed the Gourd lying beside Mania's body and tore off the multicoloured top in the blink of an eye. She pointed it in Astaroth's direction and instantly the magic that released from his scream was sucked into the Gourd. Astaroth rose to his feet, narrowing his intense gaze into a glare directed at the Queen of Hell. He looked ready to pounce when suddenly his hand seemed to melt into a puddle of floating black liquid, he gave yet another scream and instantly the rest of his body exploded into the same sticky, black substance and began surging through the air and into the Purple Red Gold Gourd. When every drop of Astaroth's shadowy essence had been collected in the multicoloured Gourd, Lilith slammed the lid in place with a heavy sigh.

Lilith jumped as Kirke gave a violent screech and got to her feet, her wings outstretched, her amber eyes fixed on the Demon before her and the Gourd in her grasp. It didn't surprise Lilith that the Dragon had reacted in such a way. She had just taken her master prisoner, the two were bonded and Dragons were loyal creatures and Kirke would do what she had to in order to protect her master. The great beast opened her mouth and a bright light began to illuminate her cavernous throat, Lilith did not know whether or not she could withstand the power of Dragon fire, but she knew better than to run from Kirke, for the winged beauty would only pursue her. The Queen of Hell clenched the Gourd tightly in her hand and closed her eyes the minute she saw the flames nearing Kirke's open jaws. She felt the violent heat as it spewed out and was surprised that she did not feel the fires engulf her, but merely felt heat above her head as though she had stepped out into the sun on a summer day. Lilith opened her eyes and turned to see where Kirke had directed her fire. She watched as it struck a number of Angels flying in the direction of the crater and melted their armour and flesh until only burned wings and charred bones dropped to the ground. The Dragon closed her mouth and turned her amber eyes back to Lilith with an expectant look. The Demon knew what the Dragon was inferring and she knew that the winged beast was correct, her army was practically diminished, her almost unkillable son was trapped in a multicoloured urn, she had been abandoned by the Faeries and her most powerful allies had been taken hostage. Perhaps Astaroth had been right when Loukas had been taken, even when the Kukan lining his soul had taken control he had still stood by his words. The attack was rushed.

"Piṉvāṅkavum." Lilith gave the order.

Retreat.

Kirke lowered her great head allowing Lilith to climb upon her scaled hide and immediately took flight, circling the crater at great speed. The Dragon swooped and crashed into more Angels as they attacked, shattering their armour and bones with the force of her wings and crushing them in her jaws before spitting them out with a loud shriek and an onslaught of bright flames. As Kirke soared in circles, Lilith sat upon her back, her dark eyes closed and her lips moving quickly as she muttered an enchantment in an ancient Demonic language long lost to the world of men. A portal spell. It was more difficult opening a portal from Heaven back to Hell as the celestial magics were potent in the realm of gods and Angels and did what they could to block infernal transmutation. Lilith uttered the last word of her incantation and a pillar of swirling black magic appeared at the centre of the crater and began to rise. As the maelstrom rose higher and higher into the endless sky of Heaven, Lilith pulled on one of Kirke's spikes and led her back into battle. They hovered over various areas of the warzone as Lilith called to her troops to make their way to the portal to retreat back to Hell.

As the members of the Stygian army began charging toward the spinning black tornado in the distance, the Angels took flight and built a wall around the crater with their glowing wings, glistening armour and shining blades. The Alium stopped as they came to the border of seraphic warriors and although many were blanched with fear, their hands shaking, not one laid down their weapon in surrender. The Angels were planning to take so much from them, but they would not take their dignity. If they were to die, then they would die fighting.

Kirke let loose another earth shaking screech as her shadow was cast over the armies of Heaven and Hell, a shadow which was swiftly washed away by the light of her flames as Lilith gave the command for her to burn the Angels where they stood. Many of the winged warriors attempted to dive out of the way but were swept up by the white hot flames as their brethren were set ablaze. The smell of melting metal and Angel flesh filled the air, as did the smoke from their charred bones which was quickly sucked up by the spinning portal in the centre of the crater.

For a moment, Lilith wondered if perhaps the war could still be won. Kirke had just destroyed hundreds of Heaven's army with one breath, perhaps if she just rode the Dragon to Olympus she could still put a stop to the Arcadian Laws. Such thoughts fell away from the Demon's mind when the Dragon beneath her gave a grunt. Lilith looked forward and, to her disgust, she saw that thousands of Angels had appeared out of Valaskjalf and were soaring toward the Stygian Army at immense speed with their blades drawn and spears at the ready.

"Go!" Lilith yelled to her troops. "Go now!" The Alium below her began rushing into the portal which swirled faster and faster with each being it transported to Hell, creating a vacuum of air which began sucking more and more of the army in by the second.

The Queen of Hell told Kirke to let her fire loose once more and instantly the Dragon complied and released a long stream of fire with a great roar. The Angels were still too far from the portal for Kirke to set them ablaze, yet her fire was still effective as a wall separating the celestials from the Alium as they made their escape. With a quick glance down, Lilith noted that the majority of her army had made it through the portal. She pulled on one of Kirke's spikes hard and the Dragon stopped her blazing breath and followed the Demon's command, taking them both soaring toward the portal. Immediately the two were sucked into the pillar of cloud and ripped through the matter of worlds back to Hell.

With a loud bang the portal closed behind Lilith and although they had fled, all eight cities in all eight realms knew that this was not the end. The Angels may have won the battle, but Lilith and her people intended to win the war.

Epilogue

"How weak," she spat. "They fled. And all because of him." She waved her hand and the image of Lilith riding a Dragon into the portal back to Hell was wiped away and the surface of the mirror before her turned back to glass. Despite Heaven's protective borders which usually blocked all magical insight into the realm of gods and Angels, the powers that be had neglected to include her teacher's realm within such rules upon its creation. Hell, however, had not been so careless, much to the dislike of the woman facing her reflection. She walked away from the looking glass and angrily picked up a goblet the same silver as her hair, filled almost to the brim with a deep red wine, from a small marble table beside the mirror.

"I did tell you this would happen." Her teacher lay on a large bed of purple and black silk sheets sipping delicately from her own goblet of wine.

The silver-haired woman sneered at the other woman before bringing the goblet to her lips, tilting back her head and pouring all of its contents down her throat and placing it back on the marble table with a grimace as the bitter liquid hit the back of her throat.

"Don't try to use your prophecy bullshit on me, you haven't been able to see anything since the day you were sent here."

Her teacher glared at her with golden-blue eyes before taking another sip of wine. Unlike the speaker, she did not express dislike as she drank.

"It has nothing to do with foresight, I know Lilith well enough to predict when one of her plans will or won't come to fruition."

"I suppose you did tell me that she would rush her attack, but you never mentioned anything about Astaroth," she paused for a second, she wasn't entirely sure what had happened with Lilith's favoured son, only that he had lost control.

Her teacher swung her legs off of the edge of the bed and stood, her bare feet touching the cold stone floor. She walked past her student and through a dark blue curtain separating the bedroom from a balcony of bright yellow stone. Quickly the student followed, she emerged onto the balcony just in time for her teacher to start talking.

"He is a Kukan, a descendant of the shadow Kitsunes with shadows lining his very soul, this makes him powerful. However, like all Kitsune descendants who are not trained in their art, he was destined to lose control at some point or another. I just didn't expect it to be in the middle of a war." The blonde smiled as she spoke, much to her students' surprise.

"Was his loss of control a good thing?" Her teacher often confused her.

"Of course it is!" Her eyes seemed to flare with excitement, as they usually did when she spoke of Lilith failing in anything or the downfall of any of her enemies.

"Mania is dead, Loukas has been taken, Estrie is Helios only knows where, and now Astaroth has aided in decimating Liliths army, which she is not likely to forgive anytime soon. All of the Cambion's are dead, missing or out of favour, which means… "

Suddenly all the pieces clicked into place and Invidia's eyes met Pasiphaë's, a clash of lapis lazuli against gold and sea blue. The eldest daughter of Sammael turned to look out across the barren landscape of Knossos Carcerem, a vast forest leading to a beach of sand and an endless sea. Her arms stretched out across the parapet, her bronze skin basking in the brilliant sunlight. She and Pasiphaë had been planning this for years, ever since Invidia had been told that her father had sired more children and that Lilith had picked them as her weapons of choice when she had so willingly cast Invidia away to a land of orphans and rejects. Since that time, Invidia had been consumed with an untamable curiosity and hatred for her siblings. She had worked harder than any other ward of Pasiphaë in order to reach power unparalleled by other magic users of her age, and with her teacher she had formulated a plot for her revenge against all those who had cast her aside and those she believed had taken everything that was rightfully hers.

"It is time I take my place by my father's side, it is time I prove Lilith should have used me, it is time I do what my siblings have failed to do."

Pasiphaë placed a hand glittering with golden rings on her ward's shoulder.

"It is time you steal back the life that was stolen from you," she grinned. "And for you to become the new Queen of Hell."

The End

Preview

The Arcadian Laws have been passed and all of the Alium world is at the mercy of the Seraphic Council.

Before she will allow further action to be taken against their enemies, Lilith insists that her children join her in her journey to rescue their kidnapped allies from a hidden location.

As old and new enemies present themselves, all within the Stygian Army are faced with one question...

Would you sell your soul to save your people.

The Salt of Angels Book 2: Pillars of Fire coming soon

Glossary

Characters

Lilith – Queen of Hell. Mother of Demons.

Astaroth – Half Demon son of Lilith and Sammael. Grand Duke of Hell.

Loukas – Half Demon son of Lilith and Sammael. Lord of the Red Sands.

Estrie – Half Demon daughter of Lilith and Sammael. Kasai Kitsune.

Mania – Half Demon daughter of Lilith and Sammael. Duchess of Hell.

Mahina Musa – Angel blooded spy.

Mariah Musa – Angel blooded spy.

Moroccan Musa – Angel blooded spy.

Sammael – Husband of Lilith. Lord of Hell.

Lucifer – Former ruler of Hell. Prince of Hell.

Amber Alarie – Eldest of the Ambrogian Vampires.

Morgana Le Fey – Queen of Faerie. Aunt of Mordred.

Mordred – Unseelie Prince of Faerie. Nephew of Morgana.

Talvi – Cryokinetic Demigod.

Skadi – Cryokinetic Demigod.

Orpheo Lenoir – Leader of the Vampire Clan, the Argentum. Brother of Ophelia.

Ophelia Lenoir – Leader of the Vampire Clan, the Aureum. Sister of Orpheo.

Theron – Prince of the Sirenus. Only known Triton (male Siren).

Lycaon – Leader of the Maledictus Wolves. Cursed by Zeus in Ancient Greece.

Ereshkigal – Queen of the Wraiths. (Eh . Resh. Key. Gal.)

Rhoda – Elected Queen of the Coxani Witches.

Pasiphäe – Angel-goddess trapped in a Sub-dimension by Lilith. Mother of the Minotaur. (Pass. Ee. Fay.)

Invidia – Half Demon daughter of Sammael. Full blooded sister of Astaroth and Mania.

Nakir – Angel responsible for recruiting the Musa's.

Persephone – Angel-goddess of the Underworld. Wife of Hades.

Nerissa – Princess of the Sirenuse.

Daryah – Princess of the Sirenuse.

Merlin – Ancient Faerie. Foe of Morgana Le Fay.

Kirke – Dragon belonging to Astaroth.
Xiuhcoatl – The first Dragon. (Show. Cah. Wottle.)

Realms and Cities

There are 8 realms within The Salt of Angels each made up of each cities. Realms are likened to Continents and are joined by portals and cities are the equivalent of countries.

Hell – Land of Demons.
Cities: Pandemonium (Capital) Fastus. Irae. Desidia. Avaritia. Gula. Libidine. Livor.

Heaven – Land of gods and Angels.
Cities: Olympus (Capital) Asgard. Vanaheim. Jannah. Avalon. Aaru. Takamagahara. Otherworld.

Faerie – Land of Seelies and Unseelies.
Cities: Cathair Órga (Capital). Cathair Gloine. Cathair Platanam. Cathair Róidiam. Cloch na Cathrach us. Cathair Adhmaid. Cathair na Salach. Cathair Chrè-umha.

The Underworld – Land of the Punished.
Cities: Irkalla (Capital.) Niflheim. Asphodel. Timoria. Helheim. Yomi. Dubnos. Duat.

Paradise – Land of the Liberated.

Cities: Elysium (Capital). Valhalla. Albios. Ame. Anum. Swarga. Zion. Summerland.

Álfheimr – Land of Elves.
Cities: Álfheim (Capital). Svartálfheim. Vatńálfheim. Bálálfheim. Jördálfheim. Íksöldálfheim. Loftiálfheim. Andaálfheim.

Acuran – Land of Monsters
Cities: Ṭirakan (Capital). Kaṭalcar. Nila. Marrutal. Irakkata. Maperum. Cari. Erintuvita.

Chaos – Land of the Unknown.
Cities: Garden of the Gods (Capital). Limbo. Tartarus. Kaṭal. Iruḷ. Pañcham. Verri. Irrapu.

Sub-dimensions

Sub-dimensions are areas, citadels and eco systems that lie within the world of Stagnants (humans) but are hidden from them.

The Sirenuse – An underwater city belonging to Sirens and creatures of the depth.

Knossos Carcerem – A realm created by Lilith to trap Pasiphäe.

Artifacts and Magical Objects

Yata No Kagami – Mirror once belonging the Angel-goddess Amaterasu. Connects the holder to Heaven.

Gjallarhorn – A powerful horn used to take the blower to a safe space. (Yal. Ah. Horn)

Grimoire of Caelum – A book of Angelic magic written by the Angel-goddess, Hecate.

Andvaranaut – A ring, once cursed by its original owner Andvari, to bring misfortune on the wearer. Its curse was diminished when the Angels split it into three. The three hold the ability to block the mind from intruders. (And. Var. A. Naught.)

Satchel of Perseus – A leather bag gifted to the hero Perseus to hold the head of Medusa.

Carnwennan – A blade once belonging to King Arthur with the ability to shroud the holder in darkness.

Sventhorn – a magical horn with the ability to put one's enemies to sleep.

Lædingr – An unbreakable chain used to bind the Great Wolf, Fenrir .

Dromi – An unbreakable chain used to bind the Great Wolf, Fenrir.

Gleipnir – A fetter said to be as light and as thin as silk, but as strong as creation.

Red Purple Gold Gourd – a magical container with the ability to entrap any entity no matter how powerful.

Spear of Longinus – The Spear used to stab the Nazarine at his crucifixion. The only weapon believed to be powerful enough to kill Lucifer.

Chain of Prometheus – a chain used by Zeus to chain the traitor Prometheus to a rock for eternity.

Species Specification

Demon:

Princes of Hell/Fallen Angels – the most powerful of Demons once Seraphim Warriors.

Greater Demons – Powerful Demons, Lords, Dukes and Presidents of Hells hierarchy.

Lesser Demons – Demons with no title used as pawns and soldiers by their superiors.

Watchers – Demons banished from Heaven for mating with mortals creating Monstrous hybrids.

Cambion:

Beings that are Half Stagnant and Half Demon.

Angels:

Olympian – The most powerful of Angels once confused in Ancient times for gods.

Seraphim – The second highest order of Angels with six wings, two covering their faces, two their feet and two helping them to fly.

Cherubim – Throne bearers and celestial attendants to the Almighty. They have two sets of wings and four heads, one of an ox, a lion, an eagle and a human; and the hooves of a bull.

Ophanim – Great Golden wheels decorated in thousands of eyes and fire charged with watching over the throne of God.

Dominations – the most mysterious of Angels known for keeping watch upon the Earth but rarely intervening.

Powers – Angels with authority over the weaker forces of evil, they are able to retrain them and prevent many from doing harm.

Virtues – Presenting themselves as sparks of light, Virtues are charged with maintaining the natural world. They have power over the elements and assist in miracles.

Principalities – Angels with the ability to guide and protect large groups.

Archangels – There are seven arch angels who are seen as some of the most skilled warriors in Heavens army. They look similar to stereotypical Angels.

Angels – The stereotypical winged warrior of Heaven.

Valkyries – The most skilled warriors of Heavens army.

Angel blooded:

Gibborim – Stagnants with remnants of Angel blood.

Nephilim – Monstrous Giants produced by the mating of Watchers and Stagnants

Kitsune

Tengoku – descendants of Japanese Angel-gods with Heavens light lining their soul.

Kukan – descendants of Japanese Angel-gods with darkness and shadow lining their soul.

Kaze – descendant of Japanese Angel-gods with Wind lining their soul.

Seishin – descendants of Japanese Angel-gods with Spirit lining their soul

Kasai – descendants of Japanese Angel-gods with fire lining their soul.

Chikyu – descendants of Japanese Angel-gods with Earth lining their soul

Kawa – descendants of Japanese Angel-gods with River lining their soul.

Umi – descendants of Japanese Angel-gods with Ocean lining their soul.

Yama – descendants of Japanese Angel-gods with mountain lining their soul.

Mori – descendants of Japanese Angel-gods with Forest lining their soul.

Sanda – descendants of Japanese Angel-gods with Thunder lining their soul.

Jikan – descendants of Japanese Angel-gods with Time lining their soul.

Ongaku – descendants of Japanese Angel-gods with sound lining their soul.

Faerie:

Seelie – Faeries who worship and draw power from the Tuatha De Danann through repeated prayer and occasional sacrifice.

Unseelie – Faeries who pray to the Fommorians once and receive dark power for life.

Witches:

Colchian – Witches descended from the Royal House of Ancient Colchis and the Sun Titan, Helios; it was from the sun they received their power.

Coxani – Witches descended from a powerful Seer by the name of Vadoma, skilled in the art of fortune telling. They travel the world cursing those who disrespect them and draw their magic from the Earth.

Mangkukulam – The most feared group of Witches originating in the Philippines known for using their own special brand of magic known as Kulam, widely compared to voodoo.

Warlocks:

Colchian – Warlocks descended from the Royal House of Ancient Colchis and the Sun Titan, Helios; it was from the sun they receive their power.

Solomon – Warlocks descended from King Solomon, skilled in the arts of craft, protection and exorcism. They are in charge of protecting the most powerful magical artifacts such as the Seals of Solomon

Hyperborean – Warlocks descended from Abaris the Hyperborean, skilled in the arts of healing magic and potion making.

Vampires:

Ambrogian – Vampires descended from Ambrogio. The stereotypical Vampire of European Myth.

Manananggal – Expert hunters with an unrivaled thirst for blood and the ability to separate their winged upper halves from their lower.

Empousa – An all female group of winged unkillable beings with one bronze and one donkey leg created by the Angel-goddess Hecate.

Vetala – The most peaceful of the Vampire species who survived purely off of animal blood. Unkillable and created by Kali. They reside high in the Gangkhar Puensum.

Werewolves:

Maledictus – Humans cursed to transform into Wolves on a full moon.

Natus – Natural born Werewolves originating from Maledictus Wolves.

Pellis – Magic users with the ability to transform into wolves using an enchanted wolf pellet.

Dragon:

Vēṭṭai – Dragons bred for hunting.

Caṇṭai – Dragons bred for battle.

Kāvalar – Dragons bred for hoarding and guarding.

Kāṭṭu – Untameable Dragons of pure magical energy

Sirens:

Siren – Enticing females with enchanting voices known to lure sailors to their deaths.

Triton – Male Sirens.

Spirits:

Ghost – Souls residing in Asphodel.

Wraith – Souls claimed by the Queen of Irkalla, Ereshkigal, to be her subjects.

Demigods:

The children of gods and Stagnants

Necrotic:

A reanimated body with no soul usually used as a slave.

Once upon a time, there was a young British lad named Connor Irving. Connor was a curious and imaginative boy, with a thirst for knowledge and a passion for storytelling. He spent countless hours reading books, delving into myths and legends from all over the world, and writing down his own tales of magic and adventure. As he grew older, Connor's love for writing only intensified. He even pursued a degree in Classical Civilisations at Warwick Univeristy where he learned about the ancient myths and stories that continue to inspire him today. Connor set out to share his love of storytelling with the world. He started writing blogs and articles for various online publications, and even landed a gig as the scribe of the Sun Titan, , Helios, for the popular online magazine "In the Patheon. But that was just the beginning. Connor had a dream to become a published author, and he was determined to make it a reality. He poured his heart and soul into creating his very own YA fantasy series, filled with demons, magic, and misunderstood characters from ancient myths. And then, it finally happened. People all over the world will be captivated by his vivid imagination, rich storytelling, and unique perspective on mythology. Today, Connor is known as a rising star in the world of young adult literature. He runs a successful Tik Tok, Youtube, and Twitter account under the name of "The Mythology Manifest", where he shares his passion for myths and legends with his followers. He also blogs on his website. Connor Irving is proof that if you follow your dreams and pursue your passions with all your heart, anything is possible.

Website: https://authorconnorirving.wordpress.com/
Tik Tok: @the_mythology_manifest
YouTube: @tehmythologymanifest1170
Twitter: @TheMythologyMa1

Milton Keynes UK
Ingram Content Group UK Ltd.
UKHW022122060923
428148UK00014B/499